the Mare

MARY GAITSKILL

This paperback edition published in 2017

First published in Great Britain in 2016 by Serpent's Tail,
an imprint of Profile Books Ltd
3 Holford Yard
Bevin Way
London
WC1X 9HD
www.serpentstail.com

First published in 2015 by Pantheon Books, a division of Penguin Random House LLC, New York

1 3 5 7 9 10 8 6 4 2

Designed by Betty Lew

Printed and bound in Great Britain by CPI Group (UK) Ltd, Croydon CR0 4YY

A CIP record for this book can
be obtained from the British Library

ISBN 978 1 78125 594 0
eISBN 978 1 78283 227 0

GRATEFUL ACKNOWLEDGMENT IS MADE TO THE FOLLOWING

Excerpt from 'Wildfire', words and music by Michael Martin Murphey
and Larry Cansler, copyright © 1975 and renewed by Warner-Tamerlane
Publishing Corp. Reprinted by permission of Alfred Music Publishing.

Excerpt from 'Obsession' by Anthony 'Romeo' Santos, as first performed by
Aventura. Reprinted by permission of Warner Chappell Music Italiana Srl.

Excerpt from 'Unchained Melody', copyright © 1955 and renewed by
North Melody Publishing (SESAC) and HUZUM Publishing (SESAC).
Reprinted by permission of Unchained Melody Publishing, LLC.

b

"F
a n
deli
to o

"A no
chara
unbri

...ouncil

"Gaitsk..... ....
intimate, and daring in her confrontation of racist attitudes and how
women view other women … Gaitskill [has an] unerring ability to
give her characters utterly believable voices, as well as complex inner
lives" *Glasgow Sunday Herald*

"Gaitskill embraces without reservation the tradition of the love between misunderstood horse and misunderstood child, then lets it loose in a modern, racially fraught world of gangbangers and domestic abuse. In *The Mare*, not just horses and girls, but also mothers and the childless are all world-weary females, abused, exhausted by life, united in their desire for safety, love, freedom, and power. Gaitskill's novel is not a children's book, but it is a book about what children long for, and how we long for the same thing many years after we've left childhood behind" *New York Times Book Review*

"A novel about the knee-smashing effects of minority poverty and the corrosive tonic of liberal guilt … here, without a drop of condescension, is fiction that pumps blood through the cold facts of inequality" *Washington Post*

"Gaitskill puts raw faith, here, in the primal intimacy of a creatureliness that is common to all who live and breathe, regardless of species, race, gender, or class. Her trust in that commonality is breathtakingly vulnerable, among the greatest risks of her career" *The New York Times*

"Gaitskill takes a premise that could have been preachy, sentimental, or simplistic – juxtaposing urban and rural, rich and poor, young and old, brown and white – and makes it candid and emotionally complex, spare, real, and deeply affecting" *Kirkus Reviews*

"I finished *The Mare* on the subway yesterday and cried. There is magic in *The Mare* though it's unclear whether the heroine, Velveteen Vargas, can actually hear horses talking to her or whether this is her intuition or a projection of her hopeful mind and heart, and it doesn't matter which, ultimately. A lot of the book is about the distance between what we think or hope or imagine other people are thinking and feeling and their actual thoughts. No one is better than Mary Gaitskill at describing moments of being able to sense what someone else is feeling, either accurately or so close to accurately that the distance between your two consciousnesses recedes temporarily" Emily Gould

The Browns . . . loved each other, deeply, from the back of the soul, with intolerance in daily life.

—*National Velvet*

Velvet

That day I woke up from a dream the way I always woke up: pressed against my mom's back, my face against her and her turned away. She holding Dante and he holding her, his head in her breasts, wrapped around each other like they're falling down a hole. It was okay. I was a eleven-year-old *girl,* and I didn't need to have my face in my mama's titty no more—that is, if I ever did. Dante, my little brother, was only six.

It was summer, and the air conditioner was up too high, dripping dirty water on the floor, outside the pan I put there to catch it. Too loud too, but still I heard a shot from outside or maybe a shout from my dream. I was dreaming about my grandfather from DR; he was lost in a dark place, like a castle with a lot of rooms and rich white people doing scary things in all of them, and my grandfather somewhere shouting my name. Or maybe it was a shot. I sat up and listened, but there wasn't anything.

That day we had to get on a bus and go stay with rich white people for two weeks. We signed up to do this at Puerto Rican Family Services in Williamsburg, even though we're Dominican and we just moved to Crown Heights. The social worker walked around in little high heels, squishing out of tight pants like she's a model, but with her face frowning like a mask on Halloween.

My mom talked to her about how our new neighborhood was all bad "negritas," no Spanish people. She told her how she had to work all day and sometimes at night, keeping a roof over our heads. She said it was going to be summer and I was too old for day care, and because I was stupid she couldn't trust me to stay inside and not go around the block talking to men. She laughed when she said this, like me talking to men was so stupid it was funny. But I don't go around talking to men, and I told the social worker that with my face.

Which made the social worker with her eyes and her mouth tell my mom she's shit. Which made me hate the woman, even if my mom was lying about me. My mom acted like she didn't see what the social worker said with her eyes and mouth, but I knew she did see—she saw like she always does. But she kept talking and smiling with her hard mouth until the social worker handed her a shiny booklet—she stopped then. I looked to see what had shut my mother up; it was pictures of white people on some grass hugging dark children. Mask-Face told us we could go stay with people like this for two weeks. "It sounds like hell," whispered Dante, but Mask-Face didn't hear. We could swim and ride bicycles, she said. We could learn about animals. I took the booklet out of my mother's hands. It said something about love and having fun. There was a picture of a girl darker than me petting a sheep. There was a picture of a woman with big white legs sitting in a chair with a hat on and a plastic orange flower in her hand, looking like she was waiting for somebody to have fun with.

My mom doesn't write, so I filled out the forms. Dante just sat there talking to himself, not caring about anything like always. I didn't want him to come with me, bothering me while I was trying to ride a bicycle or something, so when they asked how he gets along with people, I wrote, "He hits." They asked how he resolves conflict and I wrote, "He hits." It was true, anyway. Then my mom asked if we could go to the same family so I could take care of Dante, and Mask-Face said no, it's against the rules. I was glad, and then I felt sorry for saying something bad about Dante for nothing. My mom started to fight about it, and Mask-Face said again, *It's against the rules.* The way she said it was another way of saying "You're shit," and the smell of that shit was starting to fill up the room. I could feel Dante get small inside. He said, "I don't want to go be with those people." He said it so soft you could barely hear him, but my mother said, "Shut up, you ungrateful boy! You're stupid!" The smell got stronger; it covered my mother's head, and she scratched herself like she was trying to brush it off.

But she couldn't and so when we left, she hit Dante on the head and called him stupid some more. Going to this place with bicycles and sheep had been turned into a punishment.

Still, I had hope that it would be fun. The lady I would stay with had called to talk to me and she sounded nice. Her voice was little, like she was scared. She said we were going to ride a Ferris wheel at the county fair and swim at the lake and see horses. She didn't sound like the lady with the big legs, but that's how I pictured her, with a plastic flower. I thought of that picture and that voice and I got excited.

I got up and went out into the hall and got into the closet where our coats were. I dug into the back and found my things I keep in the old cotton ball box. I took them out through our living room into the kitchen, where it was heavy-warm from all the hot days so far. I poured orange juice in my favorite glass with purple flowers on it. I took the juice and my box to the open window and leaned out on the ledge. It was so early there was nobody on the street except a raggedy man creeping against a building down below us, holding on to it with one hand like for balance. He was holding the wall where somebody had written "Cookie" in big red paint. That was because this boy called Cookie used to stand there a lot. He was called that because he ate big cookies all the time. We used to see him in Mr. Nelson's store downstairs and we weren't supposed to talk to him because he was from the project over on Troy Avenue. But I did talk to him and he was nice. Even if he told me once that even though he liked me, if somebody paid him enough, he'd kill me. He wouldn't want to because I was gonna grow up fine, but he'd have to. He said it like he was making friends with me. We stood there talking for a while and then he broke off a piece of soft cookie and gave it to Dante. He said, "Stay fine, girl." A little while later a cop killed him for nothing and his name got put on a wall.

I took my things out of the box and laid them out on the ledge. They looked nice together: a silver bell I got from a prize machine, a plastic orange sun I tore off a get-well card somebody gave my mom, a blond key-chain doll with only one leg wearing a checkered coat, a dried sea horse from DR that my grandfather sent me, and a blue shell my father gave me when I was a baby and he lived with us. My father gave me two shells, but I gave the brown-and-pink one to this girl Strawberry because her brother died.

I held the blue shell against my lip to feel how smooth it was. I looked up and saw the sun had put a gold outline on the building across from us. I looked down and saw the raggedy man stop against the wall, like he was trying to get the strength to breathe.

After Cookie got shot I heard these men talking about him at

Mr. Nelson's. I heard his name and this man said, "Suicide by cop." I thought, What does that mean? so loud it was like they heard me because they got quiet. When we left, my mom whispered, "Gangbangers."

On the street, the raggedy man stretched up against the wall, his arms and hands spread out like he was crying on the red-painted word. For a second, everything was hard and clear and pounding beautiful.

The last time I saw my father I was almost ten and Dante was four. We had to leave our old apartment in Williamsburg, and my mom was staying with a friend and trying to find a new place, so he came and took us to Philadelphia in the car with his friend Manuel. I remember blowing bubbles on the fire escape with his other kids from this woman Sophia; she had soft breasts pushed together in a green dress, and she made asopao with shrimp, and mango pudding. She never liked me, but her girls were nice. We slept in the same bed and told stories about a disgusting white guy in history who cut people up with a chain saw and danced around in their skins. And the littlest girl would rap Missy Elliott, like, *I heard the bitch got hit with three zebras and a monkey / I can't stand the bitch no way.* And it made me and Dante laugh, 'cause she's so cute—she's only three. There were dogs going in and out, and Dante was scared at first, then he loved them. It was fun, but on the way back in the car, my father took my emergency money out of my pocket to pay the tolls and didn't give it back. Manuel was in the car and he made fun of me for being mad. Then he came to New York and started renting a room from us.

My father sends Dante a dollar in a card for his birthday sometimes. Never me.

I put down the shell and picked up the sea horse. I never met my grandfather, but he loved me. He talked to me on the phone and when I sent him my picture, he said I was beautiful. He called me "mi niña." He told me stories about how bad my mom was when she was little, and how she got punished. He sent the sea horse. He said one day my mom would bring me and Dante to visit and he would take us to the ocean. I remember his voice: tired and rough but mad fun inside. I never saw him and I almost never talked to him on the phone, but when I did, it was like arms around me. Then his voice started getting more tired and the fun was far away in him. He said, "I'm always gonna be with you. Just think of me, I'm there." It scared me. I wanted to say, *Grandpa, why are you talking like this?* But I was too scared. "Even in your dreams," he said. "I'm gonna be there." I said, "Bendición, Abuelo," and he answered, "Dios te bendiga." A month later, he died.

I put my things back in the box. I looked down in the street. The raggedy man was gone. The gold outline on the building was gone too, spread out through the sky, making it shiny with invisible light. For some reason I thought of a TV commercial where a million butterflies burst out from some shampoo bottle or cereal box. I thought of Cookie's face when he gave my brother a cookie. I thought of the big-legs lady in the booklet holding the fake orange flower, looking like she was hoping for someone to come have fun with her.

Ginger

I met her when I was forty-seven, but I felt still young. I looked young too. This is probably because I had not done many of the things most people that age have done; I'd had no children and no successful career. I married late after stumbling through a series of crappy relationships and an intense half-life as an artist visible only in Lower Manhattan, the other half of my life being sloppily given over to alcohol and drugs.

I met my husband, Paul, in AA. I only went for about a year because I couldn't stand the meetings, couldn't stand the language, the dogma. They tried to make it sound like something else, but that's finally what it was. Still, it helped me quit, no question. And I met Paul. It was six months before we even had coffee, but I immediately noticed his deep eyes, the animal eloquence of his hairy hands. He was fifty then, nearly ten years older than me, and still married, but living in the city separately from his wife. It made him nervous that I stopped coming to meetings, and though he'd never admit it, I think that tension gave our slow courtship a stronger charge. We eventually moved to a small town upstate, the same town he'd moved from, where he made a good living as a tenured professor at a small college. A lot of his income went to support his wife and daughter, and we lived in an old faculty housing unit long on charm and short on function. Not owning didn't bother us though. We were comfortable, and for a long time we were happy with each other; we went out to eat a lot, and traveled in the summer.

When people asked me what I did I sometimes said, "I'm transitioning," and very occasionally, "I'm a painter." I was embarrassed to say the second thing even though it was true: I still painted, and it seemed like I was better than I was when I showed at a downtown gallery twenty years before. But I was embarrassed anyway because I knew I sounded foolish to people who had kids and jobs too, and who wouldn't understand my life before I came here. There were a few—women who also painted at home—whom I was able to talk about it with, describe what art used to be to me, and what I wanted to make it be again: a place more real than anything in "real" life. A place I remember now just dimly, a place of deep joy where, when I could get to it, it was like tuning in to a radio frequency that was sacred to me. Regardless of anything else, nothing was more important than carrying that frequency on the dial of myself.

The problem was, other people created interference. It was hard for me to be close with them and to hear the signal at the same time. I realize that makes me sound strange. I *am* strange, more than the bare facts of my life would suggest. But I have slowly come to realize that so many people are strange, maybe the word is nearly meaningless when applied to human beings. Still, people interfered. And so I created ways to keep them at a distance, including my increasingly expensive habit. What I didn't see, or allow myself to see, was that drugs created even more interference than people; they were a sinister signal all their own, one that enhanced and blended with, then finally blotted out, the original one. When that happened I got completely lost, and for many years I didn't even know it.

By the time I got to AA, art had all but gone dead for me, and I credit my time in those stunned, bright-lit rooms for waking it up again.

When we finally moved out of the city, I began to feel the signal again, but differently. I felt it even when I was with Paul, which did not surprise me—he was not "other people." But I began to feel it with other people too, or rather *through* them, in the density of families living in homes, going back for generations in this town. I would see women with babies in strollers or with their little children in the grocery store, and I would feel their rootedness in the place around us and beyond—in the grass and earth, trees and sky.

To feel so much through something I was not part of was of course lonely. I began to wonder if it had been a mistake not to have children, to wonder what would've happened if I'd met Paul when I was younger. The third time we had sex, he said, "I want to make you pregnant." I must've had sex hundreds of times before, and men had said all kinds of things to me—but no one had ever said that. I never *wanted* anyone to say it; girlfriends would tell me a guy had said that and I would think, How obnoxious! But when Paul said it, I heard *I love you*. I felt the same; we made love and I pictured my belly swelling.

But I didn't get pregnant. Instead my sister Melinda died. I know the two things don't go together. But in my mind they do. My sister lived in Cleveland, Ohio. She had been sick a long time; she had so many things wrong with her that nobody wanted to think about her, including me. She was drunk and mean and crazy and would call saying fucked-up things in the middle of the night. When she was younger, she'd hung around with a sad-sack small-time biker gang, and now that she was falling off a cliff—my guess is they were too— they didn't want to talk to her. I didn't want to talk to her either, but I would, closing my eyes and forcing myself to listen. I would listen until I could remember the feeling of her and me as little girls, drawing pictures together, cuddled on the couch together, eating ice cream out of teacups. Sometimes I couldn't listen, couldn't remember; she'd talk and I'd check my e-mail and wait for her to go away. And then she did.

She had a stroke while she was taking a shower. The water was still running on her when they found her a few days later. It was summer and her body was waterlogged and swollen. Still, I could identify her, even with her thin, tiny mouth nearly lost in her cheeks and chin and her brows pulled into an inhuman expression.

Paul went with me to clear out her apartment. I hadn't been to visit her for at least a decade—she always preferred to visit me or my mother, and I could see why. Her apartment was filthy, full of old take-out containers, used paper plates and plastic utensils, boxes and bags crammed with the junk she'd been meaning to take out for years. Months' worth of unopened mail lay on every surface. There was black mold on the walls. Paul and I stood there in the middle of it and thought, Why didn't we help her? The obvious answer was, we *had* helped her. We had sent her money; we had flown her out to visit on Christmas. I *had* talked to her, even when I didn't want to. But standing in her apartment, I knew it hadn't been enough. She'd known when I hadn't wanted to talk, which was most of the time. Given that, what good was the money?

"You did what you could," said my mother. "We all did." I wanted to say, *You did what you could to destroy her,* but she was crying already. I was glad I didn't say anything; my mother died of a heart attack a month later. When my sister and I were teenagers, my mother had acted like Melinda was nothing but an aggravation who had contributed to the end of her marriage. But then she would play cards and clown around in the kitchen with her like she never did with me. Toward the end of her life, Melinda was always on the phone with our mom; she'd even pull over and call my mom on her cell if she was lost on her way to wherever she was going, which was often.

When the shock was still wearing off, I would go for long walks through the small center of town, out onto country roads, then back into town again. I'd look at the women with their children; I'd look into the small, beautiful faces and think of Melinda when she was like that. I'd imagine my mother's warm arms, her unthinking, uncritical limbs that lifted and held us. Shortly after Melinda died our washing machine broke and I had to go to the Laundromat; I was there by myself and this song came on the radio station that the management had on. It's a song that was popular in the '70s about a girl and a horse who both die. I was folding clothes when I recognized it. The singer's voice is thin and fake, but it's pretty, and somewhere in the fakery is the true sadness of smallness and failure and believing in beautiful things that aren't real because that's the only way to get through. Tears came to my eyes. When Melinda was little, she loved horses. For a while, she even rode them. We couldn't afford lessons, so she worked in a stable to earn them. Once I went with my mother to pick Melinda up from there, and I saw her riding in the fenced area beside the stable. She looked so confident and happy I didn't recognize her; I wondered who that beautiful girl was. So did our mother. She said, "Look at her!" and then stopped short. *They say she died one winter / When there came a killin' frost / And the pony she named Wildfire busted down its stall / In the blizzard he was lost.* It was a crap song. It didn't matter. It made me picture my sister before she was ruined, coming toward me on a beautiful golden horse. *She's coming for me I know / And on Wildfire we're both gonna go.* I cried quietly, still folding the clothes. No one was there to see me.

It was a year later that I started talking about adoption. At first Paul said, "We can't." Although he didn't say it, I think he was hurt that I hadn't really tried to have *his* child, but now I wanted some random one. Also, his daughter from his first marriage, Edie, didn't want to go to school where he teaches and he'd promised to pay her tuition at Brown after his ex-wife had thrown a fit about it. Even if money weren't an issue, he didn't think we would have the physical energy for a baby. "What about an older child?" I asked. "Like a seven-year-old?" But we wouldn't know anything about the kid, he said. They would come fully formed in ways that would be problematic and invisible to us until it was too late.

We went back and forth on the subject, not intensely, but persistently, in bed at night and at breakfast. Months went by; spring came and the dry, frigid winter air went raw and wet, then grew full and soft. Paul's eyes began to be soft when we talked too. One of his friends told him about an organization that brought poor inner-city kids up to stay with country families for a few weeks. The friend suggested it as a way to "test the waters," to see what it might be like to have somebody else's fully formed kid around.

We called the organization and they sent us information, including a brochure of white kids and black kids holding flowers and smiling, of white adults hugging black kids and a slender black girl touching a woolly white sheep. It was sentimental and flattering to white vanity and manipulative as hell. It was also irresistible. It made you think the beautiful sentiments you pretend to believe in really *might* be true. "Yes," I said. "Let's do it. It's only two weeks. We could find out what it's like. We could give a kid a nice summer, anyway."

Velvet

Dante wasn't on the same bus as me—his was supposed to go at seven thirty and then me at nine. Outside the Port Authority were dirty homeless sleeping against the walls; inside, mostly closed stores, hardly anyone but police, and ugly music playing. We went where they said to meet them and nobody was there. My mom told me to ask a police if this was where the Fresh Air Fund was supposed to be and he said he didn't know anything about that, which made my mom look worried and Dante glad because maybe we would just go home. I thought we were just there too early as usual, and I was right: While we were standing there, these people wearing green T-shirts came smiling at us, carrying yellow metal fences like they use to keep people back at parades. They said, "Great, you're early, that's great," and then they made a big square place with the fences and put a sign on it. They laughed and smiled with each other and then over at us. They put up tables and got out their computers and said they were ready. But then they wouldn't let us all the way in behind the fence, just Dante; he had to be inside the fence by himself. They told us he would get used to it, but that we could stand right by the fence until he left. They put a information card around his neck and gave him a coloring book, but he dropped it and ran to the fence to grab my mom, crying, "I'm hungry, I'm hungry!"

If it was me, my mom would've told me to shut up and gone to work. But Dante, she put her hands through the fence and talked to him like a baby, like "my little mother-nature boy!" But he wouldn't be quiet, so she gave me money and told me to go get him a cookie and her a coffee at this place that just opened, we saw this sad-faced man opening it.

She always pays attention to Dante when he cries, so he cries a lot. Or pretends to. Especially since he got poisoned by the babysitter. That was before Crown Heights or even Williamsburg; we lived in Queens then, all of us in one room that smelled like the garbage under the sink no matter how many times we took it out. I was eight, Dante was three. The babysitter was a girl named Rose who lived down the block, the daughter of the lady who did my mom's hair. She wanted to watch a TV show that wasn't what Dante wanted and he wouldn't shut up about it. He started crying that something hurt, so she gave him aspirin. He kept crying, probably because they were the orange chewy kind and he wanted more. She gave him the whole bottle and he went to sleep.

When I got back with the cookie and coffee, he was still sort of pretend-crying; he even kept doing it while he ate the cookie. Other kids were inside the fence by then, and they were coloring in books with the Fresh Air Fund people. I wished I could go in there, just to sit down away from Dante and my mom. I even asked if I could, but they said no, I couldn't go in until my group came.

I walked around in a circle behind my mom, dragging my suitcase until this girl in a green T-shirt said I could leave it inside the yellow fence; then I walked around without it. More people were in the station, their faces looking like they were already someplace else. More kids were coming too—the fenced-in Fresh Air space was filling up. Kids were sitting on the floor coloring in books or playing cards while the people in green shirts watched. Other moms were standing along the fence, with their children close to them. This boy came up to Dante and said, "Don't be scared. You'll like it. Where I'm going, they have a swimming pool." I felt like I could walk away and nobody would see me.

After Dante ate all the aspirin we couldn't get him to wake up. Rose called her mom to come, and then my mom came home. We were all crying, and pretty soon my mom was screaming at Rose that she would kill her if Dante died. Rose's mom defended her daughter: She screamed back that if my mom was going to talk like that, Dante *would* die as punishment. The police came, an ambulance came. They put my little brother on the stretcher; my mom cried and threw herself on his body, they had to pull her off to take him down the stairs. When they drove away in the ambulance, our neighbor Mrs. Gutierrez hugged my mom and told her Dante would be all right, that she would be praying for us. My mom thanked her and smiled at her as she walked away. Then she turned to me and said, "How could you let this happen?"

Finally the bus came and they made Dante get on it. My mom walked me up to the table inside the fenced area and they put a card on me that said "Red Hook." "Be good," she said. "Don't give them any trouble." And she kissed me, then left because she was late for work. I went in and sat down and this lady smiled and said hi and asked if it was my first time and I said yes. She asked if I wanted a coloring book and I said no. Other kids came in who were mostly younger than me; they sat on the floor and colored. A girl my age sat down and took out her phone. I didn't have a phone, so I just sat down. More and more kids came—at least I wasn't the only one whose mom wasn't there. But it did seem like I was the only one who didn't have something to look at. And the ugly music was still playing.

You're no good, said some words in my head. *It's your blood that's bad.* These are words I hear a lot. I don't really hear a voice saying them. It's more like I feel them in my brain. Over and over. When that happens, I try to listen to the people around me to drown them out. Which is how I heard the white lady standing behind us talking to this other white lady. She was saying, "They got us to bend over backward to get this kid on this bus and now they *don't even show up?*"

"They don't understand," said the other lady. "Families arrange their *whole summers* around this and then they don't even show."

"It's their culture," said the first one. "They don't understand time the way we do."

I wanted to say, *Excuse me, but we were here early?* But then they changed the subject to themselves and how they were making a difference.

". . . they come up and they see this big house and all these nice things, and they want to know, How do you get all this?" The same lady was still talking like no one could hear her. "And I say to them, We get it with *hard work.* Do you see how Jeff gets up every morning at four a.m. and goes to *work?* And then comes home and relates to his kids?"

"At least they have an example," said her friend. "We're showing them another way. What they do with that is another thing, but—"

I tried to remember the little voice of the lady I talked to on the phone. I tried to put my mind on all the things she said we would do, the fair and swimming and horses. But it seemed like there was nothing but the bus station and that it would go on forever, my brain talking shit to me and these women talking basically the same thing.

Right then a black man with dreads said, "Okay, let's go!" And he picked up some bags and walked to the door Dante had gone through. Kids finally said good-bye to their moms and we all got on the bus, which distracted my brain from talking. This bus was a dark and rumbling cave, with deep seats full of close smells and tiny jewelly lights on the arm-parts. You had to step on a platform to get into the seats and all of them had TV screens in front of them. Even the shy little kids threw themselves into these seats so they could bounce. The woman who said that thing about a "example" got on last, smiling and talking about how we were going to watch *Harry Potter*. My brain started again: *You're no good.* I told it, *Oh, shut up.*

"Hey," said a black lady in a green T-shirt. "Can I sit next to you?"

I told her yes and I was glad; she was nice. She said, "Hi, Velveteen. My name is Roxanne. Have you ever been to Friendly Town before?"

I said, "No," and the bus rumbled for real.

"You're gonna like it," she said. "I went when I was little. It's a lot of fun."

The bus backed up and turned into a tunnel. Roxanne said she wished we were watching *Freaky Friday* with Lindsay Lohan instead. "It's about a girl who switches bodies with her mom. It's funny."

I didn't know what to say, so I smiled and looked out the window. We were coming out onto the street. The Example lady was standing up and talking about the rules of the bus and the bathroom in the back. I wondered if Roxanne thought the same things she did.

The night that Dante got poisoned my mother didn't talk to me, not even when they said he was okay. I helped her make dinner and we ate it. She hardly looked at me. I cried and my tears ran into my mouth with my food. But when we got in bed, she didn't turn away from me. She lay on her back with her eyes open and said, "It's not your fault. You have bad blood from your father." I said, "Bendición,

Mami." She didn't answer. "Mami?" I whispered. She sighed and blessed me, then turned her back and let me curl against her.

"Velveteen?" said Roxanne. "Are you a little bit nervous?"

"Yeah."

"Don't be, sweetheart. Because your host family? They are gonna be so happy to see you. Trust me."

Ginger

The bus came late. We waited in a hot schoolyard for an hour because we didn't get the message. We figured it out when we saw nobody else was there, but we were afraid to go get a cold drink because we weren't sure how early we were. Paul sat in the car with the door open listening to the radio. I got out and paced up and down the asphalt. I didn't like the look of it, this dry flat line between earth and sky—who would want somebody else's empty schoolyard to be the first thing they saw in a new place? I thought about the girl's voice on the phone. Velvet—she sounded so full and round, sweet and fresh.

I wanted to give that voice sweet, fresh things, to gather up everything good and give it. The night before, we had gone out and bought food for her—boxes of cereal and fruit to put on it, eggs in case she didn't want cereal, orange juice and bacon and white bread, sliced ham and cheese, chicken for barbecue, chocolate milk, carrots. "Did your daughter like carrots when she was little?" I asked Paul. "I don't remember," he said. "I think so." "All kids eat carrots," I said, and put them in the shopping cart. "Ginger, don't worry so much," he said. "Kids are simple. As long as you're nice to them and take care of them, they'll like you. Okay?"

I paced the asphalt. Other cars driven by middle-aged white people pulled into the lot. The problem was, I didn't know if I had everything good to give. Or even anything. "Yourself," Paul had said, holding me one night. "The real self is the best thing anyone can give to anybody." And I believed that. But I did not think it would be an easy thing to give.

Paul got out of the car. "Look," he said. "They're here." And there were the buses, two of them huffing into the yard. I thought, Act normal. The buses stopped; doors jerked open and rumpled, hot-looking adults poured out, intense smiles on their faces. Last names and numbers were shouted out. Kids jumped out of the buses, some of them blinking eagerly in the sunlight, some looking down like they were embarrassed or scared. And then there was this little beauty. Her round head was too big for her skinny body, and her long kinky hair made it seem even bigger. But her skin was a rich brown; her lips were full, her cheekbones strong. She had a broad, gentle forehead, a broad nose, and enormous heavy-lashed eyes with intense brows. But it wasn't only or even mainly her features that made her beautiful; she had a purity of expression that stunned my heart.

I heard Paul's name. We came forward. The child turned her eyes fully on us. I had an impulse to cover my stunned heart with my hand. "This is Velveteen Vargas," said a nondescript someone with a smile in her voice. "Velveteen, this is Mr. and Mrs. Roberts." She was ours!

Velvet

The place they let us off at was a school, but empty, with trees around it. Like dreams I have about school sometimes, where it's deserted and I'm the only one there—or everybody's there, everything's normal, except I'm invisible. When I got off the bus, this smiling lady was standing there. Her hair was white-blond and her eyes were blue. There was a man there too, wearing shorts that showed the blond-hairiest legs I ever saw. But it was her I looked at most. She didn't look like the lady in the booklet at all. She was wearing white pants and a white top with sparkles on it. She was smiling, but something else in her face was almost crying. It was okay though. I don't know why. I smiled back. She smiled like she was seeing heaven. I got shy and looked down.

"Velveteen," she said. "That's a pretty name."

"Velvet," I said. "That's what people call me."

They said they were Ginger and Paul. They took me to their car. We drove past lots of houses with flowers and bushes in front of them. In the city when the sky is bright it makes everything harder on the edges; here everything was soft and shiny too, like a picture book of Easter eggs and rabbits I read in third grade when I was sick on the nurse's station cot. I loved that book so much I stole it from the nurse's station, and the next time I was sick I took it out and looked at it and it made me feel better even though by then I was too old for it. I don't have it anymore; probably my mom threw it out when we moved.

The man turned around in the driver's seat and asked me if I liked school. I said, "Yes." The lady turned around, smiling with no crying anywhere now. She said, "Really, you like school? I didn't think anybody actually liked school. I hated school!" She smiled like this lady in a movie I saw about a girl who everybody realizes is actually a princess. The girl gets discovered, and this lady with blond hair and blue eyes takes her into a room where all her jewels are waiting. The girl tries on her jewels while the lady smiles.

I said, "I like school because I see my friends there."

"What about the work?" asked the man.

"I like it because I get all 3's and 4's."

"Is that A's and B's?"

"Four means you're perfect, 3 means you're good, 2 means not good—1, you got nothing."

"That's great you get 3's and 4's," said the lady, and she smiled like she'd put a crown on my head.

The smile was nice, but it was starting to be creepy too. Because she was smiling like she knew me and she did not. But my face kept smiling back.

"Did Ginger tell you we have horses right next door?" said the man. "A stable?"

"Yes," I said. And then we pulled into the driveway of a red house with a big spread-out tree in front. I was surprised. It did not look like the house of rich people.

Inside it wasn't rich either. It wasn't even as clean as our house—there were papers and books on the floor, and clothes hanging on chairs. The floor was painted a big white and blue diamond pattern and there were pictures on the walls of cartoon animals and a devil smoking a cigarette. There was a deep-blue bowl on the table with apples and oranges in it. The dining room window had curtains that were blue on one side and bright purple on the other. The bowl was my favorite; I sat down and touched the shining side of it.

"Are you hungry?" said the lady.

I was, but I was too embarrassed to eat something like an apple or an orange that you tear apart, so I said no.

"Do you want some cookies?"

I did, but I didn't want her to think I was the kind of pig who starting eating first thing, so I said, "Can I see my room?"

They both came up to show it to me, the man carrying my suitcase. It was a little room, with a pink cover on the bed and a painting of a sleeping girl hanging on the wall over it. I decided I liked this house; it was so quiet, but all the pictures and bright things made it seem like something fun was happening invisibly. I thought about my mom; I wished she could be here. Then the lady said, "Do you want to call your mom?" And I started liking her.

Ginger

She was so beautiful, so solid in her body, but so shy in the way she took things. I felt excited and scared about how to act—I couldn't even respond properly to my own family, so how could I take care of a needy child from another culture? It was a cliché to think that way, but I could feel her difference. At the same time, I could feel her child's goodness, her willingness to help us, and that was more compelling. We gave her privacy to talk to her mother and when we got downstairs, I whispered to Paul, "What do you think?"

"She's a sweetheart," he said. "It's going to be fine."

She came downstairs almost immediately. Her face was sad, and the shift of emotion was profound—for a moment I thought something terrible had happened. But she just said her mom didn't answer the phone. I got her to eat some cookies, and asked her what she wanted to do. I said we could go to see the town or to the lake or the bowling alley or for a walk around the neighborhood. Or we could walk over and visit the horses in the stables across the road from us. "The horses," she said, some cookie in her mouth. "We could see the horses?"

Velvet

I said we could go to the horses, but I didn't really care. I just said that because I knew they were close—I *did* want to see horses, but I didn't feel like it right then. Because my mom wouldn't pick up when I called *twice* and I felt alone, like she was *really* gone, and I was stuck here with a devil on the wall and nice people who didn't have anything to do with me.

But I went with the lady, Ginger. She talked about something, I don't know what. I was trying to count the hours in the days I had left and trying to subtract how much time I'd been there, starting from the bus. We passed through a gate with a sign that said "Wildwood"; suddenly there was too much space around us—green and green and green with some little fences and in the distance a big building with a giant hole for a door. I wanted to reach for Ginger's hand, and that made me mad at myself because I was too old for that. Then she said, "They give riding lessons for kids here. That's something we could do if you want to."

I didn't say anything.

And then we came to the building with the giant door.

"Here's the stable," said Ginger.

It looked scary from the distance, but inside it was not. It was dark and warm. It was all wooden. The smell of it was deep. You could feel it, like it was breathing all around you, but it wasn't scary, it was the opposite. And there was a horse, looking at me from an opening in his cage. A sign over him said "Graylie," and there were pictures and a dirty red teddy bear next to his face. And then there was another one and another one: "Diamond Chip Jim" (he had a purple fish toy and a bunch of fake flowers); "Blue Boy" (he had a bunch of plastic bottles); "Baby" (she had a doll); "Officer Murphy" (he had a bunch of stuff written on some papers and a blue ribbon); "Little Tina" (she didn't have nothin'). There were some people too, walking around, but I didn't notice them. The horses were all looking at me and Ginger, and some of them were saying things: *Who are you? Come over here! Have you got something for me? I'm lonely. Don't bother me!*

"Do you like them?" asked Ginger.

I said, "Yes," and then, "Can I touch them?"

"Yes, but be careful. Some of them can bite."

I went up to one named Rocki. He was cream-colored with a short mane and a black stripe down the center of it. He was beautiful but with sad, hurt eyes. He didn't have any pictures or toys. I put my hand out to him. He let me touch his nose and his strong neck.

Ginger said, "Hi, Pat." I turned and saw a round woman with a red face and blond-gray hair sticking out everywhere. She was wearing old beat-up clothes and she was pushing a big wooden wheelbarrow like I'd seen in books about farm life; it was full of wet dirt and bits of straw. "I just brought the young lady over to see the horses."

"Hello, young lady," said the woman. It was funny, the way she looked at me; she looked past me, but still it felt like she was looking right at me. It was like her eyes were on the sides of her head. Like the horses. "What's your name?"

Her face was nice but her voice was strong, like she might beat your ass, so my answer came out like a whisper.

"Nice to meet you," said Pat. "I see you met Rocki. He's a good guy."

I wanted to ask her why he was so sad, but I just looked down instead.

"Look around all you want, just pay attention to the signs." She picked up the handles of the wheelbarrow again and began walking the other way.

"Is she the one that gives the lessons?" I whispered to Ginger.

"Yeah." Ginger smiled down at me, and that crying thing moved through her face really fast. "Interested?"

I was confused by Ginger's face, by everything that was happening. But Pat was moving away and I suddenly felt like I had to talk or my chance would be gone. "Yes," I whispered.

And so we went down to the other end of the stable so that Pat could check her appointment book. I walked slowly after them so I could look at the horses. I looked at the stable too; there was cool stuff in it: leather straps hanging everywhere, metal boxes, chains, helmets, saddles—everything was old and beat-up, but somehow that was what made it cool. It all looked like it had a *reason,* even the dirt and balls of hair and straw on the floor of the stable—even that somehow was right, and didn't seem like dirt.

Ginger and Pat were in an office somewhere off to the side when I saw a girl in one of the horse-cages by herself. It was open and the horse was gone and it looked like she was cleaning the cage with a fork. She was a white girl, thin but strong-looking, with long shiny brown hair and a chin that reminded me of a pit bull. When she looked up and saw me, she didn't say anything and neither did I. She just looked, then went back to what she was doing.

And then two other white girls came in from a hallway I didn't notice. One of them had a boy-face and hair that was half blue, half purple; the other was regular. They were leading a huge horse and talking loud, like they thought they were hot. When they saw me they stopped and stared. Suddenly there was this loud, mad-pissed-off banging, and I heard a horse making angry *wanting* noises. The other horses answered like, *We hear!* The boy-girl yelled, "Shut up, Fugly Girl!" And the other said to me, "We don't mean you." And the boy-girl laughed.

I walked away from them toward the office. One of the girls muttered, "Sorry." The banging got louder. And then I saw where it was coming from. There was a gold-brown horse kicking and *biting* the hell out of her cage. Her eyes were rolling in her head and you could see the white around them. But she was the best one so far, not the most beautiful, the *best.* There were no ribbons or toys or even a name on her cage, just a sign that read "Do Not Touch." I came close to her and she looked at me. That's when I saw the scars on her face, straight, deep scars around her nose and eyes. She turned her head all the way to one side and then the other. I thought, Your scars are like the thorns on Jesus's heart. She stopped biting and kicking. I could see her think in the dark part of her eye. The white part got softer. The girls behind me went quiet. The wonderful horse came up to me. I put my hand out to her. She touched it with her mouth. I whispered, "You are not fugly."

"Hey, can't you read?" the boy-face girl yelled at me. "That horse is dangerous, get away from it!"

"She's only dangerous if she doesn't like you," said Pat. I turned and saw her and Ginger coming out of the office. Pat came up to the horse and rubbed her on the nose. "The trouble is, she doesn't like anybody except me—and sometimes she doesn't like me." Pat looked at me, straight on this time. "So I've got a slot open tomorrow. Does that work for you?"

Ginger

When we got back to the house she wanted to eat a sandwich, so I fixed her a ham and cheese with tomatoes for health. She asked if there were any pickles and I said, No, I'm sorry. She looked at me quizzically while she ate. Tomatoes dripped out. She asked if those girls would be at the barn when she went for her lesson. I said I didn't know. I wondered if they said something racial to her, but I didn't want to embarrass her by asking. I didn't think there would be direct racism in this town. But it might come in a subtler form.

"What did you think of them?" I asked.

"I dunno," she said.

"Would you want to see them again?"

"No."

I asked if she'd brought a swimsuit. She said yes. I told her we'd gotten a life jacket for her, for when we went to the lake. She asked to see it, and when I brought it, she put it on and frowned; it was too small. My heart sank a little. We both went out to the garden, where Paul was pulling weeds, and told him we were going to the store to get a new life jacket. He said he would go with us. She wore the life jacket into the car, and I was aware of her fiddling with it as we drove. When we went over the Kingston Bridge, I sensed her stop fiddling for a moment; I turned and saw her hands still in her lap, her soft, responsive profile as she looked out the window, reacting to the huge bright sky and sparkling water. I felt pulled by big feelings, but I didn't know what they were.

When we got to the parking lot of the store and found a place, she said, "I made it fit." And she had! She had worked out the adjustable straps and fasteners that we hadn't even thought to look for. Paul said, "You're smarter than we are!" and her eyes sparkled shyly.

We decided that since we were at the mall, we would buy her a bike. It took a long time because she was so uncomfortable about choosing one. We kept asking, What about this one? Do you like this one? Do you like the color? And she would say, "I dunno" and look down, as if confused. I asked her, Do you *want* a bike? She said yes, but almost in the same way she might say no. A salesman came over and that only made it worse. I was beginning to feel we were doing some strange violence to her when she said, "That one" and pointed to a violet bike with flowers on it.

When we got back home, Paul and I got our bikes and we all went for a ride in the neighborhood across the county road behind our house. It was a short ride, but it seemed like an adventure, and it linked the three of us. We sweated up some hills, and then coasted down fast. We came to some broken asphalt—I yelled "Lumpety bumpety!"—and Velvet grinned triumphantly as we bounced over it. When we came to a little park with a duck pond, she wanted to stop and see the ducks. There was a swing set and even though it was preschool size, Velvet wanted to swing on it. We were too big to swing with her, so we took turns pushing her. Then we played on the teeter-totter and the rickety wooden go-round—then she wanted to go back to the swings. She did everything with enchanted hunger, like she was maybe too old for this but wanted it anyway, because she knew it was something she should've had. Besides, it was fun—*we* thought it was fun.

When we got home, Paul asked Velvet if she liked Celia Cruz— she said, "Yes!" So he put on a Cruz CD and turned it up loud enough so that you could hear it in the backyard. Velvet kept me company while I made the salad and got the chicken ready for Paul to cook outside. It felt good to make food for her. I remembered my mom fixing food in the kitchen, her hips solid against the counter as she moved her hands; I remembered the feeling of love and trust in it. I wanted to be that, even if it was only for a little while. When Paul came in with the chicken on a big plate, I knew he was enjoying it too; I could see the pleasure coming off his chest.

At dinner we asked about her family. She told us about her brother, who was visiting another family. She told us her mother worked as an old person's aide and also rented out a room to a Mr. Diaz, who didn't live in the room but kept his private business in there. "What business is he in?" asked Paul with too much nonchalance. She said she didn't know, that he kept the door padlocked when he was gone, and they weren't allowed to bother him when he was there. She asked if we had any kids. Paul told her about his daughter; Velvet was disappointed when Paul told her that Edie was in Italy. Velvet didn't ask me about kids, but she looked at me expectantly. When I didn't say anything, she said she wanted to try her mother again.

Velvet sounded happy when her mom answered; she said, "Mami!" But right away the woman started yelling. She was yelling so loud I could hear her from a foot away. Velvet spoke quickly, sometimes arguing, sometimes almost pleading. I heard "Celia Cruz," said hopefully; the mother just kept yelling. Finally Velvet looked at me and said, "My mom says thank you for buying me the bike." Then she put the phone down, looking mad and happy both.

We watched some videos; I had one I'd picked out in advance, a movie about a tough Hispanic girl who learns how to box and triumphs over her crappy life. I hadn't seen it, but I'd seen trailers for it; they showed one person after another yelling at the girl about how she was no good while the words "Prove them wrong!" flashed on the screen. Then they showed the girl punching the crap out of a bag while music played. I thought it was inspiring—*Prove them wrong!*— and I looked forward to sitting there with Velvet, being inspired together. We put it on, and there was the first scene of the girl's father yelling at her that she was no good. Velvet looked depressed. "It's going to get better," I said encouragingly. The yelling at home went on for a long time. Then the girl got to school and a teacher yelled at her. Other girls insulted her, and pretty soon, she was in the bathroom, beating on somebody. "Can we watch something else?" asked Velvet.

Embarrassed, I showed her the other ones: something about a Pakistani girl overcoming prejudice to become a soccer star in England and something about a girl discovering that she is a princess. Velvet picked the second one. We watched it together on the couch. Yearningly, Velvet drank in its scenes of senseless abundance and approval. An actress who was famous for playing a beautiful, fun-loving nun when I was a kid took the princess into a room and gave her tons of jewelry. In a trance of pleasure, this little girl who did not know me leaned against me and put her head on my shoulder. Shyly, I touched her hair. Paul came into the room, and I felt his warmth even though the lights were down and I couldn't see his face.

Velvet

When I finally talked to my mom, she just yelled at me. I tried to tell her about the horses and she told me that I could get kicked and killed, that a horse in DR had almost killed her. I told her that these horses were nice, and that I was going to ride one tomorrow. She said, You tell those people that I forbid it. Tell them if anything happens to you, they are going to be in big trouble. "Okay," I said. "I'll tell them."

Then I hung up and we watched movies. We watched another movie about the princess. After that, we went upstairs and they showed me my towel and washcloth in the bathroom; they were white with pink flowers. Ginger waited for me to get ready for bed, and when I got in bed she asked if I wanted her to read to me. It was embarrassing, but I said yes and she sat on the bed.

And then I felt strange. I had waked up pressed against my mother and little brother, and now I was alone in a bed with a pink cover and this blond lady sitting there, her face full of niceness with pain around the edges. Why was this even happening? I missed my mom next to me. Instead Ginger was next to me, reading with her eyes down, her voice like white dream horses running across the sky: A little girl playing hide-and-seek goes into the closet to hide and comes out in a snowy country. She meets a man with hairy goat legs. (Like Paul!) The hairy-leg says a beautiful witch has come to the land and made it winter all the time. Ginger looked at me with her blue, blue eyes and then away. Hairy-leg says the little girl has been sent to help, that only she can help. Ginger closed the book. She sat quiet like she didn't know what to do. Then she said, "That's all for now, Princess Velveteen." And she touched my head.

When she turned off the light and closed the door, there was still light from the outside on the wall with tree branches in it. I thought of my mother at home in the bed, with car lights moving on the wall and people talking and playing music in the street. I thought of Dante crying at the bus station—where was he? I thought of my grandfather. Was he there like he said he would be?

Ginger

That night Paul and I went to bed feeling close, our arms wrapped around each other. When I woke up in the middle of the night, scared and sad from a dream I couldn't remember, I reached for him, pressing myself against his back. But instead of his name I heard myself say, "M'lindie!" Which is what I called Melinda when I was five. Then I was awake enough to know it was Paul's big male back I was holding—but still I whispered, "Melinda." And then I fell back to sleep.

Which maybe isn't as weird as it sounds. Melinda and I slept together until I was ten and she was twelve.

Velvet

I woke up feeling sad without knowing why. Then I realized why. I was remembering a time a long time ago when I thought my mom was a witch and I wouldn't eat what she made me. I wouldn't eat and at first she yelled at me and then she was worried I was sick. She stroked my hair and asked if my stomach hurt and tried to give me tea with ginger. I was too afraid to drink it, but because she was talking so nice, I told her why. I said, "Mami, I'm afraid a witch might be living in your body." And then the witch came out. Her eyes got red flame inside them and she left the room angrily; Dante laughed and pointed at me, because I would be whipped, not him. But when she came back with the belt, he shut up and put his hands over his pee-pee. I tried to run, but she grabbed my hair and pulled up my shirt and she beat me until I bled, until Dante was screaming louder than me. Then she sat and dropped the belt, put her hands over her face, and cried. I heard Manuel; he was looking at me out his cracked-open door. I pulled my shirt down.

I got out of bed and went to the window. Over the field across from the house, the sun was coming up. It was perfect-round and burning red. Looking at it made my feelings pull apart.

Then I remembered: My horse lesson was today.

Ginger

I came downstairs and saw her sitting at the table drinking juice and playing Uno with Paul. She said, "When are we going to go to the horses?" It was eight o'clock and her lesson was at eleven. She wanted to go over anyway. I said she had to eat breakfast first and made her bacon and eggs. Then I got her to help me with the dishes, mostly because I could feel her attention going out the door, and I wanted to feel linked with her again.

When we were all done, I said, "What are you going to do over there for two hours?"

First she said, "I dunno," and then, "Talk to Fugly Girl."

"Be careful," I said. "You heard Pat. Stay back from the stall."

"I will. I want to see the other horses too."

I walked over with her. Pat was there leading a baby horse outside. I didn't see any other kids. "We came early," I said.

"Good," said Pat. "Want to come out to the round pen with me and Jimbo?"

I said I would be back to watch Velvet ride and left her following Pat to the corral, smiling and looking at her feet.

When I got back to the house, I was surprised to hear Paul speaking Spanish into the phone—or trying; he didn't really know the language. "Qué?" he asked. He looked like he was struggling to understand what was being said—and then he held the phone away from him as angry words poured from it. He put the phone back to his ear and then hung it up. He looked at me with a baffled face. "That was Velvet's mother," he said. "I'm not sure what she was calling about. At first it sounded like she was saying *she* was in trouble. Then it sounded like she meant to say *we're* in trouble. She was talking too fast for me to understand, but I'm pretty sure she called me 'stupido' before she hung up."

We laughed, but uneasily. We decided to call the office of the organization that had brought Velvet out. No one answered; we left a message that we needed a translator to speak to Velvet's mom.

Velvet

We went with the horse to a fenced circle. Pat told me his name was Jimbo, and that he was only a year old. She told me to stay outside the fence and then she went in and took Jimbo off the leash. She stopped talking to me and started talking to Jimbo. I couldn't pay attention to her, I just watched the horse. I could see he was a baby, not just for being small, he moved like a little kid. She made him come to her by walking away, and then if he moved away from her, she raised her arms and walked at him swinging the leash, like she wanted him away. Once when he wouldn't come, she came to the fence where I was and crouched down. I said, What are you doing? She said, Shhh and told me to get down too. The baby horse just looked at us. We waited. And then he came. He came up to Pat and put his nose near her. She told him he was good. I wished he would put his nose on me, but Pat got up and clipped the leash back on him.

When we took him back in the barn, I asked her why Fugly Girl had that name. She said, "It's not really her name, it's just what the girls call her. Because her head is a little too big for her body."

People said my head was too big too. This girl I hate calls me "Flat-Ass Fathead" and "Velveeta Cheese."

"Her ear too—one of 'em looks like somebody might've twisted it."

"What's her real name?"

"Funny Girl. Which doesn't suit her."

I agreed, it did not.

"Not much funny about the mare's background. She's an Appendix quarter horse—that's a quarter horse–thoroughbred mix—but I don't know the mix on her, and I can see both in how she's put together. Her last owners—or rather, the owners before last— brought her up from down south, where she was bush-track racing."

"What's that?"

"Rough-type racing, basically to train jockeys. Hardly any rules. People get hurt all the time."

"She ran races?"

"Back in the day."

"Can I ride her?"

"No one rides that horse. Remember the sign? It's there for a reason. Don't even touch that horse."

I thought, I already touched her. She already touched me. And you saw it.

Pat showed me the horse I would ride; she was just plain white and a little fat. But she was nice. Her name was Reesa. Pat put a halter on her face and brought her out of her cage—her stall—and "cross-tied" her, that meant she was tied by her face to both walls. And then she gave me a brush to clean her with. I brushed her whole hard body; Pat showed me the place on her back where she specially liked it, and I did it there a lot. Then we put the saddle on her; when I strapped it on with this thing called a "girth," Reesa puffed out her stomach like to push it away, but Pat said it was okay. Then Pat put a helmet on my head, meaning my head might break, and I got scared. But she gave me the end of the leash (the "lead rope") and I had to lead Reesa out into the circle. In the circle there was a wooden step-thing called a "mounting block," and Pat put it next to Reesa. "Okay," she said. "Ready?"

I stood still and breathed. Pat waited. Reesa waited. I climbed up on the top step and put my hand on her. "Keep the reins in your left hand. That's your control," said Pat. "But take hold of her mane with the same hand—it's okay, you won't hurt her—and slip your left foot in the stirrup." I took the mane; Reesa seemed like she was saying, *It's okay,* but I was scared. "Go on," said Pat. "Foot in the stirrup, take hold of that saddle, and get on your horse!" So I held the saddle and swung my leg and then I was on top of her. And then I felt her. I felt her say things, deep things; mostly I felt that she was strong, that she didn't have to let me on her, or do *anything I told her.* But she did and she would.

"She accepts you," said Pat. "She doesn't care who you are, how much money you have, where you're from. She accepts you."

I thought, I know.

"She can feel your head move; she can feel your stomach tense or relax. Her skin is so sensitive she can feel a mosquito land on her before it bites. To make her move, you tap with your calves, you don't kick. Kicking her is like screaming at her, and you don't need to do that. She can hear you."

I smiled so hard it made tears come. Pat just kept talking. With my legs, I asked Reesa to go. And she did.

Ginger

They must've started early; she was already on the horse when I got there. Pat had the horse on a lead, and she was talking to Velvet, making corny jokes, telling her to sit up straight and stick her chest out "like Dolly Parton." But when Pat led the horse around, and I saw the girl's face, I could see it didn't matter; she was in a state of joy. When she saw me and the camera I'd brought, she smiled even bigger.

Pat got her to move the horse forward, backward, then in a wide circle. She got her to trot. She got her to stand up and sit down in time with the horse. Velvet did it all, now and then giving me a movie-star smile so I could take a picture of it.

It felt so good, I completely forgot about my private radio signal, whether it was there or not. That was a metaphor that did not have any meaning in this situation. This situation was something else entirely.

Velvet

When I saw Ginger there I felt the same as when I first got in the car with her and Paul: that she was a strange nice lady with a mixed face who didn't have anything to do with me. I liked her taking my picture, I liked it that I was going to have some pictures to take back home with me. But it was strange.

And then it wasn't. I can't explain it. Just all of a sudden, it made sense, her being there, me being with her. I still don't know why. But I got it. It was like I was looking at puzzle pieces all over the floor that magically got snapped into place and I went, *Oh, okay.* I still couldn't say what the picture was. But it made sense.

Ginger

That night after dinner, instead of a movie, I asked her if she wanted to go for a walk; she said yes. It was a beautiful night, with light still in the sky, the moon glowing behind slow-moving clouds. We could see the outlines of huge old trees against the soft-lit night, and the tall grass of the field moving gently, the fireflies. The road looked pale and glowing against the dense summer foliage. I could feel her taking all this in. I could feel her enjoying the lights of the houses set back from the road, the mystery of other people's lives. At least I *thought* she enjoyed it the way I did, and I loved it that we could feel that together.

She talked about the horses. She didn't say much in words—she liked them because they were nice—but her voice said so much else. I told her my sister had loved horses, but that I was afraid of them. She asked why I was afraid. I said I didn't know. She asked if she could meet my sister. I told her my sister was dead. She said, "Oh," and we walked quietly for a while. Then she told me her grandfather was dead. I felt my mother sigh through me.

We were almost home when she asked me why I didn't have kids. I told her it was because I was an artist. I told her that if I'd had kids I didn't think I could do art. I thought art was what I did best, and I should try to do it even if I never made any money.

She was quiet a long time after I said this. I felt her puzzlement and then her acceptance.

That night I read to her again—*we* read to her. Paul sat on the bed with me, and we passed the book, reading different characters: Paul the troll, me the witch. Her eyes were golden and shining, like she was in a scene from something on TV, which is how I felt too, like this was the good thing I had always wanted and never quite got.

Which is strange because I *did* get that. Our mother read to us when we were little.

Velvet

I couldn't have another lesson right away because Pat didn't have room in her book. But I came to visit the horses the next day. I saw those other girls in the barn, but I didn't talk to them and at first they didn't talk to me. I watched the quiet one, the one with the long brown hair; I saw she didn't talk to the purple-hair boy-face or the one with the glasses either. She knew I was watching her though. I could tell by the way she moved. It seemed like she liked it that I watched, and that made me think she was a jackass, like she thought she was somebody to watch.

Still, I *did* watch: the way she led the horses in and out, how she brushed them, the way they moved with her and stood still for her. When she cleaned the stalls, she used the pitchfork like she was important, like she was saying, *If you want to be around horses, you've got to clean a lot of horse shit.* And when she went to this paper bag where the horse cookies were kept, it was like she was showing me, *Here's where the cookies are.* Finally I said, "My name is Velvet." And she put out her hand and said, "I'm Beth." She nodded down the barn at the purple-haired girl. "That's Gare Ann. She's kind of dumb, in case you didn't notice."

Pat came in and out, pushing her wheelbarrow, talking and joking. Cats walked around. There was this boy too. I don't know what he was doing; I think he was a little bit retarded. Even though it was Gare that Pat did the "brain monster" to: She put her hand on Gare's head and said, "I'm starvin' to death!" Gare ducked and turned red, and Pat wiggled her hand and went, "I'm the brain monster! I'm hungry. Where's some brains?"

I didn't care; I just paid attention to the horses. Graylie was like a old gangster with a nice personality. Diamond Chip Jim was the handsome one. Officer Murphy was like a little kid who likes dumb jokes. Little Tina knew she was beautiful. Rocki was sad, like he was when I first saw him. I asked Pat why he was sad. And she said, "Because his owner doesn't like him. Because she wants him to be perfect and nobody's perfect."

"I like him," I said.

"And he knows it," said Pat.

I smiled and I thought, So does she. Fugly Girl—so-called. I didn't go up to her when the other people were around. But I could hear her making that biting-grunt sound and sometimes kicking, and when I walked past, she got quiet. I could feel her watching me, and sometimes I would watch her back, quickly.

Late in the afternoon, when the girls were gone and Pat was out giving a lesson, I gave her a cookie. She ran up for it—she grabbed it so hard she broke it—so I gave her another one and she grabbed it again, then snapped her teeth at me and banged her hoof on the door like she was mad at me. The kind-of retarded boy put his head around the corner and stared at me. I moved away. I thought, Fuck that horse, no wonder they call her Fugly.

But later, after dinner, I walked over again, when nobody was there. I came to her stall with some cut-up apple and a carrot. All the horses made their talking noises when I walked in. I stopped to say hello to Reesa, and I gave her a piece of apple first. Then I went to Fugly Girl. She came up really fast with her ears laid back, like she was going to snap her teeth again. But she didn't. She stopped and looked at me, kind of bobbing her head. Then she came up to the bars and worked her nose. She turned her head to one side and then the other. Her brown eye thought; her white eye got soft. I gave her a piece of apple and she ate it. I didn't try to pet her, I just fed her. Then I stood there with her for a while, leaning against the stall. She bit the wood, but peacefully, and for some reason it reminded me of Cookie talking, saying I was fine.

Ginger

I was alone in the house when the agency returned our message. They had a Spanish-speaker to do a conference call with us and Velvet's mother. It was pure luck that Paul wasn't there; he would never have understood what happened.

The translator was a Latina with a young, charming voice. I said, "Tell her I'm happy she called, that she has a wonderful daughter. I love having her here." But the mother started talking—nearly yelling—before the girl could get the nice words out. I thought, She sounds like she wants to kill me. "She says Velvet can't ride horses," said the young woman finally. "It's too dangerous."

My heart pounded. I made my voice as nice as I could. I said, "Tell her it's not horses she's riding. They're ponies, little ponies, very safe." I flushed as I heard the lie translated. The silence that followed was probing and shrewd. Then came the furious reply and I thought, She knows.

But she didn't. When we got off the phone, everything was okay. I thought, How could anything be okay if she sounds that mad? The translator said, "I told her that we make sure our host families are very good people, that we know who you are and that life there is very safe. That you wouldn't let Velvet do something that wasn't safe."

I thought, She lied to the mother too. They don't know who we are. Somebody only came out here and talked to us for five minutes before they signed us up. Still, I felt justified. I felt it especially when Velvet wanted to go to the barn again that night and give the horses cut-up apples. I felt it when she came back from her second lesson, face glowing. I thought, I will tell her mother eventually. Next week, maybe. I will tell her that Velvet has gotten so good so fast, they want to put her on a bigger horse and she will say yes. And then there will be time for a few more lessons before she goes back. And the agency will be on my side.

Velvet

The third day I went to the barn, somebody new came. She was old and red-skinned like Pat, but her hair was shiny brown and cut neat. She was short and she would've been fat except her body was square and hard instead of soft and round. She wore her pants tucked into tall black boots, and when she walked she swung her arms. She looked like she could hit—like she liked to hit—but at the same time like she would only do it if there was a reason. She had a shirt on that said "Beware the Mare." She was cool.

While I was watching her, Beth came over and whispered, "That's Beverly. She's the trainer." She stood next to me and talked without looking at me. "She used to work at this fancy barn called Steeplechase where she trained horses so the rich girls there could jump 'em and look good at shows even if they don't really know anything."

I was trying to think what to say back, but before I could she said, "They fired her. I think she did something messed-up to somebody. Or somebody's horse." I almost asked how she knew, but then the retarded boy piped in out of nowhere, like a retarded person will do. "They say dogs are man's best friend," he said. "But horses are man's best slave." He looked right at me. "Are you Mexican?"

I said, "No, I'm Dominican."

"What's that?"

"Somebody from the Dominican Republic."

"I never heard of that," said Beth. "Where is that?"

Before I could answer, the weird boy said, "So why does a Mexican kid walk around like she owns the place?"

"It's in the Caribbean next to Haiti."

"So why does a Mexican—"

"Would you shut up?" said Beth.

He said, "It's a joke, and she isn't even Mexican!" But he shut up like he knew he was retarded, which made me feel sorry for him instead of mad.

The next time I saw Beverly, she was leading Blue Boy. The way Blue Boy followed her was different from how he followed Pat. With Pat, he walked normal; with Beverly he walked *sharp*—like a kid who knows he better not do *nothin'* wrong. I thought, That's how I want a horse to walk with *me*.

While I was watching, she stopped to talk to Gare Ann, who was cleaning the stall of a horse called Spirit. She was cleaning with Spirit standing in the stall with her. When I got closer I heard Beverly say, "You want to watch that one. He kicked Beth on the cross-ties last week."

That girl usually ran her mouth, but not to Beverly; she kept her head down, said, "Yes, ma'am."

"He kicked me once. Then we had a little conversation about it and he never did it again."

"What did you say to him?" I asked.

Everything stopped. Beverly turned like in slow motion and stared the crap out of me. Her strong red face had thin lips and small deep eyes. It was a face that could make you do things just by looking. "I hurt him," she said. "I hurt him more than he hurt me."

Gare was looking at me too, probably because that was the first time she heard me say anything. She wasn't gonna crack on me though. Not with this lady there. Even though she was turning around and taking Blue Boy away.

Ginger

Sometimes the three of us would do things together; sometimes Velvet would go off alone with Paul and work in the garden with him, or just do an errand, like accompany him to the hardware store. But mostly it was her and me together. We would go to the mall, make dinner together, see movies, take long walks at night and talk about "private things." I tried to get her to draw, but she was too scared of doing something wrong; reluctantly, she made cliché cats (ovals with tails and ears) and pigs, a few dull, dutiful flowers. They were the drawings of a five-year-old trying not to be messy. But I told her they were beautiful and although she probably knew that wasn't really what I thought, she smiled. At night Paul and I would both sit on her bed and read to her and her eyes would go from alert to enchanted to blurred, sweet and private as she slowly stepped down into sleep.

Her presence made everything special: a cheese sandwich cut into four pieces, carrots sliced the way my mother used to serve them, her special towel with pink flowers on it, the soap I got for her with a plastic horse in it, her favorite radio station when we drove to the store. The glow on her face when I served her breakfast and said, "There you go, Princess." The order of the house, which before I took for granted, now looked to me like something alive and full of goodness when I got up every morning and found the dishes she and I had washed in the drainer, the fruit in the bowl, the cereal and bacon ready to be cooked and eaten by somebody besides me and Paul.

It was like we were both living a dream we had known from television and advertisements and children's books, a dream that neither of us had believed in yet had both longed for without knowing it. A dream in which love and happiness were the norm.

I know this was a dream for her, because of the way she responded to idealized movies and songs. I know because I found out she'd lied to create an ideal picture for me—or at least a nice one. I found out because she told me one night when we were walking in the neighborhood behind the campus, listening to the sounds of crickets and frogs, of kids playing in the street and families in their homes. It was just dark, and I couldn't see her face, but I heard the embarrassment in her voice; I heard the trust. She reminded me of the time we'd first met, and she told me what her grades were.

"I don't really get 3's and 4's," she said. "I just told you that."

"What do you get?"

"Ones and 2's. Ones mostly."

I remembered how she'd said "1, you got nothing." We walked quietly for a moment and then, in a lower voice, she said, "I even got held behind in third grade. I should be going into middle school in the fall and I'm not."

"Do you want to do better?" I asked. "Do you want to go to middle school next fall?"

"Yes."

"Would you like me to help you? Work with you on the phone with your homework?"

She said yes again. I could hear that she was smiling in her voice.

I didn't tell her about the conversation I'd had with her mother. I saw no reason to.

Velvet

I started really liking Ginger. At first I was sorry that she wasn't more like the big-legged lady with the orange flower, then I started thinking that really, she was better. Her hair looked like Barbie-doll hair. She wore pink polish on her toes; she had rubber sandals with jewels on them, and when I told her I liked them, she went and bought me a pair. When she washed the dishes, she would take off her gold wedding ring and her diamond and put them on the windowsill. She had a gold lipstick case with blue stripes on it and she sometimes put that on the windowsill too, next to this little plant in a purple pot and these little skinny plastic giraffes in beautiful colors that she said were to stir drinks with. She didn't yell, ever. She was always nice, even when she got mad. But she didn't act "all that." The way she looked from behind, like when she was cooking food or something, made it seem like she didn't even know where she was for sure. She blinked a lot. She always forgot things, like even her bank card in the ATM. It made her seem even more nice, I don't know why.

One day she showed me her art. It was all up in the top of the house, in this small room with low ceilings, and windows, even windows in the ceiling. Her art was made out of colored shapes. She didn't like to paint real things, just these shapes. Sometimes they weren't even shapes, they just looked like things you'd do in preschool. I didn't like them, but I acted like I did. And there was one I *did* like a little because the shapes were cool—there was this round red thing like the sun when it came up over the dark line, only this was like the sun down in a hole. She said it was a picture of her sister and I'm like, *What?*

She said, "That's what my sister's personality was like."

I thought, She must've been crazy. But I didn't say it.

"My sister was very passionate. Do you know that word?"

"No."

"It means strong feelings, deep feelings. Like this."

She touched the red. I nodded. She put her hand on my shoulder and said, "You're passionate too, I think. You seem deep."

That night I took her ring. It was from this glass box where she kept rings she wore before she got married. It wasn't stealing because she showed them to me once and asked if I wanted one. I said no. But I went and took one, a tiny one with an orange flower that she wore on her little finger when she was a teenager; it reminded me of the orange plastic flower of the big legs lady. I slept with it on my pinkie finger that night.

The second week I was there I got to ride a bigger horse, a boy. Pat said that normally, she would wait till I'd had more lessons, but that I was doing so good I could ride him sooner. His name was Joker and he was light brown with white socks. He looked a lot stronger than Reesa, and he lifted his feet higher when he walked. I was scared to ride him and that made me want to ride him even more.

I came early and went to talk to Fugly Girl. Pat pretended not to see me leaning right up against the door of her stall. The horse came to me and stretched her head out like she wanted some apple, but when she saw I didn't have anything, she stayed still and licked her stall, like *thoughtfully*. I asked her if I could touch her nose for courage. She looked down like, *Oh, all right*—and flared it open; quickly I kissed it. Then I knew I could handle Joker.

Except I couldn't. He wouldn't do anything I said. He would stop and he would go, but not when I asked. He moved too fast for me and he wouldn't go in the direction I wanted. Pat was getting on my nerves, saying dumb things about sticking my chest out like Dolly-somebody. Either that or telling me to do things I couldn't do.

"Focus your mind," she said. "Pick a direction, pick a spot right there on that fence, then look at it. He'll feel your intention, but you have to mean it."

I tried and it seemed like it almost worked.

"Do it again," said Pat. Her voice was starting to sound mean. Joker walked toward the barn while I tried to turn him. Pat said, "You have a little brother, right? When he was three years old and he was doing something he wasn't supposed to do, what did you do?"

"Hit him," I said.

"You don't want to try that with Joker. Was there anything else you did besides hit?"

"Pick him up and move him."

"Then do it. That horse is just like a three-year-old. Pick him up *and move him!*"

And I did it. I picked him up with my legs and I moved him with my butt. I did it before I even picked a spot. I could feel it happening, and then I saw Ginger. She was walking toward us, smiling. I saw she had her camera again. I looked at her and Joker went to her. It wasn't what I told him, but when he did it, I tapped him and made him go faster. And when I did, all of a sudden I didn't see Ginger, I saw my mother. Not really—it was Ginger standing there. But it felt like my mother, my mother smiling at me, more than she ever really did. Then it was just Ginger again, and it felt like *I* was running to her, not the horse but *me,* on my own legs. And she was taking my picture and telling me I looked like a movie star.

I decided I would put the tiny flower ring on the blond key-chain doll with the checked coat. It would be like having Ginger in my box.

Ginger

That day was the first time it looked like she was really riding a horse. It wasn't because it was trotting—I'd seen her on the white horse when it was trotting. But then, she was just *on* the white horse and it was trotting. She was *riding* that big brown horse; even I could see the difference.

The lesson was over then, and I went with them into the barn. I stood to the side and watched Velvet secure the horse in the middle of the barn and begin to groom it. The way she moved was very different from the way she moved around the house; there was no deference or absentmindedness in her, just purpose. She looked bigger, stronger, and completely comfortable with the huge animal. "She's a natural," said Pat. "It takes most kids twice as many lessons to get where she got today. Too bad she's leaving next week."

Velvet

That night they both sat on the bed and read to me like always. The witch had hypnotized this boy by giving him too much candy, and it made him bad so that he went over to the witch's side against his family. They took turns reading and their voices made me think about my mom, singing at night: *The little chicks say "pio pio pio" when they are hungry, when they are too cold to sleep. The mother looks for corn and wheat, she gives them food to eat.* She sang that to my brother at night before we slept. She sang to him, with her back to me. Once I asked her to sing to me too, and she said, "You're too old for that!" But she didn't sing to me when I was young either. Still, I listened to the singing, and she knew I listened. *Safe under mama's wings, huddling up, sleep the little chicks until the next day.*

I tried to stop thinking and pay attention to the story. But I couldn't. I missed my mom. I missed lying next to her and hearing her. I tried to think of how I would tell her about all the things that had happened—Ginger, riding Joker, Pat, the purple-haired girl, Beverly, and Fugly Girl. But I just pictured her getting mad and finding some reason to call me stupid. I tried to look at Ginger and see my mom, like what happened when I was on Joker. But how could I see my mom reading? She didn't know how to read, even in Spanish. Right then, Ginger looked up and smiled at me. And I wondered what it would be like to live with her instead of my mom. Some of the time.

I tried to pay attention to the story again. The witch had locked the boy up and his family was trying to save him. I didn't care. I was sad. I closed my eyes so Ginger and Paul wouldn't see.

Ginger

After we put her to bed—she looked at me so longingly, her golden eyes slowly and heavily closing—I talked with Paul about keeping her longer. "We can't," he said. "It's time for her to go back."

We were sitting at the kitchen table, the little red Formica table I'd moved from my East Village studio, drinking soda from juice jars. I told him about the way she was on the brown horse. "She needs more of this," I said.

"Do you mean *you* need more?"

"I want more, I don't *need* it. But so what if I did?" My voice went from soft to sharp back to soft. "What's wrong with satisfying a mutual need?"

"Nothing, if you're talking about people in an equal position. But you aren't. She's a disadvantaged child. She has needs you can't satisfy. It's unfair to act like you can. And—"

"I can get her horse-riding lessons."

"—you have needs *she* can't satisfy. And I thought this was supposed to be maybe a first step toward adoption."

We both took drinks; he put his glass down too hard and looked away. He was mad, and so was I, but why?

"Do you even know she *wants* to stay longer?"

"Yes. If it weren't for the horses I wouldn't say that. But you didn't see her on that horse."

He looked doubtful.

"What if the organization agrees to it?" I asked. "Would that make you feel better?"

"Maybe," he said. "Though I doubt they will. At least not on their insurance."

Velvet

I dreamed that I woke up and it was day, but only for me; that it was light for me and dark for Paul and Ginger and they were sleeping. I got up and walked through their house, looking at everything: the fruit in the bowls, the colored curtains, the paintings and tiny giraffe toys on the windowsill. I went out into their yard and looked at Paul's garden; in the plants and flowers I saw a trapdoor, and I knew that it was the door to hell. I was scared, but then I realized that my grandfather was there, in the backyard. *Don't be afraid,* he said. *The devil isn't paying attention—now is your chance. I'll guard the door.*

"Grandfather," I said. "Why are you telling me to go to hell?"

Because someone you love is there and she is in danger of being lost.

"Who is it?"

I can't tell you.

"Is she evil?"

No. But she is close to evil. You can help her because you call to the good in her. You have to hurry. She is getting more lost every second.

And so I did. I opened the door and I went down the stairs. It was a long stair, and there were a lot of floors with weird things happening on them. But that is all I remember.

Ginger

When she came downstairs, sleep-dazed and a little sullen, I asked her if she wanted to stay for another two weeks, and she woke fully and said yes in the soft voice that meant she was happy and scared to trust it. So I told her, quick and soft, before Paul came, that when we called her mother, she and I, we shouldn't tell her mom everything about the horses, that it might be best to wait until she could really ride and then . . . I started to say "surprise her" but trailed off. It didn't matter. The child simply said okay.

I called the agency right at nine o'clock. I had to talk to several different people, each sounding more suspicious and displeased than the last, like parts of a machine that didn't like its operation reset for any reason. Finally somebody told me that if Velvet's mother agreed, we could keep her as long as we wanted, but that it would not be under agency auspices and that they would not insure us. If we didn't want to send her back to her mother on the bus, we would have to bring her back to the office and deliver her to her mother there. After that, we could do whatever we wanted as long as we understood they weren't involved.

Then we called her mother, who was not a machine. First Paul talked, using his Spanish, cajoling her to politely talk back. Then Velvet came on, wheedling like a teenager in a movie about adorable teenagers. Yelling came from the handset; her mother obviously thought that movie was a piece of crap. Velvet yelled, cajoled, wheedled. A slow smile spread over her face; she looked at me and nodded. The whole thing took about ten minutes. "I told her I was working at the barn," she said. "That they were teaching me how to work."

It wasn't a lie. Velvet planned to work at the barn. Pat had already agreed to give her a lesson every day in exchange for several hours of work.

Velvet

After they decided I could stay longer, I woke up in the middle of the night, I guess because I was excited. At first I thought it was late, but I saw light coming from under the door and I heard Paul and Ginger talking downstairs. Something about their voices made me feel like something was going on, and I wanted to know what it was. So I got up and went out of the room, walking quietly. I went half down the stairs and sat down right next to the wall. They were in the kitchen and I couldn't hear them all the way; it was words, then pissed-off hiss-mumbling, then words. I creeped down the wall some more and I heard Paul say: "There's a limit to what you can be to each other, and you are *mumble mumble* pushing that limit. It's taking it out of the boundaries set by the organization *mumble mumble* personal!"

"It's supposed to be personal!" Ginger mumble-hissed. ". . . families . . . the same kids up every year . . . even birthdays—*mumble mumble!*"

Paul didn't answer. They just moved around. There were dish sounds and water running, which didn't sound mad, and I thought that if they were really mad, I would hear it in the dishes: they would bang them around like when my mom is mad, when she's mad, even the *water* runs mad. So I thought it was okay. But it didn't feel okay. It felt like at the bus station, only harder to understand. Like I was in the Alice in Wonderful story where she is really, really tiny and then really, really big, like I was something tiny in their house and huge at the same time. I went back upstairs and lay down and tried to think like I wasn't really sure what they said. But I was.

Ginger

Before we got on the train, I took some pictures of her in the stable. I made sure I got as many as possible of Velvet with the one actual pony and the colt. Of course there were other pictures too; I had dozens of them. I thought, We can show them to the mother after she's met me, after she sees how happy her daughter is, how unharmed. Hopefully she will skip over the thing about the little ponies, think it's a misunderstanding. After all, the agency person hadn't really stressed the part about the ponies. She had stressed that we were nice and that everything we might give her daughter to do was safe.

Or maybe we just won't show the pictures at all. I could just say I forgot them.

Velvet

The train ride to the city was boring. It was better than the bus—there was a river outside the window instead of just a road with cars, there was more than one bathroom, and there was a place you could buy soda and chips. There were older white boys with big jackets and Converse on, their feet out in the aisle, and they cut their eyes all over my body when I went past, and one of them whispered "Rihanna."

But it was just mostly white people talking on their cell phones about boring things or people playing music on their iPods so nobody else could hear it; it was the sound of the train going and going and going. Ginger said, "Look out the window. You might see something you never saw before." But there was just water and trees and sky. For a second there was a broken-down castle in the middle of the river, but we went past it too quick to see anything. Ginger said, "When I used to tell my mother I was bored, she would say, 'If you are bored, it's your own fault.'" And she handed me the book about the witch.

I opened the book and thought about what would happen when my mom met Ginger. She would look at Ginger's Barbie hair and her pink toenail polish and her sandals with jewels on them. She would see how Ginger smiled, and how soft her voice was. She would see how Ginger liked me. She would see that I was wearing the same sandals as Ginger, that were better than anything she ever got me, and she would realize she never bought anything nice for me. She would feel like I did when she called me stupid and ugly.

There's a limit to what you can be to each other and you are—

The book fell out of my hand into my lap. My mother would feel stupid and ugly. I was glad she would feel it. Except it was me feeling it now. I looked outside.

They come up and they see this big house and all these nice things and—

Suddenly I wanted Ginger to feel it. The sun was hitting the water white-hot and putting silver on the waves. I thought of Ginger trying to make my mom like her while my mom told her she was stupid and ugly and worthless until Ginger cried. I thought of my mom scratching Ginger's face and slapping Ginger hard. The water and the light and the tree shapes kept going by and by. In my mind, I laughed while my mom smacked Ginger. But also I tried to make her hold back. I tried to protect Ginger too. Because she had been nice to me. She had smiled and taken my picture while I made Joker go to her. She had fought for me to stay. Under the water, the hitting and the smiling ran together. In my mind, my mother hugged Ginger and thanked her. I rode Joker out of the round pen, out into the field. Ginger and my mom watched me together.

Ginger

Velvet's mother was short, thick, powerful-looking. She was much older than I imagined, I thought at least forty, maybe close to fifty. Her heavy jaw and low brow had none of her daughter's lush softness. She was very light-skinned and her features were small, hard, and fine. Even if she lacked her daughter's dark beauty, she had obviously been pretty once. It took me a minute to realize that the power in her body didn't come from her musculature or size, but from her character; she sat in her body like it was a tank. When I walked in with Velvet, she looked at me first; it was an intensely focused look, rapid and bright, going instinctively from assessment to approval in seconds. She greeted her daughter, but her eyes dimmed at the sight of the child, no longer approving but acknowledging only. Docile, Velvet sat on the couch next to her. I sat in a chair to the side. In front of us were two erect, alert, smiling women from the Fresh Air Fund, one of whom was Carmen, the sweet-voiced Latina who had translated for me on the phone. But Mrs. Vargas sat there like she was alone in her tank, bored like a fighter is bored when there is no fight.

I asked Carmen to tell her, "Your daughter is beautiful," and was sorry immediately. Mrs. Vargas grimaced, as if with disgust, and made a gesture I understood as, *Don't give me that.* I flinched. Velvet didn't react. Carmen's smile froze for a moment and then she translated: "Don't swell her head, it's already too big."

And then Mrs. Vargas withdrew into herself, answering questions when asked, seeming to barely hear as the translator told her what Velvet and I were saying about the fair, the lake, the *little ponies.* Velvet glanced at me when I said those words, and her eyes were full of complicity. Her mother didn't react. I felt no guilt or embarrassment at this. What I felt was unease that she had looked at me with approval but not her daughter.

I don't know what anyone else thought of this. There was institutional friendliness (Carmen) and probing (the white social worker). Papers were filled out. When we got up to leave, Mrs. Vargas kept her head down and yanked on her skirt. She frowned. I thought, She moves like a farmhand. But she had style, even though she dressed very poor; her skirt was beige, but her high-heeled shoes were orange and so was her blouse. She gave me another glance; I realized she was checking me that way too, and liking my cheap but great sandals—which I'm sure she noticed on Velvet.

When we came out of the building and onto the street, Mrs. Vargas seemed to wake up. She put her arm around Velvet and talked to her harshly, but with warmth. Velvet and I had to wait for the train, so I suggested we get coffee and sandwiches.

In the coffee shop, Mrs. Vargas's demeanor changed. She sat across from me, next to Velvet, touching the girl with a proprietary air. When she looked at me, her face was open. I couldn't understand what she said, but she was out of the tank; I could *feel* her. I couldn't say exactly what she felt like, except that she was substantial. I liked her. I liked her even though she had made that nasty face when I'd told her Velvet was beautiful. First I didn't understand why and then I knew: it was the way she met my eyes. When I need to know who someone is and if I can trust them, I sometimes look too deep into their eyes. I don't do it on purpose, but sometimes I can feel it happening and that it makes people uncomfortable—most people just look away; some get pissed off. Some look back, but like they're scared. So I don't do it on purpose, but if I need to know, I can't help it, I look. I looked at Velvet's mother in the diner. And she looked back. She looked in exactly the same way I was looking: like she wanted to know who I was and if she could trust me. It was like, for that moment, we were speaking the same language. I could not remember the last time I'd had that experience.

Paul

Ginger was right: It bothered me more than I said that she wanted Velvet out for another two weeks, and it's hard to say exactly why. I liked the girl. I could see how much she and Ginger liked each other, and I could see how much the horses meant to her; the kid was lazy like any kid—you had to push her to help with the dishes or make her bed—yet she was willing to spend hours shoveling shit just to be near those animals. It was adorable.

But there was something unnerving about the way Ginger was toward Velvet, something fevered, with a whiff of addiction. I knew it had to do with Melinda, and with maternity, but in relation to the latter, it seemed distorted, mistaken, a version of reverse imprinting, like baby ducklings who will take the first creature they see to be their mother and follow the thing, no matter how hopelessly. In relation to the former, it was just sad and backward-looking. And there was that unmistakable whiff. I respected her for staying sober so long on her own. Sometimes I even grudgingly admired her independence. But in truth, she had not fully dealt with addiction. I could feel it.

What effect could it have on Velvet, all that coming at her and not knowing what it was about? She was poor, she lived in a shit neighborhood, and when she talked about her mother, there was something in her voice that made me think of a shadow on the wall in a horror movie. The woman's voice on the phone confirmed the feeling: She sounded abusive, half crazy. This girl had *need,* big need. I could feel it under her uncertainty and diffidence. And here was Ginger with *her* need, looking at Velvet with shining eyes, calling her "princess," and tucking her in at night. It seemed an unstable mix of things, combustible, a promise that could not be kept.

Ginger

The next week was made of tense, beautiful days, in my memory a blur of summer sights and smells: the thick flowers of the azalea bush crushed against the house, fresh-cut grass, Paul on his knees in the dark, fertilized dirt, the manure of the horse barn, barbecue sauce, the roller coaster at the Dutchess County Fair, her hair in my mouth, Paul's arms around me, the pink and yellow shacks of the flimsy fairway, our drooping plates loaded with sugared food, the heaped odors of jammed wastebaskets, the tossing cars, the roaring sludge of songs and carnie calls, Velvet's eyes on the rodeo girls her age and younger, parading on decorated show ponies, the feel of her mind going deep and intense.

I worked to give her all of this, like I was handing her each piece and going, "See? See?" I devoured it all with her and still was hungry for more. And so was she; with all of this, she could still wander into the dining room, slump into a chair, and theatrically drawl "Ahhm bored." At the grocery store, I once returned to the cart after looking for and finding a special sauce she had requested and she said to me, "I'm going to make you run around this store until you get everything I want." And I went and put the sauce back on the shelf. "You won't get anything with that attitude," I said. Her face fell, and she said, "Sorry."

I saved that moment. I did the right thing. I was the adult. But I never knew from one moment to the next if I was or not. Being this kind of adult was like driving a car without brakes at night around hairpin turns. My body tensed and relaxed constantly. I was always nearly ruining dinner or forgetting to pick something up. I couldn't sleep. I wanted to drink—really wanted to, for the first time in years. Was this what parenting was like, 24/7? My God, how did anyone do it? How did her *mother* do it, in a foreign country, in a bad neighborhood where she didn't speak the language?

Velvet

I always came to talk to Fugly Girl in the twilight, when I knew Pat was gone and nobody else would be around either. During the day I just said hello to her with my eyes when I walked by, and usually she said it back. Pat never said nothin', but she saw. I was sure she did.

Then one day when I was raking shit up from Graylie's stall, Beverly and Pat took Fugly Girl out to work her so she wouldn't go crazy. I'd never seen her out of the stall before; her tail was high up, she was trotting kind of sideways like she was trying to push on something, her eyes were bugged-out white, and her whole face looked raw, like her hair was on the wrong way, even though it wasn't. Beverly had her tight by the lead rope and I saw there was a chain across her nose. Pat was walking on the other side of her like she was a police lady, and it still looked like they barely had her. Gare Ann and the retarded boy came out of the stable to look. Right then Fugly made a twisty hump with her back and kicked out with her hind feet. "Knock it off!" Beverly yanked down on the rope and yelled with her mouth big and tight and her jaw stuck out to the side. "You hear?"

I came out of the stall and tried to catch Fugly's eye.

"Stay back, Velvet," said Pat, all quiet.

"She thinks she's the damn 'horse whisperer,'" said Gare.

"Whisper-ess," said the boy. "Whisper-ass!"

Pat threw them a look over Fugly's back. But she kept going.

I didn't look at Gare. I said, "I do not know what you are talking about."

"Yeah you do."

"Why does a Mexican kid walk around like she owns the place?" yelled the boy.

Gare said, "The way you act with that horse, and you don't even know shit about horses, like, that's dangerous."

The boy yelled, "Because her father built it and her mother cleans it!"

And Gare said, "You're gonna get deported outta this barn if you keep that up—*word*."

Ginger

I was in the kitchen getting a pork roast ready to cook when I heard her come in the front door. She came in fast, running up the stairs, and then there was a heavy thud through the floor on the other side of the house. Paul came in from his studio and started to say something; there was a crash. "Uh-oh," he said, and then we heard her scream.

"Velvet?" he yelled. There was silence, but it was humming.

"I'll go," I said to him, and on the stairs, I shouted up, "What is it?" She didn't answer. When I came in, she was sitting on the bed crying quietly and angrily. The covers were all but twisted off, and the bedside lamp was broken on the floor; she threw herself backward, staring, but not at me.

I sat on the bed. "Honey," I said, "what is it?"

She didn't say anything. I heard Paul coming up the stairs. With a hard, embarrassed motion, Velvet wiped the tears from her eyes.

Paul sat on the bed with us. He was calm, and that gave him authority. "Velvet," he said. "Did somebody do something to you?"

She reacted to his authority; she collected herself. "That girl," she said. "That girl in the barn? She basically called me a illegal. Her and that stupid boy. He said he's gonna tell Pat I talk to my horse and give her apples, and they gonna send me home."

"That's crap; they're just being hateful," I said. "I'll talk to Pat. She might scold you, but nobody's gonna send you anywhere."

She wiped her eyes again and stopped crying, though she was still not looking at us. We sat with her, feeling shame. At least I did. Her hurt felt too private for us to look at. Paul must've felt that too, because he said, "Do you want to call your mom?"

She sat up. "No," she said. She wiped her face. "She wouldn't care. She would just laugh." She said this like an adult would, resigned.

We sat for a long minute. Then I said, "Do you want me to brush your hair?" She nodded. I went and got her brush from the dresser. She sat with her back to me. I smoothed her hair with my hand first, getting at the big tangles with my fingers. Then I went to work with the brush. I could feel her concentrating on the sensation, letting it relax her. I could feel Paul near me; I could feel him relaxing too.

"I hate that girl. She was rude to me from the first day. The boy's too stupid to hate." She spoke quietly. "But that girl, I'd like to cut her tongue out."

Paul wiped his nose. He got up and left the room.

"Did you do anything to her? I mean after she said it?" I asked. "Hit her or anything?"

"No. I didn't because if I started, I woulda smashed in her face."

"Good. I'm proud of you for holding back. Not because I care about her. I don't. But because it would've been worse for you."

I kept brushing her hair. The hard, clean waves of her anger entered my body; I remembered what it was like to feel that way, and it felt good, *right,* to feel it so purely. I began to sing softly as I brushed her hair, a song I remembered from childhood: *Roses love sunshine, violets love dew. Angels in heaven know I love you.*

Paul came in with a broom and began sweeping up the broken lamp. I kept on.

Know I love you dear, know I love you. Angels in heaven know I love you. And then I couldn't remember the rest, so I just sang "La la la la" to the tune of it, still combing her hair, even though it was smooth now and untangled.

Paul

Yes, Velvet was a lovely kid. Watching Ginger brushing her hair and singing to her moved me in a different way than I had felt before in my first marriage, made my reservations seem stingy, *selfish;* Becca had always told me that I was selfish like an only child, that I was jealous of her bond with Edie. Which was true. I was jealous, even though I loved Edie profoundly; she was my blood. But this girl was not my blood or Ginger's. And poor Ginger, who'd had no child of her own, didn't seem to know the difference.

Velvet

The next day I went to the barn early, at eight instead of nine. Ginger said she would go with me, but I didn't want Gare to see me walk in with her. Because that would make the stupid bitch think I was afraid of her and I wasn't. What I was afraid of was that they took my horse away. I didn't know where they'd put her. But I was afraid I'd go and she wouldn't be there anymore.

But she *was* there, biting and kicking her stall like normal. Instead Gare wasn't there, not the retarded boy either. There was just Beth, looking at me too hard and saying hi too nice. I expected Pat to give me hell, but she didn't even say nothing. Except that we were short that day, so there was more work to do, which she said I'd be happy about because it meant I earned my lesson quicker.

I almost forgot about it. Until it was almost lunch and Beth was already outside the barn eating out of her brown bag. I was still cleaning Little Tina's stall when Pat came and stood next to me. She said, "After you left, I had a little talk with Gare Ann and she decided to take the day off. Now I need to talk to you."

I wanted to ask what happened to the boy, but I didn't say nothin'. Because I didn't know what to say. I kept my head down and cleaned extra hard.

"I see you got something going with Fugly Girl. I notice she's a lot quieter when you're around."

She didn't sound mad.

"I'd almost say she likes you."

"She's nice," I said.

"She *is* nice. She's also dangerous. Do you understand that?"

"Miss Pat, she's not dangerous, she—"

"Look at me, girl. Put that thing down and look at me when I'm talking to you."

I dropped the fork in the dirty sand.

"Fugly Girl is not a person. She's an animal. She's not a kitty or a doggie. She's a thousand-pound *horse*. That is one thousand pounds of unpredictable power. That right away means handle with care.

And in this case, 'care' isn't enough. Don't look away from me! You never noticed the scars on her face? How her one ear looks twisted? That horse has been abused. Do you know what that means?"

I didn't just look at her then, I stared. Because she *was* mad. But not at me. She was mad at something else, really mad.

"That means she can hurt you, even if you're nice to her. She can lash out at anybody just because something made her nervous. Like a person can do or say something crappy because they're in a bad mood, and they're in a bad mood *a lot*. Except most people, what they do, it won't kill you. She could kill you, like you or me would swat a fly."

I looked down. "You mean I can't feed her no more."

Pat didn't answer. I waited. On the other side of the barn, Rocki whinnied and started hitting his food bucket. I looked up. Pat was looking at me with a face I didn't understand. "I didn't say that," she said. She turned, turned back. "I think you remind her of somebody."

"Who?"

"The person who had her before. Not the abuser, the one before that. She was a girl about your age. She had a little body, big eyes, and curly black hair. The only time I saw her, she was feeding the horse an apple."

"Where is the girl now?"

"Her parents live up in Pine Bush. I guess they don't feel like making the drive to see the horse. The poor kid probably doesn't even know where she is."

We worked quietly for a while. Then I said, "Miss Pat, what happened to that boy who was here?"

"Oh," she said, "Joseph? I had a talk with him too, and it didn't go so well, so, welp—we deported him for a few weeks."

When I got back to the house, Ginger asked me what happened, and when I told her, she said we should eat out to celebrate. I asked if we could have dinner at the pizza place we went to once before and she said yes.

I wanted to go there because the last time seemed like a long time ago and I wanted to feel how different things were now. Because of that, I noticed things more. I noticed how the boy behind the counter tried to do everything right, how he asked people what they wanted like he really cared a lot. People were like that here; I saw it before. But now it was annoying me. *Do you want it like this? Do you want a little more like that?* Then we sat down and I saw there was an African-American girl about my age with a white family. I tried to get her to look at me, but she wouldn't. The white mother was smiling and passing the girl food, but the white kids weren't really talking to her and the air around her was alone. I thought, She is here like me; she came up on the later bus. And suddenly I didn't want to be there. My pizza came, broccoli and bacon like I had it before. But even though it was good and I ate it, I couldn't taste it all the way. I felt like one of my arms and one leg and half my head was there at the table and the other half—I didn't know where it was. Which didn't make sense. I should've felt good.

When we got back to the house it was barely light, but I had to go see my horse. The moon was big and it made the path to the barn shiny. Inside the barn was dark, but I wasn't scared; I could hear and feel the horses around me, recognizing me. I could hear Fugly Girl kicking her stall like she was mad as hell. I heard her kick before, but tonight was different: Tonight she kicked like she hated everything. Like there was nothing else.

"Hola," I said. "It's me."

She kicked harder, even more hating, and also something else, something I could feel coming out from my own body, coming hard. I CAN'T GET OUT I CAN'T GET OUT LET ME OUT I NEED TO GET OUT I CAN'T GET OUT. The other horses made noises: *We hear.*

I'm sorry, I thought. I want to, but I can't.

She whinnied and spun in a circle, and bucked, her jerking darkness like my mother's fists when she was so mad she'd walk up and down just beating at the air. The hate had gone out of her. Now it was just the *something else.* It was just me in the dark and her hard, jumping body making pain in the air.

I CAN'T GET OUT. I thought of the girl who looked like me who would never see her horse again. I thought of lying in the bed in the foster home where they put us that time my mom beat me with a belt and it got infected and I showed the social worker and they took us, me to a place in New York and Dante to New Jersey. I NEED TO GET OUT. I lay on the bed in the dark listening to girls laughing at me because I threw up the lady's dinner as soon as I ate it. Cars came by outside and lit up the poster of Destiny's Child on the wall. The smell of air freshener was making me want to vomit again. But I didn't and I didn't cry either. Because half of me was there and the other half was nowhere and you can't cry in nowhere.

Fugly Girl was quiet now. I could smell her sweat and feel her heavy breath. She was listening to me crying. They all were.

When I walked back it was all the way dark and there were noises from frogs and crickets. But the path was still lit enough for me to walk on. Ginger was waiting for me on the porch. She said to come inside and get ready to sleep. I asked her if she would sing to me. And later that night she did.

Paul

I heard it from our bedroom, Ginger's singing. My heart sank a little and first I thought, Oh no, not again. But her voice was so sweet I thought, Paul, don't be this way. And I came out in the hall to hear her. But when I understood her words, my heart sank again; it was too sad: *Hush-a-bye, don't you cry. Go to sleep, my little baby. When you wake, you shall have cake. And all the pretty little horses.*

Velvet

On my last day, Pat said she would have a surprise for me if I did a super-good job on my stalls. And I did. I worked really hard, mostly knowing I wouldn't be back for a long time, maybe not ever. It was only me and Gare that day and I even didn't mind her because she was quiet when Beth and Retard weren't around. I almost liked her a little because her eyes weren't fake nice, even when Pat told her to hand me the mucking fork and she did. She just looked at me the same way the fork touched my hand.

And then it was the end of the day and Pat said to me all normal: "So, you want to help me groom Fugly Girl?" And I said, "Yeah," as normal as I could. And she told Gare to go clean up Officer Murphy's stall, which was always the nastiest because he was a draft horse and made huge poops. And then she took me down and she handed me the halter. "Here," she said. "You try putting it on her." She opened Fugly's stall and the hair on the back of my neck stood up. Because all of a sudden my horse looked different, like she didn't even know me.

I went to put the halter on; she moved away from me. I tried again; she turned her body. "No," said Pat. "Not so direct with this horse."

I said, "What do you mean?"

She made us step outside the stall and half closed the door. She said, "The way you're coming right at her, looking right in her eye? It's like you're saying, I'm the biggest B here, and we're gonna do it my way or not at all."

I said, "But I don't mean it that way."

She said, "I know that, and the other horses know that. But you've got a powerful eye, did *you* know that?"

I looked down. "My mom tells me to stop looking at her sometimes."

"I'll bet she does! You have got a powerful eye. And this horse can get nervous. You look at her like that, she might decide to turn and kick you into your next life. You want to deal with her, put your head down and talk to her soft. Like she's a kitten. So she knows you won't hurt her."

"But she knows I won't hurt her. She lets me touch her."

"She lets you touch her when there's a door between you and her. That's different."

I understood. We went back in the stall, and I did like Pat said. Fugly Girl stood quiet for me this time, but when I went to put the halter on, she jerked away.

"Head-shy," said Pat. "Remember, that's where she got hurt. Be kind, but *be in charge.*"

I touched Fugly's neck and then rubbed it and waited till I felt her muscle relax. I slipped my arm around her nose and guided it down. She followed me. I put the halter on and Pat clipped on the lead rope. She handed it to me and asked if I wanted to lead her. I did; I felt her through the rope. I felt her giant heart with thorns wrapped around it like Jesus in the picture, and I'd be lying if I said I wasn't scared. Fugly Girl in the stall was not the same as Fugly Girl out, with me holding the rope. *She* was scared, scared like broke to pieces, but she was other things, too, big things. I held her. Pat got her on the cross-ties fast, reminding me to stay close to the horse so that if she kicked, the damage would be small. Fugly Girl pawed with her foot and moved sideways. Pat said, "Knock it off!" I put my hand on the horse. I noticed her eye was looking at me, thinking, not sure. I tried to tell her it *was* sure. Pat gave me the round curry comb. I rubbed the thick muscles of Fugly Girl's shoulders, working on the dirty knots in her coat. Her skin got softer as I brushed. I thought of the song Ginger sang to me. Fugly Girl pawed and moved sideways again. "Did I ever tell you about Scorpio?" asked Pat. "The first horse I bonded with?"

"No," I said.

"Well, he was not only the first, he was the only one, really. I was fifteen, and it was my first job. He was just a yearling. He came running up to me the first day, right up to the fence."

Fugly Girl cut mad nasty gas. It stank and it made me smile. I rubbed the sweet spot between her shoulders. She turned her head and I saw the beautiful long hairs she had under her eye, like horse eyelashes. She blinked and put her head down a little.

"I was the only one who could ride Scorpio, and still we almost killed each other. He kicked me, I kicked him. Which I do *not* recommend, by the way, if this one ever kicks you, because even though I got away with it the first time, Scorpio remembered. And the next time he had the chance, he kicked me so I saw both back feet coming right for my face. I saw the nails on the bottom of his shoes and I thought, I hope there's a doctor here who can put my face back together. And the feet went right past my head on either side. After that, we were good. He'd made his point."

"Miss Pat," I said. "If it wasn't the little girl that abused Fugly Girl, who did? Was it the girl's parents?"

"I'd call it more neglect than abuse on their part. They took her off the bush track circuit and were racing her as a quarter horse. They had her in a trailer with some other horses on the way back from a race. It was a long trip and one of her back shoes came halfway off, and she somehow stepped on a nail. And they didn't have money for the vet. I guess she hadn't won nothin' for 'em in a while, so they just kept her in her stall and hoped it would get better. Instead it got infected. They wound up selling her cheap to some freak, a *doctor* who treated the infection half-assed, then starved her and beat her when she didn't 'perform.' Those scars on her face? Those are from a halter he strapped to her face too tight and never took off. It was months before I could get a halter on her. She was a real big B and you know what, that's great. Being like that was the only way she stopped him from breaking her spirit."

"Miss Pat, when she kicks and bites her stall, is she lashing out like you said, like a bad mood?"

"Oh no, that—well, kind of. The biting is a nervous habit. It's called 'cribbing' and it's like some people biting their nails. The kicking, some of that is hormone issues. She's feeling uncomfortable because—well, basically, she's just being a girl. Here, watch me do her feet."

She leaned in and stroked her hand down Fugly's leg, pinching when she reached a special place; the foot came up like a button got pushed. Pat took a sharp thing and dug dirt out of the hooves. Fugly Girl made her lips like a camel's!

"So how'd you get her?"

"The freak's neighbor knew about me. I'd given lessons to his daughter. He told the freak that he'd call the cops if he kept up the abuse. He gave him my number and the doctor called me. I met the child when I went to pick up the horse. For some weird reason, the doctor called her to say good-bye to her horse. When I got there she was feeding Fugly Girl an apple out of her hand. Her mother didn't even get out of the car. The girl walked the mare into the trailer for me. I'm not sure I could've gotten that horse in without her, even with Beth. Here, you want to pick up her foot?"

Her leg when I slid my hand on it was like something with roots in the ground. Then I got to the spot; it was like butterfly bones, between the body and the wing. Her leg bent into my arm, and her heavy hoof came up.

"The kid held it together until the door to the trailer closed. Then she cried her guts out."

I held Fugly Girl's wing-hoof and thought about the girl who would never see this horse again. I cleaned the dirt out of the foot.

Ginger

When we drove to the train station, she cried. She seemed okay that morning; she smiled and said she wanted to see her little brother. She went to visit the horses one last time and came back with a big rusty horseshoe that she wrapped carefully in one of her shirts.

But on the way to the station I turned around in my seat and saw her face withdrawn and her body slumped like it had no feeling. Then when we got out of the car, she dropped her suitcase—it seemed like on purpose—and it popped open and she began to quietly cry.

"Don't cry," said Paul. "You'll be back."

"When?" she asked.

He paused uneasily and then said, "Next year."

But she heard his unease louder than his words. She stopped crying and withdrew again. She stayed withdrawn for most of the train trip, staring out the window at the bright river with her lips parted and her eyes a thousand miles away.

Her mother and little brother met us at the station. The woman surprised me by kissing me on both cheeks; Paul she merely approved with her measuring eyes. The boy eye-checked us and pretended to ignore his sister. He was beautiful too—lighter-skinned than Velvet, more inward, more visibly intense, eyes flashing privately.

"I'll call tonight," I said to Velvet. "Don't forget about the homework."

And it happened again; she put her head down and quietly began to cry. Her mother's eyes darkened powerfully. Her brother began whispering to himself with his face turned away.

"Here!" I said, my voice too bright. "Here's some pictures of Velvet's trip." Small-voiced, Velvet translated. I handed Mrs. Vargas a carefully edited envelope. She took it angrily, stuffing it into her purse. She took Velvet by the arm and headed toward the subway.

Velvet

"Those people weird," said Dante. "That ugly man and that lady like a cat food and sugar sandwich."

"They're not weird," I said. "They're like people are supposed to be. They're nice and they don't yell, not even when they're mad."

"That lady is nice because she's in the sky," said my mom.

"Her name is Ginger."

"Whatever her name is, she lives in the sky. She's nice like a little girl is nice."

"The people I stayed with were fucked up," said Dante. "The food they ate was crap."

"Mami," I said. "The place I worked? There was a horse who really liked me because the little girl who owned her before looked like me. I was the only person there that she liked."

"What happened to the little girl who owned her before?"

"Her parents wouldn't let her see the horse anymore because—"

"Because they didn't want their daughter to get killed. Listen, you think I don't know? Where I grew up, horses used to walk in the street. Now stop talking before you give me a headache."

Ginger

I called her that night. Not right after we got home, but during the soft time before bed. She picked up the phone eagerly. She asked what we had for dinner and if I went for a walk. She asked if there were any fireflies.

And then there was screaming in the background, vicious, hateful. Velvet screamed back, wild strings of Spanish words, raging but imploring too—and then she dropped the phone and the scream went raw. I shouted her name, almost hung up to call the cops when somebody else picked up the phone and said "Cat food!" at me like a curse; the brother. Then Velvet had the phone again, yelling sideways off it before sobbing to me that her mom had told her she was no good all night even though she didn't do anything bad and now she called the horseshoe dirty and threw it out the window.

I talked to her; I called her honey, darling. I said if she was with me, I'd hold her in my arms like she was a little girl. I said it would be all right. The words came out of me— desolate, helpless, and real. She got quiet; her silence felt a little incredulous, embarrassed even. I told her she could find the shoe tomorrow, sneak it back in and hide it. I told her we would do homework together and she could come to see us soon, on the weekend. The yelling in the background became angry talking, then normal talking between the mother and little boy. Velvet said, "I just decided something."

"What?"

"I'm not gonna yell anymore, not even when I'm mad."

"There's nothing wrong with yelling when you're mad. You're a fiery girl," I said.

"What does that mean?"

"That you're intense, you have strong feelings."

She didn't say anything, and I began to worry that I'd insulted her somehow. Then she said, "I just decided something else. From now on, I'm going to call my mare Fiery Girl."

When we hung up, there was a smile in her voice.

I didn't speak about it to Paul. But when we got in bed, I turned with my back to him and curled into a ball. I thought over and over of Velvet, of holding her like I said I would, brushing her hair, singing to her. I thought of the way she said "My mare," like "mah mare" or "ma mère"—my mother in French.

Velvet

I went to bed that night not even wanting to touch my mom because she threw my horseshoe out the window and started screaming when Ginger called. But I fell asleep and then I woke up and she wasn't there and I was scared. Instead of her, Dante was holding a pillow put sideways, like somebody took my mom and put the pillow there to fool him. I hoped she was just in the bathroom, but I knew she wasn't and I was right. I got out of bed and went to look for her. When I got to the kitchen, I thought she'd gone away and left us. I opened the window—I don't know why, maybe to call for help—and I looked down and saw she was standing on the sidewalk with her hoodie on over her nightgown. It didn't make sense, she was afraid of this place. She turned her head sideways so I saw her nose and forehead from above; that made her look small, like a kid who was lost. I went downstairs and opened the door. I put my head out and said, "Mami, what are you doing?" When she turned around, her face was quiet and far away. I came out and I saw—she had my horseshoe in her hand. It made me smile so much I couldn't talk. We stood together. The air was smelling like fall already. I saw that her legs were bare, but she had her sneakers on untied. "Peaceful," she said. "It's peaceful."

We just stood there, hearing the quiet, feeling the buildings in the dark and the ground humming under us. A car went by booming music and it was different than during the day.

When we went in to bed, she put her back to me like always. But when I put my arm around her, she held my hand. I said, "Bendición, Mami," and she answered with a smiling voice. "Dios te bendiga."

Ginger

I went back to my painting; classes started for Paul. The feeling of normalcy was delicious. I still went "walking at night," but alone, feeling my signal again, now big and broad and full of new things.

I found myself talking to women I barely knew—the manager of the health food store, a colleague of Paul's, somebody I'd met at a wedding—in the store, in the middle of a parking lot, at the post office; talking a mile a minute, I would confide in them about Velvet. About the remarkable things she'd said or done. About the fight I'd heard on the phone, about how I was going to help her with her homework. About how scared and excited I was. It felt like I was actually talking to women for the first time. I felt this even though the conversations were fleeting and partial. It was something about the way our eyes met, the way they took my words in; it was something that had never happened before. It was like *being* the signal rather than hearing it.

Of course, not every conversation was this way. The weekend after Velvet went home, Paul and I went to a party given by a local celebrity photographer who had just won some big award for taking pictures of Muslim kids. Paul's ex-wife, Becca, was there along with her friends, all huge women whose bodies exude importance, or as my mom used to say, "impo'ance." They sit together like a high school clique, these women in their fifties, and they walk like they're saying, "Get out the way. I've got tits." One of them is an editor in the city, one of them is an artist who shows in the city, one of them was a model about a hundred years ago; they all have kids and they all act like bitches to me. At least if Becca is there. If Becca's not there, they're basically polite. If my friend Kayla is there, they even try to be nice because she's friends with the editor. I understand the situation, but it's awkward, especially if Kayla's at the party and I have to sit with them either monopolizing Kayla or being ignored.

This time, though, I tried to connect, even though Becca was there. I couldn't help it. I told them about Velvet and the horses, especially the horses. And even *they* got interested, even if Becca got hard in the face; they overflowed like women will do, giving suggestions for activities, horse camps, children's theater, petting zoos. Until Becca spoke and they all stopped. "Sounds like a fun project," she said. "Sounds like an easy way to play at being a parent." And the conversation moved on.

Velvet

The week before school, Dante put on a pair of pants but his ass was too big and they split when he moved. We all laughed and my mom said, "What am I going to do with my little piglet?" and pinched his arm. But she got mad when I tried on my favorite blouse from last year and couldn't button it across my chest. She cursed and said she couldn't afford to buy us new clothes, why couldn't we make anything last. So we tried on all our clothes for school. She cursed again, but sad, not mad. "It's not your fault," she said. "We have to go to the ragpicker's."

By that she meant a church in Bushwick that had charity clothes in brown boxes or hung up on metal racks. They hardly had anything good. The best thing for me was a red sweater that was too big, but my mom said anyway, it would last. Also she picked out matching yellow sweatshirts for us that were brand-new but stupid, with pictures of whales on them. And a T-shirt for Dante that said "I'm the Big Sister," and she didn't even know, and neither did he because he didn't care about reading even if he knew how. I started to tell them, but Dante was acting like such a mal nacido that I decided he would be wearing it to school.

Early the next day I went to my cotton-ball box in the closet and got out pictures of Ginger and the horses and picked the ones I would paste on my notebook for school. I would put the ones with ponies on the outside and the ones with Joker and Reesa on the inside so my mom wouldn't see them. Though she never looked at the pictures anyway. I just put them in my box in the closet and she never said anything.

Ginger

Sometimes I don't care what Becca says; other times it cuts. It cuts when I feel myself small and insignificant against her and her friends and their big proud bodies, when I feel the fear and chaos that's always in me, and the nothingness, the nothing I've done with my life except to continue to live. But it's not too late. I am stronger than I was. And now I have Velvet.

I decided I was going to do a painting of Melinda, a figurative painting for the first time since art school. It was Velvet who put that idea into my head—after I showed her my sister's "portrait," she said, "Why don't you do a real picture of her?" She asked the day after she saw the red abstract, which meant she'd been thinking about it. I told her I didn't do representational or figurative work; she looked at me blankly and said, "Why not?" I started explaining to her that everything had already been painted at this point, and that there was no reason to represent figures anymore. The way she looked at me, I was suddenly embarrassed. "Did somebody else paint your sister already?" she asked.

"No, it's not that," I said, and she just looked at me.

So I decided to try. I decided to work from two pictures, one from when Melinda was ten and seriously beautiful, and another when she was a thick-necked, swollen-faced adult, some teeth already gone, her eyes dulled but still with a hard glitter deep in them. She was wearing a sweatshirt and holding a plastic take-out container; whoever took the picture had obviously surprised her. It must've been somebody she was happy to see because she was actually smiling. Which is probably why she'd even kept the picture in a drawer full of buttons, batteries, colored lightbulbs, and broken toys: It was the only one of her as an adult smiling so you could see her teeth.

I decided I'd put both Melindas in the same picture. I wanted to foreground the smiling, disfigured adult and have the pretty, sweet-faced child in the background. It was harder than I thought. I was un-practiced and couldn't make the lines properly expressive. The adult

Melinda was comic, nearly pumpkin-faced, the child wraithlike and weird. After dinner I came back to try again. This time I put them together, one half of the face a child, the other half an adult. That was worse. *Did somebody else paint your sister?* Blurry thoughts filled my head; gooseflesh came up on my arm. What was I doing to my sister? Why?

When Melinda was fifteen, our mother had her hospitalized. It was a state mental hospital and she got into fights with the other girls there; she came home for a weekend visit with a black eye and a swollen mouth. Her body was stiff and fearful, but her eyes were sarcastic and she mumbled tough, boasting things with her hurt lips. We shared a room and she sat in the corner of it listening to our little record player while I sketched in my diary. She listened to the same song over and over. It was by Alice Cooper, I think, crowing and clowning about runnin through the world with a gun at his back. Melinda listened to it hunched over and rocking intently. If the music hadn't been there, it would've looked like she was crying. But I was barely twelve. I listened to the music over her body because I think she wanted me to. She just kept picking up the needle and putting it down in the same place. It didn't even bother me.

I rested my brushes in a jar of mineral spirits and put away my paints. I turned off the lights and listened to the dense sound of bugs outside the open windows.

When Melinda was nineteen, she told me about being abused by the head psychiatrist at the hospital. He told her she had to be checked for VD. He actually did the exam himself and he didn't even wear a white coat. When she saw him come into the room, she sat up on the table and said, "But I can't have VD. I'm a virgin." And he said, "Isn't that sweet. Lie back and open your legs." She started to get off the table and he told her she'd go into seclusion if she put up a fuss. She said he shoved the speculum in so hard she bled. She said the nurse obviously knew it was wrong, but she didn't try to stop him. She just put her hand on Melinda's belly and said, "Try to relax, dear."

She was driving me somewhere when she told me. The radio was on, but it didn't matter. I heard her, but I wasn't sure I believed her. Melinda stole and she lied a lot. She even admitted it. She told me the story to explain why she stole from our mother's purse; she said it was because when she told our mother what the psychiatrist did, our mother just said, "I'll talk to him," and then kept forgetting.

Velvet

My school is in Williamsburg, where we used to live before Crown Heights. We're not supposed to keep going there because you have to go to school in your district, but my mom didn't want us to go here because she heard about gun violence. So she just pretended we didn't move and the school pretends they don't know we moved so we can go there. Which I'm glad for because I would rather stay there than go to school with new people, but it also means that in the summer all the other girls are together and I'm in Crown Heights with Dante. Everybody else is getting to know each other more and I'm not getting to know anybody because my mom is too afraid to let me out the house. We can't walk to school anymore, and because my mom can't let us go on the subway and the bus alone, she goes with us when it's barely day and drops us off in the school yard before she goes to work. We stand there and wait, even when it's freezing cold, for like an hour before everybody else comes to school together, looking at us like they're sorry for us.

I used to be friends with three girls there: Helena, who dresses straight off the truck, whose mom does her hair like J. Lo blond; Alicia, whose eyebrows grow almost together, but whose mouth is so smart she still hangs out with the cutest older boys; and Marisol, with her chubby body and sweet voice, who watches cartoons like a little kid but reads books nobody else can understand. But when I moved, Helena started talking shit about my clothes, like telling me her mom said she couldn't believe a Dominican mother would let her child walk around like that. And Alicia, if I found her alone she would talk like when we were kids—but in the cafeteria she would be grillin' me with her new girls and calling me *Velveeta* behind her hand.

The only one who's still nice is Marisol and that's partly because she dresses like me, from stores that don't have names, and her skin is bad now and she's too serious. I still like her sometimes because you can talk about private things with her and not feel stupid. But really I wish I was still friends with Alicia and Helena even if I kind of hate them.

But that was last year, and this year I had hope it would be different. Partly because of the horses, and partly because of this girl called Strawberry. Strawberry wasn't her name, but they called her that because every day at lunch she ate strawberry ice cream bars. And because of the red streaks in her long hair.

Strawberry didn't know all the girls, either. She came to our school last year when there were only a few more months left. She was special and tragical. They said she'd moved from New Orleans because of the hurricane. They said she'd been on the roof with her family without any food or water. They said she'd been sent to one foster place in Texas but something happened and she'd had to leave and go to the place she was at here. And she still couldn't go home even though the hurricane was a year ago because her family was someplace where people were acting crazy and killing each other's dogs.

If she'd been a girl like us, we still would've been nice to her. But she was not like us. She was two years older than everybody on account of being held back *twice,* and she was beautiful like a woman. She had *breasts,* and she wore flowered bras that you could see through her clothes. She wore makeup and sat kind of sideways, and looked like she was smoking a cigarette in a black-and-white movie. Her mouth smiled, smiled hard, but her eyes did not smile, ever. Her eyes watched and looked for something they knew they'd never find. I liked her; everybody liked her. All the girls who used to be my friends and then laughed at me for having church clothes wanted to be friends with her.

Then in the spring we both had detention and the teacher was new and he let us sit together. His cell phone rang and he answered it and we started whispering. She showed me a picture of her older brother, Marco. I showed her a picture of my grandfather. At first I told her he was in DR like he was alive. I told her how he called me on the phone and sent me a sea horse. Then I said, "But then he died." I don't know why I told her. But when I did, she got quiet and her eyes got different and so did her mouth. She said, "My brother's dead, too. He drowned in the hurricane. Him and his girlfriend were trapped in the attic and they couldn't get out." We both looked down and it was deep. Then she said, "What's your favorite movie?" and before I could tell her, the teacher started to yell.

The next day I gave her the pink-brown shell that my father gave me. I showed her the sea horse, too. I gave her the shell and let her hold the sea horse and it happened again: her eyes got feeling in them. She asked if she could have the sea horse too, but I said no, it was the only other thing I had from my grandfather. Her eyes changed back, and for a second I thought she was gonna keep my sea horse. But then she changed them back again, and they smiled with her mouth only not mean, and she said, "When I see one of those Ima think of you," and gave it back. "Where you gonna see a sea horse?" I asked, and I laughed because it sounded funny. She laughed too, and said, *"SpongeBob."* And everybody saw it, her talking and laughing with me with her real eyes, and all the way to the end of the year, nobody started anything with me.

The one bad thing was that being friends with Strawberry made me sometimes pretend I didn't really know Marisol. Which was a little horrible. Except really I didn't know Marisol so much anymore, all she did was read.

So I wanted to see Strawberry and show her the pictures of my real horses. I picked the best ones—me on Joker and Reesa, me grooming Rocki, who was mad big—and I pasted them inside the cover of my school notebook. I didn't put the one with Ginger in because I didn't want to explain her to everybody. Except for Strawberry. I thought maybe I'd show it to her.

But when I got to school, I didn't find her at the assembly and I thought she went back with her family. Then when I saw her in the hall and I started to go to her, she gave me a grill with her eyes like dead. Like she never knew me, or talked to me about the most private thing. It made me feel sick. I couldn't believe she meant it at first. But then in class she sat with the girls who were bitches to me. I sat behind them and I whispered to Alicia, my friend turned bitch, and she whispered to me, but turning around like I was somebody following them and then turning back to the others. That's how they were to me all day. Except for Strawberry. She didn't turn to me at all. She just talked loud like to make sure the whole room heard her, and the teacher didn't really stop her. She talked about her brother Marco in Puerto Rico. Like he was alive.

Ginger

Paul and I bickered about having Velvet up on weekends. Then we fought. He repeated the things he'd said about my needs, her needs, expectations I would not be able to meet. He said we had nothing in common. Then he started about race. He said things like "white benefactor" and "She's too different from you" and "What are you going to do when she gets pregnant?" Which made me yell, "And you think *I'm* racist?" before I left the house and slammed the door.

We made up. And fought about it again. Maybe once a month, he said. If her mother agrees. Twice a month, I said. If she keeps her grades up. *If she continues the good work, we'll make it every week,* I didn't say.

Whatever I said, I was afraid Paul might be right. Not so much about race but about need; about my feelings. A few days after we had the argument, I did something I hadn't done in years: I took the train into the city to go to what used to be my favorite AA meeting there. People I knew in the '80s go to it, artists and failed artists mostly, whom I can talk to better than anyone upstate. After I hung around for the meeting after the meeting and wound up talking with an old enemy who had been a loved friend for about six months a long time ago; someone I could not help but see as a half friend. I talked to her about Velvet, starting with the organization that had brought her to see us. My half friend put on her program face and said, "It sounds like you're really wanting to nurture yourself. I think you need to be looking at your own shit." I said, "I've spent the last ten years nurturing myself and looking at my own shit. It's time to nurture somebody else now."

She didn't push it. But her precise little needle had struck home. Because even though she spoke ignorantly, she did know something about me. She knew the way I had lived: blank loneliness broken by friendships that would come suddenly into being, surge through the color spectrum, then blacken, crumple, and die; scene after drunken idiotic scene, mashed-up conversations nobody could hear, the tears and ugly laughter quieted only by the rubber tit of alcohol or something else. Friendship was bad, sex was worse, and love—love! That was someone who rang my doorbell at three a.m. and I would let him in so he could tell me I was worthless, hit me, fuck me, and leave unless he needed to sleep over because his real girlfriend was—for some reason!—mad at him. It was not pleasure, it was like a brick wall that a giant hand smashed me against again and again, and it was like the most powerful drug in the world. Paul knows about this, but he doesn't know. Because how can I describe it? It was like being locked into a nightmare more real than anything until I woke and couldn't really remember the details or make sense of it, knowing only that it was terrible and that I would do it again.

"Sex addiction"; "addicted to emotion"; these were the sober terms by which I learned to describe this dull little hell, and for a while such terms helped me the way crutches help a broken-legged person to walk. They helped, but they did not heal.

Yes, my enemy-friend knew me. Or rather she *had* known me. She had known me in the hard, ungiving way she knew herself. She did not know Velvet's eyes when I read to her. She did not know what it was like to walk with her in soft, earth-smelling darkness or to see her on a horse. Maybe that bitch Becca was right; maybe that was playing at something if that was all I did. But I could do more, and I was willing.

I rode home on the train and I looked out the window at the shining dark water with its glowing rim of light left over from the day and I knew: Just because I had been in hell, I don't have to be there always. Love is not always a sickness, and I don't need grim, dry terms in order to walk. I have changed. I can trust myself. I love Paul. I love Velvet. I can trust it.

Velvet

This bullshit went on all week. I would sit at the end of the long table in the cafeteria trying to ignore Marisol while Strawberry and Alicia sat together laughing and basically ignoring me. It finally blew up when I told my mom what was happening and she gave me some dates with powdered sugar on them to offer at lunch. I brought out the dates and before I could even share them, Alicia said, "Gross!" and they laughed and somebody made a fart noise. I didn't even get what she meant until we were sitting down in class and then I realized and I grabbed the wastebasket and emptied it on Alicia's dirty-mouth head. Everybody laughed and she waved her arms around like a jackass and Ms. Rodriguez yelled, "Velvet, that is *it*! You get a week of detention and also you will sit separate from the rest of the class!"

But I didn't care because when I did that to Alicia, Strawberry turned and looked at me, smiling with her eyes for the first time since school started.

A few days later, she found me during recess. Recess was in two different courtyards, one for the real little kids like Dante and another one for us. Both of them had bars to balance on and there was a jungle gym for the little kids, but most boys chased each other or threw crushed-up paper at the bended-up basketball hoop because there was no ball. Girls mostly listened to their music and styled their hair and told stories. Usually I twirled on the bars or messed around with somebody so I could listen to their radio, but that day I was in the cafeteria reading this book I found about a girl who had a weird disease when she was little. I didn't want to read in front of people messing around, and anyway I liked the cafeteria when it was quiet and everything was echo-y and the old food smelled sad in a nice way.

I don't know how she knew I was there, but she came and asked if she could sit with me. She asked me what I did in the summer and I opened my notebook and showed her me on Joker and Reesa. And she took the book and her eyes got big. "Marisol told me you rode horses," she said, "but I didn't believe her."

So I told her about Ginger and Paul and the barn. The only thing I held back on was Fugly Girl. I don't know why. I even showed her the picture of Ginger. Strawberry looked at her and said, "She looks nice. Is she?" I said, "Yeah. She would get me anything I wanted."

Strawberry handed me back the notebook and started talking about going to Puerto Rico and how her cousin there had a big house and birds that could talk. I started to ask her about her brother, if he was really in Puerto Rico or if he was really dead but I didn't; like she could hear my thought, she looked down and turned away. When she turned back she asked if maybe she could come with me and ride the horses, too. I wanted to say, *How're you gonna do that if you can't even talk to me at school?* Instead I said I could ask Ginger. And she said, "Thanks. But don't tell Alicia and them, okay?" I didn't answer, I just looked away from her thinking, How could she look in my eyes and say that? She knew, 'cause she got up to go back to the courtyard. Then she stopped and turned and said, "Maybe you could come to my house sometime?"

If it was anybody else I would've said, *Fuck you. You think you can use me like that?* But she was Strawberry. So I said, "Okay."

Ginger

I waited a couple of weeks into school before calling her because I wanted her to get settled in her routine and because I wanted to get settled myself; I felt shy about talking to her. When I finally did call, I didn't know how to make my voice work right, how to fill it with encouragement and love. She said school was good, that she'd made a new friend and that she was keeping up with the work. I asked what I could help her with and she said she was supposed to write a book report about an African-American family from back when there was prejudice. So I asked her to describe the book to me; she couldn't make a coherent story line. I asked her to read to me from the book, and she had no trouble with that. I asked her if she understood it and she said yes. It wasn't until the next week that it occurred to me to ask her what the paragraph she'd just read to me actually meant; it was then I discovered that although she could sound the words out perfectly, and sometimes even understand their meanings individually, she could not really understand written sentences put together.

How could such a bright girl be so backward? "It's like her mind is working too fast, not too slow," I said to my friend Kayla. "She's jumping to the end of the sentence before she's absorbed the middle." But privately, it felt more to me like her mind just kind of went limp when she read. I stayed on the phone with her three nights a week, working on written assignments. It would take at least an hour to do one page, and then she would usually have to do it again. I kept saying, Don't you want to come up and see Fiery Girl? And I would feel her emotionally sweating over the phone, and I was just about sweating that way too. Finally she wrote a whole page that hung together and expressed something besides a garbled half summary of the plot. I was so proud. I could hardly wait to hear what the teacher thought of it. But every time I asked, Velvet would say she hadn't gotten the paper back. She said the teacher was stupid and didn't like her and was a liar. She said she probably lost it.

Velvet

I didn't need permission to go to Strawberry's. I never went home after school anyway. My mom didn't get off work until five o'clock, so I had to walk around till it was time to pick up Dante at day care, then we went home and waited for my mom there. Last year I was in day care too; I had my birthday there and they had a cake with my name on it and even my mom came for the party. There's a picture of her smiling with her eyes closed and a paper hat on her head. But I'm too old now, so I just walk around for two hours. I can't go home and wait to pick Dante up because my mom says if they find out she's leaving us at home by ourselves she'll be in trouble. I don't know why nobody thinks it's bad that I'm walking around by myself, but I guess they don't. And I'm not always alone. I see people I used to know, like these men who sit out on their folding chairs, and they say, "Hey, Velvet! Velveteen from the block!" And sometimes Mrs. Vasquez, this old lady who lives in our old building, brings me up for some flavored tea with canned milk in it. But until Strawberry nobody from school invited me over yet.

Strawberry's house was on South Third in a old building with the name Venus on it. The ceiling in the lobby was like a frosted cake with dust on it, with waves and lumpy flower-shapes painted red and green. And there were lamps hanging down and a plant that looked cool even though it was dead. It looked like a place where beautiful, strange people would live, but the lady Strawberry stayed with and the little girl, they were both normal and fat. Strawberry slept in the room with the little girl. She slept in a corner on a sleeping bag on a cot, and there was a big cardboard box unfolded and propped up by old cans of food and a chair, keeping her cot private from the girl's bed. It was spray-painted silver and had Strawberry's name on it in red. There was also a upside-down box by the cot with a silky scarf on it for Strawberry's things, like lipsticks and a rose made of glass and the shell I gave her and pictures of people in special frames. It was cool. I was expecting to feel sorry for her, but really her cot and her silver box were better than a normal room.

Except that, when we got the little girl to stop bothering us, Strawberry wanted to take the pictures of her friends and go in the closet. It was a big closet with a light in it, but still. She made us go in there and pull winter coats off the hangers and get under them. We were so close. She looked even more beautiful that close. Her eyes were strong and bright, but her skin was so soft and her mouth was shaped soft, too, not like in school. Her breast was touching my arm under the coats, and that made me want to touch her, which made me feel funny.

She started showing me the pictures of her New Orleans friends and telling me stories about them. Mostly it was stories like who she smoked with for the first time, and partied with or fought with. But then there was this one girl with big eyes, and Strawberry said, "This is Miranda. She told me she saw a deer swimming in the water by her house." And I said, "What, in a pool?" And Strawberry said, no, when this girl was on the roof of her house, she saw a deer in the water. This girl said he had horns, and he looked right at her and she saw he couldn't swim anymore, and he was going to die. The water must've carried him far. I asked where Miranda was and she said she didn't know. And we were just quiet, looking at the picture of Miranda.

I talked to her about Fiery Girl, too, how she only liked me, and how because she was abused she might still lash out at me with her hooves, like Scorpio had kicked at Pat so she thought they'd have to put her face back together. Strawberry said, "I'm sorry they did that to her, but if she tried that with me, I'd slap the shit outta her." I said, "Trust me, you wouldn't do that," and she said, "Trust me, I would. I don't care how big she is, I don't take that shit from nobody." And then she talked about somebody else from New Orleans.

I wanted to tell her more about the horse, but I didn't like her saying she would slap my mare. It was just stupid and almost made me really mad. So I just listened to her and thought about the book Ginger read to me, where the little girl went to hide in the closet and came out in a pretend world. Because that's what it was like; Strawberry's voice was like a pretend voice. She was talking like a little kid and using kid words. Which would've been weird anyway, but was really weird because she was talking about the most real things and she was older than me.

We didn't always do that; we at least a couple of times went to Grand Street, and she showed me how to shoplift from Rainbow and the Gem superstore. I would go in by myself wearing a big coat and walk slowly, leaning on the displays, and the store people would follow staring the crap out of me—and she would walk out with makeup or a manicure set and once even a purse. The one time I tried I only took a nail file, but still they almost caught me. I just got away because I ran into the traffic and the man chasing me almost got hit, and when Strawberry caught up with me, we walked to her house singing "Pon de Replay." That was fun.

But mostly she just wanted to go to her room and talk about what her friends in New Orleans said or did while we looked at magazines with stars in them. Either that or she wanted to put makeup on—except it was mostly her putting makeup on me. She put makeup on me like her friend Maciella used to wear. She did it over and over, like she was trying to make it perfect. I asked when I could do her, and she just said I didn't even know how. She let me brush her hair and then she plucked my eyebrows, which made my mom really mad when I got home. The next time, I said, "Strawberry, stop. I'm not Maciella." And she said, "Could you just pretend to be?"

And I did. It was not fun. In school Strawberry acted like she barely knew me. Even on the days I went to see her, I had to wait and meet her at a bus stop and she would look around like she was making sure nobody saw we were together. Then she'd get in the closet with me and put makeup on my face. If I didn't say the right things, Strawberry would stop me and say, "No, that's not what she was like." It was not fun. But I kept on doing it. I don't know why.

Ginger

I started calling the school, but nobody would return my calls. Finally I was told that they weren't allowed to talk to me unless Velvet's mother gave me written permission. And so I found somebody who could speak Spanish and I figured out how to make a conference call. But the call was near impossible. The translator was Kayla's aunt, who'd learned Spanish in the Peace Corps. She was religious and churchy-voiced, and worse, her Spanish was apparently too crude for her to understand Mrs. Vargas's rapid-fire style of speech. I hadn't wanted to involve Velvet because I knew she was sick of having to read and translate for her mom. But we had to get her on the phone finally. And I don't know why, but that seemed to help; Mrs. Vargas was clearly amused by the translator's ineptitude. She laughed; she said she'd sign the permission letter if I wrote it, even though it wouldn't matter because Velvet was always doing bad.

But she wasn't doing bad. When Ms. Rodriguez finally called me back, she said that while Velvet still had "discipline issues," she was definitely behaving better than she had last year. She was even turning in some homework and it looked like she was doing the reading.

"What about the book report about the African-American family?" I asked.

"The what? Oh, right. I haven't assigned a book report on that. They were supposed to write on another book. Which she didn't do. But still, I'm happy with her progress."

I was thrown only for a second. I told the teacher that Velvet had done a beautiful job on the African-American family and that she should ask her to show it to her. And I asked her to be sure that Velvet's mother knew about how well she was doing. Ms. Rodriguez promised that she would.

Velvet

So I told Strawberry I was going to the horses. I told her in front of people. Maybe I shouldn't've, but she was pretending she didn't know me and it was making me mad. The other girls got quiet and all she said was "So?" But then in the bathroom she said, "You gonna ask her?" And I said, "Yeah" like what a dumb question. Also like I might not really do it. And she did not talk back.

I went on Friday night after my mom got off work. She yelled at me the whole time, even on the subway. The people on the subway looked at us because my mom sounded crazy yelling at me about what an idiot Ginger must be and saying I stole out of her purse and I eat too much and I wore her nightgown, dragging Dante along while he talked to himself about killing some people he made up in his head. When we came up out of the train, the wind was blowing trash all over and we had to walk into it. At least that made my mom shut up. Crazy people were all over the place by then though, so nobody would've noticed her. "Look," said Dante, "there's your stupid woman."

And there was Ginger, in white leather pants and a white puffy jacket, and her white-blond hair blowing around, shading her eyes with her hand and her legs apart, so she looked powerful, like the White Witch in her book. Except that then she saw us and she dropped her hand and smiled with her sad eyes and was Ginger again. And I went to hug her.

Ginger

She was strange on the train, like she didn't quite know me. I felt awkward, too; I didn't know what to talk about with her. She was restless in her seat, asked me twice how long it was going to take to get there, was saying she was bored before we were even out of the station. I thought, *An easy way to play at being a parent;* my heart felt cold.

Then she said an amazing thing. We were leaving the city and she was looking out the window at the buildings across the water. Her lips were parted slightly and she had that dreamy look on her face. Then her expression changed abruptly and she turned to me and asked if it was true that they were planning to put a new building at Ground Zero that was even taller than the World Trade Center. And I said yes, that's what they were talking about. She said, "That is the stupidest thing I ever heard. That will just make them want to knock it down again." So I said, "But that's why they want to do it. To show we're not afraid of being knocked down." And she said, "Are you kidding me? Everybody in New York City is afraid. You should not build to be what you are not."

And I was so proud of her. I didn't care what that asshole Becca said. I was just proud to be with her, and I told her so. She smiled huge and then, shyly, looked out the window again. She was still quiet, and it was still awkward—but it was the awkwardness of people who love each other and don't know how to show it yet.

Velvet

It was dark when we got there, but still, I wanted to see the horses. I asked Ginger to walk to the barn with me because I wasn't used to the kind of dark it was out there anymore. But I made her wait outside and she didn't mind because I asked her nice.

Inside the barn was warm and right away the horses moved and said hello to me all differently. I went up to them one by one and nearly all of them came to me—Joker snorted and got his spit on me and I just laughed and rubbed him. Rocki looked even happy, and Officer Murphy moved his head up and down for me to rub his head more. Then Fiery Girl came and I saw she had this thing on her face. It was leather and metal and it was wrapped around her throat and face and it made her look like a serial killer. She came up and tried to bite the wood of her stall and the metal thing seemed to choke her. I went and got Ginger and brought her in to show her and she just said there was probably a reason for it, I should ask Pat the next day. She tried to pet the mare, but Fiery Girl tossed her head and gave her a "don't mess with me" look. I realized Ginger did not know *anything* about it.

Still, when we went back out, Ginger put her arm around me and said, "Are you okay?" and I said yes, and put my arm around her and we walked like that for a while. I wondered what it would be like if Strawberry was here now.

The next day I asked Pat about the thing on my mare's face.

"It's so she won't crib," she said. "Remember the way she bites her feed bucket and the door of her stall? It's bad for her stomach because she takes in too much air when she does it, so we're trying to break her of it. Don't worry, the strap doesn't hurt her."

"Can she eat with it?"

"Oh yeah," said Pat. "It's lunchtime now—you want to help feed 'em?"

I did. The horses got excited when they heard the grain coming. Fiery Girl kicked and neighed, and the others said, *Yeah yeah, give it now!* I thought she'd be glad when I came to give it, but instead she acted *mad*—her ears went flat and she snapped and kicked the door. Pat said, "Don't be afraid," and handed me the bucket of grain.

And I went in and she ran up on me in her killer mask like she would knock me down and stomp me. I was so scared I almost dropped the bucket, but I didn't show it. I didn't even look at her, even when she bumped me with her nose. I poured the food and she went at it, and Pat said, "Good work!" But I was scared and the horse knew it.

I think Pat knew also, but she still asked me to clean the mare's stall later that afternoon. Pat moved Fiery Girl out into an empty stall and the mare went *powerfully*, making me and Gare flatten on the walls. But after I cleaned the stall, Pat asked if I wanted to put her back. I said yes, because Gare was there but also because I felt the mare looking at me like she *wanted* me to do it. Pat put the lead rope on her and handed her to me. I led her to the stall and tried to go in first. That's when she *blasted* past me so hard she threw me into the wall. Pat came between me and the mare and yelled and took the lead rope. Beverly passed by and said, "I see you're getting to know your friend better."

Pat said, "You okay?" and I was, but still I was shaking; she threw me like a hurricane throws a house.

I wanted to tell Ginger about it, but I was embarrassed. Because this was the horse that was supposed to like me, and now she seemed to think I was crap. Also because Ginger might get worried and then decide I shouldn't see the horses and maybe even tell my mom. So I just listened to her tell me she was painting a real picture of her sister because of me.

I said, "Why because of me?"

And she said, "Because you were asking why I didn't do a real picture and I thought maybe I should."

I asked, "Could I see?" and she took me up to her studio.

But the new painting was even more crazy than the other one. It was *ugly* too, like I wanted to say, *Did you hate your sister?* But I couldn't say that and I couldn't think of anything else to say that was nice, so I just looked around. And I saw something scary: a plastic doll like for little kids dressed in leopard-spotted clothes that looked homemade with even leopard socks and a hat. It was beat-up and it had one of its eyes rolled up in its head. It looked like it was in a Chucky movie, where a doll goes crazy and kills people. Except this doll looked too retarded to kill anybody. I thought, Is Ginger retarded?

Which for some reason—the creepy doll and Ginger's maybe-retardation—made me remember when I woke up and sneaked in the hall and heard Paul say those things about pushing the limit and the boundaries, and then Ginger mumble-hissing about birthdays. It made me remember the lady on the bus talking about giving "them" a "example." I started listening to Paul and Ginger when they didn't know; I even pretended to be asleep and then creeped down the stairs again, to see if they were saying those things. But they just talked to each other like normal people, and the only times I heard my name, I didn't hear anything bad in their voices, I only heard good. It was a strange kind of good that made me feel strange. But it was still good.

Ginger

It was over very fast, but the happiness of that visit was peaceful, not so disturbed by worry and the fear that I was doing something wrong. She spent most of both days at the barn, taking lessons and working, just spending time with the animals. She came home—home!—for lunch and went back to the barn until five or so, then came back to us for dinner. I tried to get her to help me, but she would really only do that when the mood took her, and then she was wonderful, smiling while she dried the dishes or set the table. I had meant to help her with her homework, but she said she forgot it. So we walked instead and then I watched TV with her, us sitting against each other, me feeling her responses as she watched her favorite blond girls fight vampires or get boyfriends. And then she would go back to the barn to say good-night.

Velvet

I went back to the barn at twilight. I didn't have any apples. I just went to the mare to see what she would do. Which was nothing. She stood in the middle of her stall and stared at me with her ears up. I said, "I'm mad at you." I thought she looked like maybe she felt bad, but then she just put her head down to look for pieces of hay in her bedding. I said, "All I did was bring food to you and you ran at me and then you threw me against the wall." She put her head up and looked at me, then went back to eating. I said, "Okay. Good-bye."

But when I was walking away, it was like I heard her in my ear, like she was saying, *I'm sorry. I didn't want to knock you down. I just forgot you were there.*

Still, I did not go see her the next day. I went to the barn and I worked, I helped turn the horses out. Me and Beth and Gare led Little Tina and Blue Boy and Graylie out to the paddock. Beth brought Rocki back in and I groomed him and cleaned his feet. Then me and Beth cleaned buckets together. She told me about another barn she used to go to but that she couldn't go to anymore because her parents couldn't pay. It was named Spindletop, and the horses there were super clean. They got groomed every day, and their halters and bits were cleaned every day—they even got the hair *on their ears* trimmed. She said the girls there rode in a big show where people came from all over the country, and that she was going to show one day at the rodeo at the county fair. She also asked questions about Brooklyn and how I knew people up here. I told her the Fresh Air Fund and she said, "Oh, right."

And I really wished Strawberry was there. Because if Strawberry was there I don't think Beth would've said, "Oh, right" like she did. Strawberry was too bad for that. It wasn't like it was wrong for Beth to say; it wasn't a insult. But still . . . she wouldn't say it to Strawberry, I don't think. I started picturing Strawberry walking up in the barn, just looking around and how that would be. I pictured what she would've done to Gare when she said "deported" to me.

I got so into thinking it that I forgot to say good-bye to the mare.

Ginger

At the end of the visit, she asked if her friend Strawberry could come with her next time. She said the girl had come from New Orleans, that she was a Katrina survivor and that she still couldn't go home to her family. My first impulse was to say yes; even Paul was moved. Still, it seemed a lot to take on so soon, and also, it was great leverage. So I said, If your grades get better, she can come. If your report card at the end of the year is better, she can come next summer. She said, Ginger, Strawberry might not be here next summer. So I said, Easter, then. That got her attention.

Velvet

It was just after I came back that Strawberry asked me to sit at the lunch table with her and Alicia. It was like one day she's getting in the closet with me and putting makeup on my face but acting in school like I'm not good enough; the next day she's like, "Velvet, come sit with us." And I am eating lunch with these girls I don't even like anymore and Strawberry is looking like she's doing me a favor.

It happened after I walked to her house with her and told her what Ginger said. But I don't think that was why. It wasn't the horses, it was the boys. These boys that came up on either side of us. But first it was Helena; at lunch that day, Strawberry almost fought Helena. I was walking by with my tray, but I woulda seen it if I was across the room—Helena got in Strawberry's face, she knocked her soda off the table by pretend accident, and said she didn't care if Strawberry was up on no roof, she better stay away from Chris. Strawberry *smiled*, ice-cold, and she stood up and suddenly looked big enough to kill Helena even though she's smaller. "It's Chris won't stay away from me," she said. "I wouldn't touch anybody who touch you." And right then I walked slam into Helena, and my food spilled on her, and I cursed her and she cursed back and there was detention, and having to sit in the room with Helena. Who was older than me, but still, only twelve, and why was she fighting with somebody like Strawberry over a boy?

It was a few days later I was walking with Strawberry and I told her about the horses, and she looked at me really happy. And right then these three boys came up alongside of us. I didn't know them; they were older than us. First they were only by her, and they were saying things that were nice but sounded nasty. She said, "Chris, I'm walking with my friend. Maybe you can call me later." And then she didn't answer no more. And I could suddenly feel her like I feel a horse. Scary strong, and with her skin feeling everything.

The boys were still next to us, talking about us like we couldn't hear. And we were on her block but nobody was around us and her house is far down. I looked at the one she called "Chris"; he even had hair on his face. And this tall boy came around to my side and started with me.

Except his voice didn't sound nasty. It was nice and he said, "How you doing, shawty?" I looked at him. He had soft eyes that went with his voice and a little dent in his nose. So I said, "I'm fine." And he said, "I can see that." And I smiled and he said, "Aw, you sweet. What's your name?" And I told him. And I thought he was gonna say somethin' stupid about it, but he just said, "I'm Dominic." And all of a sudden I noticed his lips. They were soft too, and something else that was the opposite. I felt confused. I looked at Strawberry and she looked at me, like for the first time. And even though her house was closer now, it was as far away as the grassy field where the horses were.

Then Dominic said, "How old are you?" And I told him and his face jumped back. For a minute there was just the sound of all our feet and the pavement suddenly looking weird bumpy in a way I never noticed. Then Dominic said, "Chris, the girl says call her later. Man, I gotta go." And he didn't wait for Chris to answer, he just stopped walking with us and Chris stopped with him. And they said, "Ima call you" (Chris) and "Be good, shawty" (Dominic) and were gone.

Strawberry and me walked quiet for a while, and her body went back to normal. She said, "Sometimes I hate boys, they bring so much trouble." I could feel my body going back to normal. She said, "My first host family make me leave 'cause they say I ask their boy into my bed, but I never asked, he just come anyway."

Which was basically the same thing she said to Helena—and it was a lie because she told Chris he could call her. But right then I didn't care about that. Because I was thinking about something that happened with my father's friend Manuel, who lived in my house before Mr. Diaz, and so I said, "I know. There was this man staying at our house when I was like nine or ten, and he give me trouble even then." And she looked at me so deep she didn't have to say anything. Her eyes, her whole body, said, *I know.* Like that first time in detention.

When we got to her house, we didn't go into her closet. Instead we watched a movie about a girl who's really a princess. Not the same one from Ginger's, a different one, where she's normal in America but a princess in this other country. Us and the little fat girl all sat on the couch under a blanket, like a family. And her fat lady host, Mrs. Henry, put her warm hand on my shoulder and asked Strawberry if she wanted me to stay over for dinner.

But I had to go get Dante, and I was already late, and he was crying and mad at me. On the street, he said, "You don't care about your own family, you like those nonfiction ugly people better. You're even ashamed of us!"

I told him to be quiet, and at least those people didn't yell at me all the time. But really, I felt bad. I said, "I wasn't late because of them, I just got in a fight with this girl who's a bitch to me."

"That lady you know is a nonfiction bitch."

"You don't even know her," I said. "You don't know what nonfiction means either."

"I don't care what it means," he said and he smiled all Chester Cheetah at me.

Ginger

The next time we talked on the phone, she asked me why I still had a doll. I said, "Oh, she's from when I was like, five."

"It's not a 'she,'" said Velvet. "It's a *it*. Why do you have it *now*?"

"I have it because my sister kept it. I didn't even know she had it all these years. I didn't find it until she died and Paul and I went to clean out her place. She had every doll and toy we ever had all piled up in a box."

There was a long moment of television noise. She said, "That's sad." Except her voice said, *That's funny.*

"Yeah, I know. I threw most of the stuff away. But I wanted to keep something that Melinda kept. My friend Kayla made the clothes for her—they're cute, don't you think?"

She didn't say anything. A sarcastic feeling came through the phone. Along with television noise.

Velvet

I never even had one doll except for the broken key chain I found on the street—Ginger and her sister had a whole box? And I'm supposed to feel bad about that? I thought, Dante's right: She is a bitch. Or just dumb.

Then my mom said, "Come here. Your hair is a mess—let me braid it for you." I went to her and said, "Mami, you know something crazy? Ginger said she *likes* my hair natural." And she *laughed* and said, "Likes it! That's funny! I'll believe she likes it when she goes to the shop and pays somebody to make her hair like yours!" She worked on me with love in her quick hands; making fun of Ginger put her in a good mood. She said, "This black woman I know says she hates white women saying, *Oh, your hair is so beautiful.* She wishes she could slap some knowledge into them!" And she laughed deep in her body, working my hair so that my scalp tingled all the way down into my neck. It made me feel so soft that I thought soft about Ginger again, how her voice on the phone had a bruise on it when she told about her sister. And about the mare, looking at me with her ears up. Saying she was sorry and I didn't even say good-bye to her.

Ginger

I knew about the box of half-rotted dolls and toys for years before my sister died; she had shown them to me the last time I'd seen her. She was nearly forty then and making one of her failed attempts to get sober, and she was wondering if maybe I wanted my dolls back. The visit hadn't been going very well and when she held up the moldy and bald (I'd torn her hair out) Glinda, I lost my temper and said I thought it was crazy to keep these things, that she ought to just throw them out. And my biker-chick sister put her face in her hands and left the room, crying. I sat there for a moment, stunned. Then I got up and went to her. She'd stopped crying by then and when I said, "Sorry," she said, "No, you're right." And I helped her take the falling-apart box out to the Dumpster just before I left for the airport.

She must've brought it right back in after I was gone; the box was just about disintegrated when I came across it. I pawed through everything in it—Barbies, old-style talking dolls, troll dolls, Beatle dolls, plastic horses—to find Glinda.

Velvet

The next time I came to see Ginger, it was late, so I didn't go to the barn until morning. Nobody was there. The radio was pulled out of the office on an extension cord, and it was playing embarrassing cowboy music, but there was *nobody*. The horses had gotten watered and fed, but their stalls were dirty and they were looking with nervous eyes. Then I realized I didn't hear Fiery Girl kicking. I got scared and went to her. She was standing in the middle of her stall, but when she saw me she came up to the bars and looked at me with her eyes saying something I at first didn't understand. Then I saw: Her stall was full of shit, and she was saying *Help me*.

I wanted to, but I was scared and I told her.

Help me.

"But there isn't even anybody here in case you hurt me."

Help me. I won't hurt you. Help me.

We looked at each other without any more words. She still did not kick or bite. I said, "All right. I'm going to trust you. But if you hurt me, I will never see you again."

And I got a wheelbarrow and a fork and went back to her stall. Normally I didn't go into the stalls to clean, but I didn't want to put a halter on her. I blocked the door with the wheelbarrow and went in. She got out of my way and let me clean. When I was finished with one half of the stall, she moved and let me do the other. She didn't look at me. But her neck was soft, and her head was down. With her trembly lips she said, *Thank you*.

I stayed in the barn and talked to the horses for like an hour. But no people came until I left. That's when I saw Beth, the girl from my first visit. She told me Pat and Beverly were at a horse show and she was taking care of the barn. I thought, Not very well, and she got pink in the face like she heard me.

Ginger

The best part of that visit happened the first night; Paul and I fucked and it felt great. It was especially great because we hadn't done it for a while, and we'd never done it when Velvet was in the house, I'm not sure why. But this intimacy now made her presence more real, and I felt joy at getting up and seeing her the next day. I felt like we were all putting roots down into something deep and rich.

Velvet

It was barely light when I woke up the next day. I didn't wait; I got dressed and walked over. There was mist in the air and it was soft, and the sky was soft too, but with bright clouds. There was the so-much space and the green too, green and green. There were the little fences. There were the horses. The horses were out in the grassy place where girls had advanced lessons and they were running. I got closer; they were running wild, shining-wild. I saw Joker, he jumped straight in the air, with all his legs. Spirit kicked his back legs, Baby wiggled herself and kicked sideways, Officer Murphy jumped up front-ways, Little Tina ran in and out among them all, like she was laughing. And beautiful fat Reesa high-stepped in a circle all around them, like she was the proud grandmother. They were dancing, all different ways, and because they normally all ran together, it was crazy for them to be doing different things, showing their steps, throwing up mud and clumps of grass—*dancing*.

Pat was by the fence with her sticking-out hair and her red face. "Hey," she said. "I never saw you smile like that before."

I smiled more.

"Look at *them* smiling. They've been in for a while, so they're going a little crazy, but I've never seen 'em like this before. Hey!"

She said "hey" because Spirit back-kicked Blue Boy's leg right on the elbow part, and Blue Boy was running in a hurt way.

"You stay outside," said Pat, and she opened the gate and went in with the dancing horses. She wasn't afraid of them even though they were wild; she walked through them to Blue Boy. And he came to her, and she stood there with him, petting his nose and talking nice to him while the others ran and played.

When she came back out the fence I asked if Fiery Girl could come out.

Pat said, "Who?"

I felt my face turn red. "It's my name for Fugly Girl."

Pat smiled and said, "I like it! But no, she can't come out, not with the others. She fights with them."

"Can she come out later?" I asked. "By herself?"

"No," said Pat. "I don't have anybody here to help me with her, and she's all stirred up."

"I can help."

"Sorry." She put her hand on my shoulder.

"Miss Pat, I can handle her."

She just looked at me like, *Don't push it.*

So I went in and just talked to the mare, or tried. I saw what Pat saw: She was moving around hard and quick and her eyes were like covered up, not thinking. But she came to me right away, looking at me with thanks, still. She said, *Touch me,* and I put my hands in through the bars and put them on her head to stop her from bobbing it. I told her I'd let her out one day, I promised. She started to swing her head like she was upset, but she stopped just short. *I promise.* She wanted to believe me. But her wrinkled mouth said, *I can't.*

Then when I was back at the house, just before we ate, something happened I would never believe. Somebody knocked on the door and it was for me. It was Gare. She had her hands in her pockets and she was looking at me like, I don't know, a dog with its ears up. "Pat sent me to get you," she said. "They're bringing Fugly out."

We didn't talk when we walked over except she asked how many times I came up and I told her. We got to the paddock and the mare was already out, running. Her muscles were going like the muscles of the world, and her face when she came around was like a crazy skeleton in a old cartoon, blowing from her open nose. But it wasn't scary, it was cute, because her eye was on me like, *Check me out! See what I can do!* And then something more cute happened. When she slowed down, Beverly came out to stand with me and watch for a minute on her way out to her car. She watched and shook her head and pointed at the mare, like *jabbed* with her finger, and said, "That horse is trouble!" And Fiery Girl spun around in a circle, like a whole circle, and kicked with her back legs—it was like some nasty thing came out Beverly's finger and made her spin around and around till she shook it off. Even Beverly had to laugh, and she said, "Damn straight!"

But that wasn't even the best. When she was done running, she sank down on her knees and went on her back like a cat on the floor. She wiggled in the dirt and her lips wiggled and she ran in the air except her feet were light. She *rolled*.

There was calling over me and I looked up. There were big birds flying in a V shape and calling each other. Birds in the city fly like a moving hairnet. But these flew like a arrow in the sky, going somewhere definite. I thought, I am going to do my schoolwork like Ginger wants and bring Strawberry here. And I am going to ride Fiery Girl.

Ginger

I asked her what kind of grades she was getting on her papers. I asked her if she'd ever given Ms. Rodriguez her paper on the African-American family. And she said, Um, can I tell you what happened today with my friend Alicia? I said, Okay. And she told me that Alicia, who used to be her real friend but who was now only a little bit her friend, choked herself with her scarf in the bathroom. She said she walked in the bathroom with a hall pass and saw Alicia in there choking herself in front of the mirror. She was doing it because her mom was mad at her because she got a 2 on a paper. I said, That's horrible. At least your mom's not like that. But what about your paper? And she said it must've gotten lost.

So I called Ms. Rodriguez and eventually she called back. She said she'd never seen the paper about the African-American family, but that Velvet *was* doing the homework and behaving in class—still fighting, but not so much. I asked what did she mean, "fighting"? Physically? The teacher said no, it was verbal. The other girls teased her because they knew she would get excited and they liked to see her blow up. But it was getting better.

I hung up feeling mostly good. Except that all of a sudden I couldn't stop picturing a little girl in the bathroom choking herself.

Velvet

I hated doing homework. But I liked talking to Ginger on the phone. I liked how her voice was trembly when she explained something to me; I liked how hard she listened, how you could *feel* her listening like she was close. I liked feeling her like *me*.

My mom liked her calling me at first. If she answered the phone, she would make her voice nice and she would say, "It's Ginger," instead of "that lady." And she would even kind of be quiet in the background, moving around a little stiff and straight, like she thought Ginger was there in the room, watching her. Once she even asked, "What did she teach you about this time?"

But then she started not liking it. She said, "Doesn't she have anything better to do than children's work? Does she work at all? Or does she just lie around?" I said, "At least she knows how to read." And my mom said, "You think anybody's gonna pay you to read? I don't!" She laughed; Dante laughed. "Ginger's husband didn't marry her because she can read! Why he did, I don't know, but something tells me it was more to do with this"—she slapped me on the ass—"than that!" So Dante tried to slap too, but I swung around to slap *him* and he almost fell over his feet getting out the way. We all had to laugh at that.

I felt like saying to Ginger, *See, we laugh*. Later that night, my mom washed my hair and put relaxer and bleach on it and I felt like saying, *See?* I felt it again when I looked at my mom and Dante sleeping, the sweet way she was with him. And when I saw my mom do her push-ups every morning before she went to work, before she even made our food, before it was even light. And after we did eat, she cleaned everything in the kitchen, rubbed the counters really hard to keep out infection. My mom was so strong. I remembered how she said to us once that if anybody ever hurt us, she would come after him with her body, and I knew it was true. I knew it was more true than grades.

And I also remembered what Alicia said to me, the thing I didn't tell Ginger: "You stole my grade. And you better stop." She said it like it was a joke. But it wasn't funny.

Ginger

Maybe two weeks after Velvet went home, Ms. Rodriguez called me. She wanted to know if Paul and I could come to the school as chaperones for a class trip to the Statue of Liberty. I was thrilled for the chance, and even Paul was sorry he couldn't come because of teaching.

But when the day came, the weather was so bad that the trip was canceled. Since I was already in the city—I'd spent the night with a friend—the principal invited me out anyway, just to visit. She said it would be a treat for Velvet to see me, that they were going to make it a surprise for her. They arranged for it to be at the end of the day, during the last class. I was sad that I had to go through a metal detector and show ID to a security officer to get into an elementary school. But mostly I was happy and awkward, wondering what it would be like to see Velvet in class.

When I walked into class, though, it didn't feel awkward at all; it was easy for me to smile at these kids, to be sweet-voiced and gentle. "You know Velvet?" one asked, suspicious but also interested. "How?"

"She came up to visit me this summer," I said. "And I thought she was so great, I had to see her again." The kid looked at me, amazed.

Turning slightly to one side, I whispered to Ms. Rodriguez, "So where *is* Velvet?" Because I had not seen her.

The woman gave me a strange look and said, "She's right there." She pointed at a furious-looking girl seated apart from everyone else, her head down and her hair brutally straightened, fried-and-dyed, a horrible red color that had to have been a mistake. She looked like a completely different person than she did when she came to see me; it was like there was a sign over her head reading "Come close and I will fuck you up."

She didn't even seem to know I was in the room, so I talked a little more to the other kids, asked them what they were working on that day. She still didn't look up. Finally Ms. Rodriguez said it was time for them to pay attention to the lesson. They more or less looked down at their notebooks and I approached Velvet's desk. She didn't look up even when I was right next to her. What would she do, curse me?

"Velvet," I said. "Hi."

She smiled, but not at me. She just sat there smiling at the scribbled-up paper on her desk.

I said, "How are you, honey?"

Finally she looked at me, still smiling. "Hi," she said.

I sat next to her and tried to help her with the lesson. Which was hard because I couldn't do the lesson; it was too fast. The teacher would write something on the board, a subject like, say, spending the night at a friend's house, and ask them to write half a page about it. Then ten minutes later—while Velvet was still on sentence two—she would switch, reading to them out of a book and asking them to write a paragraph responding to what they'd just heard. It was not how I'd learned, and I wanted to say, *Stop! Can't you see this is too fast for anybody to feel anything, and how can they write if they can't feel first? Don't you know this girl needs to feel?*

On top of that, I could see how strange it was for her to have me there, I could feel her body going back and forth on whether or not it was a good thing. This happened especially when another kid would turn and glance at us with an intense, curious face. Something was happening in the room that I didn't know about, and whatever it was, that's what Velvet's intelligence was working on, or trying to feel her way through. The teacher's suggestions were something she had to feel through too, and to do that she needed time to change the channel. I would've needed to do that too, and there wasn't any time being allowed.

"It's too fast for me too," I whispered to her.

"Really?" she said.

"Yeah."

"Then why can everybody else do it?"

I shrugged. "I don't know." And I really didn't. I thought, Great. Now she'll think we're both just stupid. Then I thought, Who cares, if this is supposed to be smart?

Velvet

When the class was over, Strawberry and Alicia wanted to walk out with me. They *never* did that before, and it was because of Ginger. Her hair was white and shiny, and she was wearing pants that looked like leather and her diamond ring on one hand and her gold on the other, smiling and talking all sweet. Strawberry's eyes could not stop staring at her; Alicia's mouth was open. And Ginger seemed to like it. Who likes to be stared at? A stuck-up person who thinks they all that. But Ginger didn't think she was all that. Did she?

"Is it true you make paintings?" asked Alicia. "Are you an artist?"

So Strawberry'd talked to her even though I asked her not to.

"Yes," said Ginger. "I don't make money at it, I just do it because I love it."

"Does that mean you're rich?" asked Strawberry.

"No," said Ginger. "Just that so far I haven't made money. I would if I could." And then she stopped in the hall in front of a picture of everybody in the class. "Oh, adorable!" she said.

See how nice she is, I thought.

But I could feel Strawberry thinking something different.

Ginger

Strawberry was not what I expected. She was a beautiful young woman with a wounded, contemptuous mouth and distant, wistful eyes. Of course she had been hurt; God, she must've been hurt. But that hot blend of hope and scorn that happened so quickly in her eyes—I was uneasy for Velvet and wished that she had picked another friend. I felt bad about it because of what Strawberry had been through. But still. I wasn't sure I wanted her around.

Velvet

We walked out with Ginger and then she said good-bye to me. She kissed me on the head in front of them. She smiled at them like . . . I don't know, it felt like a funny bone. They said good-bye to her. And then they didn't say nothin'. I was thinking they'd crack on her, and I didn't know what I'd do, stick up for her or crack too. But they didn't. We just walked for a while, quiet. Then Strawberry started cracking on this boy who kept wanting to mess with her, touch her, also on this teacher who stared at her, and then Alicia talked about this boy she liked, Dominic. I said, "Is he in high school?" She said, "I don't think he goes to school." I said, "I think I know him." Strawberry looked at me. And they got quiet again.

Ginger

Right when the class got out, when all the kids were milling around, Ms. Rodriguez introduced me to the school social worker, a woman named Eliza Lopez. She had a deep, good face and she seemed very happy to meet me. She thanked me for "making a difference." In the noisy hall, I tried to express some of my doubts and fears; I wondered about how Velvet's mother felt about it all, worried that I couldn't understand her. Ms. Lopez's face darkened. "I wouldn't worry about that," she said. "That woman is like a brick wall. Nobody can understand her." And then Velvet was there with her friends.

"Here's my card," said Ms. Lopez. "Call me any time."

And I went back out through the metal detectors. Wondering what it would be like to be eleven years old and to walk through that thing every day with a guard watching.

Velvet

It was a few days after that that Ms. Rodriguez picked my paper to read out loud in class. And when she was done, this boy in front named Junior said, "That's good!" And I felt my face blush and I smiled and my head went to one side. Somebody whispered, "Look at her!" and I put my head normal and saw Alicia and them staring knives at me. Strawberry looked at her nails. Ms. Rodriguez said, "I'm proud of Velvet for all the hard work she did." "Bitch," whispered Alicia. Ms. Rodriguez didn't hear. She came and put the paper on my desk. "Velveeta cheese," said somebody else. "Flat-ass fathead." "Douche-bag." Strawberry kept looking at her nails.

Ginger

I thought the visit to the school was good. But after, things got worse. Velvet still did her lessons with me. She worked hard: First we would discuss the book she was supposed to write about, getting her focused on what she wanted to say about it. She would then write a draft and revise it after my critique. But every time I asked her what grade she got on it, she said she hadn't gotten the paper back yet.

Finally I called Ms. Rodriguez, who told me that Velvet had stopped doing any homework at all. She said her discipline problems had escalated too. I could hear the irritation in her voice; she sounded irritated with me as well as the girl. "You have to understand, you can only have a very limited impact. It's really up to her, and if she doesn't want to, there's nothing you can do. Ma'am, this girl has a lot of problems."

"But she's doing the work," I said.

"I'm not seeing it."

I talked to Velvet and she said the same thing she'd said before, that the teacher hated her and lost her papers. She continued to do work with me on the phone, *good* work. So after a few weeks, I called the teacher again.

"You need to understand something," she said. "This is a very manipulative kid."

Velvet

When Ginger called me, I told her I *did* give Rodriguez my papers.
I wasn't lying, because I did them, I did the papers and I took them
to school. Besides it *was* true, the other thing I said; Rodriguez hated
me and I knew my report card would not be good. So did my mom.
She said, "You're a dumb girl trying to be smart. You don't think I
tried too? I worked, and I still got failed and you will too. You'll see.
That kind of smart won't help you anyway."

We were watching her favorite show, and I was kneeling on the
floor rubbing her legs and her feet while she told me how shitty
everything was, especially me. *She gets what she deserves, Carmencita.
Just you wait!*

"Ginger is nice, but she's foolish. She doesn't know where you live.
She doesn't even know what it's like to get up in the morning and take
the bus to work—ah, there he goes again!" She meant the cheat Santiago, he was giving this girl a flower and saying, *Walk across a piece of
paradise with me.* Beautiful music played; he was engaged to be married,
but the music was on his side. My mom said, "More on the other foot,"
and the scene changed to Santiago's girlfriend's mom taking painkill-
ers. For a while I just rubbed and we watched, then my mom started
again. "She's got no kids and has to borrow somebody else's and I don't
know why she picked you. Probably she feels sorry for you. Well, I feel
sorry for *her.* So be nice to her. Show her manners, respect her house.
Don't let her see what you're really like. If she wants to buy you things,
let her. Give you money, even better. Make her happy, maybe one day
you'll get an inheritance. A woman like that—ow! Not so hard, idiot!"

"I'm sorry, Mami." I rubbed her foot like I rubbed my mare and I
felt her soften, like scared little hairs coming alive one by one.

"A woman like that, what kind of woman?"

"Aren't you listening? I'm telling you what she's like! She has
money, but she's empty inside." *I would've loved to have known Papa—
what was he like, Sylvie? Was he affectionate?* "Well, bless her, at least
she's trying. At least she's trying."

I rubbed and we watched, not talking for a while.

Ginger

I let her come again anyway. What could I do? I wanted it so badly, and also it seemed wrong to punish her when I *knew* she had been doing actual work. A casual acquaintance backed me up on that, a woman named Robin, Kayla's friend, a single mother who'd adopted a three-year-old Romanian child she'd named Jewel, a girl who was half out of her mind when she'd arrived and who, at five, had revealed herself to be preternaturally bright. "You need to give her something to hope for," said Robin. "Even if she can only meet you halfway, she's got to know you're always there, believing she can do it."

We had the conversation at a dinner at Kayla's house, a big spread on her long wooden table. It was me and Paul, Robin and the five-year-old Jewel, plus Kayla's grouchy sixteen-year-old, Jenny. It was festive and lovely. There was music on, and I thought, We could have this, too: children at the table. We could have Velvet's friend up. We could have maybe her mother and brother. Jewel looked up suddenly, and fixed me with penetrating adult eyes. I had seen this look on her before; it was curiously natural on the little girl. "Why do you like this girl from another family to come see you?" she asked.

"Because she makes me feel part of life," I said.

Paul looked down and I thought he was annoyed—but then he looked up with soft eyes, and put his hand on my leg.

So I got my church-y lady to get Velvet's mother on the phone and ask if she could come again. Mrs. Vargas laughed jaggedly and said something the translator couldn't understand, though she did get the word *donkey*. And then she said, sure, Velvet could come. If I wanted her.

Velvet

When we walked at night, it was cold and I had to borrow Ginger's jacket because my mom didn't buy one for me yet. There were no more bug noises and the smells were deeper and secreter.

While we walked, Ginger talked to me about self-destruction. She said she was afraid I was destroying myself by not turning in my papers. She said it made her feel bad because it reminded her of her sister who died, because her sister failed her classes even though she was smart. I didn't say anything. I just pictured Fiery Girl running out in the open, her sides shining and thick white sweat between her legs. I pictured her up on her hind legs, kicking with her front. Ginger said she was sad because if my grades weren't good Strawberry couldn't come, and it was almost the end of the semester.

"Does it mean you don't want me to come up?" I asked.

And she said, "No." She put her arm around me. "I want you to come up. But you can't bring anyone else—that's a privilege. That has to be earned."

That was the time when Joker bucked off Beverly. She was in the round pen working with him on his "manners," and as soon as I saw them I could see they were not getting along. I could see it in Joker's *skin*, in the way his body was under Beverly's legs and in the things Beverly was saying without words, *angry* things she said with her legs and her hands. I had the funny feeling she didn't even know what she was saying, but I could see it and I know he felt it; when they passed me at the fence and I saw his eyes, I felt scared—and it was two seconds after that he bucked and Beverly flew and hit the ground so bad her head bounced. Joker bucked again and kicked, I put my hand on my mouth because I felt a scream coming, and Beverly—she sat up and *smiled*. She got on her feet and shook her head and I saw her helmet was cracked. She looked at the horse and he looked at her, head up like he's proud of himself. She said, "Why, you little snot!" And he *let her get back on*.

The next day she was showing her cracked helmet to Pat and Gare and laughing about it, bragging about herself *and* the horse.

"The little SOB. He threw me high, wide, and handsome, I'll tell you! He has got one nasty sense of humor, mean and sloppy like his owner." Then her voice came down so that I could barely hear it. "You know what they say about her in town? Any man could have her and who would want to!" Pat laughed—nervous, not happy— and then she said something that Beverly didn't answer.

Maybe they thought I wouldn't hear because I was grooming Spirit on the other side of the barn. I didn't want them to know I heard because it was so ugly it was embarrassing.

I was also a little scared of Spirit; he was pissed off because his friends were outside and he wanted to be out too. He was pawing at the ground, and he even stamped his foot. I was telling him to "stand like a gentleman" like Beth told him, but he was not listening to me. I talked soft and put my hand on him, and he stamped both his feet. That's when I heard Beverly go, "Shut the fuck up and settle down!" And she was right in his face like his hooves were nothin' to her and she grabbed his halter, going, "Shut the fuck up and settle down!"

She wasn't yelling, but there was something in her voice that made it like yelling. Spirit's eyes rolled and he moved to the side, but not like with attitude. He didn't have no attitude now. I remembered that when I first met Beverly, she was talking about Spirit when she said, "I hurt him worse than he hurt me."

"I know you're not supposed to curse," she said. "But when you need a horse to back off and settle down, it helps if you say curse words. You make your voice deep and say curse words. Not because they understand the words, but because your voice will right away say those words different. And he'll know you mean it."

"I think he just wants to go out, Miss Beverly."

"I know he wants to go out. He wants a lot of things. He wants to go to a horse show where they have great big flags. Just because he wants it, doesn't mean he gets it." And then she grabbed his halter again, but not hard this time, and said, "Right?" Then she petted him and said, "That's right."

And she moved around him, scratching him with her nails, in a nice way. When she got to his butt, she stopped.

"Oh," she said. "So that's why he's got his nose open." And she pointed at these sores on his butt. "Poor fella." And she went and got this cream and she put it on him, massaging it in with her fingers and scratching his itchiness. She said, "Sweet man! Who loves ya, sweet man? Who's ya daddy?" And he turned around with his lips trembly.

I thought, Pat is nice, but Beverly is cool. Her fingernails were all broken and still she was scratching him so hard she was getting dirty all up in them. But why did she think a horse cared about big flags?

"This is how the alpha horse grooms," she said. "You can always tell who dominates by who grooms who first and how. Want to try it?"

And I did. And Spirit did his lips at me, too.

"FYI," she said, "it's right to discipline a horse. It's necessary. You see those big tears and cuts on their body when they come in from the field? That's what they do, kicking and biting each other. That's their idea of *playing*. It's really almost impossible for a human being to hurt a horse, unless it's with a nasty bit in the mouth."

"But Miss Beverly, then why do they care if you hit them with a whip?"

She tapped her head. "It's all psychological. It doesn't *really* hurt, but it hurts a little. They're sensitive. That means they get all messed-up easy. They figure if you can do that, something worse might be coming." She looked at Spirit. "And it might be, right? You control them from inside their heads. The physical is backup. Mostly."

Paul

I couldn't believe Ginger wanted to have the kid up for Christmas. It was clearly inappropriate, and I wanted—*needed*—quiet during the holiday. I didn't think I'd have to argue about it though. I expected the mother to unequivocally lower the boom—how could she not, when Ginger was trying to take her child away on the most important holiday of the year. Meanwhile, I was occupied with tension at school: a thesis student had threatened to kill herself; a colleague, a sad person who'd been kicked out of his house for having an affair, which then promptly ended, was camping out in his office, even eating there and sleeping on the floor. I would've liked to have had *him* for Christmas Eve.

But one day when Edie was visiting, I went out to do an errand and came back to find her talking with Ginger about Velvet. I recognized my wife's tone before I even understood her words; it was that fevered, too-quick voice she always used when talking about the girl. The next thing I saw was that Edie was *responding*. It took me a second to react to this; out of loyalty to her mother, Edie was barely polite to Ginger most of the time. Before I'd left for my errand, that's how it was. Now she was seemingly enthralled with my wife. I thought, Oh Christ—and that's when my daughter turned to me and said, "You're having the Fresh Air girl up for Christmas? Can I hang out with her?"

"Sure," I said, "if her mom lets her come stay with us on the most important holiday of the year, which I doubt."

"I'm not talking about actual Christmas Day," said Ginger. "I'm asking about the day after."

I said, "I still doubt it." But I was wrong.

Velvet

So I had to tell Strawberry she could not come see the horses. I told her at recess when she came to see me in the cafeteria. She was quiet and then she said, "It's okay. I won't be here anyway. My mama found a place. I'm going back on Easter break." And she went to be with the others.

Then they invited me for the day after Christmas. They were going to have a tree. We never had a tree. In school we had one, my cousin Donna had a pretend one, and there was a silver and gold one at the restaurant where we went last New Year's. But my mom never got a tree. At first Dante acted like he didn't care. He said, "Yea! You won't be here!" Then at dinner he acted like a brat, sticking out his tongue with food on it. So I stuck my tongue out too. My mom was so busy slamming dishes down on the table and talking so loud about somebody at work who criticized her that she didn't notice. Until he kicked me under the table and I said, "Mami, make him stop!" And she slapped my head and said, "It's your fault." And he kicked me and I shoved his food in his lap and he fake-cried and my mom hit the side of my head and told me to go in the bedroom, no food.

I didn't care. I just closed the bedroom door and opened the window and looked out. Outside, it was raining hard and cold. You could see the rain hitting the dirty sill and pouring in the streetlight. You could smell the wet street and see some dirty snow from before. The only thing that was Christmas was colored lights in the window across the street. I couldn't see the people that lived there, but I could see their shadows moving on the ceiling. I could feel my grandfather there saying, *She doesn't mean it. She loves you. She's letting you go have the tree.*

I believed him. Still, I wished somebody from here could go with me. My brother. Or Strawberry. I wished Strawberry could go.

Paul

We both went to pick her up at the station. Without telling me, Ginger had bought Mrs. Vargas a pair of earrings and the boy a goofy toy that stuck out its tongue when you squeezed it. I swallowed my irritation, but I was embarrassed to be bringing these things, which I pictured them accepting sullenly. But Mrs. Vargas not only smiled to see us, she gave *us* something first, wrapped in a silver and pink gift bag. The boy *was* sullen, but this time he looked up when I said, "Hey there, young man," and he mumbled something. We went to a diner to exchange the gifts and his quick, pleased glance said he was happy with the toy. Mrs. Vargas had given us a scented candle. We ate sandwiches and this time when we said good-bye to the mother and brother, we all hugged and said Merry Christmas; Mrs. Vargas kissed Ginger on both cheeks. She took my hand and gave me a look that was not flirtatious, but that nonetheless acknowledged me as a man. I thought, Well, she is polite.

Then the boy suddenly stepped close to me and said, "Can I come too?" Ginger spoke quickly: "Maybe next year." And Velvet frowned; I frowned too, and put my hand on the boy's shoulder to cover it. His mother frowned also, quietly but deeply; she and Velvet exchanged words. Then, with a sideways "Good-bye" in English, Mrs. Vargas pulled her son away from me and down the street. And Velvet smiled again.

While we walked to the train, I asked her what her mom had gotten for her. "The same thing she gets me every year," she said flatly. "A mug with a flower on it."

I pictured the tree we had waiting at home, all the gifts Ginger had piled under it. And I felt uneasy, nearly ashamed.

Until we got home and she saw the tree.

Velvet

I thought there would be snow up where they were and there wasn't. I thought I would see snowmen. But it was the same cold wet with old pieces of dirty snow on the curb and the grass, except lonelier than my street. Right away when we got out the car, I asked to go see my mare, and for the first time Ginger said no, it was late, didn't I want to see the tree? I said please and Paul said tomorrow. And I felt mad. Because it was my Christmas and I even said please.

But then we came in the house. It was dark at first and then Ginger went in the living room and the tree went on and—it was like being in a room I never saw before. Their tree was big, much bigger than the one at the restaurant or even at school; it was like the only thing in the room. And there was all different things on it, colored balls with designs on them, glass birds, candy canes, and angels and animals, and you could see they put them together in a way that was on purpose. There was tinsel hanging on every branch. And there were little white lights, but also big lights in soft colors that reminded me of the game I played at day care, Candy Land; there were wrapped presents underneath. My blood started moving really fast in my body, like music that's too fast to dance to. I thought of Strawberry then, how she talked like a little kid, because that's what I felt like.

"Do you want to open them tonight or tomorrow?" asked Ginger.

"I don't know."

"How about one tonight and the rest tomorrow?"

I picked a little one and when I opened it I found a silver ring in the shape of a blue butterfly. It was more beautiful than anything I ever had. It made my blood run faster, like something too fast for me to hold.

Ginger

I remember that night and the next day in a soft haze of joy; the look on her face when I turned on the tree lights, then again when she opened her first present. And Edie, acting like it really was Christmas Day, opening her present, taking part. It was slightly unreal somehow and yet at the same time more real than anything. It was like my own childhood come to life again, my memory of Christmases cleansed of the disappointment and anger, the fighting and silent unhappiness that sometimes was there. What I remembered now was the goodwill, the effort made, the cookies my mother baked from scratch, my father bringing in the tree, Melinda and I putting on the ornaments, saving the most delicate for last. I felt all that as a child, but I took it for granted as how things ought to be. Not now.

Velvet

That night I couldn't sleep. Everything in me was still going too fast. Also, my stomach felt sick from the food at the restaurant, like I might have to go to the bathroom. I thought about my mom, especially her cooking, how you could feel her in her cooking. I thought about my horse: her rough mane, her powerful shoulders. Her wise wrinkled mouth. Her thinking dark eye. I sat up and turned on the light. I took my cotton-ball box out of my backpack and laid my things out on the blanket: the plastic bell, the red heart, my father's blue shell, my grandfather's sea horse, my one-legged Ginger-doll in her checkered coat and her orange ring. I put my new ring in with them. I thought of my horse. My grandfather said, *Go.*

So I made sure their lights were out and then I got out of bed and put on my butterfly ring and my clothes. I went downstairs really quiet and out the door quiet too. I walked on the dark path to the barn. I would've been scared normally, but that night I wasn't. I wasn't scared even when I went into the barn and it was so dark at first I couldn't see at all. The horses moved and asked me to come say hi, and the fast thing in my body got slower. I didn't talk to anybody else, I just went to her. She was curled on the floor of her stall, her head even curled down with her nose resting on the floor like some little animal. When she felt me there she raised her head; I spoke soft to her and she uncurled to stand and come to me.

When horses are curled up and then they stand, it is beautiful and funny, like babies walking. They put their front feet down like it's the first time and they don't know for sure how, they need to go slow and feel on each foot, their body going one way and the other until they find the strong spot and *boom,* they are proud on their legs again. Watching made my heart soft, made me want to hug her. So I did something I never did; I opened her stall and came in it.

Which I should not have done. She wasn't expecting it, and she came to me too fast. I held up my hand like I saw Pat do and I said, "Alto!" like my mom when she means business. And the mare stopped. And I made my head and shoulders soft. I petted her, first her shoulder, then her neck. I told her how much I'd missed her and promised I'd clean her stall the next day because I could smell it was mad dirty. I tried to sing her a Christmas carol but I couldn't remember all of one, so I sang, *Safe under mama's wings, huddling up / Sleep the little chicks until the next day.* I sang it to her until the fast thing was gone. And then when I walked out, I sang it so they could all hear it.

Paul

Edie came over that afternoon. Velvet was shy and sweet around her and Edie was nice in a way that seemed unnatural to her. Not that my daughter isn't nice; she is. But there was a subtle theatricality about her manner that, to my surprise, Velvet seemed not only to enjoy, but to match. Each seemed to know her role and to fall into it easily—though what those roles would be called wasn't an easy thing to put a name on.

"Do you want to come to the stable with me?" asked Velvet, her voice lower and sweeter than the one I knew.

"I'd love to!" cried my daughter. And then, when Velvet was up in her room getting a sweater, Edie turned to me and said very soberly, "Dad, I am so glad you are doing this."

"I am too, I guess," I answered. "I just wish I knew what it was."

Velvet

My best present was from Little Tina. I rode her without a saddle. It was cold and so muddy I slipped and fell off the ramp at the end of the barn and that was even before I got on the horse. Pat said when it was this cold, she used to like to go bareback to feel warm from the horse. And I said, "Can I do it?" And she told me yes, because it was Christmas. And we took off the saddle and when I got on Little Tina it *was* warm all up in my legs. The cold air was on my face but I was warm. I could feel her muscles; it was like I could feel her blood. We only walked and practiced steering, going backward and in a circle and zigzag around things.

But then she started to go at a trot. She did it without asking me. "Whoa!" yelled Pat, but she kept going. So I pressed my butt deep into her body and I talked soft and pulled back on the reins and said, "Whoa" *soft*. And she stopped. Pat came running up and said, "Excellent!" And I was in the sky.

I got some other good stuff too. A pink radio and CD player that said "Princess" on it and earrings in the shape of tiny red flowers and a Celia Cruz CD and a blue Gap shirt with a big zipper in the front. And I met Paul's daughter from his other wife. She was nice.

Ginger

On the train I tried to talk to her. I told her I knew how hard life is, how cruel people can be. "People are assholes," I said. "They will say whatever they think will hurt you. You can't listen, and you can't try to please them. If people at school don't like it that you're doing well, it's because it scares them. If you don't want trouble, hide it. Act like you don't care about school. Just do the work quietly and act the same in class. I'll talk to Ms. Rodriguez; she should understand."

She listened and looked out the window, sort of smiling. I talked about when I was in school, how I didn't fit in. A black woman one seat up across the aisle glanced at me with a curious face. My mother floated into my mind and out. I had only half listened to my mother; I hated the way she was with Melinda, and I did whatever I could to make her *not* be that way with me. My mother was very flawed. But even half listened to, her words built me, and I'm glad she said them. Velvet was already built, but still it seemed she needed words, even dumb ones. So I talked until I ran out of words. Then she put on her headset and played her new radio and I read a book.

When we got to the station, I looked forward to seeing her mother, to connecting with her like we had at the diner, showing her the pictures of Velvet opening her gifts. But her mother wasn't there. We waited outside like always. Snow was finally coming, light and wet, whipping around in the wind. It was getting dark. We stood near the Thirty-Third Street entrance, and the big doors blew hot dry air on us as they opened and closed for the many-faced people trudging in and out of them. Christmas music played from speakers. Dirty, ragged people sat on the ground under the concrete overhang of the building, some with bulging garbage bags. The digital red clock on the side of the station said Mrs. Vargas was fifteen minutes late.

I called her home number; she wasn't there. I called her work number; they said she had left over an hour ago. Velvet looked afraid. I bought her a hot dog from a vendor. A woman with dry dark patches on her face had pulled up her pant legs and was scratching at sores with both hands, her mouth open in concentration. I began to be afraid too. I said, "What kind of neighborhood does your mom work in?" And she answered, "There's white people there." I wanted to say, *That's not what I asked.* But I understood her. We had understood each other. Mrs. Vargas was half an hour late.

I asked Velvet to go into the station to look for her while I stayed outside with her paper bag of Christmas presents. I called the home number again. Velvet took so long that I began to be scared I'd lost her too. When she came out, she looked like she'd been crying. "We'll wait until it's been an hour," I said. "Then I'll call the police."

"No," she said. "You can't do that." Her voice was tearful and I knew she *had* been crying. "They might take us away."

I didn't argue. The hour came. Tears ran down the girl's face. I put my arm around her. "Don't worry," I said. "We'll go back upstate if we have to."

"I don't want to go back upstate," she said. "I want my mama. I want my brother."

I wound up calling a friend, Julian, an editor at an art magazine, one of the few people from my past who actually had made a plush life for himself—and who, not coincidentally I'm sure, had come from money. I explained the situation and he told me to bring her over, he and his wife were sitting down to dinner.

Velvet

We went to stay with these people who lived in a building with a glass door and a shiny stone hallway. We went up in a big elevator with too many buttons and came out into a hall with a sign somebody wrote in crayon that said "Take off shoes, please." Ginger's friend was the only apartment on the floor. The door was open and the man that came out was dressed in white and he was smiling and I wanted to cry.

Because this place did not look like a house is supposed to look. It was too big and bright and everything was white, all the furniture and even the floor. The windows were so big you could see buildings everywhere; it was like being outside up in the air in the middle of buildings. We sat in little white chairs at the white table and the lady put food on the white plates. She was pregnant and she was nice, but I couldn't eat. I was thinking of my mother and how it felt to be next to her. I was thinking these people knew I was a girl whose mother did not come for her. I was thinking if I could only get back to her, I would never go to Ginger's again. Even if it meant I would never see my mare. Everybody was staring at me. I was crying. The pregnant lady tried to hide it, but she was starting to cry too. Ginger was looking like she always did, only more. She said, "Please eat something. It will make you feel better." I said, "I want to call my mom."

So Ginger gave me her phone again. And finally my mom answered.

Ginger

So after that she relaxed. She ate and even talked with my friends, smiling, wanting to feel Carolina's pregnant belly. They found her delightful. Mrs. Vargas told us a story about having to take the brother to the emergency room because his stomach hurt. I didn't believe her, but I was just glad she was all right. Even if she said it was too late for Velvet to come home, and asked if I could keep her for the night.

Julian said we were welcome to the guest room. We had to sleep in the same bed, but Velvet didn't mind. We got under the covers and settled in back-to-back, with the excited feeling of a sleepover. "Good-night," I said.

"Good-night," she answered.

"Good-night!" I said.

"Good-night!" she replied.

We were quiet and I thought I could feel her sinking into sleep. Then she said, "I need to ask you something."

"What?"

She didn't answer right away. I turned my head to encourage her.

"Why is it . . ." She stopped. Her voice came very earnest in the dark. "Why is it that white people can walk their path in a way that black people—and people of my color—cannot?"

"Honey," I said. "You just don't know enough about white people."

"What do you mean?"

"The white people you see where we live have money. They all know each other. They're not going to start trouble, because they have something to lose. White people start with advantages, you know that, right?"

She said, "Yeah," but uncertainly.

"And still, sometimes they wind up going down the toilet anyway. Have you ever heard about the Hell's Angels? They were worse in their day than any gang you've heard of. Murderers, rapists. And they were all white. They had the advantages. They became what they were because they wanted to, not because they had to. My sister was like that. That's what I mean when I say 'self-destructive.'"

I felt her thinking. I knew she wanted to say something but didn't know what. I waited. She didn't say anything. I said, "We can talk about it in the morning if you want."

"Okay," she said.

"Okay, then. Good-night for real."

Velvet

That night I dreamed of horses running together like they were water with a brain that could decide where to go. Except you could see their faces and their feet and tails coming out and then going back into the water of themselves. Ginger was there and so was my mom and Strawberry and Alicia. But I don't remember them. I remember the horses and that they were running toward a giant red sun and that nothing could stop them and that I was with them.

Ginger

The next day I asked her if she wanted to ask me any more questions like she did during the night. She said no. So we went out of the room and ate breakfast with Julian and Carolina.

Then I took her to meet a cousin at Penn Station. Dante was with her, but he barely nodded at me when I said hello. The cousin was an exhausted-looking, heavyset woman with eyes that were hard, quick, and reactive. Without looking at me, she patted Velvet and greeted her in Spanish. She didn't seem to realize I was there until Velvet hugged me good-bye. She finally said good-bye to me and then, as they were walking toward the subway, she added, "Thank you," as if she'd realized she hadn't even greeted me.

People of my color.

Her tone when she said that: forthright, courageous. With the purity of expression I had recognized at first sight. It made my heart hurt.

I went into the station and sat down to wait for my train. It was not very crowded; the usual businesspeople were at home, celebrating with their families still. The people seated around me were slumped and threadbare, carrying their possessions in shopping bags or cheap canvas totes. A bearlike young black man in baggy too-long pants with torn filthy hems paced around cursing at somebody on his cell phone. A dry-haired stringy white woman my age sat very erect, gripping a purse and a computer bag. I knew none of them were homeless because you had to show a ticket to sit in this area. But somehow even this stringy woman with a purse had a homeless feeling about her.

Velvet

When we first left Penn Station there were people in the subway with happy faces: people with nice clothes, and kids with parents that had bought them things who were laughing and playing with each other. I had my things too, but my cousin and Dante were quiet and looking up at the ads about Dr. Zizmor taking pimples off your skin and people on TV. I was getting a sick feeling. The happy-looking people started getting off. More and more dark people were there, sitting and staring quiet. The farther we went, the more there were. A lady across from me had a shopping bag that said GET MORE JOY!! but under her glasses she looked like she was going to cry and not stop.

I remember what I said to Ginger about people like me not walking our path and I did not like myself for that.

Then a man got on and sat next to the woman, and I could tell he was Spanish. He was by himself, but he did not look sad or quiet. He looked strong and happy in his body. He was looking at me like he liked me, like he *knew me.* I looked at him and my sick feeling opened up and became a deep feeling. I remembered my dream of the horses, running into the bright red sun, moving in and out of each other. The subway ran faster and faster in the underwater tunnel. We moved into Brooklyn toward my cousin's house. My feeling went deeper. It was like we were the horses, moving together, in and out of each other, going someplace we needed to go. Even though Dante told me my ring looked like something you get from a gumball machine and I smacked him and my cousin said my mom gave her permission to whip me, so quit it.

Even though my mom screamed at me all night that I was lazy and she wished she didn't have me and then took my CD player in the bedroom and played Celia Cruz on it with the door closed.

Even though when I tried to show Strawberry my ring she wouldn't look and just walked past me. Even though I saw her on the street and she was with Dominic with their arms around each other, which I wouldn't even care about, except she was smiling her evil smile at me and I knew she *wanted* me to care so she could laugh at me for it.

Even though when I put my ring with my cotton-ball-box things it didn't look nice anymore because it made everything else look ugly.

Because when we got up in the morning and my mom did her push-ups and we all got washed and dressed and my mom made our oatmeal with brown sugar, and we all went out—we were moving like the horses. And I was going to let my mare out again one day and she was going to run too. With the others or alone or with me riding her.

I wanted to tell my mom this, but I couldn't. It didn't make any sense. And also my mom thought the horses would kill me.

Ginger

When I called her for our homework session after Christmas, she told me she got spat on. She said she wore her blue Gap shirt that we gave her and her new ring. All morning people stared at her and then while she was waiting in the cafeteria line, girls walked by and spat on her. They spat on her while she walked to her seat with her tray. So she waited till nobody could see, and then she hit somebody. They told, she said they lied, then she got detention. I said I didn't care if she got detention, I was glad she hit the bitch who spat at her. I told her how I'd hit somebody in school once too. I asked if she had any friends who would help her. She said, "I don't got no friends." I asked about the friends she'd talked about, Strawberry and Alicia. She said they were the ones that spat on her. I told her she was better off without them. We read then, a book that was technically under her age range about a little boy who meets a dragon. I kept thinking, But that shirt wasn't even very nice. I listened to Paul; I didn't buy something that was too fancy. That shirt was cute but normal. They spat at her for wearing a normal shirt.

The next day I called the social worker, Eliza Lopez. She said she knew Velvet had gotten detention, but she didn't know anything about spitting. She said that Velvet talked instead about her mother hitting her. I asked if she thought it was true. She said she knew the mother was verbally abusive, but she couldn't be sure about anything physical. A year ago she said her mom beat her; they brought in Child Protective Services and Velvet took it all back. So now the woman didn't want to call anybody unless she saw bruises and when she asked to see bruises, Velvet couldn't show anything.

I thought about why Velvet had not wanted me to call the police, that she didn't want to be "taken away"; I did not tell Ms. Lopez that Mrs. Vargas had not come to meet me. Instead I repeated to her what Velvet had asked me about how white people "walk their path"; I told her my answer, that she didn't know enough white people. "Do you think that was appropriate?" I asked.

"Oh," said Ms. Lopez, "I think it was perfect. I've told her the same. I told her I've been in poor white neighborhoods and they are so disgusting she wouldn't *believe it*. More disgusting than anything she has ever seen in her life. That's what I tell her."

When I hung up I thought, Now we are really in it. We can't go back. It was the first time it occurred to me that Paul had been right.

Paul

She came up every few weeks all spring. She went on long walks with Ginger; she was over at the barn; she spent time with Edie. I saw her mostly at dinner and after, when I would make sure she helped out with the dishes—she washed, I dried or vice versa. The three of us went to the movies together sometimes; she liked to sit up front in the car with me, and the soft curve of her brow rhymed with the roundness of her stomach and early breasts and also with the soft hilly landscape rolling past in the dark. I began to feel that Ginger was right, that in spite of all the dangers, this really was a good thing to be doing.

And then Edie said to me, "Is she going to come and stay with you? She said Ginger was going to homeschool her."

Velvet

I fell off Little Tina. We were in the round pen, and we were cantering and I was making her stop and start and sometimes walk backward. Then somebody started shooting. Behind me Pat said, "What
the hell?" and I got scared and Tina started moving too fast. I turned
around in the saddle to ask why they were shooting, and the rein
came loose in my hand, and then they shot again and Tina moved
sideways *hard*, and I slide off her and I hit the ground; her back legs
kicked up and I rolled over and *prayed*. But she just kind of moved
off sideways and Pat was there saying, "You okay?" and I said, "Why
are they shooting?" And she said it was idiots target shooting out of
bounds, was I okay? And I was. So she told me to get Tina and get
back on her. I didn't think I could, but Tina let me. I walked to her
and turned around like, *Follow me*, and she did. That's when I took
her bridle and took her back to the mounting block.

Paul

Ginger just said, "Oh, I know where she got that. In this movie I saw with her, the character is homeschooled. She asked what it meant and I told her. I guess she liked the idea."

She insisted she said nothing to make Velvet think she was coming to live with us, that the girl was just "experimenting with scenarios in her head." She said she would speak with her—God knows if she did.

And then the girl turned twelve and Ginger took her shopping. Velvet came back to the house with all these bright bags, but she had to catch the train and I never saw what "we" had bought her. I heard about it later, though. From Edie, not Ginger.

Velvet

Ginger took me to this store. I told her I was going to a party, and I was. It wasn't my party; nobody gave me a party. But Alicia was inviting me to a party. I didn't know why. Maybe because I gave her the paper I wrote with Ginger and because we got in trouble together and I made her laugh. Maybe because Strawberry wasn't there anymore. Really, I don't know why. She still acted like she hated me, mostly. But she invited me and I wanted to wear something good. Ginger said, "Let's buy you something, it's your birthday soon." And she took me to this store with things in it nobody in my neighborhood would wear. I said, "This is too fancy," and Ginger said, "No it's not."

But when I came out of the dressing room in this shirt she gave me, the lady in the store said, "A twelve-year-old shouldn't wear that." Ginger said, "I'm clueless." And the store lady picked something. She picked out a short blue skirt that showed my legs and then this shirt. I felt weird, but the store lady said, "It's very cute." I said, "It shows my body." And she said, "But not in a bad way." I didn't understand because it showed as much of my body as the other thing that she said a twelve-year-old shouldn't wear. But in a way I did understand because it didn't have lace and it wasn't black.

I looked in the mirror and I was ugly and stupid. I looked and I was pretty. In the store I *did* look pretty. In my house I knew I would not. At the party I didn't know. But I wanted the outfit. I wanted it.

I wore it to the party. And nobody spat. They looked at me. I could see they were looking like I looked in the store: I was ugly and stupid and then I was pretty. That is how the girls looked. The boys looked different. And I wished Ginger had not taken me to that store.

But then that boy Dominic walked in. And I was glad that she did.

He wasn't alone—he was with Chris, who Helena got in Strawberry's face about. Also this thin tall boy with very dark skin and long straight-black hair who walked like he was somebody famous. And a girl, somebody older than us. She was black but light, with red hair and a silver belt with a buckle that spelled SONDRA, and she walked and turned her little head *so* beautiful. My gladness turned sharp in me; I remembered Dominic's arm around Strawberry with her red-streaked hair. Sondra looked at me, but Dominic did not. I looked back at her, then looked away, and then the boy who acted famous was next to me. Up close he had nasty teeth; brown and rabbit-y, but two of them long on either side, like he's a vampire. His eyes, though, were like warm candy, like a song where the singer sounds like a liar, but you believe it anyway.

He said, "Hey, shawty. Who got that dress for you?"

Across the room, Alicia and Helena were looking like they didn't believe.

"It's not a dress. It's a skirt and a top."

"Your boyfriend got it for you?"

This song came on: *Supersonic, hypnotic, funky-fresh*—and I just smiled.

"Aw, your boyfriend got it for you. That's nice."

—*beat flows right through my chest*—he touched my arm. "But I could get you something better. What's your name?"

"Hey, Shawn," said Dominic, "what you talkin' to my little cousin about?" He was there with Sondra, who looked at me very chill. "Sondra, this my cousin Velvet."

He remembered my name. My glad was back, big and soft; I looked down and mumbled hi to Sondra's hi.

"Just inviting her for a smoke, thass all."

"She too young for that." He looked at me with the little dent in his nose and his eyes soft like—

Suddenly I felt Sondra standing there, strong and perfume-y, with covered eyes. Not saying anything. Not having to.

"She old enough for a boyfriend," said Shawn.

"That don't mean old enough to smoke." Dominic punched my arm real soft. "But you can hang with us if you want."

So we went to somebody's bedroom with clothes all over their bed. Shawn went to sit next to me, but Dominic moved too fast for him, between me and Shawn so close that his leg was against mine. Shawn didn't say nothin'; they just talked about something else. Sondra talked to me separate. She said, "Your boyfriend bought you the outfit? It's cute." Her voice was nice.

"I didn't say it's from a boy. My godmother got it for my birthday just today."

"How old are you?" she asked.

"Twelve."

"It looks like money. She rich, I guess. Really, you don't look twelve." And then she passed me this sweet-smelling rolled cigarette, but I didn't take it. Because Dominic was there and he didn't want me to. So I just sat and felt Dominic's leg like it was breathing his life into my leg, up into my whole body. What they talked about after that didn't matter. I was just breathing in life. When we walked out of the room, Alicia and Helena gave me eyes like they did not know who I was and hated me anyway. But I didn't care. Dominic was walking in front of me. He had his arm around Sondra, but he turned his head to look at me. And his look was not candy. It was tight and hot, joking and serious. Like a song I never heard before.

Paul

They attacked her and beat her. That's what Edie said. Not at the party, but later, they swarmed her and beat her. She didn't even try to fight back; there were too many of them. Her little brother was there, but he didn't help. He actually stood there and laughed.

Between me and Ginger, there was hell to pay. Leave the girl alone, I told her. What do you want to do, get her hurt worse? And she went *nuts*. She beat the wall and screamed that if it weren't for me, she *could* come stay with us and nobody would hurt her again and I told her she was crazy and selfish and she ran out the door. It was raining and she just ran out into it. I waited and she didn't come back for I don't even know how long. So I went out in the car and found her walking in her sopping pants.

I opened the door; she got in. We drove around, up in the neighborhood where we'd first taken Velvet bike riding. I waited for her to talk. She said, "Please don't take her away from me. You wouldn't let us adopt, so at least let this happen. Can't you see how good it is for me? Don't you see how even Edie finally respects me? She finally sees me as a normal woman. I *am* a normal woman. I want to be normal. If we can't adopt, this is the closest I can come to having a child."

I told her I was willing to consider adoption. She said no. She said, "I love her."

I struggled to control my voice. I said, "If you love her, think about her safety. She's already been hurt. The truth is, she could get more hurt on those horses."

She didn't answer until we were almost home. Finally she said, "I know."

But when we talked to Velvet, she said it wasn't about the clothes. She said those girls just didn't like her. She said the clothes made them respect her. She said she was friends with some of them again.

Velvet

It wasn't all of them right away. It was Alicia that called me a pig at recess and told me to "go hang around with the rich people." I hit her and knocked her head to the side; I was strong because of working in the barn and she did not dare hit me back or even talk, she just held on to her face and stared at me.

It was later that her friends came up on me when I was walking to the train with Dante. Dante laughed while they hit me, but what else could he do? He was only seven. If he didn't laugh, he'd have to put his head down and feel like shit. So he laughed, and when they were done, he picked up my backpack and carried it for me. And when I got home, my mother looked at the places somebody'd cut my face with heavy rings and she put medicine on it. It made me remember when I was little and she would wash me and comb my hair more softly than she does it now. Sometimes she would hum a song and her touch and her voice would wrap us up in a place where there was nothing but her and me. I would be very still and I would want her to keep doing it forever. It was like that now, except it was even better because she was angry too, and not bitch-angry like at Mr. Nelson at the grocery. She was deep angry, but not at me; she was angry *for me*. This angry was big and warm like a horse, and it felt better than her nice. It was better than anything Ginger had, and what Ginger had was *good*. My mother said, "If this ever happens again, if they do this to you again, swear to God, I will hurt them like they have never been hurt before." She said what she said before: "I will come after them with my *body*."

Except that she didn't. It was Shawn that helped me the next time. They were following me down the street, and not even Dante was there. They were saying they were gonna beat me down, put me in the hospital this time. I looked at the buildings and cars going by and it was like everything was normal, like me getting beat down was normal. I thought of Ginger and my mare; that didn't make me feel stronger. It made me feel weaker. The girls got closer. And then like in a movie, Shawn came up beside me. "Hey, girl," he said. "What's

good?" I said, "Nothing good now. You see those girls?" He looked,
I looked. "They gettin' ready to jump me like before." All he had to
do was look their way with a hard face. They stopped; him and me
started. He asked if I wanted to smoke some weed with him. And I
said yes.

Ginger

On the phone, I asked if those girls were still bothering her. She said they were not. I told her a story from when I was her age, how a bunch of girls attacked me, how I knocked one of them down and they didn't bother me anymore.

She said, "I wouldn't do that." She sounded amused.

I asked her, "Why not?"

Instead of answering, she asked if I believed in hell. At first I said no. Then I said, "Honestly, I think it's possible. Though I don't think you get sent there. I don't think God would have to send people there. I think they would go there by themselves."

She asked, "Why do you think that?"

I said, "Look at how people act. They walk right into horrible things all the time. They actually go out of their way."

I told her about the time I dreamed of going to hell on purpose. I was only seven, and in my dream, I went to hell to take the devil's treasure. I got lost, but finally I succeeded and I came back up and put the treasure under my bed. The dream was so realistic that when I woke up, I looked under my bed to see if the treasure was still there.

"Was it?" she asked.

"I don't remember. But really, those girls, they aren't bothering you?"

"No," she said. "Not anymore." And then, "I dreamed I went to hell too. Because my grandfather told me to. There was a door in your backyard."

The hair on my arms stood up when she said it.

Velvet

I went with Shawn because I wanted to get away from those girls and also show them what I could do—walk away with a boy who looked famous. And because even though he wasn't Dominic, he was close to Dominic. Maybe Dominic would even be there, where we were going.

But he wasn't. There was only Shawn's grandmother there, and I could see where he got his dark skin; she was very black with her gray hair up in a net and she did not look happy to see me. The TV was on really loud; we sat on the couch and watched it. A woman was in the hospital and she had cancer and her man was with another woman. Shawn's grandmother said there would be dinner in a minute and we went into his room.

This time I did smoke. The smoke filled my body like Dominic's leg, only this time it was Shawn's leg. And then it was his hands. He kept trying to kiss me with that mouth of vampire rabbit teeth, and it just made me want to laugh. He kissed my lips soft, but it felt angry. He said, "You not really his cousin, are you? How old are you?" I said, "How old are *you*? What grade you in?" He said, "I'm not in no *grade*," and the smoke filled my body again. He started kissing my neck. I said, "Your teeth are funny." But he just said, "That so?" and then he took my hand and said, "Girl, you ever felt a man before?" And I pulled my hand back and said, "I've felt horses." He laughed in this nasty way. I said, "I ride horses. Horses are bigger than a *man*." I said *man* like he said *grade*, and he pulled back and said, "I don't see no horses here. It's me here."

A lot of minutes had gone by and dinner was not ready.

Silvia

The clothes that woman bought my daughter! They were nice, but too nice, like the woman was saying to me, *What's wrong with you, you can't even dress your child right?* I know that's not what it was supposed to be, but that was my first feeling and my first feeling is always right; whenever I've gotten into trouble, it's been because I didn't follow my first feeling. Besides, when Velvet put them on, she just looked conceited, a bitch royale, and she looks like that anyway. Maybe where Ginger lives girls can go around looking like that, but here you're gonna get *hurt* and *I knew it.* But everybody keeps telling me I'm too hard, I yell, I don't understand it here—okay, fine. I can see she hates the clothes I can get for her, she always wants better and more—okay, fine. Let her have it. Let her see. And she did see; she never wore those things again. But how stupid was this Ginger that she didn't even talk to me? How *disrespectful,* did she think she was dressing a doll? I knew she was silly, but I believed her to be good, or good enough. Was she? There *was* something strange in her eye, es rara—but it never stayed long enough for me to know what it was. Mostly she looked immature, more girl than woman—a sad girl trying to be happy. Una sufrida—what else could she be, married but not one child? I could see the sadness and emptiness in her eyes and I'd feel her, that surely she's been through some real hell. Then she'd stare at me, and I'd know she was also something else. But what? She acted so big, walking up to me like she knew my daughter better than I did. But then the next second she'd seem so *lost.* Who was she? Why was she being so nice?

Then she sent me fifty dollars, and whatever she was, I had to take it. Mr. Diaz was moving out and I didn't know what I was going to do.

Ginger

She passed her grade, even though she failed. Her grades were crap, but they pushed her through anyway. If the school passed her, did it make any sense to punish her? She was going on to middle school! So she came up again for the summer, this time for six weeks. I was going to tell her mom about the horses at the end of it, but I didn't. I sent her money instead. I sent it in a greeting card with a picture of horses on it. I said it was for Velvet's graduation, but really it was because Velvet told me that her mom was so broke a woman gave her money on the subway. The woman gave it to her mom because her mom was crying. The woman was Dominican, and she asked Mrs. Vargas why she was crying and she said, "I have no money for my family." And the woman opened her purse and gave her five dollars. She said she wished she could give more, but she had a family too. Which I don't.

Velvet

When I went back to the barn, Beth wasn't there anymore. Some of the horses weren't there either: Blue Boy and Baby were gone. Instead there was a new girl named Heather and her horse, this weird pale horse she called Totally Crushed. Heather wore gold things, rings and little chains, and she had short, shiny nails and Barbie hair. I thought maybe she was one of the rich people Beth told me about, the ones who Beverly trained the horses for just so they could look good. But Heather already looked good on Totally. She was everything right and did everything right and everything that wasn't right made her sick. She didn't like Joker because "he doesn't want to work." She didn't like Graylie because he was "wimpy." She didn't like Fiery Girl because, besides being "psycho," she had "ugly ears." Who she liked was Beverly. And Beverly liked her *a lot*.

I hated her worse than Gare and I think Gare hated her too. After Heather came to the barn, Gare didn't eat her lunch with everybody anymore. She went out and ate her sandwich on a feedbag, her shoulders curled up and her dumb purple head down in them.

The day Joker got loose was the day Heather finally did something wrong. It was mad hot, we were all sweaty and the horses were sleepy and all the big fans were going, and I was pushing this wheelbarrow of dirty sawdust to dump it when I heard Heather scream, "Loose horse!" And it was Joker. He'd gotten away from her when she was going in to clean his stall, and he was running, heading for the door, with his eyes going *Hee hee hee!* Pat yelled, "Get out the way!" and I threw myself flat against the wall and he went past like a smiling tornado, heading right for the door where Beverly was. I thought, Now *she's* gonna learn some respect—even her.

But I was wrong. She saw him coming, and she grabbed a rake somebody left and stuck it right up in his face. He made a scared noise and turned around, and she followed him with the rake, chased him back into his stall.

"Good goin'!" yelled Pat.

"Watch what you're doing next time," Beverly snapped at Heather, who turned red.

Which I would've liked except for what happened then. When I first rode Joker and he didn't do what I asked and Pat said, If he was your little brother, what would you do? I said, Hit him, and she said, I wouldn't try that with Joker. I didn't try it. I was nice and he did what I wanted and I was proud. Now Beverly was in his stall hitting him, like it was nothing. Like he was nothing. And Pat didn't say nothin'.

So I stood around Beverly and waited for her to say something about it. And she did, kind of. She told me a story about a boy my age at a place she used to work at in Texas. She said he worked in his father's stable and one day this stallion got loose. She said this boy knew that horse, that it was unpredictable. Still, that boy was stupid when he knew better. He saw that horse running right at him, and he stood in front of it and tried to stop it by waving his arms, and that stallion stood up and knocked the boy out with his hooves.

"The kid was out of it for days. They weren't even sure he'd come back to normal," she said. "And he deserved it. Even his father thought it. People thought he'd put the horse down, but he didn't. It was a valuable horse and the kid did a dumb thing."

"His own father?"

"Yeah." She looked at me the way she looked at the horses when they were starting to make her mad. "It wasn't the horse's fault. He was just saying, 'Get outta my way, you idiot.'"

Then I really didn't understand. I still thought Beverly was cool. But like you think somebody scary is cool. Because she thought horses should be hurt if they acted up. And she did the same as the boy did, she got right up in Joker's face. But she was still on the stallion's side, and all I could think was, she felt that way because he was the one who hurt somebody. Like she did.

Ginger

After just a week with us, she came back from the barn one day and asked could she please, please, please take a bareback riding class. I said, "Let's see," and we went over to the barn. Pat introduced me to the woman who she said would be the trainer and I thought, *no*. The woman had a powerful body, a hard, blunt voice, and an *insane* face. Her eyes were simple mentally but emotionally snarled, aggressive and shrewd like an orangutan's. She looked out of her eyes so hard you couldn't look into them. She was verbally polite to me while her face dismissed me with the fast scorn of a teenager. She looked like the kind of person who could really mess up a child.

But then I saw: She respected Velvet. Or at least she was paying attention, she was interested, and I felt the woman wasn't interested in much. I could feel Velvet change around her, come to attention in a way I hadn't seen before. So I decided to risk it. It was a four-week class, just enough to take Velvet through the summer. It was a thousand dollars, which would be hard to explain to Paul. Unless I took it from the private money my mother left me. Which is where I got the money I'd started sending Velvet's mom every month. Two- or three-hundred-dollar checks that she never asked for or acknowledged but always cashed.

Velvet

The bareback class started early in the morning before it was hot. I woke up even before the alarm, swimming like a fish out of sleep, making clouds of mud come up from the bottom. Clouds of dream settled down and I remembered: Shawn. I was dreaming of his hands on me even though I'd said no. Except in the dream, he turned into Dominic and I said yes. And then the alarm beat my head and I slammed my hand on it and got up to go, feeling the dream still in my body while I ate scrambled eggs.

The class met in the barn. There were six girls and they all knew each other, but except for Heather they didn't know me and she acted like she didn't know me. Then Beverly came in carrying a whip. Not a crop or a lunge whip, but a black whip so big she had it looped around her arm. My heart pounded; something swam out of dark privacy and swam away. We went outside and she said, "Meet my friend and helper," and she cracked her whip hard, like black lightning, and the cats ran with their tails low. Everybody was very quiet when she told us to go get our horses.

I didn't have a horse so I said, "Which horse should I get, Miss Beverly?"

She said, "I think Joker."

Which made me feel funny because . . . she didn't like Joker. Because he threw her high, wide, and handsome.

Ginger

The bareback class was something to see, and I didn't even see all of it. That crazy woman was so completely in her element that she didn't even look crazy. They started out in the small ring I'd seen Velvet ride in; they mounted there and then walked the horses to a larger ring, where they trotted in a circle for ten minutes at a time before slowing to a walk, then picking it up again. The trainer kept them trotting with a bullwhip, which she used with gloating skill—she hit each horse precisely on the crook of its back leg with a rhythmic flick that was almost hypnotic to watch. The whole time she would bark out military-style instructions—"Sit up straight! Stay with him! Give him his head! Sit on your seat bones, Jessie; let go that mane! Seat bones, crotch, seat bones, crotch! Legs, legs, legs!"— while the girls bounced on their fannies so hard they got sores, holding on for dear life.

Velvet

She did not hit the horses hard, but still you could feel how big that whip was. You could feel something else too, something big and *oily* in the air around her when she used it. I realized then what she'd meant when she talked about controlling them from inside. When I was on Joker, I could feel something *psychological* happen inside him, like he was mixed-up and didn't know which way to go. It wasn't the whip. He understood the whip. It was the *something else,* and I had to use my legs not just to stay on but to tell him, *It's okay, you're okay.* It made me feel like I was riding against Beverly, even if she was the one teaching me to ride.

Then one day we went on the trail into the green that I used to be scared of a long time ago. The bushes and plants were fat back there and *thick,* like beautiful songs are so thick in your brain sometimes you can't think. We walked until we came to a river. I thought we were going to turn around, but Beverly didn't stop, we went up to the river and I made a scared noise, and Joker slowed up, nervously. Beverly said, "Steady! They know how to swim!" And I felt Joker telling *me* to relax, and then we went into it—we went into the water. My heart hammered; the water went almost up the horses' backs, and our legs went under the water too. All the girls were screaming about the cold, but I wasn't. Not even when it got deep and I could feel Joker's legs running in the water under me, his body moving incredible, like a *snake.* I just closed my eyes and felt: cold water. Hot sun. Thick green. Shawn. His hands on me, his mouth, his voice in my ears. The snake-moving feelings of the world. *You so beautiful, I wanna kiss you all over, touch your breast, feel your legs holding me real tight.* But where was the one I wanted? We reached the other side and I held Joker with my legs as he climbed out onto shore, rocking back and forth, horse-strong and heavy under me again. Shawn's lumpy dick like a crocodile in his pants, his grandma knocking on the door—but where is the one I want?

It was later that day that I asked Pat why she said I should not hit Joker when she thought it was good that Beverly hit him. She said, "Because you don't have the authority. Not then you didn't. Beverly *does* have the authority and also that time he got loose was a particular situation." We were grooming Joker together; she'd just been out working him, and he was all wet and peaceful. He was on cross-ties almost right in front of the mare, and she was right up against her door, watching us. Not kicking, *quiet,* almost like she was listening. "You hit only as a last resort," Pat said. "Or at least I do. Some people do it different."

"Beverly told me that hitting doesn't really hurt them. She said it's more psychological."

"That's kinda true. You can make a horse crazy hitting him, especially if he can't figure out what you're hitting him for. But he *did* know in that case. It made sense."

"So if hitting is okay sometimes, what is abuse?"

"You know Little Tina, right? She used to have this issue with cleaning her hooves. I'd pick up her hooves to clean 'em and sometimes she'd go like to kick me. That's dangerous. So I'd hit her with the crop. Once, maybe twice the next time she did it. Abuse is when you don't just hit once, but over and over. I've seen people do things like beat a yearling to the ground 'cause it reared up 'cause it was young."

We took Joker off the cross-ties, and I led him back to the stall. As soon as he was in, my mare went to the side of her stall then and put her nose up where Joker was. He came to her; I noticed they were talking more this summer.

"You think anybody ever beat Fiery Girl that bad?"

"I don't know, but I doubt it. The thing about mares? They will always draw a line in the sand. Stallions, geldings, they can be tough. But while a mare'll take a lot of shit, eventually she will draw a line in the sand, and when she does that—cross it and she is going to take you down, even if she has to die doing it. Just like a woman. It's why some people don't like mares."

I smiled and Pat said, "You think I'm joking? People say you can tell a gelding, discuss it with a stallion, ask a mare. I say beg a mare is more like it. Unless she likes you. And sometimes even then."

Ginger

I dreamed I went to hell, just like I told Velvet. In the dream I was little again, and again, I went looking for treasure. I found it, but in this dream I lost it; I got lost in hell. I met a naked old woman carrying love wrapped in pain. But I wasn't afraid of her. There were horrible things happening all around us, all the terrible things that can happen in the world—but most of them I didn't even notice. The old woman took me to a terrible hallway where living human heads protruded from the walls, talking incessantly in every language, unable to understand or hear each other and crying in desperation to be heard. One of them was me and one of them was a beautiful young man. The old woman said, "He is your love." And he was. He was Michael.

I fought to wake up. I fought to run. An iron hand was holding me; there was a spider that was also a person. And then someone came to help me. An old man and someone else I couldn't see. The old man carried me in his arms over a field. But I said something he didn't like and he dropped me. And I woke up, turning violently on my side and remembering: Velvet had dreamed of going to hell too. Through a door in our backyard.

Velvet

Beverly and Pat were always saying somebody didn't want to work. They said it about people and horses. They told stories that ended "he just didn't want to work for it." It could be about a horse who didn't win a contest or a horse that didn't want to pull Beverly around in a circle while she sat in a buggy. Or a person who couldn't ride very good or somebody they knew in school who flunked like about a hundred years ago. Once Pat said it about her own father, that he didn't want to work to get a better job. Once Beverly said it to me. She put her hand on my shoulder and said, "Your trouble is, you don't like to work."

It was the same thing my mom said to me. And I thought the same about Pat and Beverly as I thought about my mom: Look what your work got you. Shoveling shit and carrying it back and forth all day in hell-heat and half the horses standing pissed off and hot in their stalls while the other half go out and play because they can only use one paddock because they're trying to grow out the grass in the other one, and they can't all go out at once because they fight. That's why Beverly wouldn't let Diamond Chip Jim go out even though he was rearing up and wanting to be out; he'd fight in the same paddock with Rocki and Officer Murphy. And besides, there's not enough room. And Beverly's going, He don't like to work, like that's got anything to do with it.

He don't like to work. It was like flies buzzing at you all day, like Fiery Girl banging on her door that she could not open, because they let her out hardly at all. "She has to go out by herself because she fights and there's not always time or room to let her out by herself. Besides which, listen to her." She meant, listen to her banging and cursing, probably snaking her head around. "Do *you* want to turn that horse out right now?"

"No, but—"

"I didn't think so."

"But it's not fair. She hasn't been out for like, days."

"Guess what, life ain't fair. But you know that already, right?"

I looked down so she wouldn't see the expression on my face.

"Look at me," she said. I did. She saw what I thought. We stood for a minute. And then she said it: "You're right. It has been too long. We'll take her out early evening."

We had to argue to get the halter and the nose-chain on her, and when we did, she came out her stall feeling like the A train running even though she just walked. Pat said, "Pull the chain if you need to." I said, "Does it hurt?" and Pat said, "It reminds her that you're there." We stepped outside and I saw Heather and Gare and this other girl Elizabeth were still there, hanging around in the driveway. I didn't like them being there. I especially didn't like it that when we walked out to the arena they stopped talking and stared at us. I lost my concentration; Fiery Girl picked up her pace, like she wanted to trot. Pat said, "Be in control!" I tugged the chain and the mare slowed, but her engine ran and she pushed on me with her shoulder. Pat snapped, "Cut it out!" but the horse lunged, jerking me almost off my feet. I heard somebody giggle. I remembered "Why does a Mexican kid walk around like—" and I yanked on the chain. I didn't care if it hurt. Fiery Girl rose a few inches off her front feet. Pat said, "Give me the lead." But I did not. Fiery Girl yanked me and I yanked her, and my mom reached out of me with her fist, *she* grabbed the rope, and I swung around in front of Fiery Girl and yelled, "Oye, slow up NOW!" And she jumped back so fast, it was funny. I came back to the side, my heart pounding, and we walked, her still a bit ahead, still all fresh, but for show; I had her. There was no giggling. I didn't even have to look to know their eyes were all on me.

Pat put her hand on my shoulder. "I'd say I didn't think you had it in you, but I knew you did."

I smiled and felt my face turn red, proud and embarrassed to be that way.

"But FYI, that's not a great idea, getting in her face like that. Next time, she could dance on your head. Next time, just use the chain."

When we walked past, Elizabeth and Heather turned around and walked away. But Gare didn't. She stood there and she didn't talk, but her face said, *Awesome.*

Ginger

I thought: What if her mother could move up here? Mexicans live here; I see them, mostly working in restaurants or biking on the roads with plastic bags of groceries hanging from their handlebars. Down the block from us, in a boatlike three-story house, live a couple of Mexican families. One night, when Velvet and I walked past, we saw they were having a lawn party with colored lights and music and food. A woman looked at us and smiled as we passed. After that I noticed the Mexican grocery store in the little strip mall by the Laundromat. I went in and bought some candy, sweet red peanuts and sugar animals dyed green. I asked the guy behind the counter if he would be willing to talk to Mrs. Vargas. He looked at me like I had three heads and said sure.

I asked Velvet too: "Would your mother like to move up here?" It took her a long time to answer. When she finally said, "Yeah," she sounded like I had three heads too. Still, I asked, "Would you talk to your mother?" and she gave me the three-headed "yeah."

But later that night, she asked if she could see where the middle school was. So I drove her there. The school was up a hill, on a windy road. It was very visible in the moonlight. Its name was written on a stony mound thick-grown with tiger lilies that looked pale and velvet-gray in the dark. We sat in the car and looked for some minutes. I said, "Will you talk to your mom about it?" And she said, "Yes." Different word, different tone.

Velvet

One day when Gare was eating her sandwich on the feedbag, I was going past her on the way to the house for lunch, and she said, "Hey."

I stopped and looked.

"Heather's a cunt, right?"

I just looked at her.

"Calling her horse *Totally Crushed*?"

I stayed quiet, looking.

"She told me she wanted to call her Totally *Fucking* Crushed, but they wouldn't let her register the horse that way. *Duh*."

I said, "Why *did* she want to call her horse that?"

"Fuck if I know. It sounds like nail polish or something."

"It don't sound like nail polish. It sounds like she hates her horse."

"I dunno." She looked down and ate her sandwich. She looked up again. "You don't curse, do you?"

I said, "No." I thought about her saying I was gonna get deported. I thought, I could curse you out so hard, you'd fall down.

"Why not? Don't you think it's cool?"

"No," I said. "I think it's stupid." But I sat on the feedbag with her anyway. We didn't really look at each other.

She said, "Are you in a gang?"

I looked out at the paddock and at the path going out into the meadow beyond. But I was seeing the street where I lived, and the word almost faded off the wall: Cookie. I thought about him giving my brother some cookie. I thought about the man reaching up to touch his name on the wall. Some kind of feeling came up in me. And I said, "Yeah. Yeah, I'm in a gang."

"Awesome," said Gare. "I wish they had gangs here."

Paul

It wasn't about her being younger. I was never one of those guys. She wasn't a kid; she was almost forty, a National Guardswoman who'd driven a supply truck in Iraq, and had gone back to school to get her MFA in writing. She was worn for her age, tough-skinned and rigid-backed, but with a beautiful mouth and strong, calm eyes—green, with hazel flecks. It *wasn't* about her being younger. In fact, in spite of her relative youth, it was her maturity that appealed to me, her strength; I felt she was a woman who understood things without too much talk about them. I was at ease with Polly.

She wasn't my student either; she was working with a colleague of mine on writing her memoir about her service in Iraq, especially her relationship with a translator whose brother was, like Polly's, schizophrenic. I met her at a graduate-faculty tea and discovered she was also writing about Blake, whom she'd discovered while on her tour; she wanted to juxtapose his imagery with her experience and also with her brother's. I invited her to come by during my office hours and she did. We talked about Blake and Iraq. We talked about our lives. When I told her about Velvet and the horses, tears welled in her eyes. "Sorry," she said. "I never cry. But that is very moving."

It wasn't until a month or so into these conversations that I realized, while telling Polly about Velvet, I was using the pronoun *I* instead of *we*.

Velvet

I woke up thinking about his nose, the little dent in it. About how his eyelashes and eyebrows made his eyes soft, but how inside they were strong. His lips were tense like a muscle, but still his mouth looked full of kisses. Soft, strong, tense, full; he had everything I knew about, with secret things sparking in between: Dominic.

Then my grandfather's voice came in my ear and made me jump out of my dream. He was saying, *Lo prometiste!* I hadn't heard it in a long time. But I knew what he meant right away. It was my last night and I still hadn't taken her out like I said. I was treating her the same way everybody else did, and for the same reason as them; if it was just me and her, without Pat or Beverly, I was still a little scared of her.

I made myself get out of bed. I got dressed with music in my head: *Amor no es amor / Son las cinco de la manana / Y no puedo dormir.* The voice like a live ribbon unwinding, giving feeling. I walked out on the path and the song ribboned up in the sky, in the clouds, dark and with moon behind them. When I got in the barn, the music left my head but stayed in my blood. The horses woke up around me and started talking to each other. My horse was looking like, *Girl, what you thinkin' about?* I took the halter down from the hook and opened her stall. She put her head up like, *It's night. We don't do this at night!* I came to her with my head low; I talked to her like she was a kitten. She let me come to her and touch her neck: She seemed like she was trying to decide and then, like with shiver inside, she put her head down for the halter. When she came out of the stall, the air around her rolled like water when a boat comes by, and it felt good to me and I wasn't afraid; I felt her with me wondering what I would do. All the horses watched and wondered too. I could even see a cat watching at the mouth of the barn, its ears against the sky.

But when I put the saddle pad on, she moved sideways. She pushed out her belly so I could barely get the saddle on. I went to put the bridle on over the halter, but she fought the bit, tossing her head even with my arm around her face. I got the crop from the wall, but then I felt stupid because what was I gonna do with it? Her eyes stared and I smelled my own sweat; I felt the scars on her face like they were on me. I put the crop back and made my body quiet, stroking her shoulder. I tried again and again until she finally took the bit. I put the chain on her nose and led her out.

In our eyes and on our skin we felt the night. I felt her fear of it, felt her start to walk backward, and I turned her in a circle to the indoor ring. She calmed and let me take her there, but when I turned on the light, birds flew in the rafters and again she walked backward. I forgot how big she is and pulled her like a dog on a leash, and—damn!—she reared up and beat the air with her feet, killing hard. The lead line burned through my hands, but I held it, and she came down and I turned her in a circle, two, three times. She followed, and I felt our minds pressed together, each feeling where the other was. I remembered: *Tell a gelding. Discuss it with a stallion. Beg a mare.*

I got her to the mounting block and worked to make the girth right, over and over thinking, Beg a mare, beg a mare. Then I worked to get on—first just standing with my left foot in the stirrup, then both feet in, sitting very soft, just sitting, no legs on. Finally walking, thinking I won't beg, I won't beg, and then wind came through the arena, and she spooked, and I couldn't turn her fast enough, and her head came up, she reared under me. I grabbed her mane, and prayed forward, my feet out of the stirrups, her body wilding under me like a snake, like Joker swimming. She came back down and I was ready, I turned her hard, right into my thigh. We went forward again, walking, trotting, walking. Each feeling where the other was, except it kept moving and changing. Was this what Pat meant by *begging*? Because that's not what it was, it was like *finding*—no, not that either. It was—I tried to think what it was so hard that my mind grew like a forest with everything in it: my mom and Dante and school and Dominic's eyes, Shawn's hands, Strawberry so close in the closet; Ginger. My grandfather said, *You can walk your path better than that lady ever could. She loves you, and you should respect her love. But she doesn't know your path. You can walk it. She can't.* And somebody else was there too, a twisted-up face coming at me sideways through a crack in the forest floor; Manuel, my father's friend who lived with us. *Walk your path!* The forest closed up and I was just on my mare and for a long moment, I found her.

When I walked her back to the barn, we were both sweating. The moon was out from behind the clouds. In its light, I ran the hose between her legs and wiped her with a rag. When I took her to the stall, she stopped for me and then followed when I led her in. She turned herself around so beautiful. I stood in the barn for a long time, just looking at her.

I was almost asleep when the face came again, like a witch coming out the crack. When he first moved in, Manuel acted nice; he even gave me a dollar to make up for my dad taking my money. Then he started to get me between the legs and rub until it felt like it was burning. All day it felt like I needed the bathroom and like everybody could see. I told my mom and she told me to quit lying. But when she locked him out because he didn't pay, and he was banging on the door and cursing, she said, "And what you did to my daughter!" And he shut up. Dante looked at me and looked away. Manuel started banging and cursing again. But I could tell he would go away. I could tell my mom was not afraid of him. If anybody was afraid, it was him afraid of her.

Ginger

I got my translator to do a conference call to tell Mrs. Vargas how much I'd enjoyed Velvet's time with us. At the end of the conversation, I asked if she'd ever consider moving the family here. If she could get work. There was a long silence and then she asked me, "How much does a carton of milk cost there?" I said I was sure things were more here, but that it could be worth it if she got a job that paid more. If she cleaned houses, she could make at least ten dollars an hour, maybe more. There was another long silence. I thought of the lawn party down the block, the lights, the smiling woman who glanced at us as we passed. I asked if she might want to come up for Christmas with Velvet and her little boy. She laughed. But she said, "Maybe."

I hung up feeling good. Even though it was embarrassing that I didn't know how much a carton of milk was.

Velvet

Middle school was so big I hardly knew anybody. The halls were too big and if you walked alone, your feet echoed. The boys were suddenly big and they stank big too. There was broken glass on the playground and there were men guards and metal detectors in the halls, not just at the door. There were a lot of different classes with different teachers. There was at least some of the same girls, Alicia and Helena and Marisol and this other girl, who I was friends with before I got held back. And they were all mad bugged about their hair. They always were, but now it was like *war*, who had good or bad hair, whose hair was smooth and straight, whose color was ugly, which meant me, these new girls followed me in the hall going, "You need some foster care, your mami let you walk around with that fucked-up hair, it is *abuse*." Marisol, they called her "nappy wilde-beest," even girls who used to be her friends, because her hair wasn't done. And Marisol, when I said to her that Ginger liked my hair natural—even she looked sarcastic and said, "She's white. She don't know nothing about hair."

It felt like people were acting in a show and they didn't even pick the show, somebody else did, but who? I would hear things they said, shit girls fought about, things teachers got mad about or liked you about: stories we had to "discuss." The first week there was a special assembly where people who used to be in gangs came to talk to us about how it was bad to be in gangs, and at the end of it they gave us shiny buttons for not being in gangs, but how did they know we weren't?

These things were the show, and underneath was *something else* that you couldn't even tell what it was—it was too big to fit in our words or in the things you were allowed to do, but I could feel it all the time trying to get out. Once I talked to Marisol about Fiery Girl, how she was so powerful but still so sensitive that Beverly's sick-ass jabbing finger made her spin around so hard she had to kick it out. You could say things like "sensitive" to Marisol, and she totally got the story; her face lit up, and the *something else* was there. I could even see it sometimes in the eyes of people on the bus, or feel it in my mother's hand; I could hear it when she screamed at me that I was a puta, mal nacida. I could feel it when I curled against her back. But then we would wake up and the show would take over again.

When I thought about Ginger and Paul it was the same, just the show was different where they were. There was the crying in Ginger's face all the time, and she didn't even know it was there because if I asked her why she was sad she would say, "I'm not sad." There was riding the mare and then sitting at the table with Ginger and Paul or sitting at the table with my mom and Dante; being on the mare happened on another planet, someplace beautiful but with outer space all around it. I couldn't even tell it to anybody. I was locked away from everybody. I couldn't even beat on the door because there was no door.

Then one day I was helping my mom make dinner, tearing up lettuce for salad. She was making pork and tomato sauce that we would eat with pan sobao. It smelled so good, it made my mouth water and my stomach weak. Her food was so much better than Ginger's and I wanted to tell her that, but something stopped me. Instead I said, Mami, I'm hungry. Could I have some bread now? and I took it before she answered. She said, Put that bread down! I said, Please, Mami, I'm hungry, and she answered, I don't care! And I crushed the bread in my hand and she hit me. I yelled, I didn't do it on purpose! And she yelled, You did! And hit me again. I thought, That is not abuse. Because I did crush it. And then she did it again. And I ran.

Silvia

Crushing that bread and pretending she doesn't know! And that look—not only in her eyes and her mouth, but her *body*, the way she moves. Doesn't she know everybody sees it? Why does she think those girls hate her? She's conceited, spoiled by that sad rotten-belly woman.

I leaned out the window and saw the top of her head, like a little dog on the porch, turning to look at the people going past. People playing music, the girl with her red head scarf across the way, talking on her cell with her baby in her arms. I looked and I remembered sitting on the stoop in my aunt's lap, watching a storm moving through the mountains, heavy clouds pouring dark rain, coming toward us but me safe in the lap. My mother looking with faraway eyes; half her body was somewhere else. Not that girl in the red scarf; she is right *here* with the music banging in her body, shouting in her phone, walking up and down . . . I remember music too, coming down the street on a summer night. My boyfriend coming on his bike. Vegetable smells in the heat. The bell on his rusty purple bike. My mother's prayers when she thought I couldn't hear. *Please don't let me hurt my child. I love her so much.* The horses walking in the street.

Well, it's her time of life too. Her body's an alarm about to go off; she'll be needing her own room.

Velvet

Once a teacher asked the class if we had to show the whole world in just one picture, what it would be. A boy said he'd show a picture of war, a girl said she'd show a baby being born. I didn't say, but I thought, All the feet walking past my building. Like these old-lady feet with a cane and quick boy feet like rubber running past her and this girl in strappy red shoes and this man walking after her trying to make her smile. And sometimes somebody trying to make me smile.

Like Mr. Nelson at the store downstairs. He's old and so dark he's black, with a big stomach, but he has happy wrinkles around his eyes, and he's kind to my mom—he gives her extra sandwich meat sometimes. She says it's garbage, but still. He comes now and says, Hello, Sweets, what's good? So I tell him, Nothin'. I'm hungry and my mom wouldn't give me nothin', not even bread. So he says come to the store, he'll fix me something. I ask him to give me a egg and cheese sandwich and he says yeah. I go to the store with him and he makes it on the grill behind the counter. People come in and out the store. He talks to them and me. He asks about school. He asks if I went to "those people" in the country. I say yes. I tell him I rode my favorite horse. I tell him I rode her at night when nobody knew. It was the first time I told it to anybody, and when I told it to him, his eyes changed, like *he's* a child listening to me give him a story for bed.

I think that's what made him want to kiss me. He gave me the sandwich on a paper plate and waxy paper and I said, Ima go eat it on my steps and he said, You not even gonna stay with me? And I said, Noooo, but I smiled so he would know I still like him and he said, At least Ima walk you out, and he did, but before we were out, he put his hand on my head and kissed me on my mouth. I kissed him too. Even though his mouth was old with gray hairs around it. He said, "Keep ridin' that horse," and I smiled.

Then I went and sat back down on the steps and ate my sand-wich. I watched the people. It was between day and night, so both day and night people were out. I remembered when Manuel grabbed my head and pinched my jaws till my mouth came open and put his tongue in. I remembered him banging and cursing at the door, me being scared, hiding behind my mother. But I wasn't nine now, I was twelve, and I was watching the whole world get ready for the night.

I finished my sandwich. My mom shouted out the window, I thought you were hungry. Don't you want some food? So I went up and she told me I was going to have my own room where Manuel and then Mr. Diaz used to be.

Silvia

She came back in and the night was like always. Lying in bed but feeling like I'm walking in mud up to my chest with Dante in my arms and Velvet on my back like a monkey, with her hands around my neck going mami this, mami that. Street noise keeping me awake, music, people yelling, strings of angry words I don't know except *money* and *bitch* and *money*. Money, always money. I can't get enough shifts, and they say they'll turn the lights off if I don't pay. I can't pay, if I do there won't be enough for rent. I'm supposed to send money for my sister in DR. I'm supposed to make cookies for a sale at the school. The only thing that makes me feel better is talking to the one person who's really my friend, a black woman named Rasheeda who even speaks Spanish. And I can't go to her now because her pregnant daughter tested positive for HIV and now she won't even talk to Rasheeda; how can I come to her with my problems?

I turn on my back for just a moment. Dante stirs. I think, Just a minute. Just a minute away from him and from her, remembering: my father's soft cheek at night, the smell of his body, tobacco and sweat. The time I went to a party when the hostess had a tray of prizes for the kids, and I reached up to it and got a tiny doll with no face in a big dress. The horses walking in the street; the horse.

I rode a horse when I was six. Because my father was friends with Mr. Reyes, the man who ran a store down the street, and Mr. Reyes had a horse. One day my father held me up so I could see the horse's face, and he had rough skin but soft eyes. I put my hands on his neck and it felt good. I wanted to get up on him, so my father laughed and put me on his back. And on that horse I saw the world: sky, trees, buildings, streets going in different directions. My life, going in different directions. My father was talking to Mr. Reyes with his hand on the horse; it was right by my leg. But then he turned and his hand came off the horse. And the horse began to move! He walked and then Mr. Reyes yelled and the horse ran, and the world was shaken so hard my teeth rattled. I grabbed the mane and watched the world clatter by, I clattered by my mother running out the house waving a towel. Somebody stood in front of the horse, and it reared up and I fell off. I banged my head; it felt like all my bones broke. I cried, Mami! A dark hole closed over me and I fell down into it.

In the hole people were yoked to machines, thousands of people, naked, bent, and pulling, so angry that they bit the shoulders of those before them. Voices said, "You are lazy and selfish"; the voices came from faces joined together in a breathing darkness, one dark, expressionless face made of many faces, a black field of nose-holes, eye-holes, and many mouths. People fell down the slippery holes and mouths and into working guts; they were shit out into dreams of people who did not even know them. I was there, with the shit-people. We crawled in the dirt of dreams, the dreams of those who cursed us without knowing us. Above were signs, telling us what we were: crosses, dollars, flashing lights, thousands of quick-moving pictures showing pain and ugliness.

And then my mother grabbed me up by my arm and slapped me awake, crying. My father said, "It's not her fault!" but still she got me home and whipped my legs. Later, my father got me a piece of candy.

Now he's gone. When he died I could not even be with him to say good-bye because I had no money to get on the plane.

Paul

I had an aunt named Bea. She was a strange, frightened person. She was small, with a pretty, big-eyed face, but also huge, clumsy hands that I think she picked at. She was a terrible cook and once when my sister complained about a soggy grilled-cheese sandwich, Aunt Bea went into the bedroom and cried. She could play the piano and she acted in a community theater version of *The Cherry Orchard,* playing a jilted servant girl; she actually thought this was going to be the start of an acting career. My uncle went to see every performance and sat proudly in the front row; he was too charmed to notice the pathos of the ambition, not even when they wouldn't let her act in another play. He reminisced about *The Cherry Orchard* for *years,* every single time we went to visit, while she just sat there and stared. Then their marriage went through a crisis and she got a little crazy, would hide under the bed sometimes and refuse to come out.

Both she and my uncle are dead and I don't normally think about them much. Then Ginger decided that she wanted to act in the children's community theater; they were doing *A Christmas Carol,* and she wanted to play either the beautiful Ghost of Christmas Past or the depraved hag who steals Scrooge's curtains when he dies. I thought it was wonderful until she told me why: She wanted to invite Velvet's whole family up to see her perform. She was hoping Velvet and her brother would want to act in the theater too, and that Mrs. Vargas would realize what a wonderful place this was to live. And she couldn't even tell the woman how much she'd have to pay for a carton of milk!

My God, I thought. Under the jaded, ex-addict exterior, the wan, toughened survivor I'd fallen in love with, who could listen to and talk about the saddest, most brutal experiences at meetings—under that was Aunt Bea! I'd married Aunt Bea!

Ginger

The Cocoon Theater was on the second floor over the liquor store. When I came up the stairs, kids were running up and down a hallway full of hats, masks, robes, swords, helmets, wigs, and sparkling crowns. In the foyer, teenagers stood around a huge papier-mâché fortress and a rack of goofy dresses on cockeyed hangers. A sexy middle-aged lady with a bossy young butt burst in and yelled us into a big room with a linoleum floor and punched-up walls hung with black drapes. We had to sing a Broadway song while a small, intrepid man with a mild mouth and a teardrop nose played the piano. In an English accent I sang, *All I want is a room somewhere / Far away from the cold night air.* The kids stared at me. I tried to pantomime and my voice wobbled; the piano player sighed and started again.

But it was perfect: The man who played the piano (Yandy) was married to the bossy middle-aged lady (Danielle); he was a dancer from Cuba and he spoke Spanish.

Paul

I hate to admit it, but in retrospect it's clear: I didn't put up enough of a fight about her plot to get the family upstate because I was sure it would never happen and also because I wanted her focus on something else besides us. I wanted to be feeling the resentment. I wanted a reason to look for Polly. Because that's all it was, looking. And often finding her, walking alone across campus where I could come up beside her and touch her elbow and talk. That was even better than the times she came to my office.

Velvet

When I was walking around before I had to pick up Dante, this older boy I don't know came up to me, going, "Hey, lil' mama. What's good?"

I didn't like his voice, so I just said, "Hey."

"So what's good?" he say.

"Nothin'."

"No? I got somethin' good. You wanna come smoke it with me?"

"No."

"Why not? You on your way somewheres?"

"I don't know you."

"I hear that don't matter, shawty."

I looked at him long enough for him to get embarrassed. I said, "I do not know what you are talking about." And he said, "Well, you better figure it out, girl. You play your position or it play you." There was no friendly in his voice at all. He looked at me to make his point, then walked away.

Ginger

I didn't get what I auditioned for, but I did get several minor parts: solicitor for the poor, drunk, debtor, beggar, tortured soul. It didn't matter; I loved it. I got to make faces, sing, and even dance in the crowd scenes. Danielle and Yandy ran the theater with their five kids; the whole family acted, sold tickets, ran the concession stand, and made costumes. Because they couldn't come up with full costumes, Danielle decided we'd wear pajamas under our meager bonnets, skirts, top hats, and dressing jackets; then she decided we should all paint our faces blue. Rehearsals were like a cross between Dalí and Dr. Seuss: chaos, with sudden ecstatic bursts of order. Kids ran everywhere yelling their lines, waving props, having tickle fights, and slapping paint on each other while Danielle yelled about acting philosophy and Yandy played the piano. There were two other adult actors, an out-of-work female psychiatrist about my age and a male nurse in the middle of a divorce. We'd stand around together during the chaos and the psychiatrist would bitch that Danielle and Yandy were sloppy professionally, mentally ill, and probably drunks. I said, Oh, it's just supposed to be fun. The nurse sucked on his cigarette and ogled my breasts.

But I took it seriously too. I really tried. It actually hurt when Danielle criticized me in front of everybody because she thought my debtor's reaction to hearing of Scrooge's death was too nice. "You think she'd be *ambivalent* to hear that the guy who's been putting the screws to her is dead? Are you *nuts*? She'd be overjoyed and nothing else!"

"But wouldn't you feel ashamed to think you'd come down so low on the food chain that you'd gloat over somebody else's death?"

Both Danielle and her husband cracked up. "You are some Goody Two-shoes," he said.

So I went back and tried to be more bitter for them. I tried to picture what Mrs. Vargas would feel if she heard about her landlord dying and not having to pay back rent. I thought she might cackle about it at first. I thought she might say pious things too, then laugh. But when she was alone, I thought she'd feel weird. I thought she might even pray for the person. I don't know why, but I did.

Velvet

Then one day I'm sitting in class and I get a note passed that says, "Kwan likes you." I look over and Kwan is staring the gloopy-eyed hell out of me. Which I don't like because he's sixteen and still in my grade, and because he's the boyfriend of Brianna, who's fifteen and café au lait beautiful and basically the baddest bitch in the school. And I can see he knows about this note, but I don't think it was his idea. And I can feel every girl in the class watching to see what I do. Which is, walk up to him in the hall and bitch him out so everybody can hear, and tell him to leave me alone before I tell Brianna.

My mom said, "That's what you get for being a troublemaker." But Ginger said she was proud of me for handling it. I got a 3 on a paper that we did on the phone and I went upstate and jumped over a low pole on Little Tina. Pat told me she was proud of me too, and we went on a trail ride together. The leaves were changing color and the evergreen was alone in the sky. There were birds with huge wings circling over everything like searching eyes. Pat said they *were* searching; they were hawks out for prey. She said they caught mice, chipmunks, rabbits, sometimes even little dogs or cats. I looked up at them and my back tingled.

Then I came back home and it was on everybody's phone, the phone everybody had but me. This picture of a girl kissing what's supposed to be Kwan's naked chest and reaching her hand down his pants. You couldn't see her face, but her hair was *not* good like Brianna's, it was damaged, like mine was when my mom bleached it, but not now. And there was a message with it that went, "Here she go, slurpin' away."

Marisol was the one who showed it to me. She said in her little voice, "They sayin' it's you. But I know it's not." She looked down instead of at me and her shoulders were turned in.

"Who sent it?" I asked.

"I don't know."

I said, "I don't care about this shit," and she said, "I don't either," but we knew we did. We sat quiet for a minute. I was remembering something else Pat told me on our ride: "The dominant mare drives the troublemakers to the outside of the herd. Because that's where the predators are."

Ginger

The woman called my cell phone Saturday morning when I was at the grocery. Her voice was friendly and hopeful but with a push behind it; she wanted to know if I was Velvet's godmother. I had no idea where *that* came from, but I said, Yes, who's this? Lydia, she said, down the block from Velvet. The girl had come to her, crying 'cause her mother was abusing her, and she had taken her in. I put down my wire basket and went out into the lot. There were orange and yellow paper turkeys in the windows and little evergreens. There was a Humvee with a sticker over its windshield saying GET THE FUCK OUT OF MY WAY. "Does she have bruises?" I asked.

"No," said Lydia. "But I don't think she's making it up; she's too upset. Some girl at school is saying Velvet tried to steal her boyfriend, and they're following her home from school. Somebody threw a glass bottle at her. Velvet says the girl's lying, but the mother believes the one she doesn't know over her own child, and she's been hitting the child and calling her a *ho* in front of her brother."

"Where is Velvet now?"

"She's in the other room sleeping still. She spent the night; I didn't have the heart to send her back."

"How do you know her?"

"Just from the block. She sits out on her front stoop like a little *puppy,* trying to talk to whoever talks back, and a lot do because that girl is *pretty* and she needs the attention. Last night while we were looking at the TV? She just leaned on me the same way, like a *puppy,* like way younger than fifteen. I hate to see her treated this way, and when she told me about you—"

"Wait," I said. "She *is* way younger than fifteen. She's twelve."

There was a silence on the other end. "Maybe I'm mistaken." The voice was harder, the friendly hope gone stiff and artificial. "But everybody thinks that's how old she is. I don't know why she would lie."

"She *looks* older than twelve. Maybe people just assume—"

"Well, whateva. I got my own family to consider." She said she was going to take Velvet back home as soon as the girl woke up so that her mother would know she hadn't been doing anything wrong. She was going to see the situation for herself. She said she couldn't really get involved because she had her own problems with the state system. But me being the godmother, she thought I should know.

I thanked Lydia. She gave me her phone number. I put my cell away and stood in the lot. *Why she would lie.* Because she lies all the time. Because it's the only way life is bearable. A big, angry-looking woman with gray hair came out of the store with a full cart of groceries plus a bag hanging off her arm. She went to the car that said "Get the Fuck out of My Way," unloaded her groceries in it, and drove off.

Velvet

I listened to Lydia talking about me like I was a telenovela that she cried over and got mad at. *I got my own family to consider.* I thought about walking with Ginger in warm dark full of smells and fireflies past houses with decorations in their yards and sounds of children in them. I rubbed the Ginger-doll key chain with my thumb, down its sharp nose, checked coat, one leg and back. Now Ginger would know it wasn't just me talking. An adult had told her and she would have to believe.

Ginger

Later that night I tried to call Velvet's house. Mrs. Vargas answered, spoke angry-normal Spanish, then sad-brightly said, "Okay?" It was the first English word she'd ever said to me. It was also the first time I'd heard any sadness in her voice. Or brightness.

I called Lydia. She said as soon as she walked in, the mother started crying and thanking her, and that Velvet did nothing but curse and yell. She said, "I told her, if you talked to me that way, I'd hit you too."

When I got Velvet on the phone, she said, "She acts so nice in front of everybody else! I am so sick of her bullshit!"

Paul said, "And you want them to move up here? Really?"

Velvet

When I went back up there it was night and there were white Christmas lights in all the little trees on the main street of the town. But the next day it was rainy and cold with mud. I went to the barn. Horses stood outside, wet and streaked with mud, bony like dinosaurs, their heads like dinosaur birds with wings. Inside, they felt angry and bored. Fiery Girl felt worse. Fiery Girl would not even talk to me. She stood away from me like she didn't know me. I said, Hey, don't you remember when I brought you out? And she didn't look.

I walked through the barn to the office and I saw two more horses were gone: Rocki's stall didn't have his name on it anymore, or Officer Murphy's. Their toys and ribbons were gone too. I looked for Pat, but I didn't find her; this girl I didn't know told me she wasn't there but that Beverly was schooling a horse in the indoor ring. I went there and saw she had the horse on long lines, and a whip in her hand, and she was talking in her hard voice. "When I say whoa, I mean whoa! I don't mean let's talk it over, I mean you stop and no backing up, no nothin'! No! Don't move, don't think it!" But the horse did back up and Beverly whipped it and it ran and she dropped the lines and laughed. It ran around her and then it ran *at* her, but she raised up the whip and it ran in a circle on the outside of the ring while she followed it from the inside, shaking the whip at it. "You think running is a good option? Now it's *my* option. This is my option!" She struck at the air, again and again.

The horse's coat was dark with sweat and its eyes were scared.

"Whoa!" said Beverly. The horse stopped, trembling and panting. "That's right, whoa! Good girl!" She went to the horse and touched it. "Look at this poor thing, she's scared to death. It's okay, sweet pea. That's nice, that's nice, that's a pretty girl. Thank you. I'm gonna thank you." She looked at me. "Always remember to say thank you. Always remember your manners."

I left, but I did not go back to the house. I walked around the block, breathing hard. It felt like I was in an ocean looking at lights on a shore a long way away.

The next day Gare told me that before I came, Heather's horse, Totally, kicked this girl Jessie and broke her ribs. I said, "Why?"

Gare went, "I don't know, maybe because Jessie's a bitch? I didn't see it. I heard Jessie came up behind Totally too fast while Heather was giving the horse a hard time about something. I was like, way to go, Totally."

I thought, If I was a horse, I'd kick too. I'd kick whenever I could and even trample.

Ginger

On the phone I said, "Listen. I want to invite your mom and brother up along with you around Christmas. I'm acting in a play and I think it would be fun if you all came to see it. It's a children's theater."

"Why are you acting in a theater for children?"

"Because it's fun. Do you think you would want to act in it if you could?"

"I dunno."

"Could you ask your mom if she'd like to come?"

She didn't answer. I felt her like she was next to me breathing.

I said, "I'm thinking if she had a chance to look around up here, it might make her think about coming here to live."

I felt her, but I didn't know what she felt.

"Just a minute," she said. I heard her talking to her mother, her mother answering back. They talked awhile. There was no anger or cursing. Velvet came back.

"She says yes."

Paul

I picked them up at the station because Ginger was getting ready for the show. They were standing there like a bundle, outwardly ragged but powerfully linked inside: the woman holding the boy close to her, the boy tensely looking down with his fist by his mouth, Velvet trying to pull his jacket down and pants up so his butt-crack didn't show. The platform was crowded with people walking quickly past them, but the mother looked straight ahead as though she were alone.

When I got closer, I saw why. She looked exhausted, too tired to smile, though her eyes saw me with pleased relief. She took my outstretched hand, but when Velvet came to hug me, Mrs. Vargas snapped at her and pointed at the little boy's feet; his shoe was untied and though he looked at least seven years old, Velvet knelt to tie it.

I took them straight to get dinner before the play. It was a big casual place with pictures of the owner's pit bulls on the wall; as we waited to be seated, Mrs. Vargas stood with her arms across her chest and viewed it harshly with her brow pulled down like a cap. She and Velvet exchanged hard/entreating words. We were seated; Mrs. Vargas sat with an incredibly erect posture and snapped her napkin open on her lap. I conferred with the boy and decided we should both get burgers. Velvet got mac and cheese. Mrs. Vargas ordered the chicken by pointing at the menu imperiously.

The boy and I talked about the dogs on the wall; he wanted to know if maybe they'd come out and walk around. His voice was sweeter than I'd heard before. He said he liked fighting dogs. Velvet and her mother fought in a low furious mumble. Her mother glanced at me with a laughing string of words meant to link us as adults. Dante said, "This man's dog where I live acted bad and the man made the dog scream." I said that was wrong; the boy looked rebuked and confused.

When the chicken came, Mrs. Vargas took one bite and grimaced. "She says it's disgusting," said Velvet. Mrs. Vargas made them take it back and cook it some more, and even then, she cut it in two and put the bigger part on Velvet's plate. Velvet said she was too full, but she made the girl eat it, all of it, hectoring her the whole time. When I took out my wallet to pay, she cut her eyes at my money, seeing just how much this lousy meal was.

We walked to the theater in silence. I thought I saw Mrs. Vargas looking approvingly at the Christmas lights. I saw she'd put lipstick on. The boy's shoe came untied again and she made Velvet stop to tie it. I asked, "Don't you know how to tie your shoes, young man?" He said, "She does it for me. I'm only seven." I said, "A seven-year-old man needs to tie his own shoes, and before you go home, I'm going to teach you."

The boy looked down. Mrs. Vargas gave me a sharp look, and I thought, She understands. But we were at the ticket booth by then, and there were people with their radiant children. Her sharpness deserted her; she put her hand on the boy's shoulder. The boy frankly looked the other kids up and down; Velvet led the way upstairs; she looked back and smiled at me. There was a burst of happy voices and then children running up and down a hallway in half costume, rosy families getting out of their coats, a vibrant little girl handing out programs amid papier-mâché castles and trees with brown trunks and balls of green sitting atop them. A girl recognized Velvet and spoke to her. Mrs. Vargas sank back into herself.

"Hola! Bienvenidos!" Mrs. Vargas blinked and looked up. Bearing down on us through the crowd was Ginger wearing pajamas and a bonnet with a man in blue face-paint holding out his arms and gesturing at his heart like to long-lost friends.

Body and eyes, Mrs. Vargas rose to the welcome instinctively. And then she sagged back, bewildered. The blue-faced guy put his arm around her shoulders and began talking to her in Spanish. She talked back, but her body still sagged. Ginger was talking to somebody else in a bonnet. Dante was slowly wandering forward, looking with great interest at plastic knight's armor, assorted masks and weaponry.

Silvia

He said, I hear you might be moving up here, is that true? I said, It looks too expensive for me. That depends where you go, he said. You can live simply here. Me and my wife moved up here from the city and at first she cleaned houses. I painted houses, she cleaned. I'm not somebody who needs to live fancy. I can have a simple meal of beans with a little meat and be happy. I said, The place we just ate was simple for a lot of money. He said, Ah well, I don't know where you went. I have to perform, but let's talk later.

Everything he said was a boast and he wanted me to join him. But I couldn't. I didn't sleep the night before, and in the morning I accidentally dropped this old lady on the floor and she broke her ribs. I called 911. I told her, You know, I have children. I said, Please. But I don't know what she's going to say.

Ginger

I went backstage and I said, "Listen! There's some people here who came all the way from the city to see this. I want you to act your guts out for them!" And somebody said, "Okay."

Velvet

It was something I used to see on the old movie channel, except it was done ridiculous funny, people painted blue and wearing pajamas underneath dresses and hats. Ginger came out in a old-timey hat being a dumb nice woman who wants this mean old man to give money. Little kids ran out and sang Christmas songs; one of the little kids messed up and started crying, which made me on her side. I looked at my mom; her eyes were soft, her lips coming open like she's dreaming. This guy who looked like the science teacher everybody bugs on came out wrapped in bike chains, groaning and yelling. My mom's mouth was still open, her eyes closed. Dante whispered, "He's going to say, 'You're nothing but a bit of undigested beef or a piece of cheese!'" That's when I realized it was that story about the mean old man who hated poor people until ghosts came to him on Christmas Eve.

Silvia

Painted people came out onstage; Ginger led little girls around making faces, singing, like weird prayer cards come to life. A little one forgot to sing, just looked at us, smiling—sweet. The old lady I dropped on the floor has whole walls covered with prayer cards, pictures of grandkids, crayon drawings, and presidents, yellowing away or bright as Easter. St. Clare with full ruby lips, St. Lucy with her eyes on a plate, a snowman drawn in orange, a boy, a dog. I close my eyes and disappear in the wall of pictures. "Mami!" Velvet jabs me, and I jab back. Boring; an old man is on the stage eating from a bowl. The pretend clock is striking. This lady keeps her dishes in the oven and her refrigerator full of disgusting dry cakes like they have at the food pantry. I scold Velvet and pinch her. The old man looks up; someone is moaning, rattling around. I pinch myself, wake up. The old man shouts, Who's there? The old lady thinks the neighbor boys are coming to steal her panty hose, but she's got her purse open on the table. She wants to know, What kind of person would take your panty hose? I hold my tongue, wash her scabby ass. Easy, easy, she whines. The old man clutches the other man in pretend-chains, begging. She says the same thing every time: came to New York, job at the candle factory, lost her husband, had a child, lost the child. The stage goes dark. Music starts. I feel my head drooping. There's music on the subway, people singing and begging. Velvet jabs me. A girl stands in the spotlight, holding a doll and crying out, trying to sound unhappy, but she obviously has no idea what it is. People, singing and crying in rags, crawl from behind the black curtains. The subway beggars tell their stories, play guitars; one man has cats riding his shoulders. They do tricks, their faces smart like people . . . wait, that's Ginger's face, she's on the floor, crawling, making a face that is—well, that is funny, worth coming to see. Now she's holding up play money, they're all giving play money to the girl with the doll, but she won't take it, doesn't see it. She screams, "Help, help!" but doesn't take the money—what in hell is this thing about? In the subway I saw a man with no legs stuck in the door. Somebody took him here to beg and now he's stuck in the door, how did he get there? I try to turn around and help him but it's crowded; they push me in. I look again and he's not there. The stage goes dark again. Velvet and Dante press near me. A lot of people *do* steal from the old ladies. But I don't. Not unless they leave it right out on the table. That's just stupid. The light goes out; the subway goes into the tunnel. I speed along on my belly. Above me, they carry crosses and dollar signs. Above me there are songs of love; the ugly woman is transformed by love. I speed on my belly down the side of the road. Leave it on the table, that's not even stealing. That's— Suddenly I am lifted up. My love is here, our hands are about to touch—that's not even—but I don't remember who he is.

"Mami, you snore!" Dante pokes and I sit up among strangers. The old man is singing alone in his pajamas. As he sings, he turns the crank on a little music box; his voice is beautiful and broken. Three young girls in white gowns turn with the music like they are inside the box; they face each other, turn away, face each other, step away.

I looked at Velvet, shining with her eyes, picking at her nose. My poor daughter. My poor worthless girl.

Ginger

I peeked out once between the curtains to see how she was enjoying the play. It was during the scene where Scrooge sings about the past love he had forgotten, and three girls mime the ideal figures in a music box; Mrs. Vargas's face was upturned and enchanted. The nurse couldn't really sing, but that only made it sweeter, and she felt it, I could tell.

When I'd asked Yandy how it was to talk to her, he'd shrugged and said, "She didn't seem all there. Like maybe not too bright." But her face when I looked *was* bright, bright, soft, and alive.

Paul

When we got home, it was past ten and they wanted to go to bed. They all slept together, so we gave them our bedroom. The upstairs thermostat was in that room and when I went in to turn it down for the night they were already asleep: the woman holding the boy to her breasts, he embracing her fiercely; Velvet with her back to them, rolled as far away to the other side of the bed as she could go. I thought, That says it all.

I went to tell it to Ginger, but she was already in bed with the light out. When I lay down with her, I could feel her rigidity even before I touched her; she was inaccessible, locked. Like I did not exist. And not for the first time. "What is it?" I asked.

She said, "Human love is the vilest thing in the world."

"What's wrong?"

"I just said it."

"Why?"

"Because she loves them. I can tell she loves them. But when they were getting into their nightclothes, she made Velvet come stand out in the hall in her gown and she talked at me. And Velvet translated. She said, 'My mom wants you to look and see how ugly I am.'" Ginger breathed hard and slow, like she was pushing with all her might against something that would not give.

Ginger

When I came down in the morning, Velvet's mother was there, already dressed. Her face was so clear and calm; her cruel words to Velvet evaporated in her clear gaze. Paul was in his pajamas, making coffee. He handed her a cup and she said to us, "Pretty. You house is pretty." She said it earnestly, like she'd asked somebody the words and then rehearsed them. I thought, Velvet, and said, "Thank you." Then we were all quiet, like we'd reached some place of strange and yet natural peace, where we could for a moment be more real than our real lives allowed. Paul made us scrambled eggs with herbs. She ate and looked out the window at grass wet from just-melted frost. I thought: Eye of the storm.

Later she took a shower with her son. They were in there a long time. Velvet looked at me and said, "That's not normal, is it?" I said, "Not for me, but . . ." The girl watched my face. She said, "Can I show them the horses?"

Velvet

My mom came but like she didn't really want to, like looking at horses was stupid. Like I was stupid and Ginger too. On the way over, she basically looked at the sky and the trees like *they* were stupid. Dante too. He said in Spanish, "Horses are boring." I said, "We haven't gotten to the horses yet." He said, "And last night was boring too." "Shut up," I said. "It wasn't that bad." I remembered the part where this little girl who had something wrong with her leg came out and sang by herself and then ran away when the old man yelled at her. It made me think about Strawberry. It made me picture being in a movie where I would sing that song in front of people and Strawberry would stop and remember me and how we used to talk. And everybody would see it. I don't know why, but it seemed like a song about something you forget and then the song makes you remember. Dante said, "I kept waiting for the commercial. I wanted to see that commercial where Santa gets stuck in the chimney and then he has diarrhea."

I didn't say anything. We were close enough to see the horses were out, and they looked big and brawling. Dante stopped talking and looked. I could see my mom looking too, her head up like *she* was a horse. I thought, Now she will smile. Joker and Totally ran around each other; they kicked up dirt, they got hard and curved in their shoulders. "Ho, snap!" said Dante and *he* smiled. Joker and Totally faced each other and stood up on their back legs to fly at each other with their fronts. *Mami, smile. Please, Mami.* Like she heard me, Ginger turned to me and smiled. She smiled like a mother. My mom stood with her hands on the fence and her back to me.

Then Pat came out of the barn. When Ginger introduced my mom, she said, "Good to meet you. Your daughter's an excellent worker," then said hello to Dante. I didn't translate, but my mom understood anyway like she does. In Spanish, she said, "Thank you. Your animals are beautiful." She still did not look at me.

Suddenly from around the side of the barn, there was this woman I never saw before. She was dressed in high boots and tight pants and she was leading Diamond Chip Jim. She was tall, with the sun hitting her eyes so they looked silver. Her nose was like something carved. In her helmet, she had a face like a square block with curly blond hair and perfect lips. She looked down at us. She looked especially at me. "Who's *this*?" she said.

I felt like a thing, poking up from the ground. My family felt like small, dumb things. I felt angry. Then numb.

"This is Velvet," said Pat. "She's the talented young lady I've been telling you about. And this is her mother and little brother, who came all the way from the city."

And the square face smiled and said, "Oh, the little Fresh Air girl!" She took off her helmet and shook out her hair; her eyes shined all over me. I did not want to like her, but her eyes raised me up; I felt myself shining in her eyes.

"Velvet, meet Estella Kadner. Estella, meet Velvet and Ginger and . . ."

My mom just stood there. I could've helped her. Every other time I would've helped her. But now I didn't. Ginger said, "Mrs. Vargas." I said, "And Dante, my brother."

Estella Kadner shook my hand and said, "It's so wonderful to meet you." She shook Ginger's hand and thanked her for making a difference. She reached for my mom, who shrank behind her hard eyes. She reached for my brother, who stared at her, so she dropped her hand. She tried my mom again; she said, "You must be proud. I hear your daughter is a very talented rider."

My mom looked at her like she wasn't there.

"She can't speak English," I said.

"Oh! Well then—" And Estella Kadner looked straight at my mom and said, "Pat me dice que su hija tiene mas talento para montar que cualquier otra."

My mom's face went dark with blood.

Ginger

Her face filled with blood; her eyes went hot. Sweat came out my armpits. Estella just kept talking. Pat looked at Mrs. Vargas, then at Velvet, at Estella, and at me, stopping on me. Estella turned to Velvet and said in English how much she'd love to see her compete one day. And then I guess she said that to the mother too. Who smiled with her dark face, through her hot eyes; an enraged and cringing smile. I saw: She was helpless before this woman. I saw: Velvet grow ever more animated and glowing as her mother shrank.

"Do you have a favorite horse?" asked Estella.

"Yes," said Velvet in her glowing voice. "I like Fugly Girl."

"Really!" said Estella. "Shall we go see her?"

And we all walked into the barn, Estella and her big horse with Velvet by her side, Pat behind Velvet. Well behind the horse, I walked with Velvet's family. Velvet's shrunken mother looked at me and her eyes said "Judas." "Forgive me," I said in a low voice. "Por favor."

She didn't answer or look at me. It was like she'd disappeared.

Velvet looked back and the triumph on her face was unmistakable.

I saw: Dante was afraid.

Velvet

She cursed Ginger to her face, but she took the sandwiches Ginger made and laughed. Paul drove us to the station and she was laughing then too. He didn't even know, I could tell. His eyes kept going in the mirror, like, What the hell is this? At the station, Ginger got out the car, she kneeled down and hugged me. She said, "We'll work it out. Call me." My mom took my arm and yanked me up on the train. She told me to sit. She took Ginger's sandwiches out of her purse and threw them at me. "Mami," I said, "that lady was just being nice. I'm not riding horses."

"Liar!" She dropped my ticket on the seat and walked away with Dante, her back hard and hating. I wanted to call for her, but I was ashamed. I sat forward in the seat and tried to act not ashamed. People looked at me, their eyes stretched and sorry. I turned my body back around and watched them walking down the aisle. Dante looked back at me with a scared face. I tried not to cry. They left the car. I thought, She'll have to come back. If she doesn't, the court will take Dante away. Then I thought, What if she says she lost me? I got up and followed them, not crying. A man in a uniform came out of the other car where they went. He looked at me like it was my fault and said, "Where is your ticket? Who are you with?" I said, "It's on my seat. I'm trying to find my mom." He took me to her and made her be with me. She told him I was a worthless liar and didn't deserve to sit with them because I didn't even want to be part of the family anyway. Everybody could hear. He didn't care; he tore my ticket and went away.

Ginger

She humiliated her mother. It wasn't her fault. It was mine. The look on her face when she looked back at us, walking with that obnoxious woman! I didn't blame her. Her mom was a bitch, and she was getting back. But I couldn't forget the way the woman shrank and then just *went away*. Like she was the child and her twelve-year-old daughter had all the power.

Velvet

She closed the door and knocked me down in the hall. She said, "Get up."

Dante went away down the hall.

She said, "Get up, bitch!"

Dante turned the TV on and up loud.

My mother kicked me and yelled, "Get up!" I tried to stand; she kicked me in the stomach and I sat back down. I heard Dante talking to the TV, cursing and calling it "bitch." I held back crying.

"Understand," she said. "I will knock you down until you don't get up. Every time you get up, I will knock you down again. Maybe you're the boss with that fool woman, but here I am the boss."

"Mami," I said. "Mami—"

Dante talked faster, louder.

"You want to ride those horses, fine, ride them. You want to die, die. I don't care."

There was more, her cursing and kicking and then Dante ran at her yelling. "I don't want Velvet to die!"

Then me running out the door, down the stairs. My mother was yelling at Dante and he was yelling back. I ran out into the street. It was snowing, and I ran in front of a car with music blasting out of it. People laughing at the crazy girl, but stopping, caring if I died. Laughing on their way somewhere else. I was never out this late before and the street was full of people I didn't know. Lydia; I knew Lydia. I ran to her; I rang all the doorbells on her door. A man said, "Hey, lil' mama," but he saw I was crying and went away. I rang and rang but Lydia didn't come. I sat on her steps and stopped crying. I looked at all the people going by. Some looked back, some kept going. I thought about the play where people were singing and dancing and pretending to be poor. I thought of Fiery Girl. I wanted to go into the stall with her and feel her body, see the snow falling outside the barn while I was beside her warm body.

A woman passed by carrying plastic bags full of bottles. She wore a winter coat, but instead of shoes she wore furry house slippers with socks that were soaking wet in the mushy snow. I realized she was the lady my mom called "the Haitian." But I liked her; her hair was gray under her scarf and her eyes were deep and kind. "Young woman," she said. "What's going on with you? You look sad."

"My mom hit me and said she doesn't care if I die," I said. "I don't want to go home."

She came close to me, but her eyes didn't look at me. She looked past me, but like she was seeing me. Like Pat and the horses. "Don't be afraid," she said. "You are blessed. Don't forget, you are blessed." Then she brought her eyes to mine. "But you need to go home. Your eyes are older than your years, but I can feel your heart is very young, too young to be out now. Go home. Your mother won't hurt you any more tonight."

Ginger

Her thirteenth birthday fell on a weekend, so she came. Paul was away at a conference and it was just the two of us. Waiting at Penn, she looked like she did the first time I saw her: tender, pure-eyed, with that gorgeous hair free and unstraightened. I knelt to hold her and I thought with my body, *I love you.*

I said, "Your mom says it's okay for you to ride."

The light left her eyes. She said, "I know. She doesn't care if I die."

I said, "She doesn't mean that. She was angry because she felt disrespected."

"She hit me, Ginger. She knocked me down."

My mind went blank. I saw Mrs. Vargas's face when she heard the love song in the play. I saw her telling Velvet she was ugly. I said, "I'm sorry. You did not deserve that."

That evening she was sullen and snappish; she went to the barn, came back, and looked at me like she had nothing to do with me. On the second day, we fought because I asked her to help me with the dishes and she refused. I told her we would not go out to celebrate her birthday in that case and she stormed upstairs, I thought to her room, but when I went to use the bathroom, I found she was lying sprawled out in the hallway, face turned sideways so I could see its aggrieved expression. I stepped over her, to and from the bathroom. Eventually she got up and went out to the horses. I went for a walk. When I came back, she was sitting on the porch. I sat next to her and put my arm around her. She sat there staring straight ahead like she didn't know me. I kept my arm there anyway. I asked her if she wanted to have a good time or a bad time. She looked at me like I was an asshole. I was about to say, "Maybe you should just go home," when she said, "A good time." I said, "Okay. Help me with the dishes and we can go out for your birthday." She looked at me blankly. I put my hand on her shoulder and said, "I'm sorry about your mom and the horses. It was my fault. I should've told her." We went in and she started running the water.

Velvet

We went to a fancy place to eat. The people there were fat ugly pigs who thought they were great. Their expressions were ugly and fat even when they were pretty and thin. I remembered this disgusting thing I heard a boy say about somebody: "She thinks her shit smells like ice cream." I felt glad I don't live where people think their shit is ice cream. I looked at Ginger. Why was she even here? We sat down and next to the table was a shelf of olive oil marked thirty dollars a bottle. I remembered something Ginger said to me about Republicans, how they were on the side of the most greedy rich people in the country. Right now, Ginger was looking at a menu while behind her greedy pigs laughed and stank up the air with their slit eyes and hairy hands and little red nasty mouths. I said, "This place is full of Republicans." She said, "No, honey, probably not. This is a mostly Democrat county." I said, "There's a bunch of Republicans right behind you," and she said, "How would you know by looking?" "Trust me," I said. "They're Republicans."

Ginger

How adorable was that? Wondering what she saw, I turned to look: jowly guys with big arms spread out on the table, women in flowered dresses, a certain expression of . . . "Um, maybe," I said. "Those might actually be Republicans." I nodded at another party across from us. "But those are likely Democrats."

"Why?" she asked. "They don't look different."

I tried to think of how to explain. A tray of red cocktails went past. Our waiter appeared. Velvet looked at the menu and frowned. "How about the steak?" I said. "It's good here." A roar of enjoyment swept the room; there were drinks, red drinks riding a sudden, bitter wave. What was I thinking bringing her here? "I'm going to have the calamari. Do you know what that is?" She shook her head. Her tight-curled hair fell over her lush cheek. "Octopus. You can tell people you know somebody who eats octopus."

"Darling! Oh my God!"

Two guys wearing flowered shirts strutted into the room. Velvet gaped. One of the "Democrat" women stood up, clutched her heart, and screamed, "Oh, it's been so long!" A flowered guy clutched *his* heart, "fainting" against the door and crying, "Darling, I want to *smooch* you!"

And Velvet cracked up. I mean, she really did *burst into laughter.* Flowered Guy Two looked over, ready to bitch slap, then saw he was apparently being laughed at by a black teenager. The other guy looked; the whole table looked. I giggled behind my hand. Velvet slapped the table and laughed. The Republicans smiled benignly. It was too ridiculous and Flowered Guy One knew it. "Ladies," he said as he magnificently swept past, "have a wonderful night."

I said, "Thank you." And ordered a Cosmopolitan.

Velvet

I said, "But you don't drink," and she said, "I'm trusting you. Don't tell anyone, all right?" I said I wouldn't, but I didn't like it because right away she wasn't the same. Her eyes were different and she laughed like there was something wrong with her, like she was out of breath. But the steak was good and it was *big*. Also it *was* fun to watch her eat fried octopus.

Then she wanted to go for a drive and I said, "You will get in a lot of trouble if you get caught driving drunk with me." She said, "There won't be trouble. I only had one." She turned down a tiny white road with black sky but also something glowing at the end of it. I felt like I used to when she read that book to me, like we were in a place I could only be with her; a place where nobody hit or yelled at anybody. Then Republicans didn't matter anymore and the drink didn't either. "Can we play music?" I said.

She put on this tape of old music by a group called the Shangri-Las. She said it was the name of a place where people didn't get old, and there was a story about people getting lost there. Life was so perfect there that it made them crazy, so they couldn't stay even though one of them fell in love. They tried to go back over mountains, but a huge snowstorm came and the Shangri-La woman who came with them turned old and died in front of her boyfriend while he cried. I asked if that's what they were singing about, and she said no, it was just the name of the group. We were quiet for a while and I tried to like the music, even though it was corny. We drove into fog and everything got weird-beautiful: the red taillights on parked cars and numbers flashing on mailboxes, and sometimes deer-eyes. Ginger started singing, really soft. Her drunk voice was embarrassing, little and pinchy like a funny bone. But still, my neck tingled like when my mom did my hair. I said, "Can we drive a long time? Can we get a little bit lost?" And she laughed and said, "Honey, we already are a little bit lost." I said, "Really?" She reached out and took my hand. "No," she said. "Not really. Because we're together."

Ginger

I tucked her in like she was still a little girl and then walked around straightening the house and whispering, "Mistake, mistake, mistake." I poured myself a large glass of water, slowly drank it, then brushed my teeth. I got into bed. My heart raced; my brain filled with clashing words and silent, hectic music. Yes, the drink was a mistake, but a healing one. Our beautiful time in the car; a moment of forgiveness; a way to *the in-between place*. The drink helped me to get there.

I sat up. *The in-between place.* It was my term for the tenderness that sometimes happened between me and Michael, usually when we were trying to get out the door in the morning in time for work; a time when our exhausted eyes would acknowledge the stupidity and nastiness of the night before, but would still say wordlessly, "It was not really that. No. It only seemed like that. Really, it was this."

I got up and drank some more water, leaned over the sink absorbing it, then made myself throw it up.

Paul

I thought Ginger would know, would sense it when I got back. I flew into Manhattan and took the train in a daze of Polly, hip-deep in the feeling of her, the way she never stopped looking me in the eyes.

But then there was Ginger at the station and the meadow just outside; the cows as we drove by, tearing hay from the broken feed cart, working their jaws. And there too was Polly; my wanting to turn her over to see her that way, but thinking it might be just the one time, and not being able to give up the look in her eyes. The feeling was so intense, I thought Ginger would read my mind, thought she would say something.

And she did. She said, "Velvet told me her mother beat her. She said she knocked her down and kicked her."

"I'm not surprised." I was ashamed at the lack of feeling in my voice. But I had no room for more feeling. "Did you call social services?"

"No. She doesn't want me to."

"Then why is she telling you?"

"I don't know."

I said, "Ginger" and thought, *Polly*.

"I think it's because she wants me to invite her to come stay with us."

"That's out of the question and you know it. *She* knows it."

"If it wasn't for you, I'm not sure it would be out of the question. We don't know what her mother thinks."

"Did you say that to *her*?"

"No," she said. "I didn't."

"You know, we did this because we were thinking about adopting a child. We can do it. We can adopt a child who can really be ours."

"I don't want a child. I want her."

"You can't have her."

"If I can't have her completely, I'll have what I can."

It was what Polly said to me. *I know I can't have you completely, but—*

"Is this a Democrat county or Republican?"

"Republican. Dutchess County's voted Republican for the last thirty years. Why?"

She smiled and told me.

I wanted to say, Please. You know what you're like. You gravitate toward pain. If you want to get hurt, use a grown-up, not a little girl. But it wasn't fair, and anyway, how could I talk that way now?

Velvet

The last week of school I got the sea horse from Strawberry. Alicia told me she had something for me, and I almost said fuck you but she said, "It's from Strawberry." I saw she had a real letter with pink script on it. She handed me the envelope and watched me open it; a picture cut from a magazine fell out. It was a glass sea horse cut with scissors, and there was a folded note in *her* handwriting that said, "I told you I would think of you when I saw one and I did. Friends 4 Life." And then "Strawberry" in pink script with a heart.

I didn't want to smile, but I did; I looked at Alicia and she was looking back like she used to. She said Strawberry e-mailed her but hardly ever, and that when she got an e-mail asking for her house address, Alicia didn't even know why until she got the card for me. We walked down the hall like in elementary school. She asked me if I wanted to go to a party. I asked, whose party and she named a girl I knew was friends with Brianna. I said, "She helped spread lies about me." Alicia said, "What, you mean the picture?" And her voice was like a animal about to eat something. I stopped walking and said, "You know that wasn't me." She put her eyes down. I thought it meant she was sorry. She said, "I do know. Brianna knows too." She looked up and said, "So will you come to the party?" And then, "Dominic gonna be there."

Ginger

She called me and told me her mother was going to die. *"What? How? What happened?"* She has a disease, sobbed the girl, in her stomach. The doctor said she'll die and she couldn't even tell Dante because her mother made her promise not to. Because Dante would be scared.

She was calling from school, from the social worker's office. I asked to speak to the social worker, but it turned out she had no idea what was going on. She'd called Mrs. Vargas at work and was waiting to hear back. She said she'd let me know when she did.

"What are we going to do?" cried Velvet. "Ginger?"

"I'll do anything I can to help, baby."

I hung up and walked from the kitchen to the dining room to the living room and back, over and over. Maybe we could take Velvet and her brother could get into foster care here so they could see each other. Maybe it would be better to keep them together in foster care but up here so Velvet could stay with us on the weekends and ride horses. Maybe we could become foster parents and they could both live with us. Maybe I could divorce Paul and become a foster mother.

Break apart, come together, break apart. The rooms and their furniture were there before me. But invisibly, it all seemed to break, re-form, and break again and again.

The phone rang; it was the social worker. She said she had spoken to Velvet's mother, and she was not dying; she just had irritable bowel syndrome. When the social worker asked why her daughter thought she was dying, Mrs. Vargas laughed. She said she was teaching the girl a lesson.

"About what?" I asked.

"I didn't ask," said the woman. "I've been doing this upwards of five years and I've never heard anything like that before."

Break apart, come together, break apart.

Velvet

I put on the outfit Ginger gave me for my birthday and the butter-fly ring and the red earrings shaped like flowers. I took the Ginger-doll out of the cotton-ball box and put it in my front pocket where you couldn't see it. I put the picture of my grandfather in my back pocket. I put clothes under my blankets until it looked like maybe I was under them. I turned off the light and walked down the hall quiet. I walked quiet all the way out the house and down the block and then ran for the bus that Alicia told me to take.

I'd never walked on the street or rode the bus that late at night, and it was scary, but it got me interested. The people were mad rude but funny too. In the seat behind me these older girls were talking like: "An' then I said to her, 'Bitch, all that ring means is he paid too much to fuck ya waffcake ass,' she just stand there and look stupit!" And the other one laughed and went, "That bitch best get her weight up if she want to step to you, girl, you are a bossalina next to her!" And men were talking to me, and looking, their eyes soft or hungry or both. I sat next to a older lady all the way and she talked to me like she knew me to keep them off, and she said, "You take care, sweetheart!"

And I remembered that restaurant me and Ginger were at and I thought, Everybody on this bus is a bossalina next to them, even the old lady. Because she has something in her face and her voice nobody in that place had, even if they do eat thirty-dollar olive oil.

When I got to the party, I thought it even more. There was a evil-looking dude guarding the door and people all around waiting to get in, and they were rocking the hell out of it—I never got what that meant until now: gold high heels, chain belts, brand-name skinny jeans, shining lips, dyed blond braids tight up on the head, shining ironed hair rolled up in a bun to the side, white eyeliner, nails out to *here*. My heart pounded. I wanted to turn around and go home, but I couldn't stop looking: they were heaven-beautiful with a little hell added for flavor. The women like lightning hitting the ground, the men like thunder calling back. I knew somebody who called his mom "my ol' bird." Next to these people, Ginger in her white leather pants was a ol' bird even if she did have a diamond ring. Next to these people I was . . . in middle school.

But so was Alicia, and she invited me.

I stepped up to the evil man and he checked me like *What the hell?* But when I checked him back, his eyes changed and he wasn't so evil. He said, "What you doin' here, Miss Pretty? You look like you need to be home in your twin bed."

"Alicia invited me," I said.

"Alicia? Alicia who?"

"And Dominic."

"Dominic, huh." He turned his head like he might go inside and talk to somebody—but then he saw more people coming and just scrunched his face like, *Whateva.* "Okay, shawty," he said. "Slide through."

Silvia

I was late for work. The subway was speeding much too fast; it was boiling hot and barely lit and the people were all too close to me, so close their faces pressed against mine. Their bodies were crushed and wrong-shaped, their faces frowning with eyes crunched closed and lips pushed out like animal noses. They pulled at me and I saw I *was* at work, with Mrs. Somebody pulling at my clothes and whimpering because her saggy little tits were coming off, her hands were coming off. Her own hands were trying to put her hands back on. She said her children had died in a fire and there was the building burning while the children cried. Oh God, my daughter was in the building, I could hear her crying for me, she was only five! She had died when she was only five! I stood up and screamed for the subway to stop, I had to save my daughter, but no one could understand and it kept going.

I woke up sweating bullets. I loosened Dante's grip and went to down the hall to Velvet. I found her and put my hand on her; I found her in soft pieces. I clawed through them, my breath clawing through me. Fear came like a hurricane and went out my mouth.

Velvet

The music was so loud, it was like it was moving us, moving everybody. It was dark, but still I could see rooms like regular rooms in somebody's house, people drinking, talking, dancing, except in one room I saw a girl with her back to a man, her hands on the wall, dress and leg up, him grabbing her butt and shoving at her. I looked away quick. I saw girls maybe my age in one corner, talking and smoking something. Alicia wasn't here. No way she was here. This guy started talking to me, he said, ay, memba me? We were up against a wall, people pushing past. He said he knew Dominic. I knew his face but I didn't know from where, so I said no to the smoke at first, but then I thought, At least I will be doing something and took it. The music got louder; I saw his mouth moving but couldn't get what he said because the music was pulling me down a tunnel, and I was in the good feeling of Strawberry and the sea horse and that feeling *did not* belong here. I could see the boy was watching me very close, but I was thinking how once me and Pat were putting out these ponies, Nova and Sugar, and Nova got away from Pat and ran around the fence alongside Sugar, and Sugar ran with her inside the fence, her eyes bugged and her mouth foaming. The boy waved his hand in front of me. And then I knew him. He was the boy on the street who had told me I needed to play my position. I moved off the wall and said, "Where's Dominic?" He said, "I don't know where he is, Ma, but I'm here," and put his dick against me. I said, "I'm not your ma," and moved away, but he pushed against me, saying no bullshit he knows I'm feelin' him. That's when I saw Brianna and her girls mean muggin me right in the eye. He took my hand and put it on his dick. I yanked it back and said, "I'm feelin' you, all right—you make me feel sick," and he slapped me hard enough I hit the wall. Somebody shoved Brianna out the way. "Get off that girl," said Dominic, and he was taking up the whole screen.

"Ay, I'm not hurtin' lil' chicken head."

"Bitch, this girl is twelve and she ain't no chicken nothin'. You touch her one more time Ima lay you out, that's my word."

"I ain't gonna be no bitch," he said like a bitch.

Dominic didn't bother to answer the bitch, he just took my arm and pulled me out the door. "What in hell are you *doing* here?" he said.

"Alicia invited me."

"Alicia? Who—oh, *that* lil' skank? Since when you hangin' with that?"

"Since when *you* know me so well? I know Alicia since third grade, and FYI, I am not twelve. I turned thirteen last week."

He tried not to smile. "Oh, so you a big girl now."

"Big*ger*."

He looked around; there was people there, but they weren't looking. He crouched down with his hands on my shoulders and his legs open. His legs were long, and warmth came from them. He said, "Okay, big girl," and I felt myself open to let the warmth come in me. "You know your girl played you by asking you here, right? So now don't play yourself. Go home, a'ight?" We weren't moving, but I felt something come from him to me, heavy and delicious. I looked at him from the bottom of me; something came up in me and met him strong. Inside his eyes, he fell back. "Ay," he said. "You *are* a big girl ain't you?" He touched my lips with the back of his thumb; my lips kissed it before my mind thought. He stood, moving his hands over me, over my breasts. I stretched up to him, my lips open. He bent to me, his mouth open too, his hands feeling my butt.

"Girl, you need to stop that *now*." It was a man's voice; Dominic stepped away quick and turned his mean face out ready to fight. But it was a old man—even in the dark, I could see he was old. He said, "Young man, my granddaughter is out too late and she's too young for that anyway."

And I will never understand this: I said, "I'm sorry, Grandfather."

Dominic looked at me, confused. The old man came closer. He was wearing a cap with a brim low on his head and I couldn't see his face. I checked Dominic; I was surprised to see him looking almost scared. "I'm sorry, mister," he said. "I was only trying to take care of her."

"Sure, that's all right. But her mother is angry. She needs to come home. Come along with me, chica. I'll take you to the bus."

And he did. He walked me to the bus. We talked and I don't know if it was the smoke, but I forgot what we said right away. Except for this: He said, "I want you to tell your mother you love her." And I said I would. I took his hand and said, "Bendición, Abuelo," and he blessed me.

When we got to the stop, the 47 was there, so he said "Go," and I didn't have time to ask him who he was or anything. I got a seat up near the driver and then I thought, How did he know what bus I took? I whipped my head around to look at him, like he could answer through the window. But he wasn't there.

He wasn't there, but his voice was in me. Not just in my head, in my body, like part of me. It was still saying "Tell your mother you love her."

I came home and saw lights on. My mom must've seen me out the window because when I walked in she grabbed me around the throat and shoved me against the wall. I flashed on the boy and his dick; I tried to push back. She crushed her whole body against me, even her head bone crushed on mine. She didn't yell. She didn't hit. She said very soft that I wasn't worth hitting because if she hit me now she wouldn't be able to stop and then the police would come back and see and they'd take Dante away and she wasn't going to let me do that to her. She whispered, "I could kill you right now. But you aren't worth it."

I said, "Mami, I'm sorry. I love you." I looked in her eyes. "I love you."

She jerked back her head like I was a snake that bit her. She laughed hard and nasty and then jerked me off the wall and dragged me into her bedroom, where Dante lay curled up and scared. "Mami!" I cried out, and she put one foot behind my leg and then pushed me so I fell on the floor. I started to get up, but she put her foot on me and pushed me down, held me down. "Don't you try to manipulate me, you little puta," she said. "If you love me, act like it. Don't play bullshit stunts like you just played and then come at me, *Oh, I love you*. That drama might work with your social worker. I'm sure it works with Ginger. But it don't work with me." And she pushed her whole body weight on her foot, pressing into my chest like she was gonna *stand* on me. "You'll sleep here tonight. On the floor like a dog. If I get up and you're not here on the floor, I'll come get you, and I'll put you back down until you stay there." And she got back into the bed with Dante. I heard him whisper something to her; she whispered back like he was the sweetest thing in the world. And then they were sleep-breathing like nothing had even happened.

I lay on the floor like I was paralyzed. Why did that old man tell me to say that? Was I crazy? Was the smoke so strong I saw somebody who wasn't even really there? But he had to have been there—Dominic talked to him! I lay there for at least an hour with the floor hurting my head, too afraid even to move. It was like I could still feel her standing on me, on my chest. But I kept thinking that I had to find out, I had to ask Dominic—I had to see him, feel him. I wanted him to hold me. That's what finally made me strong enough to stand up and quietly, quietly go outside.

I thought I would take the bus back and look for Dominic, but I realized it was too late now; the bus might not even run. Instead I sat on the steps and watched the street: boys on corners, sometimes other boys coming to them. Men coming by in cars, this one car stopping and the boys coming up to it. A woman was there in the car, and she looked at me; big earrings, flashing eyes. The boys went back to their corners, but the car sat there, the man and woman talking at each other. I thought of Dominic touching me, felt my body as different now. The man yelled at the woman so loud I could hear, "You wanna smell my dick? You out you fuckin' mind?" Boys looking away, trying not to laugh; one of them looked at me, trying to catch my eye. The woman yelled, "If I could *trust* you, I wouldn't—" These little kids came running down the street laughing and I felt sick-sad 'cause no way should they be out this late. But they just laughed and ran around the corner, like Nova getting away and Sugar inside the fence rearing up like, *Fuck this shit.* I smiled at nothing. The car sped away so fast the woman's head snapped back. I remembered the Republican restaurant again; I thought of walking at night. I thought, upstate is nice. But compared to here, upstate is like somebody dreaming to themselves.

I took the Ginger-doll out of my pocket, rubbed it with my thumb. I thought, My mom is right: She's nice but she's . . . I couldn't think what she was, except that she wasn't *here*. My grandfather too.

He was nice, but he wasn't here either. I went out to the street. Somebody banged into me and said, "Watch where you going, stupit lil' bitch!" I stepped out of his way, and he kept walking. I went to the curb and I threw Ginger down the sewer. I took the little flower ring off first, though, and put it on my pinkie finger; it was too cute to throw away. I kept my grandfather's picture too. I did take it out of my pocket, but I put it in again and went back into my house and lay down on the floor.

Sugar said, *Fuck this shit* and slammed through the electric fence, her body tight like a cat going through a little hole. It must've hurt like hell, but she got through and ran, ran with Nova and nobody could stop them. My eyes shot open; I thought, The horses have what the people here have. They get beat down and locked up but still, when they run, *nobody* can stop them. I lay on the floor thinking about it over and over. And when I went to sleep I heard my grandfather's voice, very weak but clear. *You did well. I won't be talking to you like this again for a long time. But you did well.*

Ginger

I had not thought of Michael for years. Then suddenly, he was there again, floridly. At night, when Paul's back was like a wall and I couldn't sleep, I would think of him: the numb, hard way we were with each other, the deep touch of his deadened hands, his broken childishness, the cartoon-cruel expression of his mouth. The time his body trembled and he made a soft noise, and I took my hands off the floor to touch his thighs and he hit me in the face. *I told you, don't touch me!* The time he stroked my eyebrows and lips, his strange eyes glittering as if amazed to discover that I *had* a face. The time he said to me, "You are so lost." Numb and hard, but with something else inside it; I remembered it with grief and love. Because I had always been haunted by that pitiful feeling, that there had been love between us. Secretly.

These picture-thoughts scrolled past while I grocery shopped or made dinner or walked at night, planning Velvet's next visit. But I had not had such thoughts for so long that they seemed significant. They seemed related to the drink the night of Velvet's birthday. Because it was not just a drink; there was a wish that came with it, a need for something I couldn't put into words. I was afraid to talk about it with Paul. I was afraid he would lecture me, and also that he would associate the slip with Velvet's presence. And so I decided to go again to my old AA meeting in the city.

When I walked into the room, he was there. At first I couldn't believe it; I had never seen him at such a meeting or ever imagined he would go to one. The coincidence seemed so impossible, I thought it must be someone else; he was potbellied and pouch-faced, but the eyes and mouth were the same even so. He had the same restless body, the same insouciant posture, though with exhaustion now too. And who else would stare at me like that, as if shocked to see me too, also ashamed and unsure—but glad? He looked glad to see me! He looked glad, then avoided my eyes. I insisted, and finally he looked back. Then he raised a finger to his lips, and with smiling eyes, went, "Shhhh."

Velvet

My next time back I wanted to tell Ginger I threw her doll away. But it was too mean and anyway she didn't know about the doll. So I told her I could see the bald spot on her head.

"Thanks a lot," she said, "but I knew about that already. Do you know you got a big-ass head?"

I asked her if she'd been out drinking again. She whipped around and said, "Don't *ever* mention that again. Mention that again, our relationship is *over*."

"I'm going to the horses."

"Honey, I'm sorry."

Before I got to the barn, I saw Beverly in the round pen with Joker and she was using her bullwhip. She was excited. I could feel how excited she was. I could feel how scared he was. She was scared too, and that made her more excited. She yelled at him and made him run, but then she changed the whip from behind to in front and he turned and ran and she hit from behind again. He didn't know where to go. He stood up in front of her and I thought he would stomp her. But he didn't. She used the whip and that's when he screamed.

I wanted to kill her. I wanted to take the whip away from her and use it on her. I wanted it so bad I couldn't see.

I went in the barn. Gare was standing there so quiet I didn't see at first that she was watching Beverly and she was crying. I felt even more mad to see that. I went to the office. Pat was in her plastic chair eating old takeout with the cats stretched up on her front. I said, "Why is Beverly doing that?"

She sat up; the cats hung there looking pissed. "First, get the attitude out of your face."

"Why is she hurting him? She's always hurting him. Why?"

"She's not seriously hurting him. What she's doing is psychological. She's—"

"So she's hurting him inside."

"She's psychologically *disciplining* him, she—"

"He's screaming, Pat."

"Listen, it's not my way. I wouldn't do it. But I don't run this place and—"

I walked out of the office. Gare was still standing there. Nobody else was. "Come here," I said to her. "Help me."

"Help you do what?"

"Come here, I'll show you. Get a bridle."

She followed me. I went to the other side of the barn, to Fiery Girl's stall. The mare came forward as we came. I took her halter down. "I'm gonna bring her out right here. I'm gonna get the bridle on her while you hold her."

Gare stared at me. "You're fucking crazy," she said.

"She won't hurt me. We don't have time to get her on the cross-ties."

Like she knew what I was planning, Fiery Girl shook her head, stepping fast and light from one foot to the other.

"What're you gonna do?"

"Help me get the bridle on. Help me get on her."

Gare's face lit up. She went to get the bridle. I opened the stall door enough to get in. The mare put back one of her ears, stretching her head to me like she wanted to lip me. I lightly pushed her face back and touched her neck to get her to take the halter. She put her head down. I opened the door and led her out, her step high and *springy*. Gare came back, strong now. The mare's back was trembling under her silky skin, but she let us get the bridle on. Then it was scary: Gare couldn't hold her *and* help me get on her. I had to make her be still with just my hand on her. I said, "Whoa. Be with me. Whoa. I've been with you. Be with me." Gare's eyes flashed. She let go the horse and stood with her hands locked for me to step on and get a leg up.

I took the reins and went from Gare's hands up on her trembly back; the mare took off at a strong walk. Gare gave a holler, Pat came out the office and yelled, "Shit! Whoa!" She went for the reins, but I tapped with both heels, then barely had time to duck my head before we were out the barn door at a trot past the round pen.

And then it all happened: Beverly saw me and spun so she damn near hit herself with her own whip—just before Joker reared up on her from the back and she fell down. Then Fiery Girl took off almost out from under me, running down the trail toward the water. I grabbed her mane with both hands, but I could barely stay on. Was Beverly dead? The mare went off the path into the neighbor farm's orchard. The trees came at me with black claw-arms and rushed away, green leaves and rotting fruit. I ducked; she took me through. I yelled, *Whoa!* but she didn't even slow. Everything was flying past and I would go to jail, my mom talking forever about what shit I was. I pulled the reins, feeling for her mouth, but it was no good; I was already slipping when I saw the fence coming. I screamed, "Whoa!" and pulled the reins hard, she came up on her back legs, and I saw nothing but sky that went forever until I slammed down on my back so hard my head bounced. The sky blurred and black came in on the edges. I pushed it back and made myself sit up. My horse was trotting slowly alongside the fence. I felt vomit coming. Ginger's voice said, *Our relationship is* over. I called to my horse; she ignored me. My eyes blurred; my horse blurred and then she was gone. Dominic was there, his arm around Brianna. We were outside the school. He was walking with her and at first I thought he didn't even see me because he had turned his back to me, both their backs were to me. But then he turned his head back around and looked at me that same way he looked a long time ago, when he was with Sondra, joking and serious. But it was horrible now. Because he had touched my breasts and my lips and his eyes mentioned that while he turned away to be with someone who hated me. Alicia saw. Other people saw. I was all of a sudden a tiny hurting center of something huge that had nothing to do with me.

I felt dizzy. Grass and trees stretched away. Now I was not at the center of anything. I wasn't anything. Grass and trees stretched away from me, not touching me. The mare ate grass, ignoring me. Far away was a road with cars and people that had nothing to do with me. The sky was like the ocean, full of things I couldn't see. Birds flew, hunting for invisible things to kill. People said this was beautiful, but it was not. It would kill you if you were alone in it and I was alone. I was alone everywhere. There was nothing to stand on, nothing to hold. My mother wouldn't even hit me because I wasn't worth it. I bent over and vomited.

The next time I saw Shawn, I went with him and I did what he told me. I wanted Dominic to hear and be mad. When I finished, I don't even know why, but I said, "So you love me?" He said, "Sure, you cool." The next time I saw Dominic he was with another girl, a friend of Brianna's named Janelle. He didn't even look at me.

Any man could have her and who would want to?

Beverly would say it about me if she knew. It wasn't true. But she would say it. Maybe even Pat would. Why? Why did they talk like that about somebody? I bent over again, but instead of vomit, pain came with a sound that was horrible to me. I fell onto my knees and the sound became words. I hit myself and said them: *Ugly stupid chicken-head bitch. Worthless, stupid. Nobody wants you. Even the horse doesn't want you. You're worse than shit. Even the horse knows. You're not worth it.*

I wiped my mouth with my shirt. The black closed in and then parted; the grass was so green beneath me. I felt her breath on me. Then her nose against my shoulder. The grass was so green. I lifted my face and she lipped my hair. I almost laughed because she had come back, but then I saw she was scared. She was scared, but she still came back to see if I was okay. I could not make her more scared.

The blackness cleared. I stood up and touched her shoulder with both my hands. She shied away. I made my voice softer and I talked to her like she was a kitten. I said I was sorry I said those things, that I wasn't talking to her. I said I would never say those things again. I tried to kiss her and to hug her. She shied away again. I tried again, and she moved away again, stronger this time, like I was scaring her. I didn't understand and it hurt me. I needed to feel her, but I couldn't make her more scared. Her skin was shining, and her head was up, nervous, even though her eyes were trusting me. I put my head down and moved close enough to put my hand on her shoulder. She stayed. I felt her muscles, her blood. I felt *her.* I remembered suddenly how it was when I walked to the barn with Ginger that first time, how all the green was too much, too open, and I knew: She didn't feel safe enough to hug in the open. Like she knew I understood, she put her head down and began to eat the grass. I petted her neck and then picked up the reins. I let her eat for a few minutes—it made me feel calm to watch her eat, looking a little piggy with her snout. Then when I was ready I said, "Come on" and pulled her head up.

I led her to the fence like it was a mounting block. I climbed up on it. She shied away at first, but I talked her back. She saw what I was doing; she let me. I sat on her and swung my hair behind me. The sky was huge and bright, but it was touching me now, it was friendly, and the huge brightness of the grass stretched before me. I started her at a walk. This was my place. No one would ever be in this place but me and my horse. No man, not even children; they would never come here with me. This place was only for me and my mare.

We were going at a trot when we saw Pat on Graylie and Beverly on Diamond Chip. I slowed to a walk. They stopped and they stood there waiting, Pat with her face like she just saw God, Beverly like somebody'd stuck a rake in *her* face.

"Get off that goddamned horse," Beverly said, "before you do any more damage."

I got off. Pat got off Graylie. She was trying to make her face mad, but I could see she was really something else and she was barely holding it back. She said, "Do you realize how lucky you are that you didn't get hurt?"

Beverly said, "Do you realize how lucky *I* am that I didn't get killed? He came up on me and hit the back of my knees. He could've kicked my skull in."

"Both of you could've been killed," said Pat.

"I'm sorry, Miss Beverly," I said. "I'm sorry, Miss Pat. But Fiery Girl wouldn't kill me. She loves me."

"Don't be a fool!" Pat said. "She's an animal!"

"I know. But she loves me." Then I fainted.

Beverly

Jesus Christ. Even her, the tough black girl from the city—or Puerto Rican, or whatever she is—even she's been ruined by the Disneyfied horse-snot they sell in the multiplex. Love and self-esteem, love and self-esteem—love is good for babies and that's it. Yes, you make a horse good by raising it up with a little love and a lot of discipline. But you make a horse great by making it feel like shit. Because it knows it is *not* shit and it will turn itself inside out to prove it to you. Sure you give it love, just a touch. And then you make it crave the love, make it try to please you for another little taste—it will turn itself inside out to show you it's good; you make that horse prove it over and over, every time. If that horse is worth anything, it will pull up everything it's got for you and it *will* find what it's worth and be more and more proud. It will know it can take whatever you got and sometimes it will give it back. But it will know its worth. And it will do *anything* to make you know it. It will die to make you know it. Not that I'd go that far. That would be stupid. Because that horse is worth more than me. The dumb animal just doesn't know it. It's me that's shit. Not him.

Ginger

When I saw Pat and Velvet come into the house I thought, She's won a prize. Because that's what their faces said, even when Pat said, "There's been an accident." Velvet smiled and said, "I'm okay. I just fell off."

I felt a lump forming under her warm hair; there was a little blood. I asked if she'd blacked out. She said yes and I told her to go get her Medicaid card. I thought of Mrs. Vargas and began to sweat. Velvet went up the stairs and I said, "What happened?" Pat said the girl had broken the rules of the barn and that she'd been expelled.

"What did she do?"

"Improperly handled a horse, rode *bareback* without permission or supervision, endangered herself and others. She fell off the horse and passed out. She's probably got a concussion, but she could've broken her neck."

"My God!"

As Anglo as she was, she suddenly reminded me of Mrs. Vargas; powerfully in her body, peering out of it with the expression of someone looking at a world she didn't fully understand and didn't think much of. She said, "I'm pretty sure she's okay; she was only unconscious for seconds. But call me tomorrow and let me know."

On the way to the hospital, I asked Velvet what she'd done and she said, "I rode my mare." Her face was withdrawn, like into some powerful dream, but something exalted and private radiated from her. Consequences, I thought. Why doesn't she understand?

"They're not going to let you go back to the barn."

"Miss Pat will. She told me I can even come to her house."

I thought, Yeah, like I'm going to homeschool you; my heart went dark and sore. We pulled into the hospital parking lot. She said, "I stopped this other horse from being hurt," and I gathered the crazy trainer had been distracted by Velvet's antics and gotten knocked down. Which was, I guess, the idea.

As we parked, I flashed on all the movies I'd taken her to or rented for her: movies where some stupid mean adult is basically knocked down by the heroine and everybody thinks it's great. I said, "This isn't a movie, you know."

She looked at me and said, "*Wha?*"

At the desk they said they couldn't treat her without her mother's permission. I said, "Does anyone here speak Spanish?" and the receptionist said, "I'm sure there's someone."

I thought, It's all over now. And Michael came into my mind with the force of despair. I looked at Velvet; I should not have brought her here. Clearly there was nothing wrong with her; she was alert and even looking rather pleased as the receptionist called for someone who could speak to her mom. I thought, I've lost her. I pictured my life with Paul before she came into it and it seemed intolerably bleak.

Velvet smiled as she picked up the phone and said, "Hola, Mami."

I thought again of Michael, of the way he touched his finger to his lips: *Shhh.* We barely even spoke when I saw him, yet he seems closer now than Paul. How is that possible? How could something I barely remember, that happened in a small room so long ago, seem more real than my real life?

The translator arrived, a helpful girl with PANIC AT THE DISCO on her shirt.

Velvet

Ginger looks like she's about to cry and I'm like, *But I'm okay*—then I go, Right, she's scared of my mom. But I'm not stupid enough to call my mom. I call my cousin and say, "Hola, Mami." Nobody who can speak Spanish is even there yet, so I tell Donna I can't bother my mom at work, but I bumped my head and Ginger wants to be sure I'm okay, could she be my mom and give permission? She asked questions, but then the translator came, this girl who hardly knew Spanish, and I knew it was okay, and they let me see the doctor. He tapped my knees with a little hammer and made me balance on one leg and count my fingers. He asked if I knew where I was and where I was from. He wanted to know the name of my horse; he smiled when I said, "Fiery Girl."

"When can she go to sleep?" asked Ginger. "I heard you can't sleep after a concussion."

"She can sleep at bedtime," said the doctor. He thought a second. "Maybe wake her after a few hours. I think she's fine, though."

But I couldn't sleep. I stayed awake feeling Fiery Girl run under me, and seeing the branches and rotten fruit fly past me like time and outer space. At first it was a good feeling, but it turned sick and bad, like black coming in on the edges of the sky. What if they would never let me see her again? My brain had a bruise on it, that's what the doctor said, because it hit against my skull. "Crap for brains, but she can ride, you gotta give her that." That's what Beverly said. I pictured my brain pressing on my skull and I felt like there was something invisible pressing in the dark, trying to get visible. Was this what happened to my brother when the babysitter gave him the aspirin? I was afraid if I slept I would dream of hell and I would not wake up. Why did my grandfather tell me to go to hell that time? Was he in hell? Alicia said almost everybody went to hell, it didn't even matter if you were a good person or not. Gare said, "You rode the hell out of that bitch." I said, "Don't call her a bitch." But maybe I sent her to hell. Because if I couldn't see her, who would take care of her? Who would love her? The way she looked at me when Pat put her away in her stall—even though she did not turn her head, I know she looked and loved me with her dark eye. I thought of Dominic, turning to look at me while he was with Brianna. My heart hurt. I held my chest, and it hurt.

Ginger came in her nightgown and shook my shoulder. I said, "You don't got to do that. I'm awake." She kissed me. I said, "Ginger, when can I see my horse again?" She said, "I don't know. Don't think about that now." "But I want to see her!" "You will," she said. "I promise you will. But right now try to rest, get better." She kissed me again. "That's more important right now."

She left, but still I could feel her. I felt my mare, her body standing quiet for me in the field, her muscles and skin, holding me. Still, I felt alone. And there was still the invisible thing, pushing through, and I was scared.

Silvia

I woke in the middle of a dream I forgot as soon as I knew it was a dream. Voices outside argued and laughed. It was one of those dreams that make you think you've realized something, that all the stupid shit in life finally makes sense. Police lights flashed on the ceiling; there was cursing. The stupid shit, same as usual. I rolled over and closed my eyes and remembered: cartoon pictures of wrapped-up gifts, toys, sweet voices, and happy faces. *The Velveteen Rabbit.*

I opened my eyes and saw Dante's little sleeping face. I watched that cartoon when I first came here, in Providence, Rhode Island, with a little boy named Raul, a poor child with a narrow back and a twisted foot he couldn't walk right on. I couldn't understand the movie except that it was about toys; Raul said it was about a toy made real by love. He watched it over and over.

I was pregnant, and I had come to the country alone to wait for my lover, Jesus, to leave his wife. I was staying with Jesus's brother, Miguel, and his little boy. Raul was only six, but Miguel was almost fifty. His fiancée had disappeared, and so far he had no other woman. He was strange; he didn't talk much, he just worked and took care of Raul. He had two televisions on mute all the time, one in his bedroom, one in the main room, both of them on crime shows. Most of the time he didn't even watch, but when he really did watch, it was video movies of women being murdered. At night, in his room, painful light flickered from under his door and women screamed their asses off. In the main room on the couch, I fell asleep to TV screaming and dreamed of being with my husband and child, and watching things like *The Velveteen Rabbit* together.

But it was funny about all the murder movies, because—Miguel was gentle! I cleaned the house and cooked for him and we ate together like a family. He read to Raul from *The Hulk* comics, and, on Saturdays, let him watch cartoons instead of crime. He took us to the ocean. We walked to the edge of the cold water, Miguel carrying Raul so he wouldn't stumble on his bad foot. The water was dark and the sky was dark too. A slit of cold light separated water and sky. I picked up shells, blue and brown ones that I mostly lost.

Then one night Jesus called me and told me his wife was pregnant and he wasn't coming. Just like that. I went to Miguel's room. He turned down the sound on the TV and he told me that his brother cared for me, it was just too hard for him to get away. He held me and talked to me and watched the show on the silent TV. He said not to worry, that he would marry me at city hall and I would be legal. When the show was over, he asked me if I wanted to see a movie of his fiancée. I said okay, and he put it in the machine and it was a video of her taking her clothes off and rubbing herself. He held me and ran his hands up under my T-shirt. He wasn't in the movie, but his cock was, and she was kissing it. It sounds disgusting, but I understood; he missed her. He turned me around and pulled up my T-shirt; I watched his fiancée suck him off. He moved behind me; he was lubricating himself. I resisted but not very much; I wanted something too. He put it up my ass, like his brother did at the beginning. So I wouldn't lose my virginity to a married man, though of course I eventually did. Miguel was gentler, though, very slow and careful. He kissed my shoulders and tried to make me enjoy it and I almost did. When it was time to sleep, he turned the TV off for me.

But in the morning, I felt numb. Miguel said we would get married, but then I had to go. I had no money and no man and I spoke no English and the child was due. There was my aunt in New York City, but I hadn't been able to reach her yet. I looked at myself in the mirror and I thought, Who would want a child who came from this?

Then the child came and she was dark. It made no sense. I'm light, Jesus was light, and here she is, nearly negrita. Aunt Maria said, "Black Velveteen!" and shook her head. Because the child would have hard luck all her life.

The police were gone and it was quiet out. I took the pillow that used to be hers and put it close behind me, like it was her. I held Dante and closed my eyes. I thought of Raul with his little foot and I slept.

Ginger

It was true: Velvet was invited to ride at Pat's house. She was barred from the barn indefinitely, but she could visit Pat's home after four o'clock. She could ride Pat's mare Chloe.

"Do you think that's a good idea?" I asked Pat. "Given how reckless she's been?"

"She's not going to be reckless at my house. Listen, there's an element of danger any time anybody gets on a horse, just like there's danger any time anybody gets in a car. Velvet plus that horse she fell off of are a particularly volatile thing. Velvet plus a certain trainer are even more volatile. But one, there's only two horses at my house and both of them are angels—"

I felt myself smiling into the phone; my heart rose with the cadence of her voice. Because in spite of the danger, my question had been pro forma.

"—and two, I'm the only other person she's gotta deal with at my house. Three, that girl is a genius horsewoman. That kind of talent should not be ignored; in my opinion, ignoring her talent will be putting her more at risk than letting her ride. Because that girl *needs* to ride for her sanity."

"That's what I think too."

"Impose some discipline on your end; she needs that as well. Make her do chores for a week, hold something back, whatever you want. Make her realize that what she did wasn't okay with you. If she's good for the week, I'll drop by and take her to my place."

So I laid it out for her: dishes, math workbooks, and the three extra-credit essays for school. I said, "And don't ever endanger yourself like that again. If you do, you can't come back here anymore. That would break my heart, but—"

"I stopped Beverly from hurting Joker."

"If Beverly was abusing Joker, you should've told somebody! Instead of getting on another horse bareback and riding it out with your ass halfway on it!"

"I told Pat, and she didn't listen!"

"Then you need to say it differently or say it to someone else or accept that you can't do anything about it!"

"I did do something about it! She stopped hitting him!"

"And you know what? The next time she looks at Joker, she's going to remember that you got her knocked down and guess who she's going to take it out on?"

"I don't care. I'm not afraid of her."

"Not you. She's not going to take it out on you. You won't even be there. She's going to take it out on the horse."

Her face went into a wounded full stop, mouth and eyes open.

"Maybe that won't happen," I said. "I'm just saying it could. But I don't care that much about the horse. I care about you. You could've broken your neck and that would've broken my heart. And by the way, it would've destroyed your mother."

"Trust me," she said, "it would not destroy my mother."

I said, "Just don't do it again."

But I was thinking: It would be a relief to have a mom who could not be destroyed. My mom used to say that Melinda was going to destroy her and that if I ever "went like Melinda" it would destroy her. It was a very annoying thing to hear.

Velvet

Before I could go to Pat's house I had to do chores and read books for a week. I had to apologize to Estella Kadner for causing trouble and apologize to Beverly again in front of Estella. It was disgusting, but I had to do it and I was going to do it. But when I went, Pat took me into Estella's special office and it was only me and her there, not Beverly. It was the first time I saw her since Christmas. She was sitting down and her hair was tied back, but her shiny skin and her carved nose still made her seem like she was looking down at me, and maybe she would lift me up, maybe not.

"I wanted you to ride in a competition," she said. "I wanted you to represent us. Why did you do such a foolish thing?"

And I told her. I said that Beverly was hurting Joker inside. She said, "I see" and looked at her desk. Lines came on her forehead.

Then Pat came, and Beverly, and I had to apologize to Beverly. I said, "I'm sorry, Miss Beverly," but I said it with my head down and Estella Kadner made me raise my head and look at Beverly and say it again. And then I had to say *what* I was sorry for, just like in school, basically feeling like a piece of shit for no reason. Except that the lines were still on Estella Kadner's forehead because of what I said before.

"How old are you now?" asked Beverly.

I looked at her for real then. "I'm thirteen," I said.

"You look older. Even if you *were* older, I'd be wondering. Just what do you think you know about *psychology*?"

Nobody said anything.

"How do you know anything about *psychology*?"

And then I did something I've seen my mom do. Except I didn't *do* it, it just happened. Instead of looking *at* Beverly, I looked *in* her, like looking down a dark hall with doors.

"I know like everybody knows. *Miss.*"

Beverly looked at me like we were the only people in the room. "You know, you used to be able to beat a kid who acted bad," she said. "And guess what, kids learned fast, just like horses. They figured out,

I act like a jerk I get the crap beat out of me, maybe I don't want to act like a jerk. Not anymore. Everybody's worried about 'self-esteem' and 'hurting inside.'"

Estella Kadner said, "That's enough."

Beverly didn't say nothin'. It was still like, just her and me in the room.

I said, "My mom does beat me."

Estella's forehead went more lined.

Beverly said, "Then your mom does you right."

Silvia

The lord is my shepherd / I shall not want. Today a man went into a movie theater with guns and started shooting. He killed five people and hurt lots of others, and I understand. Because I am tired of being the one in pain. It says *I shall not want.* But I want; I want somebody else to feel pain. I want to hear them screaming.

What I don't want is prayer. I hate prayer. It's what people do when they have nothing. I have never had anything and now I don't even have a job. I am on the crowded subway but I am alone in darkness. I want to send bullets into the darkness, send knives. They won't strike anyone because in the dark no one is there. And I am praying. *He makes me to lie down in green pastures.* I see Velvet's horses, running in the grass. They are beautiful; my children smile and reach for them, thinking they can have them—their smiles, their hope destined to go black and die. Tears come up under my closed lids. *He leads me beside the still waters.* Last week I hurt Dante by crying in front of him—better for him if I'd given him my fist. *He restores my soul.* The horses run again, swerving together. I open my eyes. Across from me there's an old woman with a sad face. In her body she carries a small flame. I look around; all the people on the car, no matter how rough, have a flame. I want to be like them. But I can't. I am locked inside hardness and nothingness and I can't get out. Like the horse Velvet talks about, the one who kicks the wall. Striking the hard thing, trying to break it. No one sees, no one hears. *Though I walk through the valley of the shadow of death, I will fear no evil for—.*

But I fear. I fear. I am ill with fear.

Velvet

I thought Pat would talk about it in the car, but she just put the radio on. We drove over the bridge and took a road I didn't know, like a dirty tongue going up a hill with no houses or even trees on the sides of it. The Iraq War was on the radio and people were being blown up. Pat said the war was a horrible mistake; she said it like she wanted to know what I thought. But I was thinking of when I showed Ginger's picture to Shawn. I wanted him to see how nice she was, but he said, "You know why those people can act nice? Other people do the violence for them. That's how they have that nice world." I said, "Ginger doesn't have anybody doin' violence." He just tossed her picture back at me and said, "She must think you some lil' Orphan Annie."

Pat changed the station to a song I didn't know. Suddenly I thought, I don't know *her*. And she is Beverly's friend. Hard feelings banged together in me. *You used to be able to beat a kid who acted bad.*

"Where are we going?" I asked.

"My place," she said. "Where did you think?"

We went up a bumpy driveway. I remembered a long time ago when I rode my bike with Ginger and she said, "Lumpety bumpety!" and we flew.

Pat said, "Just so you know, my place is primitive compared to Estella's."

"What's 'primitive'?"

"I mean there's no toilet in the barn. When I don't feel like walking to the house I use a bucket."

We drove past a little house with tin patched on it and colored plastic flowers twirling in the yard. There was a vegetable garden with wire around it and a barn behind a bunch of pale trees. Two horses in a jelly-bean-shaped paddock came running at us, then away; they were both light brown, one with a blond mane and low, round, ripply shoulders. "Chloe's the blondie," said Pat. "The gelding's Nut. See the difference in the way they're built?" I looked. Nut looked stronger to me; he was tall and his back was very wide. "Chloe's built what they call 'uphill'—and her back is nice and short *and* she's got a strong rear. See how long her shoulders are, that long neck? She's a good jumper partly because of how she's built—but the main reason is, she actually likes to jump."

"Is Fiery Girl a good jumper?" I asked.

"I don't know. I haven't seen her jump. I don't even know if she's been jumped. She does have the build for it, though. Got a beautiful neck."

I thought we were going to bring the horses in, but they didn't want to come in, so we went to clean their feed and water buckets instead. We brought the buckets out of the barn and ran the hose. It was still hot; plant and vegetable smells spread in the air like invisible color with dark horse-smell underneath. I remembered Shawn in my mouth. I remembered Dominic in front of me with his legs open and soft heat coming from between them. I remembered his eyes when he was holding Brianna and looking at me over his shoulder, sharp like the arrow in the valentine, sharp in my heart, my real heart, like in the science chart of your body, the heart-muscle in the dark of my body. Soft/sharp. Love. We scrubbed while the horses played.

"Miss Pat, do you think Beverly would hurt Joker because of me?"

She didn't look at me or answer right away. Then she said, "No. I can see why you would ask. But no."

"Would she hurt my mare?"

"No. Beverly is crazy, but she knows horses. She knows the mare would kill her. Even if she had to bide her time. She'd kill her."

What I thought was, Good. What I said was, "If you think Beverly is crazy, why are you friends with her?"

"We work together. It's not my choice who Estella hires." She dumped soapy water from a bucket. We rinsed the buckets and took the water buckets back to hang. We filled them up. While we were running the water, Pat said, "I've known Beverly a long time. We went to school together. She's Estella's half sister. Here." She handed me the hose so I could fill Nut's bucket.

"What's a half sister?"

"Beverly's mom married Estella's dad when Beverly was like ten. Estella was born something like five years later. Beverly's dad wasn't in the picture anymore."

I said, "Oh." And I felt a little bit sorry for Beverly. Because it would be hard to have Estella for a sister, especially if you had to work for her.

"It was Estella's dad who had horses. He used to own the place."

I said, "Oh" again.

When we were done with the buckets, we got brooms and swept the floor and cleaned cobwebs. We got forks and cleaned the stalls. I wanted to ask if I could still see my mare sometimes, but I was afraid of the answer. So instead I said, "Miss Pat, what's a competition?"

"There's different ones. Hunter paces, eventing, hunter-jumper shows."

"Estella said she wanted me to be in one."

"Yes, she did. I did too. We were thinking you could do a hunter-jumper schooling show next spring."

"What would happen if I won?"

"It's complicated. You'd basically get a ribbon and points. Schooling shows are awarded in points; girls go to different shows and build points within the Equestrian Association. At the end of the year, if you have the most points, you get a big honkin' ribbon."

"Oh."

"It means you're recognized as the best in the county. And you can show bigger after that."

"Do you ever get money?"

"There's cash prizes for some shows, yeah."

"Could I still do it?"

She stopped cleaning. "I don't know, you tell me."

I didn't answer, or even look at her, but I stopped cleaning too.

"Can you stop putting yourself and other people in danger? Can you respect what I say to you and follow instructions?"

"Yes."

"Can you? Because I went out on a limb for you and you made me look like an idiot. Truthfully? If I was your mother, *I'd* smack you."

I wanted to say, *That's not what you looked like when you saw me on my mare.* I felt mad and I put my head down so she wouldn't see.

"You could never see the mare again, you know that?"

My head shot up, pain on it.

"Glad to see you still care about something."

"I'm sorry. I told them I was sorry!"

"Then show it."

"How?"

She didn't answer me, she just went back to cleaning. The next thing she said was, "Come with me. Time to bring the horses in."

Ginger

Back when she still talked about Strawberry, I asked her, "What's she like?" Velvet smiled and said, "Like every girl." I said, "What's every girl like?" She answered, "Like, they see a boy and they see heaven." I smiled at her twelve-year-old coolness; I hoped she'd hold on to it. But at thirteen she'd lost it already. I could feel the loss of it: in her sudden attention to romantic movie scenes, in the music she played on her princess boom box, in her soft, suddenly yearning eyes. I asked, "Honey, are you in love?" We were in the car, coming back from Pat's place, and she took her time answering. She said, "I like somebody. A lot."

Michael: his finger to his lips. "Shhh." Sweet like high school, middle school even.

I said, "It almost hurts, doesn't it?" She glanced at me—face grateful and shining—then away.

It did hurt the first time I "liked" someone, mostly because he didn't like me back. I remember telling my mother and she said, "What do you like about him?" I blushed; the only things I could think of were the way he smelled and the sound of his voice, the expression on his face when he thought no one saw.

"What kind of person is he?" she asked.

"Nice."

"Have you talked to him?"

"No."

"Then you don't know him. You can't like somebody if you don't know him."

I said I knew he was nice because he looked away and didn't join when his friends laughed at the ugly girl.

I didn't tell her about the time I bumped into him on purpose, because I wanted to talk to him. I wanted to talk, but I didn't know what to say, I just looked at him, hoping he would say something. Which was, "Get out of the way, dope."

She shook her head. "Sex. That's all it is. I hope to God you're not going like Melinda."

But I was nothing like Melinda. Boys liked Melinda. She always knew what to say. She always seemed like she was moving even when she was just standing with her hand on her hip, like her skirt was swinging though it wasn't. When I was in elementary school and she was in middle school, I asked her what happened when you liked a boy. She said, "It's like when you see him you feel this big warmth and he does too. It's like there's nobody else there. Except when you slow-dance together too long and you know you stink and then you wish he *wasn't* there!"

Warmth; stink. My sister was natural. I was not. I didn't feel warmth, I felt painful burning and tenderness so big it made me want to run and hide because how could something so soft live with such burning? Of course boys didn't like me. Burning and stunned, I hid inside myself, stiff as a glass doll. Melinda went outward, smiling and warm.

Smiling and warm. Why was she hurt? She rode horses, she sat with her legs confidently open, she made funny animal noises in class sometimes. Her first year in high school, she was so popular that when my friends came over, they asked to look in her room, then stood at the threshold, peering in as if awed. Our father adored her. When we would go in the car as a family, Melinda sat up front with Daddy, her hand and her head on his chest, while Mom and I sat in the back. Two years later, she ran off with an older guy who worked at the barn. When the police found her, it was determined by somebody that she be sent to a mental hospital for evaluation. After two months at the "place" she came back still-faced and watchful. She returned to school and people who used to be her friends picked on her while I pretended not to notice. She got fat and hung out with skanks. Our mother called her a pig loud enough for the neighbors to hear. My father was gone by then, so there was no one to stop her. When Melinda shouted back, my mom would try to hit her, but Melinda was bigger; she warded off the weak blows just by raising her arms, yelling, "Mom, cut it out!" Sometimes my mom cried, and when that happened my sister would run from the house with her hands over her ears. My mother would walk around angrily praising me for not being "a pain in the ass." Eventually Melinda would come back and stomp upstairs, or sometimes play cards with my mom, while I watched TV in the den with my homework in my lap.

Why did these things happen? I can understand why I was hurt; glass begs to be smashed. But why her? Why?

Velvet

Driving to Pat's horses was so different from walking over to the barn; it was like someplace foreign. Chloe and Nut were different than the horses at the other barn; their coats were dirtier, their eyes were softer and more people-y, and they ran happier. Nut liked to take Pat's hat off her head and run, then Chloe would run with him trying to get it. Chloe *did* have a long rounded neck and a high head and when I got on her I thought, High, wide and handsome in Beverly's voice.

When Pat finally let me ride instead of just working, I started working on jumping almost right away. We started out trot-jumping little fences, me in the two-point, holding her mane, her body jerking me forward and then back when she landed, running until I slowed her to go again over the next fence. My heart pounded, but my legs were calm on her and Pat's voice yelled, "Stay with the motion, don't hang behind!" and I went over right and Chloe ran.

And then I washed her with the hose and scraped the water off her, and even though her face was sweet, I missed my mare.

I said, "Miss Pat, how is Fiery Girl? Do you think she misses me?"

"Well, she's an animal. It's hard to know what they think."

I soaped Chloe with mint between her legs and I thought, I would know.

"But I have noticed she stands at the door of her stall every day. Like she's looking for somebody."

I stopped in the middle of rinsing Chloe. I said, "I know I can't see her, but why don't you have her here if she's yours? Why do you keep her at Estella's place?"

"Because I don't have a stall for her and also I don't think she'd get along with Chloe. I'd have to build a fence to divide the paddock."

"Oh."

"But I've been thinking about that. She's lot better now than she was. If you'd help me build a stall, maybe—"

I dropped the sponge and hugged Pat. I felt her be embarrassed and then just like me, and hug me back. "When?" I asked.

"If we can get the stall together by the end of the month, then. It should only take a few days, then a few more days for a fence in the paddock. You can pay for the lessons that way—not much mucking to do around this place."

I told Ginger and she started letting me come almost every day, even though sometimes I had to wait extra time for Paul to get back from his "office hours." On the extra-time days, Pat invited me in her house to put my feet up. Her house was dirty. It was normal-dirty, like plates with old food and yellow-y rags and clothes piled up, and also strange-dirty, with little broken things everywhere: toys and a glass cat head with jewel eyes and a scissors stuck in the door where the knob was supposed to be, and the toilet couldn't flush; you had to stick your hand down in the back of it and pull on the chain. It was like the house was falling down in pieces and Pat didn't even notice! The first time I came in, her mom was there, sitting in it. She was watching something about horses on TV and when we came in she said, "The queen flew into Lexington last night. She is very excited about the new foal sired by Abdul." She was a strong old lady with a long neck that came out of her body like a person trying to escape out of a tree trunk. She did home care like my mom. Pat would rub her legs so her veins wouldn't hurt, like I did with my mom. And she would tell stories about how the other care workers stole but she didn't, and how she "blew the whistle" when she found this one old man's good things packed up in boxes on his back porch and he didn't even know the other shift worker was about to "snatch him bald-headed."

Pat's barn was dirty too. All the combs and brushes were filthy in filthy bags, and so were the spray bottles and nasty jars of horse-rub, clipboards and plastic boxes of cards and the greasy towel covering the toilet bucket. Really, there were *pieces of dirt* on everything, even the old dead webs covering the bars on the stalls and the windows so crusty you couldn't see out of them. It was also covered with bird shit. There were these birds shaped like fat arrows in nests under the ceiling, and they flew in curves, going on the horses when they came in or out and diving at us while we worked nailing pieces of wood together to make the walls and door of a stall. I was scared of them at first, that they would peck my face, but Pat just smiled and said, "Get back, brother bird!" and they swerved away and out the door.

But mostly me and Chloe jumped. She was different from my mare, lighter, like she never cried in her life. When she jumped, she rounded her back so strong it almost pushed me off, pulled her legs up into her body so soft, and landed on them like a cat. Once she didn't take the jump, she ran around it, and I fell off and banged my head. I got mad and yelled at her and Pat yelled at me. "That was you, not her," she said. "She saw you missed the distance and she wasn't going to hurt herself *and you,* heinie over teakettle."

I started loving Chloe. I loved the feeling I got in my legs sometimes when I was on her, like the spot where my legs touched her sides was the best place in the world and we were both in it. I never felt that with Fiery Girl. I didn't know why and it made me feel bad. I didn't want to ask Pat about it because I didn't want to admit it.

I went to see my mare, but only once. Because I wanted to respect Pat's words, and also because I had to sneak out when Ginger and Paul were asleep and I *really* didn't want to get caught this time. When I got the courage and went, the mare seemed like she didn't like me. I brought her an apple and she ate it. But then she turned her body away from me and looked at the wall even when I hugged her neck and begged her to turn. I said, "Come on. I want to get you away from here!" And I thought to her about Pat's place and the stall we were making for her. And the leg-feeling, that I wanted to feel it with her. Still, she wouldn't turn. It was like, even *she* was mad at me for disobeying Pat.

I talked to Ginger about the leg thing. We were in the car at night, "getting lost" on the same roads we always drove. I told her how I could feel it with Chloe and not with my mare. She didn't answer for so long, it was like she didn't hear me. Then she said, "Just because you can't feel it with Fiery Girl doesn't mean it's not there. Before my sister died, I didn't feel love for her. I didn't even like her. But I did love her. I just didn't feel it."

"How could you love somebody and not feel it?"

"I don't know how to describe it."

I didn't say anything. The same trees and houses went past, slanty and shadowy, the same but still strange. Ginger's music was on, this grown woman singing like she was my age. It was ugly and fake, her making her voice like that, but I didn't care. I was remembering something from a long time ago.

Ginger said, "Before Paul there was a, a . . . boyfriend who I had a bad relationship with. We were bad to each other."

"How?"

"We just hurt each other all the time. It was awful and I always felt bad about it. But I ran into him a little while ago, and I realized there was love between us, even though we acted horrible. I was glad."

The thing I remembered: being in the car with my father. His free hand under my clothes feeling me all over for money until he found it and he took it. Because I lied and told him I didn't have it, he kept it all.

"So I'm saying, just because you haven't felt that thing with Fiery Girl yet doesn't mean it's not there. It's just not right on that spot where your legs are."

I lied. Why did I lie? The money was for emergencies—was the toll an emergency? Was he right not to see me again or even send anything?

"I used to feel something like that," said Ginger. "I felt it when I painted."

"In your legs?"

"No. In my brain. I used to think of it as a radio signal that I had to be alone to hear. I don't hear it now, but I'm hoping it's still there."

"What did it sound like?"

"I didn't actually hear it. I more felt it."

"That doesn't make sense."

"I know." There was a space between songs and I heard her breathe in, then out. The music started again.

I thought, Did my father love me but not feel it?

Ginger said, "I wonder if I can't hear it anymore because I'm not alone?"

She said it like she *was* alone. That made me feel alone.

"If so, then I'm glad I don't hear it," she said. "I'd rather hear you."

Does Dominic love me and not feel it?

Ginger reached over and put her hand on my leg. "What're you thinking?"

"Nothing."

But I was thinking, No. He feels it. He feels it.

Ginger

She made good on our deal: She filled up her math notebooks and wrote her essays with a minimum of groaning. And she'd improved, no question. It was still hard for her to read and write, harder than it should've been, given her intelligence. The one book review she did—on *Black Beauty*—was stilted and showed her boredom. The essay she did on what it was like to come and visit the country was better. The one she called "My Horse" was wonderful.

I knew she still wasn't turning her homework in. We still did it almost every week during the school year, but whenever I could actually get through to a teacher, he or she would say—with rare exceptions—that they never saw it. I stopped saying anything about it because it didn't help and at least she was learning.

Then I talked to Edie. Velvet and Edie spent time together nearly every weekend. I was very pleased by it, even if I didn't think they were true friends. The age difference was too big for that, and Velvet was subtly guarded around Edie; I almost had the impression that she was somehow "acting" for the older girl.

I was right. When Edie came by the house to pick Velvet up one day, she had to wait a bit for Velvet to change out of her horse clothes, and while Edie was waiting, she and I talked out on the porch. She said, "You must be so proud."

I said, "I am."

"For her to go from failing to the top of her grade? That's extraordinary, and it's because of you and my dad."

She must've thought I turned my head out of modesty.

"And on top of that, she's even competing at the county fair? I wish I could see her, but I'll be up at school by then."

Velvet

Ginger asked me why I said I was at the top of my grade when I wasn't even giving in my homework. I told her that I did give it in; that the teacher was lazy or just lying. She said, "*All* your teachers?" I didn't say anything. She said, "You *would* be at the top of your grade if you were turning it in." I still didn't say anything. We were sitting out in the backyard in plastic chairs. The grass smell was in our noses and the crickets were out. The neighbors were behind their fence talking about the Iraq War, how it had to happen because of the Bible. Paul was away somewhere and Ginger was drinking something, I wondered what.

She said, "Why did you tell Edie that you were going to ride at the county fair?"

"I didn't tell her that."

"Then why did she say you did?"

"I said I know somebody who's riding at the fair."

Ginger said, "If you're going to lie, you should learn to do it better than that." She said, "You keep lying to me, we aren't going to stay close. Lying creates distance between people."

"I'm not lying."

She didn't say anything. The crickets went, *I'm a boy I'm a boy, I'm a girl I'm a girl.* Ginger sipped her drink. I thought about what Shawn said, why she could be so nice. I thought about the dream of a trapdoor in her yard, and how she went down the stairs to steal treasure from hell. I thought, It's you who's the liar. "It all started in the Bible," said the neighbor man. "With an Arab woman named Hajar."

Trapdoor. I got up and walked in the back door, through the house, and out the front door. Ginger called to me, but I didn't stop. I went directly to my mare. No one was there. I opened her stall and went in. This time she didn't turn her back to me. I rubbed her neck and thought of when I took my paper for school and put it on the counter where water had spilled; I watched the words I wrote with Ginger melt and then I went to school. I thought about myself giving the clean, dry paper to the teacher and getting it back with a 4 on it. My horse put her head on my shoulder. I thought both things, the clean paper and the ruined one.

Pat says, "This mare tolerates no bullshit," and she is right. It wasn't bullshit; I was telling her the truth just standing next to her: destroying the paper but giving the teacher the paper. The county fair. Me and Fiery Girl at the county fair. It hadn't happened. But it would. I could feel it. So could my mare.

Ginger

I didn't talk to Paul about it because of how provoked he could be about what I was "doing." Sometimes he was so remote, it was like he was wearing a "Keep Out" sign on his back. In some ways I was grateful for it because it meant he was out of our way, but it was also painful.

Still, I respected the sign. So I tried to talk with Kayla, and a lot of other people too, whether I knew them or not. I got more advice than I wanted at the drugstore checkout from Danielle, the woman who ran the Cocoon Theater—who just happened to be there with Laura, a member of Becca's clique, the *artist*. I should've just kept my mouth shut, but I couldn't help it: I told them about Velvet not turning in her papers even though she did them.

"What do you expect?" said Danielle. "You're competing with her mother."

"No, I'm not."

"Oh, you are," said Laura. "And you're not going to win."

I flushed; the conversation was now about something else. "What are you saying?"

Laura answered me with a look. Danielle said, "The message you're giving her contradicts the message she's getting from her mother."

"What message do you think her mother is giving her?"

"That she wants her to fail," said Danielle. "That's why she doesn't turn in her homework. She's doing exactly what her mother wants her to do."

I thought, She's right. But it made me mad. Because she didn't even know Mrs. Vargas *or* Velvet. I said, "I don't think that's what her mother wants."

"I doubt that's what she wants either," said Laura. "She just may be highly ambivalent about somebody else messing around with her kid. Somebody white, with money, who doesn't know anything about their culture."

Danielle touched my hand. "I think you're doing something good. I support what you're doing. It just sounds . . . complicated."

She was innocent, I was pretty sure. Laura, I wanted to kill.

Velvet

When we were finished with the stall and the fence, Pat told me we could bring the mare, that I could go get her and lead her into the trailer. We hooked Pat's car to a little trailer that looked like a toy from a machine, and I was afraid to think about my horse in that thing, with nothing but a piece of metal moving between her and the road going faster than she could understand. But Pat said not to worry about it, and we got in the car.

Beverly wasn't there, but Estella was. She said good morning to Pat and nodded her nose at me. Pat positioned the trailer outside the barn door and I helped her put out a ramp for the horse to walk up. Estella stood and lit a cigarette, smoking with flat eyes, thin lips wrinkled.

Pat went into the barn first and got a small whip that was different from a crop. "You're gonna lead her, and if she doesn't go up the ramp, I'll tap her with this. Don't worry, I won't hit, just tap. Only if I need to. Maybe she'll go without it. Estella will be on her other side just in case."

Fiery Girl came out with her head up and ears forward; when she saw the trailer, her neck got stiff and she pulled on the chain. I put my hand on her neck; there was something in her I hadn't felt before, something little and *hurt,* too hurt to be bad. I tried to find it with my hand, and talked to it soft. "Just come with me," I said, "like before." She listened; she put her head down to study the ramp and snorted at it like she recognized it and did not like it. It was almost funny— then I remembered the little girl. The girl she loved brought her to a trailer and she thought she was going home and—that was the hurt. Right then the mare shied off to the side, pulling me off balance.

Estella put her cigarette in her mouth and held her arms out, blocking the mare. Fiery Girl turned back to the ramp, but crouched and tensed in her legs. I got my balance back and tried to lead. She moved away from the ramp again. Estella held out her arms and Pat clucked with her tongue, then she must've tapped with the whip because the mare whinnied and started forward. I relaxed my lead arm and fixed my eyes on the trailer. Her head went up and I felt her mind on me, but she didn't follow me. I told her it was safe. She looked to be sure I meant it, then calmed, her eyes deciding to trust me. "Good girl," I said. "Good, beautiful." Pat said, "That's right." Head high, the horse looked at the ramp again. I touched her neck. She relaxed and dropped her head a little. I rubbed her neck like I'd rub my mom's legs. I got onto the ramp. So did she. Then it was like she took a deep breath and banged up it with high, wild feet.

Estella looked at me fully then, and not like I was a little girl that she had to lift up. She took her cigarette out of her mouth and said, "Good job."

Ginger

We took her to a party that night, to celebrate bringing the horse to Pat's. It was a faculty party and normally those are terrible, but this was supposed to be for kids. There was going to be music, and Velvet wanted to go.

When we entered, the room was full of music and laughter, but the first people we saw were Becca and her editor friend, Joan. They greeted Paul, not me. My attention was pulled away by singing; in the corner, a young professor's wife was playing a guitar while a tiny, charming child sang a pop song for a circle of children. Joan was saying, "I hear you ride horses. You should come to the barn where my daughter rides." Velvet looked down, maybe confused by the friendly unfriendliness. Oblivious, Joan continued, "Edie could bring you over sometime. Would you like that?" and Velvet said, "Yea-uh," with a tinge of mockery only I heard. Becca's face softened on the girl like she was actually about to speak when there was a burst of energy and a gang of kids ran around us like happy water, pushing us a little apart. They were all younger than Velvet, much younger, with quick, animated faces, confident that they belonged and were loved above all, and they flashed around Velvet like she was a rock while right in front of me she became one. My heart sank. A writing teacher I was actually friendly with started talking to me, her smiling eyes on Velvet, trying to get a smile back. Joan touched my shoulder and said, "Let's talk about it"; Becca turned away and Joan floated after her. Paul saw someone and abruptly excused himself; Velvet's eyes followed him. "Let's get some food," said the teacher, and we did, but Velvet's face disturbed me; her expression reminded me of her mother when I first met her in the Fresh Air Fund office, sitting in her body like it was a tank. We loaded our plates and sat down with a beautiful dance instructor who seemed to be friends with the writer. I listened while they talked, and Velvet sat silently beside me, her attention elsewhere. In another part of the room, a man was somehow playing a classical song on a garden hose. Children were laughing with delight. I followed Velvet's eyes and saw she was looking at Paul, who was talking to a woman with red hair. I hadn't seen her before. She looked old to be a student; was she a new instructor? The writing teacher was saying: "My kids are taking synchronized swimming and ballet *and* tap while all the other kids are taking soccer and basketball. Laurel so excels in swimming that it affects everything else she does, and the ballet, that has given her body a special awareness as a swimmer—"

"Yes, that body awareness, it's part of everything," said the beautiful dancer. "It translates into every single aspect—"

It was lovely conversation; its loveliness was so shaped and perfect that I could not touch it. Probably there was soft feeling inside, but the outward expression was so shaped and perfect that I could not feel it. It was so shaped and perfect that it hurt, and I thought I must be very ugly to be hurt by something so lovely. I wondered what Velvet felt. Did it hurt her too? She was standing there like her mother: alone in her tank, looking like a fighter when there is no fight—or at least no fight she could understand.

"She has really blossomed in tap, the way she moves! It is *so* different from ballet, she's so serious in ballet! In tap it's like she becomes a runway model; she *vogues*! It's *dazzling,* her personality comes out in such an inventive way!"

"Velvet rides," I said. "She handles a very difficult horse that nobody else can manage."

"Oh!" said the dance instructor. "So then you know what we mean about body awareness!"

Willed goodness showed in every muscle of the woman's smiling face. Velvet looked at her and said nothing. I looked for Paul. I did not see him or the woman he'd been talking to.

"How has riding affected the other parts of your life?" said the dancer.

Velvet dropped her eyes. "Ahh dunno." Her words said, *I'm too stupid to say;* her tone said, *Your question is too stupid to answer.*

I looked for Paul again and still did not see him. Or the redhead.

Velvet

On the day after the party, Ginger and Paul took me to the county fair. It was so hot the air was fat and you could smell everything, not just the people and the food but the greasy machines that made the rides go. Paul's forehead looked like one thick wrinkle melting into the other and Ginger was sweating herself practically invisible. People were still eating warm food and ice cream that dripped down them, and throwing balls or shooting plastic guns to win toys. There was this one guy shooting at worn-out green balloons; I even remember his hot eyes and purple pimples and his shirt wet under his arms, the way he glared through his sweat and shot like he was in hell and had to do it forever. We were there to see girls racing horses around barrels and boys on bulls, but I just kept thinking about Paul standing with that red-haired woman and then they went down a hall and I didn't see them no more.

People were waiting for the barrel race on bleachers, eating and talking while music played like teeth biting at the air. Paul and Ginger sat like they were drawn in pencil; the other people on the bleachers ate and yelled and moved like they were drawn with big pens and colored in. The night before, when we got home, I expected to hear fighting—I even listened for it. But there was nothin'. I didn't get it; Ginger had to see him with her. Then a fat-assed silky voice came on the loudspeaker to make us stand up and say the Pledge of Allegiance and sing that song nobody knows and then shit happened: The bulls in deep pens banged around and this boy I'm sure was Mexican straddled the wall and looked up at the crowd like he wanted somebody to look back at him. Music came on, that song with stamping feet: "We Will Rock You." People shouted and a bull ran out with a boy on it, one arm holding, the other waving, the bull's head down, its legs mad-dancing its back up into a fist that right away punched the boy on the ground, running for the fence as soon as he hit, the bull chasing, but not really, it was like they were friends, clowns came out and pretended to bother the bull, and the bull pretended to care. The fat-ass speaker voice said these brave riders could take a cash prize back to their families in Mexico or Texas, but when the Mexican boy came playing *sharp-dressed man,* and he stayed on longer than anybody, they said he couldn't win the prize even though he didn't even get punched off, he jumped off and grabbed the fence.

"That's why," said Paul. "I think that's why. He took advantage of the fence."

If I could see it happening between him and Redhead, probably everybody saw it. Maybe that's why those women didn't respect Ginger. The ones that talked to us first.

Girls came out in flowered blouses and cowboy hats, on horses with huge muscles. I saw that one of them was Beth. I remembered how when I first saw her, I thought she had a chin like a pit bull's—her chin had basically taken over, and on her horse she was like the biggest bitch in the world. Woman-music came on and she paraded in a circle with the others while Ass-Voice said how pretty they were. *That body awareness translates into every aspect—*

And Ginger had to know—she had to—but instead of being mad at Paul, she was mad at the women that talked to us, the nice ones. On the way home from the party, she was telling Paul what a bitch the dancer lady was, and then he was annoyed at *her.*

Beth and her horse ran around barrels nearly sideways and sprayed dirt, the horse's eyes cold-hard and its legs crazy, and I was glad when her leg flew out and smacked the barrel and then her hat fell off.

Ginger said, "Do you think you'd like to do that?" I said, "No," and she said, "Why not?" I said, "I just don't." And then I said, "Remember that lady that said I could come to the other barn? Could I do that?"

Ginger didn't answer, but Paul did. He said, "I think that's a good idea. It would be interesting to see what another barn is like."

I looked at Ginger to see if she heard that like I did—but then everybody went "Wahhhh!" and I saw this bull was going to kill a boy for real. He was running for his life while his goofy music played *Bored! Born! Bored!* and he barely got over the fence—*Born to be alive!*—before the bull slammed its horns into the wall just under the boy's butt, then went after the clowns. I said, "Damn!" and Ginger and Paul both smiled at me. The bull got tired and decided to go back into the pit.

Then out of nowhere, I heard Shawn's voice, like *really* heard it, like in my ear, saying, *Lil' Orphan Annie.* Which did make some sense because I felt alone.

Ginger

She didn't call me when she got home that night and when I called her she didn't really want to talk. She sounded happy to hear from me, but she was quiet. She didn't respond when I mentioned coming to ride on the weekend.

When I called her the following week, her mother talked harshly at me and then handed the phone to her brother. He said, "She's asleep"; he said it the same way Velvet said "Ahh dunno" at the faculty party. There was cartoon noise in the background; I pictured him in the dark with a flashing television. "Can you ask her to call me when she wakes up?" "Sure," he said. Then he put the phone down. He didn't hang up, he just put it down. I thought maybe he was going to wake her right then so I stayed on the line. Cartoons talked, commercials flashed in the gaps, there was running water and Mrs. Vargas talking to someone somewhere in the jumbled distance. I thought it must be Velvet until I heard the boy answer. Still, I waited several minutes before hanging up.

Velvet

The night I came home I asked my mother why I never heard from my father. Why he sent money and birthday cards, but only sometimes, and only to Dante, not me. Even though people say mothers love their sons more, but fathers love their daughters more. At least that's what Mrs. Vasquez from our old building said when I told her my mom liked Dante better than me. I didn't get into that with my mom, though. I just asked why I didn't hear from him. She said, "Sit down. I'm going to tell you something." I sat down. She said, "The man you call your father isn't your father. He's Dante's father, but not yours." I said, "But I called him Papi and he answered." She said, "I asked him to do that."

I said, "But he gave me the shells."

"No he didn't. I did. I found them on the beach at Providence while I was pregnant with you. I kept them for you."

I couldn't talk anymore. She came to me and put her arms around me. My head went against her; she smelled to me like she used to, like safety. My body trembled, but I didn't cry. It felt too bad for that. She said, "I'm sorry. But you are old enough to know the truth. I haven't seen your father since I left DR. He said he would come for me, but he didn't. Now you know what I mean when I say 'bad blood.'"

I moved away from her and her arms came off me. I stood up. "Just because he didn't come for you doesn't mean I'm bad."

She looked like she was going to slap me, but she didn't. She looked like I slapped her; she even put her hand to her face. I was going to say I was sorry, but then she said, "Something else you need to know. I lost my job and I need to rent your room out. When I do, you'll have to sleep on the couch."

Ginger

I called again the first week of school and nobody answered the phone. But the next day a teacher from Velvet's school called me. She wanted me to know that Velvet had turned in a beautiful paper about a horse; she said it was probably the most beautiful paper she'd ever seen from a student. Technically, she wasn't supposed to call me, but she knew it would really matter to me, and she wanted to tell me. I said, "How did Velvet react when you told her?" "I haven't yet," said the woman. "Velvet hasn't been in school all week and I can't get her mother on the phone. Do you know what's going on?"

Velvet

My first week at school they beat a old man and made him crawl on glass. If I said that to Ginger she would say, "'They'? Who is 'they'? Be specific." And I would be thinking, What difference does it make? They beat a old man. Anyway, I didn't know who they were; they weren't in my grade.

But I saw them doing it. It was the morning before the school opened. Most kids stand by the door waiting to go in, but I walked away from them that day because I was missing my horse and also thinking about what my mom told me, and how she looked at me when I said I wasn't bad just because my father didn't want her. Or me. I walked to the side of the school and I saw these older kids in the back, way at the end of the basketball court, crowding around. Even from far away it looked like something bad. But I mind my own business, and anyway the doors were open and my homeroom teacher, Mr. Stamford, was yelling at me.

They next day the homeroom teachers yelled at all of us. They used words like *vicious* and *decency*. They said the old man was small and crazy and the boys said they would burn him and made him crawl on the glass while they kicked him; Mr. Stamford yelled about jail. Teachers have been yelling at us about jail since first grade, so somebody just said something funny in the back and people laughed. "That could've been your father or your grandfather!" yelled Mr. Stamford. But it couldn't. Not mine. I didn't have a father or grandfather anymore.

Ginger

I finally got her on the phone. I told her how proud I was that she turned in her essay. I asked her what the teacher said to her about it. She said, "Nothin'." I said, "What do you mean? How could she tell me it was great and tell you nothing?" She said, "Ahh dunno" and then, abruptly, asked me if I could get her into a better school. How could I do that? I asked. What kind of school? She said, This girl Marisol is going to Catholic school next year. "What kind of grades does Marisol get?" I asked, and she snapped at me. "If you can get your grades up, I'll talk to Paul about it," I said without hope. "And then we can talk to your mother."

She didn't even mention her horse.

Velvet

After school I walked around looking for Dominic. I went to the block where I first met him with Strawberry and walked around it, like, three times. These little kids were staring the crap out of me. I kept my hand on my cell, hoping he might call, even though how could he? I never gave him my number.

I kept thinking, What would he do? I knew he wouldn't kick a old man, but would he just walk away or would he try to stop them? What would it be like to crawl on the ground while people kicked you? What would it be like to kick somebody like that, with everybody else doing it too? I went back to the school and went to look at the place. There was still glass on the ground and something that was maybe blood. I *felt,* but not a normal feeling that you can say what it is. It didn't come from inside me, it came *to* me, like a echo, far away, but from *everywhere.* Except I didn't hear it, I felt it on my skin and in my body.

What Shawn said, that Ginger could be nice because people like her got other people to do the violence for them; I didn't understand what he meant, but it felt true. Ginger in the car, talking to me about Fiery Girl loving me and the thing she could only hear by herself—that was true too. I knew because now I was hearing it.

Paul

When Ginger mentioned sending Velvet to Catholic school I said, "We can't take that on; it's too much." She said she thought something bad was happening at the school, that Velvet was acting strange. I said bad things are always happening at school at that age; bad things will happen at Catholic school too; we can't protect her from her life. She pushed and I blew up. I didn't say anything I hadn't said before, but my voice was more angry than my words and I could see her shut down inside. She didn't storm out of the room, she just got quiet and looked away. I knew I should put my arms around her, or at least touch her; if I'd done that, it would've been all right. But I couldn't. Polly had broken with me just hours before. She'd gotten her degree and she was going away.

Velvet

The truth of Shawn and the truth of Ginger were both real, but I couldn't be in them at the same time. I wanted to talk to Shawn about it, because he was the only one who might understand. So I called him. But he didn't call back. He blew up my phone all spring, but I never called him back. Now he didn't pick up the phone at all.

Ginger

I told her we couldn't do Catholic school because we couldn't afford it. She was quiet and then said, "I understand." I don't remember what we talked about then, just that she kept stopping to scream at her brother, who was screaming at her. I asked when she wanted to come ride. She said she didn't know, she needed to help her mother at home. Her mother didn't have her job anymore and they needed to get the house clean so that they could get a boarder.

I wanted to talk to Paul and I couldn't. I couldn't even feel him when I lay next to him that night, except distantly, like something chaotic happening somewhere far away from me.

Paul

They say that your partner always knows when you "cheat," even if it's unconscious knowledge. But I don't think Ginger did. She was too focused on that damn kid. It was almost insulting.

Velvet

Shawn never answered, so I thought his phone got lost or stole. I went to his house. I knocked at the door for a long time and his grandma finally came. Her face was deep, her eyes were so deep I was scared to look at them. I saw she didn't remember who I was and, looking at her face, I didn't want to say.

"What you want, girl?"

"Is Shawn home?"

Her eyes remembered me; they remembered and they hurt. I said, "When will he be back?"

She said, "Baby, Shawn's dead. You didn't know? They shot him."

Music played from cars driving by; *supersonic, hypnotic, funky fresh.* A chill went through me. *This beat flows right through my chest.* I said, "Who shot him? Why?"

"There is no 'why.' He was with a boy had a beef with some other boys. He was just there. That's what they told me."

I said, "Sorry," but it didn't come out. Still, she heard.

"It's not your fault, baby," she said. "Thanks for comin' by. Now you go home." She started to close the door.

I said, "When was it?"

"Fifteen days ago. Saturday before last."

Saturday before last: that was the day of the county fair, when I heard Shawn in my head saying "lil' Orphan Annie."

Real soft she said, "You look older than you are, don't you? You probably no more than fourteen years old."

"I'm thirteen."

"Thirteen," she said, shaking her head. "Thirteen." She closed the door.

I went away from the house and sat on some steps a few doors down. Music still played from cars, different songs crossing each other. I tried to hear the song that played when I met Shawn. But it was gone. People walked by. I touched my face with my hand; my skin felt thick and numb.

I thought: I want my mare. I want to put my arms around her neck and feel her feeling me.

I didn't have Pat's number, so I called Ginger. She wasn't there and Paul didn't answer either. I called twice and then I called Ginger's cell. She didn't pick up. *Lil' Orphan Annie.*

I didn't leave a message. I put my cell in my pocket and went to pick up Dante.

Ginger

I didn't go to the New York meeting to find him. When I did find him, I didn't approach him. It was enough to know he was there, and that no harm would come, that goodwill lived between us. But, at the tail end of the meeting after the meeting, he came to me. He said, "I'm sorry. I'm sorry for how I was, everything." I said, "I am too." He put his arm around me, and without thinking, I put my hand on his heart. I said, "Can we go somewhere and talk?" His eyes thought off to the side and then he said, "Yes."

As we walked out, my enemy-friend from a long time ago stared me in the face. But I didn't care about her.

We walked for blocks looking for someplace quiet; every restaurant or coffee shop was loud and crowded. I talked nervously. I said that when I had met him I did not know how to be part of life. He said, So now you know? I said, I'm figuring it out. I'm married and I'm fostering a child. I felt this statement touch him, though I wasn't sure how. He said he lived nearby, that if I wanted, we could go to his place.

I realized I was afraid like this: He offered to make us tea, and when he opened a drawer, instead of spoons, he took out a large knife and held it up in his fist. I stood and shouted, "Put that down now!" He laughed and said, "It was a joke." I sat down and we had tea. His phone rang and he answered. I checked my phone; Velvet had called but left no message. He was talking to a woman; I could hear her angry voice. He was telling her that his plans had changed unexpectedly; he said, "Trust me." She hung up on him. He said, "That was my girlfriend." I stood and said, "I guess I should go." He said, "No. Let's go into the other room."

The trapdoor opened and I went down the stairs.

Velvet

I tried to sit and watch *Napoleon Dynamite* with Dante, but I couldn't, not with Shawn dead, sit there and act like nothing happened. I couldn't talk about it to my mother and I didn't want Dante to hear it anyway.

So I waited until just before my mom would be home and then I went to Lydia. I had not been there for a year, but I saw her sometimes on the street and she was nice to me. So I went to her door. Her daughter Kristal answered wearing a shirt with Tweety Bird on it; she was only a few years older than me, but in a year her body had grown up all the way even in that shirt. She didn't let me in; she went to get her mom. Lydia opened the door, but she didn't let me in at first either. She just went, "What up, sweetheart?" with not much sweet. When I told her why I couldn't go home, her voice got so hard she almost shut the door with it. "Then you have to go to the police," she said. "I can't help you."

"But the police know," I said, and I was crying then. "It happened while I was up riding horses and I just found out. His grandmother told me."

"Why don't you go home then, baby?" she said. I told her because my mom lost her job and had too many bad things already, and she opened the door. She put her hand on me and asked if he was my boy, and I said no, he was just a boy, but we talked sometimes, and she said, "Come in and sit with us, then. We just sittin' together. Don't talk about it—my babies don't need to hear it. But just sit and watch some TV with us." And she let me stop crying and then we went in with her family and she sat with me on the couch with her arm around me while a little boy and his girl twin watched Madea.

Ginger

When I called her back, her mother put her brother on the phone again. He said, "She's not here." It was dark by then, so I said, "Where is she?" And he said, "I don't know." His voice wasn't scared but almost high-spirited, as if he were delighted by some funny thing. He said, "My mom says Velvet's going to live in a box on the street." I said, "But she's not doing that now, is she?" And he said, "Nooooo." I said, "Then tell her to call me when she comes back, okay?"

I got off and felt how bad I wanted to sit outside in the cold and drink. I put on a jacket and a scarf. I poured myself some pomegranate juice, mixed it with lime, soda, and a ton of sugar. I went outside and drank it and thought of Michael.

We kissed with our whole mouths, but the feeling was delicate, too delicate for sex. He touched my face and we held each other. I sang a song to him, a nonsense song from when we were teenagers, and he looked it up online to see who it was by because I didn't know. It was so gentle, like something young springing from inside age, smiling and sweet like I was never able to be in middle school, or high school, or when I knew this man nearly two decades ago; in that foolish moment, the hard glass of my girlhood became flesh as if for the first time.

Middle school; where Velvet was.

Velvet

Kristal said to come in the kitchen and help her get some soda and chips, and when we were in there, she said, "You can stop by on Friday if you want to. Lydia's goin' out that night, and I'm taking care of the kids. You can come. Maybe you can stay when I go out. I'll give you a little cash."

I said, "Okay, let me find out."

Madea said, "Sometimes I look at you, I don't know if you got a mirror or a friend."

I wanted to ask Kristal why she called her mom "Lydia," but I didn't. I was tired, and everything was strange. I wanted to see the old Haitian lady. On the way home, I hoped I would see her. If I knew where she was, I would've gone to find her, but I didn't know.

Ginger

The phone rang in my lap; I picked it up and said, "Honey, what's going on? It's late; why were you out?"

"It's before ten," she said.

I said, "It's still late for you."

She ignored that and said, "When can I come up there? I want to see my horse."

"You know you can come whenever your mother says it's okay. But your voice sounds different. Why haven't you been talking to me?"

She was quiet a long moment. Then she said she hadn't been going to school, that she thought I'd be mad at her.

"Honey," I said, "why aren't you going to school?"

"Something bad happened."

"Listen," I said. "Something bad happened this summer. You got thrown off a horse and got a concussion and you got kicked out of the barn. But you kept riding and now you've moved your horse to a better place where you can ride her again. You *walked your path*. You asked me how to do that; now you know because you did it. Keep walking your path."

She listened to me. I could tell. Because I believed my words and she could hear it in my voice. Of course I believed it. If a man who had told me I wasn't worth anything could hold me and kiss me and I could sing him a song, then any good thing might happen. If what I had longed for, blindly and brokenly, and struggled like an animal to find in the most unlikely form, if it had really been there and was now simply, gently revealed—any good thing might happen. Anything.

"Ginger," she said, "somebody I know got shot. This boy who didn't even do nothing."

Velvet

I went back to school. Ginger said, "You've got to, you've got to," and she sounded so fucked-up I felt bad for her and also I needed to see my horse. I didn't act different in class or in the lunchroom and I didn't take bullshit from anybody. But I paid more attention to teachers even when everybody else was clowning and throwing gummed-up paper at everything. I did some work and gave it in.

When school got out, I went to the block where I first met Dominic and walked around there until it was time to go get Dante. I saw the same little kids who stared at me before. Once I saw Mrs. Henry, who took care of Strawberry, and she talked to me. I saw boys who said, "Dayum, you need to break me off a piece of that, girl." Except for one who said, "Charlie, I don't think so. Look at her eyes, that girl is a hundred miles away, she is aficionado, she belongs to somebody for sure, she's in love."

That even made me smile. But I didn't see Dominic.

I tried not to think about it. I thought about my horse instead. I thought about her following me up into the van, the way her feet looked confused and almost funny, like somebody acting scared by running with their feet high. But my mind kept coming back to his lips and his hands touching me, his open legs, his eyes flashing as he turned to look at me over one shoulder and then the other; feeling flashed at the memory, all through my whole body, moving and breathing, coming out my skin and eyes, quiet and wild in the air. *Where are you, where are you, where are you?*

I thought, This is stupid. This is the last day I'll do this.

That was the day I saw him.

He was with the boys who said break off some of that, and he looked at me like they did before he saw me. I stopped; his face changed. He turned from the other boys and said my name. The other boys looked away, then moved away, just a step, but it was like a mile. He said, "How you doin'?" I said, "Okay. How you doin'?" He shook his head and said, "Like hell." And we started walking like we planned it. He said, "You know about Shawn?"

"Yeah. You know what happened?"

"Yeah, it was crazy. He was just standing next to Angel on the corner—"

"What corner? Where was it, in Williamsburg?"

"No, Bushwick. On a corner of Harmon, Irving—I dunno. This guy Juan, he's beefin' with Angel, he come up with his crew and had words and they shot Angel and Shawn."

"That's crazy."

We didn't talk for a minute. He said, "So, you were with him?"

"Not really. Once or twice. I—"

"Wha'd your grandfather say about that?"

"Dominic, my grandfather's dead."

"That old man, that night? He died?"

"No, my grandfather died three years ago. I never even met him. But that night, that man called me granddaughter, and I called him grandfather before I knew what I was saying."

"You a strange girl."

His eyes flashing while he walked away with Brianna and some girl, one shoulder then the other. "Vete pal carajo," I said, then *I* turned and walked away.

"Hey, no, wait," he said, "wait, you want to get something to eat?"

"I'm not strange."

"I don't mean it bad, I mean more like, you complicated."

"I have to pick up my little brother in an hour."

"We can be quick."

"And why you asking me about Shawn when you with that nasty ho Brianna and also with her equally nasty friend, that is some ratre-ria shit."

His face was surprised, like, *You funny,* but *soft* too, his open lips and eyes and even his nose so soft they were *blurry.* But when he closed his lips, the shape of them was *cutting.* "I don't know what friend you mean—"

"Janelle, for one."

"Oh, she—" He smiled, like embarrassed. "She seventeen. And Brianna's almost seventeen. I'm seventeen, and Shawn is—I mean *was*—older than me, and you a little girl."

"No, I'm not."

"You the same age as my little sister."

"I'm not your little sister."

He smiled and my body flashed sick-hard.

"Okay, big girl, why don't you come eat with me?"

I thought he would take me for pizza. But instead we went blocks away to this place on Grand, with Christmas lights, where my mom took me and Dante once for New Year's a long time ago. I got a mango drink; he got salami and cheese.

"Why do you call me complicated?" I said.

"I don't mean nothin' bad." He moved his chair around so he was next to me. I was embarrassed, but the man behind the counter looked with nice eyes. Dominic said, "I just mean you diff'rent. I felt it the first time I saw you. It's in how you carry yourself—even when you was *eleven!*"

"That's why they say I'm a conceited wannabe."

"You think I care what girls in school say? I can see you ain't any a that. You just diff'rent. I don't know how. But it ain't about white people or horses neither."

And then he kissed me on the side of my head. "But I'd like to see you on a horse!"

Paul

Ginger wasn't even going to tell me about the boy. She wasn't going to tell me because she thought I wouldn't want to hear it, but it woke her in the middle of the night; I could feel her body pulling against itself as she turned and turned in place like some old animal.

"You're helping her," I said. "Ginger, you're doing everything you can. It's amazing what you've done. It's amazing what *she's* done, and she knows it, and that will hold her in good stead."

I held her close and stroked her heart, and I felt her slowly become right again: fragile, strangely young, but strong, with the fanatic strength that thin girls sometimes have, more fierce nerves than muscle. I remembered that night she said, "I want to be a woman! I want to be a normal woman!" It was as if her whole body said that now, that she wanted to be a woman, she wanted to protect this girl.

I wasn't sure I believed what Velvet had told her: that the murdered boy had done nothing wrong, that the girl didn't know the people he'd been with when he'd died. But right then, it didn't matter. If she'd asked about Catholic school then, I would've said yes.

Ginger

I thought: I have a good man. What happened with Michael was a blessing. But his body has no feeling like this. Even now, even though he's better than he was. It was wonderful to see him. But I'm not in middle school. She is and she needs me. I may not be a normal woman. But I can pretend. I can try.

Velvet

When Ginger dropped me at Pat's, Pat waited till Ginger drove away—then she took my shoulders and looked in my eyes. "What happened to *you*?" she said.

"Nothin'."

"*Nothin*'? Then why do you look like you got hit by a truck doin' sixty?"

I looked down and didn't say.

She let go of me. She said, "Make that a truck doin' eighty. C'mon, let's get to work."

And we went and worked on jumping Fiery Girl. Who did not want to jump. Chloe and Nut watched from their side of the paddock while we trotted around and around and I tried to make her go over the jump and she would not go. Pat yelled, "Be clear! You're not being clear! You decide and you get your legs on her and tell what you want to do!" But I couldn't be clear because nothing was clear. There was Dominic's lips on me and an old man crawling on glass and Shawn dead and his eyes and Dominic's eyes and my body burning all the time and the noise coming in all night while I lay on the couch, some idiot yelling. I kicked Fiery Girl and told her to jump, but all I wanted to do was look at my phone and see if Dominic texted, even though he hadn't even once. The only clear thing I could feel was that Fiery Girl was scared of jumping and she was getting pissed at me, and still I couldn't focus right. She was starting up with this crazy jog-dance when Pat yelled, "Whoa!" and came and took the rein sideways in her hand.

"What are you doing?" she said. "This poor horse looks like she's hearing ten different things from five different riders, and she's getting ready to say, 'Shut the F up!'"

"She's scared of the jump, Miss Pat."

"I see that. I also see you're doing one thing with your hands and another with your legs and your head is all over the place."

"I'm sorry."

"Dismount. We're going to get focused and work on trust."

What that meant was leading Fiery Girl where she didn't want to go. First I walked her through mud puddles, which she did not like. Then we walked on this piece of shiny tarp that Pat brought out. She didn't want to. I had to make her, gently. It sounds boring, but it wasn't. Because I felt her through the line, at first just her normal mouth-self and then something that was soft and round and just starting not to be afraid. And there it was: the leg-feeling. It was in my hands, but it was the same. Dominic and the poor man and Shawn and everything else was there, but it was in the distance and this feeling was here now.

Girl, where I am now is basically a trap house. You don't wanna come there. But give me your number. Maybe I'll come see you one night when you're over at what's her name, Lydia's? When the other girl's got something else to do, maybe I'll be up around your way.

I thought: He will. He hasn't. But he will. I don't have to worry; it's over there in the corner, waiting to happen.

Then Pat gave me some peppermints and I got my mare to follow me without the line. We walked on the tarp again, and in the puddle, sometimes me giving her a mint. Then Pat lowered the pole on the jump so it was almost on the ground. My horse hopped over the pole and broke into a run. Across the paddock, Chloe tossed her head and ran too; Nut chased her, bucking and farting.

"Can you come next weekend?" said Pat. "Next weekend I bet she takes the jump."

I said yes, and I meant it.

But I didn't do it.

Silvia

"You don't need to ride a horse—you need your own feet on the *ground*. Take your dumb face out of the mirror and listen to me! There's no man out there you can trust, and if you forget that, next thing you know, your belly's out to *here* and you're watching the door for somebody who never comes."

She said, "Mami, I'm thirteen," and put on more of that greasy lip gloss, which I grabbed away so hard I crushed off the tip. She yelled like she does, like a stupid animal, like she can't even talk, "Na-urhhh!" like an elephant or a cow. I mocked her and laughed at her. I said, "You think I don't know how old you are? The day I gave birth to you was the loneliest day of my life. No one was here except your aunt Maria, she was the only one, and she was already half dead." She didn't care, she just grabbed for the lip gloss. "Listen, you ungrateful girl, I'm trying to educate you. Watch yourself! Men are babies screaming for love. They get it, they throw it across the room until it breaks and then start screaming again. And always some dumb woman comes running. It makes no difference to them if it's you or the one before you or the one after you or the one down the street."

She said, "Just because my father—!"

And I took off my house slipper and slapped her face good. She started crying and I said, "You think that hurts, llorona? Wait till *he* hits you."

She said, "*He* wouldn't hit me," and I hit her again. Because I knew it. I was right. If I push her enough, she always lets the truth out. She can't hold anything back.

Ginger

The next weekend she was supposed to come, she didn't show. I waited at Penn Station for half an hour before calling her at home. Her mother yelled into the phone; it was somehow comforting, like she was yelling on my behalf. Her brother came on and said Velvet was asleep. He said she'd been out late and a social worker was coming. I asked him why a social worker was coming. He said, "I don't know, she's from the school. She comes when my sister does something bad." "Like what?" I asked. But I guess something interesting must've happened on the TV because he didn't answer me. I said, "Can you go wake your sister up?" and he said, "Okay."

I waited on the phone for almost ten minutes. I was about to hang up when a tornado of screaming voices came up behind the cartoon noise. I waited, thinking that Velvet was coming. The screaming went on. The cartoons got louder. I hung up. It was nearly winter and my toes and hands were cold. I went into Penn Station to get a hot chocolate and walked around drinking it. I stared at the jumbled food nooks and windows filled with cheap shit: crazy-print panty hose, boxes of chenille gloves and hats, teddy bears, glass roses, Empire State knickknacks, magazines crammed with exhausting opinions and worthless pictures it cost thousands of dollars to take. Pretzels. Pizza. Squashed sandwiches and big, biliously iced cookies. Lights buzzing, music pumping, people yelling orders and wiping surfaces; so much honest effort put into so much ugliness, everyone worn out by it but still doing their job to push it out the chute. All of it probably overrun by rats at night. A crazy guy pointed at me and laughed.

What was I going to tell Paul?

I called her again. She picked up the phone and said she was sorry. "I'm sorry too," I said. "I spent time and money to come all this way for nothing and you can't even come to the phone?"

She was silent.

"You know what, we don't have to talk about it," I said. "I'm too angry to talk." I hung up.

I would tell him she texted and canceled because she was sick, and that I didn't get the text until I was already halfway into the city.

Velvet

The next time I came, Pat was mad at me too. She said she made time for me that weekend and that Fiery Girl was expecting to see me. She said, "You ever read something called *The Little Prince*?"

"No." Really, I was supposed to read it last year in school, but I didn't.

"Okay. In that book it says once you tame something, you are responsible for it. You tamed that horse, you understand?"

We walked to the barn. The ground was cold mud in hard, frowning shapes. The long grass was smeared with dry mud and the garden was nothing but dirt and dead plants bent over and broken, with bits of green trying to live.

I felt the hardness of it even more than I felt my horse. Fiery Girl was warm under me and she snorted peacefully. But she would still not jump. She wasn't afraid—that wasn't why. It was because she could feel I had no jump in me. All I could feel was the cold hardness and stillness of the ground.

At least Pat wasn't mad at me for that.

Ginger

Mrs. Vargas's friend called and asked for me. Mrs. Vargas was in the room, I could hear her, but it was her friend who spoke English on the phone. She said, Silvia wants you to know Velvet's report card had an A on it. They wrote a note on it saying she's done better than ever, even though she didn't come enough. She says because of that, please have her for Christmas. She's getting into trouble here and Silvia knows she'll be safe with you.

It was the first time she'd ever said please. It was the first time I'd heard her first name.

Paul

The day before Christmas, the family met us at Penn Station and we went to eat at the same diner we'd gone to before. Ginger gave the boy a Hot Wheels car and his mom a gift card from Macy's. Mrs. Vargas presented us with candles.

"Ahh," said the boy, "the tradition continues!" He said it in English; he also said it sarcastically. He was much sharper this year.

I sat across from him and, while his mother and sister triangled with my wife, he and I talked about horror movies and cartoons. I asked him what he thought he'd be when he grew up and he didn't miss a beat. He said, "I'll be a statue of the suffering of hell."

"I don't think they make statues like that, Dante." Though of course, they do.

"Then I'll make it myself," he said. "I'll make it out of the junkyard."

I said, "That's great," and he burped, which made his mom slap his head.

It wasn't until much later that it occurred to me he was referring to the kind of elaborate graveyard statue you see in horror movies. That he was saying, basically, I'm going to grow up to be dead.

Velvet

The tree was still beautiful and they still had my favorite striped glass ball. But I kept thinking of that night we went to the party and Paul disappeared with that red-haired woman. I didn't know if everything was the same with them or if they were pretending, and so nothing seemed the same to me. So I pretended and waited until I could walk to the barn. Even *that* wasn't the same since Fiery Girl wasn't there anymore, but still I walked over in the cold, steam coming out my mouth like I was a horse. Half the sky was full of white clouds; the other half was black with a lot of stars. There was ice in the paddock where I first rode.

It ain't what it was with Shawn. You know that.

The horses moved and breathed when they heard me, but I didn't hear them talk. I realized I hadn't heard them talk for a long time. Maybe because I wasn't a kid anymore? I went to Joker because I hadn't seen him since the day me and Fiery Girl rode past. He was glad to see me but too nervous to pet; he kept moving around and then he sneezed in my eye. It made me almost laugh, but I wanted to touch somebody, so I looked for Reesa, my first horse. She was lying down and I wanted to curl up against her, even though it's not safe. But I couldn't because she got up when I opened her stall. She looked at me with such soft eyes and stood quiet and let me get warm on her. I remembered how it felt that first time. I felt love for her. I rubbed her and scratched her back where she liked it and looked out her window at the night. It started snowing.

You know I have love for you. You love me?

It was late when he finally came. The kids, Rochelle and Jason, were asleep. He came in looking angry, then I realized, no, scared. Something happened, but he wouldn't say what it was, said I shouldn't know. He kept walking around. He said they wouldn't come here because nobody knew about here. They'd go to Brianna's place; he needed to stay with me. Did I know when Kristal would come back? I didn't know exactly, but I knew it would be late, he could stay until then. Jason heard us, I guess, because he came in the room holding his little three-year-old dick and looking sleepy-bug-eyed at Dominic until I kissed him and put him back in bed. When I came back in the living room, Dominic had calmed himself down. He sat close to me on the couch, but he didn't look at me; he texted. I could smell him, and the smell of him scared me and I didn't know why. I tried to bring back the warm feeling of when he crouched down with his legs open, but this was not like that. His sideways face was hard, and his hands didn't care about anything but texting. He worked his phone. I didn't move, but still I went toward him in waves, hurting to touch him. He closed the phone and put it on the table. He looked at me; he started to talk, then he stopped. His eyes saw my feeling, and I let him see it all the way. He said he had to do something and he picked up his phone again. He opened it and stared at it. He put it down and looked at me. He touched my face with his hand. I had words I couldn't say, but he heard and answered by kissing my mouth—quick, like he meant to move away. But he didn't. For a second he pulled back and I felt him soft, waiting like a horse, waiting for me to tell him which way to move. Like a horse, he heard my answer before I knew I gave it, and we kissed for real, and he made these noises, little noises that said *Please, please let me close, please let me inside,* and because the noises were so baby, I touched the back of his head like to protect him. Next thing I knew, he kneeled and pushed my legs apart, and put his hands and head on my breast. I pulled my shirt up and he touched them and kissed them. It felt so good I got scared and my body trembled. He rose up and kissed my face and said, "Don't be scared. I ain't gonna hurt you, boo. We ain't gonna do it all, I can't, I'm with Brianna."

"If you with her, why you with me like this? Why you callin' me 'boo'?"

"I don't know, I shouldn't. But I need to touch you. I wanna feel you next to me. We can at least do that, right? You know I have love for you. You love me?"

I said yes by kissing, and we went in the next room, where there was a bed. We took off our shirts and I saw words on his chest tattooed in BIG mad-beautiful letters, like: *You humbled my adversaries* and *I destroyed my foes* and *18:39*. It was so wicked serious I almost put my shirt back on. I said, "Is that, like . . . from the *Bible?*" "It's from a letter my uncle wrote me," he said. "From prison. But yeah, he got it from the Bible." "You believe in that?" I asked. He said, "Not in a bible-ass way. I ain't even read it mostly. But this I like. And my uncle, he like a father to me." I touched his chest with my hand and kissed it. I took off my bra and we pressed hearts together. We talked about his uncle and about Shawn and how my grandfather talked to me, and what happened that night after I went home. About his sister and how he got split up from her when his mom moved in with this boss up in Washington Heights. Also about Fiery Girl; the time I talked to her and she talked back to me and I cleaned her dirty stall. He told me about how he used to think he could be an actor. He said he acted at this charter school he used to be at before he got kicked out for assaulting a teacher; they put on plays and he was Romeo in one of them. I laughed. I said, "You mean like *wherefore art thou?*" and he said, "Yeah, you don't believe me?" I said, "No!" just to be that way, and he promised the next time he saw me he'd show me the picture of it that his teacher took.

And the whole time we were talking, we were touching everything. I took off everything except my panties and he touched everything until it was like a dream. He unzipped his pants and I saw him. There was nothing ugly or crocodile—no. Because it was *him*, even more than his face, and I kissed it like it was his face. I heard him laugh very soft and I looked up. Was kissing it stupid? But I saw his eyes soft and his lips smiling, and I smiled too. He said, "Go on, beauty, don't be afraid. It ain't what it was with Shawn. You know that. Open your mouth, love me. Show me love."

Reesa lay down again, curled with her nose down almost in her bedding. I went and sat against her body for heat. Out the window, the snow was like the beginning of a old black-and-white movie where they show the outside of the house in the snow and then the inside where everybody's living the story. I took out my phone and looked. Nothing.

Ginger

We drove at night, but she didn't talk and she frowned at my music, like it was distracting her from disappearing into her music—this goopy Spanish stuff, all love songs except for one with snarling dogs and gunfire and guys yelling *"Ronca!"* That song was the best, all threat and flash in the dark, but when I told her I liked it, she just stared straight ahead, and I remembered her friend who died.

Something else was different too. She stopped leaning against me when we sat to watch TV. When I put my arm around her, she went still under my touch. I thought she was rejecting me, then I realized it was worse: She had lost her trust in touch. Not just *my* touch, all touch. I still touched her, out of habit; my hand on her back, her arm, her forehead when I said good-night. She stayed remote. Someone had made touch into something else for her and I could not change it back.

Velvet

That Christmas Fiery Girl took the jumps—not just one, but four in a row. It was cold, but the ground was firm and dry with no ice or slush, and I put my legs on her like *business,* not feeling. Because I was going to find a way to be in a competition, get points, and be in a bigger competition where I could win some money and buy clothes and do my hair and go to that club and find Dominic.

That's all I thought about back home, trying to sleep on the couch with people brawling at each other outside and their cars pumping music so hard it pumped up in the walls of my building. That's all I thought about when I was on the mare, and damn, she seemed to get it. The one time she gave me trouble in the stall, lifting her head and resisting the bit, I slapped her mouth and *she minded.* "Real smart," said Pat. "You just smacked somebody that outweighs you by a thousand pounds." But when I took her out, that horse took the jumps better than ever, better than Chloe, fiercer, like she's gonna *eat 'em.* When we were done, she cantered proudly, and I remembered that on the couch, watching lights and shadows tangled on my ceiling, hearing voices and music tangled with pretend pictures of me at the club; Dominic's face when he saw me looking bad—everybody would see it.

That's what I was thinking when we were in the subway going to Macy's. Normally that is not a place we would ever go, but Ginger had gotten my mom a gift card. I had to go to translate, and we couldn't leave Dante, so there we were on the subway, my mom complaining that she could only get junk with this card, Dante dumping potato chips on her head, me waiting for her to hit him, her not even noticing but bitching at me instead. Then the train broke down and we had to get off in Manhattan and wait for another train. My mom started laughing over these stupid white girls wearing colored sneakers in winter, but I wasn't listening because these Indian-kinda dudes with scarves on their heads were playing for change on little wooden flutes with a machine on the floor making the song like it was from a movie. *Oh my love, my darling, I hunger for your touch. I need your love, I want your love.*

That's when she hit me in the face. "You stupid girl, you give everything away! In front of people!"

The train came in screaming. We got on it pushing. Huge tired people pushed in between me and my family and I faced the flying tunnel out the back door of the last car, hiding my hit face.

My mom got a purse and crap gloves that day. That night I got up off the couch. I waited until they were asleep and I found my old birthday shirt Ginger gave me. I saw it wasn't any good; it was made to go with a summer skirt and also it was only cute, not hot-cute. If I couldn't be fly with my clothes, I had to make it like I'm so fly I don't even have to *try*, work my face instead. So I put on my black jeans and my Puma hoodie with the silver cat and the silver hoops I stole with Strawberry. I made up my face in the kitchen, by the window where all the light came in, I put gold around my eyes. I left my North Face jacket open so you could see the silver on my chest. And I went out to find that club again.

The street was poppin', not too cold for people to be mobbed-up around cars, music and powerful feeling up in the air. I walked with my head down and myself pulled in—people looked, but left me be. Until I got to the bus stop. I had to wait and then it was like, Hey, Mami, what's up? Can I talk to you? Oh, you waitin' for your boyfriend, that's awright. Except this one dude, he's like So is your boyfriend a black man? Where is he? Why he keep you waitin' here? It was starting to be aggravating when this woman suddenly came down on the dude like a Rottweiler, pulling the whole show away from me, but screamin' about me, You can't wait two minutes to work on some underage pussy? I looked away. She's going, You said you loved me! And he's, You crazy ho-bag. I as good as told you, you were just emergency pussy till the real shit come back!

I thought it was just boys who fronted this shit, boys in my grade acting stupid. This was a man and he was not acting.

Anyway, at least the bus came before they did anything else, and nobody was on it but some asleep bad-smelling people and a lady my mom's age who looked like she was coming home from work. I looked out the window and wondered why I was doing this. It was stupid, but I had to. I had to try.

Except it was even more stupid than I thought. I got off a stop too late because I didn't see no party and when I walked back I saw why: there wasn't one. The building was dark and shut up and it looked broke and poor, like somebody hit it with a wand and turned it back into a place for rats and homeless. I felt disappointed but also relief, and then my neck hair stood up. Men were talking, close. I saw them come around the side of the building, dark moving in dark, arms, legs, jaws. They saw me and stopped. I kept walking. They didn't call out. But I felt them looking and their look was like a animal following me. I made myself not run. I felt animal-breath on my neck. I made myself not pee. Then one of them laughed and the animal turned away.

I got to the bus stop. There was a old man there, talking to nobody. I sat close to him like we were together and he was talking to me. I was still feeling the animal-eyes of those men and I wished he would pretend to be my grandfather, but he didn't.

I got home and went to the kitchen to change back into my sleep clothes. From the window, voices and lights talked on my skin. There was a noise down the hall and I jumped, but it was just Mr. Figuera coming in. He came out of the hall, his dark shape moving in dark, like the men back there, not like someone who sat next to Dante watching *Family Guy*. The dark shape saw me and I was a stranger to him too; I could see because he stopped with a tiny jolt and then he relaxed and said, "Chica, what are you doin' up?" I said, "Nothin'. I can't sleep." He sat on one arm of the couch and I could see him, except he didn't look like him. Mr. Figuera had sleepy eyes and a friendly, hairy face; the man in front of me had a hard mouth and eyes like a cur between shrink and bite. I asked him where he was comin' from, and he told me, "Bushwick."

"You know people in Bushwick?" I asked.

"Yeah, sure. Why you ask?"

"You know a boy there named Dominic, half Dominican, half African-American?"

"Sure. Everybody knows him. You ain't messed up with that boy, are you?"

"Not really. Why? He bad?"

"Nah, not bad, just, if you a young lady, you know, a lil' tiguera like that liable to be trifling. Also liable to be into shit he really don't know how deep it is until it's too late, you know what I'm sayin'?"

"Yeah."

His face looked more like his day-face now, but that animal feeling was still on him like a cloud. He could feel me seeing it and he said, "What you lookin' at, girl?"

"Nothin'. I'm just tired."

He put his hand on my head and rubbed it. "Try to sleep," he said, and then he went to my used-to-be room and unlocked the padlock that he kept on it.

Except he had to fool with it in the dark, and while he was fooling I said, "Dominic in some kind of trouble, that what you mean?"

Mr. Figuera stopped fooling with the lock and stared at me. "You not messed up with him?"

"I'm not, it's just somebody else told me he might be in trouble, so I thought you—"

"Who?"

"Just this girl who knows his sister."

He shook his head. "You shouldn't listen to people who talk other people's business. Or talk it yourself."

He went into my used-to-be room. I lay down and tried to sleep, but I couldn't because I knew that in just a few hours my mom would be up in the kitchen with the radio on. And because I kept hearing *liable to be trifling* and *You were just emergency pussy.* And I thought, I'm gonna beat the brakes off any man who talks to me that way. Ima beat the brakes off any man that even *thinks* it.

Ginger

Because I got the phone call from Ms. Johnson that first school week, I called her, maybe once every month. I knew she wasn't supposed to talk to me, and usually she didn't. But every now and then she would return my call and let me know how Velvet was doing. At first it seemed she was back on track; then I could tell Ms. Johnson was being optimistic for my sake; then she told me Velvet had been given detention for bullying a teacher. I thought I hadn't heard right. I had. Velvet had joined a group of girls who ganged up on and bullied a substitute teacher.

"They didn't hurt him," said Ms. Johnson, "it's more like they—"

"*Him?* They attacked a male teacher? *Girls?*"

"They didn't attack, its more like they picked on him."

"*Picked on him?* A man?"

"He's new and not so young, and he's small and real nervous. They were just, you know, calling names, knocking his things off the desk, flicking at him with their fingers, just basically challenging his authority. I know Velvet wasn't the instigator. But you might want to talk to her about it, let her know you disapprove."

Paul

We had her up to confront her about it; that was my idea. Ginger was ready to cancel the next visit and deal with it on the phone. It was me who said, No, face-to-face. I think it felt like an ambush to her, but that's what she did to some fool—I could just picture the guy—and I wanted to do the same to her, both of us get right on top of her, jab our fingers at her, call her names, see how it felt.

Of course we didn't. We waited until after dinner and then I asked her if it was true. She said no. I said, Then why is Ms. Johnson saying it? She said Ms. Johnson didn't like her. Ginger said, "Stop lying." Her voice was ice-cold, and Velvet looked down, scowling. Ginger said, "Tell the truth. Just tell the truth." In Ginger, anger is cold, and I could see anger coming up in Velvet too. I spoke just to assert normal feeling.

"You know I'm a teacher," I said. "Do you know how hard it is to go into class sometimes? When you know the students don't like you and don't want to hear anything you say and still you have to try to make it good for them, make it exciting? When you don't feel excited at all?"

She looked at me and said nothing.

"Why did you treat somebody like that?" asked Ginger.

She said, "I don't know," and Ginger stood up and *shouted*, "Don't use that tone with me!"

"It's you that's using tone!" cried the girl, and she stood too.

"Easy!" I said.

"Ahh dunno," mocked Ginger. "You think I'm an idiot? Answer me! Why did you treat somebody that way?"

"We didn't do nothing!"

"Call him bitch, do this shit"—Ginger triggered her index with her thumb—"at his face?"

"We didn't hurt him!"

"You did! You hurt him like that woman hurt that horse!"

"He's not like a horse, and I didn't have a whip!"

But Ginger had hit home, and she kept at it.

"Was it because he was weak?" she said. "In his body and also here?" Ginger put her hand on her chest.

Velvet looked down; I realized with strange distress that she was upset.

"Look at me!" cried Ginger.

The girl looked, alarmed. Ginger sat down and spoke quietly. "*I'm weak,*" she said. "I'm small and I'm weak."

Velvet's eyes changed powerfully; I could not define their expression except it was like something in her had stood erect.

"Do I deserve to be treated like that?" asked Ginger softly.

"I'd never treat you like that!"

"That's not what I asked."

"No! But you don't come around acting like you gonna tell people what to do! If he's too weak to be there, then he shouldn't be there!"

"He probably had to be there," I said. "If he's doing that and he's not a kid, he really needs the money. And they aren't paying much."

Lots of things were said; the upshot was that, because of what she'd done, she couldn't see her horse this visit. She accepted that but asked if she could go visit the horses at the barn next door.

"No," said Ginger. "We can't let you do that because you aren't allowed there and you know it."

Velvet looked angry for a minute and I thought she was going to explode. But instead her shoulders sagged and she said, "Then what *am* I gonna do?"

"Read," I said. "Write."

"I want you to write something specific," said Ginger. "I want you to write about why you behaved that way to the teacher."

"*Huh?*"

"Write it and be honest. Then we can do something fun. We can go see a movie. Or walk at night."

Velvet

I didn't want to walk, I wanted us to ride in the car and play music. But she said No, we're going to walk. It felt sad because I remembered how much I used to like it, and she still wanted it to be that way. But my mind was different now and the little things in people's yards, their decorations I used to think were so cute—I didn't care about it anymore. There was nothing going on *at all*, except a old person walking his dog and no music, just some kids' voices talking from somewhere in the park. How could anybody stand it? And Ginger was trying so hard, like we walked over a little bridge and she said, "Remember the time we shined a flashlight in the water and we saw an eel?" I was basically ignoring her until she asked: "You're having periods, right?"

"For a year now, Ginger."

"Do you ever get really, really mad when you have your period?"

I tried to think and couldn't remember.

"Because when I first started? I remember sometimes I would get unbelievably mad. I was once so mad at my mom I remember looking at the back of her head and wanting to kill her and she hadn't even *done* anything. It was scary. And then I started my period and I was like, oh, that was why."

I pictured Ginger staring at her mom's head and wanting to kill her. I didn't know what to say.

"It's normal, if you feel that way. I feel it too sometimes, but in a different way."

I said, "Different how?"

"Because I'm on the other end of it. You're starting to have periods and I'm starting to stop. You're coming up and I'm going down."

And I don't know why, but that made me smile. Not because of her going down. More the way she said it. It made me feel her again, and I wished I could explain: You can't go into a barn weak and tell horses what to do. Horses are real. They don't care who deserves what. They do what they do and if you can't handle it, you shouldn't be there.

Ginger

When we got back to the house she said she wanted to write some more about what happened with the substitute. She'd written something already, saying she was sorry, that she just did it because she wanted the others kids to like her, that she was afraid to stand up and not go along. It was fine, and when she didn't give me anything new the next day, I thought she'd forgotten about it. But she hadn't forgotten. She handed it to me right before she left, and made me promise to wait until after she was gone to read it. I finally opened it when I was on the train, going back home from Penn Station.

You said I was doing what Beverly did to Joker beat him down inside. But that is not true. A teacher is like a trainer its us who are like the horses. The subsitute was like a trainer acting like he know what he is doing giving commands. But if you give the wrong command or in the wrong way the horse knows its bullshit and they won't do what you say. They ignore you or throw you off of them. I saw Joker throw off Beverly once because she was mean with the bit and also her voice the subsitute wasn't mean but he was stupid saying "Go away! Go away!" like we were bugs he should've said "Go back to your seats."

And something else, if you are riding horses in a field and one breaks out and starts running they all do. They don't follow you they follow each other. They forget they have riders and they run together maybe so fast everybody will fall off. Like what happened last summer and I didn't tell you. I was the last to fall off. One girl got hurt.

I'm sorry if I was bad to the subsitute. I would not be that way with you ever. But that's what happened. We ran together.

Velvet

I went to look for him like I always did, walking the block where I met him, and also where we ate. It was so cold it was hard to look sometimes because of keeping my head down in the wind. It was like that when I saw him finally. He was in the restaurant where he took me and he was sitting with Brianna. I went to the other side of the street. I got in a doorway and put up my hood. I got out my phone and I texted, "Hi why don't u call me u ok?" I watched him take out his phone, look at it, and put it away. I saw him sit over his food with his head down, then look up at her. I couldn't see his face.

On the way home with Dante, I saw the lady who went off on the dude that night at the bus stop. She didn't know me; she just went by. But I knew her even though she didn't have her long weave in and her hair was so short she was almost bald, and her eyes were back in her head like she never had the heart to yell at nobody. And I remembered what I heard a girl say at school, that her mama said to her, "Any time you see a bitch with no hair, that bitch ain't got no love neither."

That's when I heard the text hit my phone. I looked and saw "Hey mami sorry it been crazy get u soon miss u—d"

I should've been pissed off. But in my head I heard that beautiful song on the subway the time my mom hit me in the face.

Then I went home and she threw a envelope at my face. She said, "A letter for you." She watched while I opened it and read.

Dear Velvet: What you wrote about the teacher was beautiful, especially the part about running together. But you are not a horse. You are a person. We'll talk more soon. Love, Ginger

I put the letter down, smiling. "I got a job today," said my mom. "So you *should* be happy."

"Mami, I am happy."

"A job at the candle factory. Just like that crazy old woman with all the saints." She laughed. "But Mr. Figuera is still renting his room. So you're still on the couch."

Ginger

She called me and told me she got the letter and then yelled at her mother, who yelled back. She yelled at me that her mom got a job but that she was going to let Mr. Figuera keep sleeping in her room and make Velvet sleep on the couch.

I said, "Your mom must really need the money."

She said, "I don't care what she needs! Why doesn't she sleep on the couch?" Her mother yelled again and Velvet said, "Can you talk to Dante?"

I said, "About *what*?"

Dante said, "Hi."

So I said, "Hi. What are you doing?"

"Watching *The Simpsons*." The yelling went up and came back down. "Do you want to know what's happening?" he said.

"Yes, please tell me."

"Bart went to church and sold his soul! To the devil!"

There was a snatching of air and Velvet said, "Can I come live with you?"

"Honey," I said, "I don't think you'd really want that."

Velvet

When I saw her again, Fiery Girl came to me with love. She made the nicker noise. When I went in the stall with the halter, she put her head down and forward to show me what she felt. I couldn't ride her or even lunge her because the paddock was icy. So I groomed her, brushed her, scratched her, rubbed her. She wiggled her lips.

Ginger said she didn't think I really wanted to come live here because I would miss Dante and my mom. Her voice when she said it was high and hard with no love in it. She was right; I knew it wouldn't be any good for me to live with her. Still, I wanted her to say yes. I wished she had said yes.

I rubbed my mare's legs. Her head was down and her eyes were soft. I remembered how she was when I first got here, how she bit her stall and they had to put that strap on her face, how hard it was to even touch her. I kissed her scars, and I know she felt the love in my lips. Whatever happened with me and Ginger or Ginger and Paul, I had to keep coming here so that I could take care of my mare, always.

"The next time you come, Estella says you're welcome back at her stable," said Pat.

"Why?"

"I've told her how responsible you've been, and she could see it when you got the mare into the trailer. It probably helps that Beverly's not around."

"Why is she not around?"

"Let me count the whys! I'm sure you've noticed between the time you started coming and the time you left, there's fewer students, fewer horses boarded. Which is another reason Estella would like you to be there. She'd like you to represent her place at an event coming up—you'd make the place look good."

I was embarrassed about how I smiled, but I couldn't stop. I said, "I could ride Fiery Girl?"

"I don't think she's the best choice. She *has* jumped before, I'm sure of that now, and she looks good taking the jumps. But she's not consistent like Chloe; she's temperamental—but on the other hand, she *has* competed before so . . . maybe! If you work hard on schooling her, maybe Fiery Girl."

Ginger

I didn't dare say how much I wished she could live here, how I'd dreamed of it, prayed for it. Because then I'd have to tell her that it was Paul who blocked it and she would think he didn't like her—that's how she would feel it. I couldn't talk to Paul about it either. He had changed since the confrontation about the teacher, and I felt him accept Velvet's presence more sincerely. I didn't want to mess that up.

Velvet

But the next time I came, I didn't go to Estella's stable or even to Pat's house, not the first day. Because that lady at the party, her daughter Joanne invited me to come and see where she rode because she was Edie's friend. I could visit and watch and Joanne would give me her lesson. I wanted to go, especially when Ginger said the name of the place was Spindletop—I remembered that was where Heather went, and Beth before their parents couldn't pay.

Spindletop at first didn't look better than Estella's except it had a big sign with a fancy horse on it. You could see the barn from the road and it did not look scary like Estella's place the first time I saw it even though it was a lot bigger—maybe because it was winter and there wasn't thick green secluding it. Or maybe because I wasn't young. Anyway, it was two big buildings with a big parking lot in front and big paddocks with horses in them.

Then Ginger dropped me off and I went in the office and saw how different it was. In this office there were no bags of horse treats or horse medicine or boxes of horse combs or boots or blankets or dirty rags—no dirty *anything* really. There was no radio playing country music and no cats hanging off anybody. There were desks with computers on them and neat-dressed ladies with manicures. When I asked for Joanne they smiled and took me back into this big stable that was warm and bright-lit and so clean it didn't even smell like horses. I was starting to get nervous when this smiling girl wearing tall boots and tight pants came and said, "Are you Velvet? What a great name for a rider!"

That was Joanne, and she took me into the tack room, where everything was hanging *so* neat, bridles all tied the same way with the nose pieces standing out, on hooks with horses' names on them— not just hanging on the stall door like at Estella's or Pat's. There were so many horses and their stalls were all clean and they looked perfectly brushed and *chill*, like yeah, they had something to say but you needed to be *somebody* to get their attention.

Joanne's horse was named Major Tom and he was big like Joker, but different, not wild or funny, more like a soldier at attention, like he was clean on the inside too. While Joanne groomed him, she told me what a great horse he was, and how much he loved her, that he would jump in her lap if he could. While she talked, girls in the same kind of tall boots and tight pants walked by; their hair was so perfect that if Alicia saw it she wouldn't know whether to bow and worship it or rip it out. Men wearing work clothes walked by too, Mexican men pushing wheelbarrows and carrying buckets and mucking forks. Joanne smiled and said hi to them the same way she did to the girls. But they were the only ones who looked at all dirty.

"So where do you ride now?" asked Joanne.

"At Wildwood. Pat teaches me."

"Oh, yes," she said. "I know her and Estella. They're sweet."

And I thought, *Sweet?*

Ginger

When I picked her up she didn't look triumphant or even happy like I expected. She seemed troubled and subdued. I asked her how it went and she said, "Fine." I asked if it was different from learning with Pat and she said, "Not that much." We rode quietly for a while. Then she said, "Those women we met at the party in the summer, one of them is Joanne's mom?"

"Yes," I said. "And Joanne knows Edie."

"And that was Edie's mom there too?"

"Yeah. Becca."

"Who was that other lady? The one Paul went to talk to?"

"I don't know," I said. "I think she's probably a new teacher at the school." And I turned on the radio.

Velvet

The Spindletop trainer was not like Beverly or Pat; she was more like Estella, but smaller in her body and face. Her name was Jeanne and when she asked what I wanted to work on, I said jumping. We warmed up like usual: walk, trot, canter. About two minutes in she said, "Good hands, excellent hands!" and when she did, these two girls stopped to watch. It made me nervous, so I missed my diagonal when we went to the trot—but I sat a stride to fix it and Jeanne said "Good!" again, her voice surprised and her mind *on* me then.

But then she said, "Let's see your two-point" and suddenly everything I did was wrong. "Stretch, don't lean," she said. "It's bad form." I even grabbed the mane bad form-ly. The girls walked away from the fence like they didn't need to bother watching. She made me two-point for *half an hour* until she liked how it looked, walking, cantering, posting, then going from two-point to sitting trot and back. When we finally jumped I felt good, but she said I was too far forward in the saddle and I was releasing too much and I was supposed to *stop* after the line of jumps, that the horse couldn't just canter. Pat *never* said that.

Joanne and those two other girls were watching again toward the end, and I felt like shit—even when Jeanne said, "That was outstanding. I hope you come back soon." I didn't believe her until I saw the way one of the girls was looking at me. Like I was a problem. The blond one.

The next day I went to Pat's house. I wanted to talk to her about Spindletop; I wanted to hear what she had to say. But I couldn't because there was an emergency and Pat had to stick her arm in Nut's ass to save his life. It sounds funny, but it wasn't. She had to do it because he was sick with colic and could die, and the only thing she could do was try to pull shit out of him herself. It was freezing and windy, and when I came, she was in the barn wearing rubber gloves almost to her elbow. She said it would be "educational."

I was first afraid he would kick her, but then I saw him with his head way down, looking so weak and hurt he could hardly stand. I thought he would cry out when she went in, but he didn't; his poor body just got crunched up and horribled, like when the dentist is getting in your mouth. Pat talked soft to Nut and worked her arm. The wind got bad and started shaking the barn and the mares talked to each other. Pat pulled out the shit and handed it to me. "Feel that," she said. I did feel it—it was like a cooked rock.

"At least it was warm in there," she said.

Then we cleaned the stalls and groomed Chloe and Girl. By the time we were done, Pat said Nut would be okay. Later when we were in the house getting warm, Pat told me you shouldn't do what she did. Her face was sick-white when she said it, and her fat cheeks were hard. She said she could've killed Nut by tearing his butthole. I asked why she did it, and she said she couldn't afford a vet. She said she had to face reality. She said she had to do that a long time ago. She said it old and tired, like she forgot I was even there. "I have the ability," she said. "I have the quality animals. But I don't have money, and it's all about money in this business."

I didn't know what to say. I felt the dirt and the broken things around us. There was wind and the sound of the furnace. There were all the ribbons on the wall saying "First prize" and "Scorpio" and "Handsome." I didn't know what to say, but I did know not to talk about Spindletop. Not then, maybe never.

But at night I was wondering, Why was I at the poor, dirty place? I used to think it was so cool, but now it just seemed like crap—as Ginger would say, *literally*, like it had to be pulled out of the horses.

Ginger

Something happened at Spindletop. Not something bad—I would've known if it was actually bad—she wouldn't be able to hold it back. No, it was something confusing. She was trying to understand it, that was the most obvious reason she would ask those questions in the car.

But it felt like something else was going on. It felt like she was being aggressive with me. Like she did with her mom that time they came up for the play, the subtle way she sided with the tall blond woman at the barn and shut her mother out. Velvet knew all about weakness and power, and it felt like she was pressing on my weak spot, just to see what would happen. She didn't push it; she didn't have to. She was just letting me know she saw it. And that she was curious about it.

Velvet

Before I left I went across the street to look at the old barn again. It was freezing cold but still I thought someone would be there, maybe Pat giving a lesson in the arena indoors. But nobody was there except the horses chewing grain and giving out heat. Then Gare came around the corner singing something corny—she saw me and got her friendly shy-dog face, which made me feel embarrassed but sorta happy. She said she was going to ride in the arena, did I want to?

I liked Gare, even if she was dumb, because of how she helped me get up on Fiery Girl and also for how she cried for Joker when Beverly was a bitch to him. But I still didn't know what to talk about with her. That I lied about being in a gang made it worse, but I couldn't take it back, it would be too embarrassing. She'd say, "What's it like being in a gang?" and I'd say, "We don't talk about it unless we know you." And she'd say nothin'.

But we didn't have to talk about anything to ride together. I tacked up Little Tina while she tacked up Joker three stalls over and she yelled to me that it was better now 'cause Heather wasn't at the barn anymore since she had a fight with Pat about never cleaning Totally's feet and he got thrush. Then we led the horses out and the talking was all in their eyes and soft-up necks and our hands on the reins and the heavy gate coming open.

Then we were riding, Tina following Joker until I passed on the outside, Gare yelling, "Bitch!" but laughing. Some of the lights were out, so the arena was dark and like a place bats would fly, except for broken parts that let in the cold and light, you could see tiny branches covered in ice. We warmed up, walk, trot, canter, and even though we were going in different directions and not following nobody, it was like we were together at the *stomach*. And then I did the two-point, stretching, not leaning. She said, "Horse whisper-ass!" I put my leg on Tina, made her feel me, counting my strides, rushed seven, then slow seven. I sat back and controlled my release, and she took them easy, three in a row; I could feel her happiness like I can smell *perfume*. Gare couldn't make Joker take any jump and she fell off trying. But she just cursed and got back on him. She said, "Damn, you really *are* the horse whisper-ess!"

And I felt good again. Everything felt right again. Nut was okay and even if Pat didn't have money, she had the ability. And I had Fiery Girl. And I had new things to teach her. And Ginger didn't care about that woman at the party, so it must not've been what I thought.

Ginger

When she left, I walked alone. Snow and brilliant light poured through splotchy clouds. Family things were heaped on porches: boots, cheap round sleds, statues, hidden flowers sleeping in red pots. Somebody still had their Christmas lights up. Because there was no traffic, I walked in the middle of the road.

"You and she have nothing in common." Paul always said that. But what did I have in common with these houses and the people in them? I thought of Velvet's powerful music, the song of guns and dogs—"*Ronca!*"—and the song we sang in the Christmas play that time, Danielle running around with her blue face, Yandy pounding the piano, Mrs. Vargas looking out of her tank. The horsewoman who ruined the day with her bad Spanish, the horses running, Mrs. Vargas cursing me like I couldn't understand her, then taking her daughter home and beating her. The time we biked on the broken pavement, me yelling "Lumpety-bumpety!" What did any of it have in common?

I told Kayla I was not sure I should keep sending Mrs. Vargas money if she had a job and a boarder. Kayla didn't think I ever should've started. "When you have to cut that money off, trust me, she will feel anger at you. It'll be like now you *owe her*, not the other way around."

But I knew that wasn't true. She wasn't like that. I knew because of how she'd looked me back in my eyes.

It was Velvet I wasn't sure about. Because it still felt like she asked me that question in the car out of aggression. Or anger. Or scorn. Because of something she saw.

Paul

"So I heard your young lady rode out at Spindletop," said Becca. "She made a good impression."

We were on the phone talking about Edie's spring break visit when she dropped that in.

"Joanne said they'd maybe have room for her as a work-study—apparently that place she's been training isn't the best quality."

"What in the fresh hell?" I said. "You've been aggressively icing Ginger for years and now you're interested in her . . . her—"

"I'm *not* interested in messing with your wife's project, although I was under the impression it was your project too. Spindletop wasn't my idea. It was Joan who suggested it, and because she knew I was going to be talking to you today, she asked me to mention some event they're going to in the early spring, a big show that a lot of people from all over the country come to. It's called EQUAL for some reason—anyway, her daughter was thinking Velvet could come along, act as a groom, get a look at a different part of the horse world. She asked me to mention it. That's all I'm doing, mentioning it. I'm not trying to sell it."

We spoke about other things, and almost got off the phone. Then I felt bad for my attitude, so I apologized.

"No, it's okay," she said. "And partly I was okay mentioning it because when I met the girl, she seemed nice. Not just nice, interesting. Which is what Edie's always said, but Edie can be . . . romantic about people."

"Edie's very perceptive."

"I know, and I trust her in general. It's just that Joanne's heard gossip about Velvet that wasn't so nice."

"She *did*?"

"Well, she knows horse people, so yeah. Apparently some friend of a friend had talked about being afraid of Velvet, said she glared at people and—"

"Afraid of *Velvet*?"

"Well, there was some story about her getting kicked out of a barn because she caused a trainer to get trampled, even something about her being in a gang."

"That sounds like teenage BS!" But then I recalled that Velvet had somehow abruptly stopped going to that barn.

"Well, I thought so, yeah. Edie's said nothing but good things about her, and like I said, Joanne had a good impression of her, and the trainer at Spindletop was struck with her talent. So . . ."

I thanked her for telling me about Joan's offer, quietly guessing that one, the conversation had been a chance to feel me out about the gossip and two, she'd really enjoyed the idea of Ginger's cluelessly taking up with a menace.

"And you know what? If it's awkward, I can just have Joan call Ginger."

"No, Becca, it's okay. I'll tell her it came from you."

"And just so that you know that I know that you know—I'm not the only ice queen at the party. That woman has a thousand-yard stare that could stop a truck. She does not make it easy."

I wished I could say I *didn't* know what she meant. But I did. Which I did not share with Ginger when I brought it up that night.

"Becca," she said. "Becca? Becca, who insulted me to my face about Velvet, now wants to get involved? Get involved with sending Velvet to a place that's better than the place I've found for her and now to some ridiculous—"

"Ginger, you didn't find the place, it was just next door. It's not a reflection on you."

"You don't understand how I feel? That she's trying to—"

"I do! My first impulse was to question her. But I think she essentially means well."

"I don't."

"Ginger, give her a break! I know she's been unpleasant. But I was technically still married to her when I met you. You're younger, you're better-looking, and you're living in the same town. And it's only been six years."

"That's exactly why I don't think she means well." We carried our dinner into the living room to eat while we watched a TV show about a likable gangster.

"Whatever she means, it's an opportunity for Velvet. If Velvet wants it."

She didn't say anything.

"And if it really bothers you, we don't have to bring it up."

We stared at the TV; the gangster was in the middle of an argument with his daughter in the family car. Ginger stared at it as if absorbed and then out of the blue said, "I have a question for you. Are you having an affair?" She turned from the TV to look directly at me.

"No," I said. It was the truth.

She turned back toward the television. The gangster had left his daughter sitting in the car so he could follow somebody into a gas station bathroom and kill him. She looked at me again and said, "So fucking predictable."

I felt my face go hot. "What do you mean?"

"Becca. The main thing she has over me is that she's a mother and now that I have something a tiny bit like what she has, she wants to come in and show me up. What a fucking bitch."

"So you don't want Velvet to have this opportunity."

She looked at me angrily. "Of course I want her to have it! If she even *wants* it. I just wish you were more—" She stopped, and her expression changed. Then she said, "You're blushing."

Ginger

I didn't think she would want to go, especially because it turned out that Joanne wasn't even riding on the day that we could go. It would be two girls she didn't know. But she did want to. She had to think a minute before she said yes, and she didn't smile when she said it. But I could feel she really did want to go. I respected her for it. Whatever had made her uncomfortable about Spindletop, she wanted another look at it.

So I made her a sandwich the night before and we got up at five a.m. and drove through the in-between time of dark and light, no cars on the road, just us. She was tired and quiet, but I felt her sensitivity to the in-between time. I remembered when my mom made me go to camp with this organization called Camp Fire Girls; I hated it, and she said I had to go anyway because it would "build character." I thought that was the stupidest thing, and I didn't even believe she meant it, I thought it must've been what somebody else told her. But this, the drive at dawn to an unknown situation—it felt like that. Character building.

Velvet

I knew it was going to be weird when they put this thing like a giant clothespin on this horse's face. It didn't seem like there was a lot for me to do. There was that blond girl who watched my lesson—her name was Lexy—and this other one, Lorrie, going around in tall black boots and little jackets, doing everything really fast, and it seemed like I didn't do anything fast enough. Finally they let me take over grooming Lorrie's horse, Spectacular, while she did something else, but before I was done, Jeanne walked past and said, "Look at his ears! He can't go out in public like that!" I said, "What's bad about his ears?" and she said, "They're hairy." And she brought a electric shaver and tried to take the hair off his ears, but he wouldn't let her. So she asked somebody to bring her "the twitch"—that was the giant clothespin that pinched his mouth and nose so hard you could see his teeth. She used the twitch to pull his face where she wanted it and ran the razor and he didn't say nothin', or even move.

"It looks like it hurts," I said.

"It's a distraction," she said. "It's releasing endorphins so really it feels good."

Then they told me to put the saddles and pads and everything in the compartments of the trailers, but when Lexy came out, she looked at it and made a face and did it different. They got the horses in the van, Spectacular and Lexy's thoroughbred, Alpha, who did not want to go. These two Mexican men had to lock arms under Alpha's ass and shove him in like that.

Ginger

On the drive back I thought about the broken-off conversation with Paul, how he'd blushed and I did not press him because after all he had said no, he was not having an affair. And Becca, I thought about her too. The next time we saw each other, how would we talk about EQUAL? If Paul *was* having an affair, how would she look at me then? How would I look at her?

Velvet

We drove there slow on curved roads with trees and bushes growing almost into the road; it was light but darkish anyway because of wet mist coming up. It took almost an hour to get there, and it seemed like the whole time Lorrie and Lexy talked about their boots, Lorrie said some boots called Tuff Riders had a knockoff that looked just like Parlantis, but Lexy didn't believe it, she would never buy Tuff Riders. Jeanne tried to talk to me about Brooklyn, where she used to live, but it was hard to pay attention because I didn't know any of the places she talked about. We turned onto a road with just one big gray building on it and then nothing, like somebody tore a hole in the trees to make it that way. It was the place. It wasn't twice the size of Spindletop, it was five times the size of Spindletop, and we were just in the *parking lot,* which was full of cars and trailers and big curtained places for horses, and horses being walked, and also people speeding around in tiny carts.

We parked at the end of the lot next to a place where people were lunging horses. We got out and all three of them started putting black polish on their boots; Jeanne talked on her phone with one hand and polished with the other. I just stood there noticing Lexy's manicure and jewelry. Nobody at my barn had a manicure, not even that bitch Heather. Lorrie smiled at me and said, "Is Velvet your real name? Because—" But Jeanne started talking to her too quiet for me to hear, and then Lexy was taking Alpha out and suddenly Jeanne got on a bicycle that was lying in the grass and rode away going, "Meet me at Hunter Ring 3!" Lexy pulled out her phone and told Lorrie to lunge Alpha, and got on her phone with her back to me. A lady with big earrings and bigger lips went by on a cart with a little dog in her lap. I watched Lorrie exercise Alpha next to a woman whose horse was lunging with a brat-ass attitude and even rearing up on her. I could hear her say, "Oh, stop it!"

"Excuse me?" said Lexy. "Maybe you could tack up Spectacular?" She didn't even wait for me to answer, she just turned her back and talked on the phone. I did it, but I had to work to keep my hands soft and let Spectacular know I wasn't mad at *him*. Which I wasn't. He seemed like a nice horse who didn't understand why people sometimes all of a sudden wanted to run a electric thing on his ears so bad they had to clothespin his face. When Lexy got off the phone she thanked me, but her voice was more petting itself down the middle than saying anything nice to me. Or even anything to me. Which made me feel pissed off, like sick pissed off. Even when she said she had to be on the phone because of a personal crisis, which she said mostly to Lorrie, who lunged her horse for her.

Anyway, she got on Alpha and rode him to where we were going, and Lorrie led Spectacular and walked with me. She told me Jeanne had left the bicycle there the day before so she could ride on it today, that Jeanne had to ride fast to find out when Lexy's event was, because sometimes they changed them. She told me she wasn't competing; she was just there to help and to ride in the practice arena. Her parents couldn't afford to pay the entry fee for her to compete, it cost them two hundred dollars just for her to practice. I asked her why this was called EQUAL. And she said it stood for something, she could never remember what it was, though. We went over a little stone bridge to a place like the fair, with buildings made of flat walls that sold food and also horse things; there was a sign that said "European Fashion Horze" next to a sign for pizza. Horses walked and people rode them, and there were more women with little dogs. We turned and instead of stuff for sale, there were rings with people riding horses, and the jumps in the rings were all bright colors and covered with flowers. I saw a lady holding a little dog up to a horse's nose like it was a bunch of flowers.

We came to Hunter Ring 3, but I didn't see Jeanne or Lexy. Lorrie said Lexy was warming up, and she was going to warm up Spectacular. She said I could come watch, and I went over with her, but I only stood by the fence for a few minutes watching this gray horse with beautiful spots curving his neck against the bit while his rider made him canter around the same jump again and again. Then I walked down the path and sat on some empty bleachers in front of a empty ring. Because I did not want to be here. There were horses all around me and I did not feel them at all, it was like they were part of machinery that I didn't know how to work, and they were controlled by this machinery. All of them were beautiful, more beautiful than any horse at Pat's or at Estella's, like models compared to people you see on the subway. But I couldn't feel them. Horses usually make me feel calm, and these were making me feel something else.

Voices started coming into the air, people were talking into speakers. A girl rode into the ring in front of me and a voice said, "Miss Mumble Mlech from New Jersey!" and she rode like hell even though nobody was watching her but me and I didn't care about her. And I was going to have to be here all day.

Ginger

She called me sooner than I expected and said she was getting a ride back to Spindletop early, could I come get her. When I got there she was sitting blankly on a bench outside the office. I asked her why she left early and she said they didn't have anything for her to do and Jeanne had to come back to drop off a horse and pick up two more, so Velvet rode with her. I asked if she had fun and she said, "It was okay" and then, "Ahm tired" and then, "Can we listen to the radio?"

When we got home she took a nap and then wanted to watch TV. Paul asked her questions about the event and she talked about women with dogs and some woman holding a dog up to a horse's nose. And a gray horse whose rider took him in circles around a jump. That was it. She didn't go to the barn, not that day or the next.

That night I sat on her bed like I used to do when we still read to her. I asked if anything was wrong. She said no, but that she'd decided something. She didn't want to ride in a competition.

"*Why?*"

"Ahh dunno. I just don't think I do. I don't want to make my horse jump over things with a lot of people watching, I don't care about that. I just want to ride her by myself and take care of her."

"But you can still ride her by yourself. The competition is like an accomplishment; it's out in the world. It's like . . . you can read and write at home, but at school you take tests and then—"

"It's not like school."

"But it is. It's important to show what you can do, to be tested. It's important in life. It . . ." *Builds character.*

She didn't say anything.

"I think you would feel really good about it. Because I think you could win and then—"

"I don't think I would win."

"Why not? Of course you could win. I think you *would* win!"

"No, Ginger, I wouldn't!" She sat up as if yanked, facing me in a twist. "All those girls today were better than me and their horses were better!"

"But Pat says you're really good!"

She didn't answer immediately. She lay down. Then she said, "Maybe she's just saying that."

"Why would she say that if she didn't think it?"

"To make me feel good about myself. To 'make a difference.' "

And she turned her back to me.

After she left the next day, I went to see Pat. It was late in the day and when I first walked into the barn it seemed like nobody was there. The horses were quiet; maybe they'd just finished eating. I stopped to look at a white one—I think it was the one Velvet had ridden first. It didn't look at me; it stood facing the back of its stall smelling of shit and brute personality. When it finally looked at me, its body said, *Oh. You.* "Hi," I said. "I know I'm not her. But I—"

"Excuse me?" said Pat. She'd just come around the corner with an empty wheelbarrow. There was nothing sarcastic in her tone; she seemed pleased when I said that I'd been talking to the horse, and I don't think she realized I was being whimsical. "By all means, go ahead," she said. "Don't let me interrupt you."

"It was a short conversation," I said. "I really came to talk to you."

"About?"

"Velvet."

"Yeah?" The woman walked the wheelbarrow down the aisle to an open stall and went in with it. I followed.

"I was hoping you could talk to her. She . . . I think she's feeling insecure. She's not sure she wants to ride in the competition you talked about."

"Huh." She began methodically and gracefully shoveling shit. "You have any idea why? Did something happen?"

"Yes, it did. I think it did. Do you know Spindletop?"

She kept working, silently. Her silence answered yes before she did.

Velvet

I texted him over and over and told him I needed to see him. He kept saying he would get back to me, but he didn't. Until finally I told him I was at Lydia's and he came to me. But then he wouldn't kiss. He hugged me back but said he couldn't kiss me. I dropped my arms and waited for him to explain. He just stood there, so I said, *Why?* He sat on the couch and said, I told you it could only be once. I said, Then why you here? And he looked away. The heat was still on high even though it wasn't cold out, so the room was hot. He took off his hoodie and he sniffed all wet in his nose. I touched him on his leg and said his name. He said, "Brianna's pregnant." I pulled my hand away.

He got up and walked around. Brianna lived with her aunt, who was taking care of five other kids and a retarded girl from the neighborhood and also this other girl who tricked the retard into getting raped by a man with AIDS. He said it was like some rape crisis center over there, Brianna could not be bringing a baby into *that* reality show, he had to take care of her.

"You gonna support a *family?*"

He said, "I have to try." And he put his head down, but not ashamed.

"You can still see me." I said it real quiet. "Like now."

He looked at me and looked down. "If you was like some hood-rat puta, maybe I would. Even with you bein' young. But you not that. You not that, and you would hate me if I did you like that. You'd hate yourself. I don't want—"

"What you think I *am?* Where you think I live? I live down the block!"

He came and sat close enough that I could feel how warm he was. "I know where you from. But it feels like you from someplace else."

"What place?" I tried to make my voice mad so I wouldn't cry.

He looked me in my eyes. "I don't know. Someplace I can't picture. Someplace I can't be. Even if it's beautiful."

I looked down and bit the inside of my mouth to stop crying.

I was thinking about the barn and Spindletop and Ginger and that gray dappled horse riding in a circle around the jump. I'd wanted to talk about it with Dominic, talk like before. Now I wished I'd never seen any of it. Because it was "someplace else." He sat next to me like he felt what I was thinking, not saying anything. Then he took something out of his pocket and said, "Look."

It was the picture he told me about, where he was Romeo in the school play. He was wearing pants that looked like velvet, and slippers and a silky shirt. He was smiling and holding his arms out like a girl was about to run to him. He looked even younger than me. The picture was so wrinkled and old, there was a crease right across his face. Still, he looked beautiful. Like he came from "someplace else."

"So you know I don't lie," he said.

I took the picture and put it on my knee to smooth the wrinkles from it. "How old were you?" I asked.

"Twelve," he said.

"Can I keep it?"

"Naw," he said. "It's the only one I got. I never even showed it to nobody else except my mom and my sister."

I wanted to ask, *What about Brianna?* But I didn't.

He took it from my hands and put it back in his pocket. He said, "You tell anybody you saw it, Ima say you a liar, right?"

I said I wouldn't tell nobody.

He said he had to go.

I said, "But we can still talk, right? Like friends?"

"We friends," he said. "I won't forget that time." He looked at me when he said that. "But for right now, don't call me or text me, okay?"

Ginger

My cell rang and somebody wanted to know if I was Velveteen Vargas's godmother. I said, Yes, why?

Because there'd been a girl-fight in the Catholic school yard. Three girls on one, but the one fought so fiercely the others got the worst of it. When the social worker ran out to break it up, she saw the lone girl had one of the three by her hair; this lone girl looked so wild that for a minute the social worker thought *she* might be attacked—but the girl just spewed obscenities and then they all ran. The social worker's car had gotten keyed, Velvet's school was called, Velvet was ratted out and dragged by her ear over to the Catholic school. Where she was immediately recognized as the ferocious fighter.

"When we tried to call her mother about paying to repair the car, nobody answered. She says her mom can't pay anyway. She says you might."

They said it would cost four hundred dollars, and I said I'd pay for half, I don't know why. Maybe because the car-keyed social worker had a kind, harried voice. Even when she said she'd never heard such ugly language come out of a young girl.

"When they brought her over, I confronted her. I said to her, You know I am a mother of two young children. How would you feel if somebody talked to *your* mother that way?"

"She's actually very nice," I said. "But in fact she talks to her m—"

"I know! I know she is! When I confronted her, when I said 'How would you feel if someone talked to your mother that way,' she just looked down, ashamed."

I said, "You know, I'm not a mother, but I wouldn't like to be talked at like that, either."

"No, no, of course not. No woman would. I just thought, if she could think of it in those terms, she'd—"

I asked where I should send the check. She expressed gratitude.

I hung up and thought, Maybe they really *are* different from us. More violent, more dishonest—nicer in some ways, yes, warm, physical, passionate. But weak-minded. Screaming and yelling all the time, no self-control. Do her homework with her on the phone, she doesn't turn it in and lies about it. Give her all the special treatment in the world and she throws it away because she can't follow through. Just *different.*

So Paul was right. Everybody was right. I'm racist. At least now I know.

Velvet

She said, You think I'm rich? You think two hundred dollars is pocket change for me? Why do you do this shit? You're almost fourteen! I said, I'm sorry, but she didn't even say, It's okay, it's all right. She said she's afraid. She's afraid because we're drifting apart. I wanted to say, *No, we're not,* but I couldn't because we were. She said I couldn't come for the weekend, making it happen more. I told her it didn't matter. I wasn't riding in any competition anyway, so I didn't have to come up. And she's, Mwah, mwah, mwah. Is that why you keyed that lady's car and got them to call me? Because you don't *want* to come up, you don't even care about your horse anymore? Why you acting like this? Mwah, mwah, mwah!

I decided then that I was going out to find Dominic and make him talk to me. And if I couldn't find him, then I'd find something, somebody, I didn't care. At night I lay down in my clothes with my eye makeup on thick. But my mom suddenly got up and went past my room, bumping on the wall like she's blind and not even cursing. She went into the bathroom and I heard a thump and then she puked *horrible,* like her gut was coming out. It scared me, but I thought, Good, she definitely won't hear me leave, and I went out into the hall. I got to the door and stopped, waiting for some noise to cover me. The sink water ran; I flipped the lock. There was another thump, like maybe she fell; I stopped and listened. She groaned and it yanked me inside, she sounded so weak, I never heard her weak. She puked more, but weaker, like it was hard even to puke. I flipped back the lock and went to her.

Silvia

I felt it coming on at work, sharpness in my stomach, light head, hard to stand. Juanita next to me said somebody'd been in the bathroom already, sick from the food truck salad, did I have it? I did, but my body is good; if I tell it to hold on, it does. Still, it made me dizzy to keep moving my hands in the same stupid puzzle, the same sounds I hear every day driving me like a pain motor. I broke into a sweat and this woman Lena told about how she used to work for, basically, an ass doctor and she was sometimes in the room when people, *white people*, were examined. *The look on they faces, when they realize what's going to take place, that they are going to be on their knees with their face and pants down, getting they ass thoroughly finger-fucked in front of a black woman!* Everybody laughed, and for a second the motor was beautiful motion, like we were all walking inside a conch shell spinning like a wheel, our feet in exact grooves like gold threads. *And he had arms like a white gorilla, and I think he lo-o-ved his job, because he went at it!* We laughed, and she said it again: *The look on they faces!* And my sweat passed. I came back to the line, hot then cold, my fingers moving without my telling them.

I got home to fix food. I had crackers and ginger tea instead of dinner and for once Velvet didn't act like a malcriada, just sat and read her book in a corner. I lay in bed coming in and out of sleep while street noise patterned up and broke. Cars, voices, music, lights, subways rumbling in their dirty holes. Except that sometimes there was a forgotten passage and a crack to hide in, or a flight of stairs, and I ran down, and there was a young blanca running too. She was looking for something and she was in danger and she did not know it. Street noise filled my ears; good voices forced into vicious shapes by iron hands, whose hands? Dante came into bed with me and I held him tight. Where was my daughter? God, with the white girl! And the white girl walked in a hall with living heads sprouting from walls and they spoke all languages but not one could understand the other and their talk split our ears. I screamed, *Shut up!* And woke with truck poison coming up my throat.

Velvet

She was on the floor with her gown way up, reaching to pull a towel off the rack. "Mami!" I said. "Here!" And I got the towel for her, then went to run cold water on a cloth. I looked in the mirror—*oh shit*—I was dressed in my street clothes and makeup. But she just sat with the towel around her like she was cold, so I kneeled and put the cloth on her forehead; she looked at me with strange eyes. I said, "Mami?" and she had to puke again. I held her hair away from her face and remembered making rivers of puke in a blue rubber pail, how she held me. My ragged toy that somebody gave me, I would lean it out the window and pat its back and pretend it was puking, *plah plah plah*! What happened to that toy?

I stayed up with her all night. She saw my clothes and makeup; I saw her look and felt it. But she didn't say anything, not that night or next day. She yelled like always. But not about that.

Paul

My sponsor advised me not to tell Ginger about Polly because it was over and unless there is some *very* good reason to do otherwise, you don't tell the truth if it's going to hurt the other person.

"But she asked me," I said. "And—"

"And you told her no. It's still no, right?"

"Yes, but then she asked why my face was flushed. She knows. It's sitting there waiting to happen. She's going to ask me again; if I keep saying no, it'll start to sound more and more false. If I say yes, it makes it worse that I said no to start with."

"Worse for her or for you?"

"Both of us. Listen, Ginger isn't someone who cares about discretion or, or dignity. She cares about truth."

He didn't say anything for a minute. My sponsor is a manual laborer with a degree in philosophy. He's been impotent for years because of a prostate operation. He can't take Viagra because of his heart condition, but he's recently been using a penis pump and it seems to be working for him. He cares about truth too. He also cares about dignity and discretion. Mostly, though, he wants things to *work*.

"Well," he said, "I don't think you need to throw the past in her face. But you could always ask her why she asked the question. If you really want to have the conversation."

And so I did. And she told me. She said even Velvet noticed something.

Ginger

Like I didn't already know there must be a reason that he'd suddenly become so kind and understanding of Velvet and me, that he'd stopped with the racial piety about how really, while I think I love her, it's actually *white guilt* or something even more perverted and sick; it can't possibly be what it looks like or feels like to me. Frankly, it was such a relief not to hear that shit anymore that I'd rather he shut up and "cheat" if it meant he could leave us alone or even actually show support and back me up like with the substitute. *Cheat.* What a stupid word, like you're playing cards and your partner cheats and the whole deck has to rise up and attack you, both of you, him because he didn't play right, and me because—why? Because I didn't catch him? Because therefore I'm now "humiliated," *officially*? Well, guess what? Here's the good thing, the one good thing, *the one good thing* about being the girl on the side where the guy goes to act like he can't with his main squeeze: you realize it doesn't mean anything much except he feels like doing it with somebody else. The wife isn't "humiliated" or unloved or anything. If that's happening to anybody, it's usually the other one. He says he's not even seeing her anymore, but still here he is with his AA face on talking about amends and wanting to feel close again. All of it, the piety, the careful examining and blaming of himself for daring to want sex, of me for being— what? A guilty white person who must be doing something wrong? That attitude is so much more disgusting than his wanting strange pussy, not to mention his hard, fake self-righteous friends. Starting with that bitch he used to be married to.

Paul

She stared at me a long moment, then looked away. "I guess it's normal," she said.

"Normal?"

"My dad did it. Everybody makes a production out of it, but every time you turn around somebody's doing it. It didn't mean anything, right?"

Her sarcasm was cheap but sharp, and though I meant to humble myself, it made me mad. I said, "Actually, it did mean something. It meant that somebody was paying attention to me and holding me like she meant it."

"Then why is it over?"

Because Polly ended it. "Because I wanted it to be you."

She frowned like she heard the unsaid thing, then shook her head, almost twitched it, like she was shaking something from her ear.

"I want *you*," I said.

Her chin quivered; as though to hide it, she raised her hand to her face. The gesture was piercing, and for a second I was sure she was crying—though I knew that Ginger has not cried since childhood. I moved closer to her. "Ginger," I said. "I wanted you to know because—"

She raised her head and dropped her hand. "Velvet is coming this weekend," she said. "I can't cancel it. I didn't let her come last time because she messed up at school. But she needs to practice for an event." And she stood up, like to leave.

"Ginger," I said. "Where are you?"

"Where I always am, right in front of you."

"Listen," I said. "I know what I did was cowardly and fucked-up. But I love you. Do you love me?"

She looked at me then and her eyes finally showed her. "Yes," she said. "But I don't feel it now." And she left the room. I heard the front door open and softly close.

Ginger

I went to the park where we took Velvet those years ago and sat on a picnic table with my knees up and held close against myself. A short distance away there were little kids on the swings, their father pushing them, the mother getting something from the car, watching them as she closed the door with her hip, guardian care visible to me in her neck and jaw even though I could not make out her face. The light child-voices sounded so far away in the cold spring air.

Cheating. Of course I know why they call it that. I hate it, but I know. So much of what happens between people is comparable to a game. There is a deep, soft core that everyone longs for, too deep for games or even words. But to get to that, you have to play and play well. And I did not know how. Art, society, relationships, simple conversation—I couldn't understand how to do any of it. I don't know why; I don't know what was wrong with me. I tried, and when I was young and good-looking it could at least sometimes seem like my failure was actually an interesting *artistic* version of some special game. But now the truth is so plain that even Velvet's illiterate mother can see it. It's clear even to her—somehow *especially* to her—that I couldn't even do the thing every woman on the planet knows how to do. I can see her contempt, the question in her eyes: *What is wrong with her? How did she even get a husband?* And still, it was her child, the lovely girl that she *doesn't even want,* the child I finally loved, who somehow allowed me a way in, who made me feel what everyone else felt; finally I could join, be part of the play—except everybody thought that was wrong too, that somehow I still wasn't doing it right.

Everybody including my husband. I got up off the table and my movement caught the eye of the mother at the swing set. She waved at me and I realized I knew her; she was the aunt of one of the Cocoon Theater kids. I waved back at her and she came toward me.

Please God, I thought. Not now. I resisted the urge to put my hands over my face. She kept coming. But what is doing it right? What in hell can I do that's right?

"Hey," she said, smiling. "Weren't you in the *Christmas Carol* a couple of years back?"

"Yes," I said. "Yes, I was."

"I thought so! You were really good!"

"Thank you," I said. "It was a lot of fun."

Great, something I did right—act in a play for children.

Velvet

My mom said about Ginger once that she had a crazy eye and I always thought, No, she just looks sad a lot. But now her eyes shined like a animal in the dark and I didn't know their expression.

I said to her, "You're different."

She was making me cucumbers with white vinegar, and when I said that she stopped and said, "How?"

"Your voice is different, everything is different. You say things like it's in a book with quotes on it. Even to Paul."

For a second she looked like herself, and I missed her. Then she went back to the salad. "Something happened," she said. "But I can't talk about it."

"Why can't you talk about it?"

"You're too young. But don't worry, it was nothing horrific. It'll be okay."

I went to see the horses and it *was* okay because it needed to be. I didn't want to think about whatever was wrong with Ginger. I couldn't stop thinking about Dominic, but for once I felt like, he says I'm from *someplace else* and he can't be there—and he's right. He can't be here. Here is like coming back to my country, and not sneaking in like a illegal. Fiery Girl was back too; her stall had a sign on it, but instead of "Do Not Touch," it had her name carved on it and inside it was *cleaned*. She was not wearing the cribbing strap even if she sometimes bit her stall, and when I came with the halter she put her head down like YES.

Pat took Graylie and we went out by the paddock. I saw Sugar and Nova running together, and all the others bucking, clowning, and talking loud at each other with their heads and backs and legs. Fiery Girl raised her head and called to them and somebody called back. She got turned out with the other horses because she learned how to be with Chloe and Nut; now she could go out with everybody but Spirit and Diamond Chip—she still fought them. I could feel her shivering toward the other horses inside herself, but I pulled down on the lead and she lowered her head, sending softness and obedience to me. The air had new smells and sounds, and the horses said it with all the muscles of their backs and legs: *Spring, spring, spring!*

We mounted and went out down the path where I'd run with her bareback; my legs remembered and it felt like she did too, like under me she bunched and sighed. I remembered how the orchard was all rotting fruit flying past my face; now the trees were getting buds, and there was a feeling of something about to happen in the ground and even the air. The path was first big enough for the horses to walk side by side, but Fiery Girl walked faster than Graylie and when the path narrowed, we led the way. We had to stay on the path because of holes where the horses could break their ankles, or maybe snakes.

When the path got wide again Pat said, "We've missed you the last few weeks."

I said, "Me too."

"You know you have to keep up your practice if you want to compete."

I said, "I know. I'm sorry." I could feel her expecting me to say more. But I couldn't tell her now. *Now* didn't have anything to do with all that.

"You know, if you don't want to compete, that's your business. But if you don't, I hope it's not because you think you can't."

My heart went quiet in my chest. Still, I couldn't speak.

"When I used to compete—I liked to win, I liked the applause, I liked the prizes and trophies. I especially liked to beat certain people, that's the truth. But what felt best was the reason I won, when I did. It was because of my bond with my horse. Because under pressure, I could put my mind and my body together with his, and I could feel it, like he would go through the wall for me if I asked him to and he knew I meant it. And I would go through the wall with him. And everybody could see. You know what I mean?"

"Yes."

"I think you do. I *know* you do. I know you *can*. But it's one thing to do it out here. It's another thing to do it in front of people, with other riders who're all doing the same. It's powerful, more real. Even if you don't win. If you don't try it, you'll never know."

I didn't answer her and she didn't try to make me. We just rode quiet, feeling her words. The only time I talked was when I asked her about this covered-box shape up in some trees; she told me it was a blind for hunters left over from hunting season. That they would hide in there and shoot.

We stopped when we came to the fence where I fell off before. Pat dismounted and walked Graylie to the fence and tied him. The fence was wood posts with torn-up rails stuck through holes in the posts. Pat took one end of the top rail and pushed it out the hole so it came down on the ground. Fiery Girl moved like a five-year-old that needs to pee, wanting to eat grass, talk to Graylie, run, *something*. I had to pull her back, turn her in a circle, sit her firm. Pat took the second rail down and said now we were gonna gallop to the jump. Gallop not like in the arena, but all the way. Fiery Girl's back legs moved all over, like she knew something was different, then we cantered away from the fence. When we found a place to stop Pat asked me, "Have you seen racing on television?" "At your house once," I said. "Okay, it's not gonna be like that. You want to be more grounded in your stirrups, not forward like the jockeys on TV. You *do* want to lean forward in the gallop. You want to get off her back and kick her forward—but just before the jump? Sit deep in the saddle with your shoulders over your center, but I mean *just* before. Got it?"

She looked in my eyes and I said, "Yes."

"And remember, look ahead of the jump, not at it."

"Yes."

"Okay," she said. "Now. Through the *wall*."

Ginger

When I was in kindergarten there was a series of books meant to teach kids how everything in the world was put together. At least I guess that was the point of them. In the one I remember, each cardboard page showed a picture of a farm animal—I think there was a farmer too—and each of the pages had three sections: instead of turning a whole page, you could turn them section by section and make a rooster with a pig's body and farmer's legs. That's what it felt like trying to act normal around Paul with Velvet there. It felt that way even in the days before she came, like a hand was grabbing my midsection and turning me into a cow with cat legs, and something hairy and disgusting in the middle, and it kept happening, pictures flipping randomly. How could I even bring her into this shit-storm—but if I didn't, when would she ride? "Listen," said Kayla, "I've had to smile and put food on the table when I was so depressed I didn't want to move. Ginger, that girl isn't made of china and neither are you. You can handle it." Paul said the same. "We can do this," he said. "Even if we break up right after she leaves." I said, "We can't break up until after the event." "Okay," he said, "we won't."

Because I had not told him the event was off. Because as far as I was concerned, it wasn't.

So we got up together and made eggs and bacon and orange juice; the picture split and got joined with the first time I made us bacon and eggs in that house. He had looked at the food and said, "Breakfast!" so softly, like it was the dearest thing, and that's what it was to me too. But now that feeling had been divided into pieces and stuck together with the impossible present and something else down below it, something hard, misshapen and too big. I laid the dishes out, and through the chaos came the special feeling I had whenever Velvet was there and I made food for her. Well now here was the other side of that privilege, a tiny, tiny taste of what people mean when they say parenting is hard. I remembered my mother, *our* mother; the day after Dad left she made us pancakes, exhaustion and will mixed up in the sweet taste. It was maybe a year later that she sent Melinda to a mental hospital for running off with a married man when she was basically still a kid. When we were grown I confronted my mother about it and she said, "I didn't know what else to do!" and I despised her. Well, now I didn't know what to do either. So we ate and smiled and asked Velvet about the horses, and then she went to the barn, and I went upstairs to my laptop to look at sites about cheating spouses with lists like "5 Reasons You Should Take a Cheater Back" and "10 Reasons You Shouldn't Take a Cheater Back."

Velvet

When we galloped, there was nothing but me and her. I felt the sky above me but I didn't see anything but her ears and her neck and the ground flying toward me and Graylie's butt and Pat's butt on top. Graylie's legs flew and he rose up over the fence, switched his tail, and came down. The fence flashed up at me and I remembered, sit back. Fiery Girl came up under me like nothing was even there. The fence disappeared. It was so beautiful-easy and at first I didn't know why.

Ginger

How do you respect yourself staying with a man who can't or won't value you?

Yes, it's hard if you run a business together, but the cheater is the one who must change and prove love.

Don't even touch him till he begs and pleads; make him vacuum and clean the toilet, make him call and text you constantly.

You won't forgive yourself if you don't at least try to move past it.

We're all human.

You'll save on therapy bills.

You didn't make him do it.

You have a strong foundation together; don't throw it away. You might never find anyone else.

"Ginger!" The door banged and she came up the stairs. Guiltily, I closed the cheaters window. She came into the room, rosy and exultant, lifting me up.

"What is it?" I said. "What?"

She said, "I saw the distance! I knew where it was, and I don't even know how! I saw it for the first time and I jumped perfect and we were going fast! Ginger, I am going to be in the competition!"

Paul

I saw her ride for the first time. She'd spent the weekend practicing and she wanted us to come. She and Ginger were getting ready to go when she looked at me and said, "Could you come too?" The walk over was heartbreaking, me talking too much about how beautiful everything was and them not saying anything.

The horse surprised me at first—the way Velvet talked about it I expected it to be big and beautiful and it was not. It was built somehow a bit strangely, with a narrow chest that from the side was deep in breadth. But its muscles were fine and distinct under its glossy, moving skin and its steps were springy, like it had elastic ankles. Its head was overlarge, but there was something noble, *senatorial,* in its boniness and size. As Velvet rode it quietly around the arena, I guess warming it up, I began to see its personality and to understand; the horse was rippling with nerves, like its basic forward movement contained fierce motion in all directions, which Velvet controlled seemingly without effort. Ginger and I stood against the fence to watch and every time the horse passed us, it looked at me sideways like, *Check it out—see what I can do!* and I smiled to remember Velvet describing how it looked exactly that way. Once, the horse broke into a nervous jog, which Velvet smoothly corrected without so much as a glance at us.

A fat, tough-looking woman was in the ring too, giving a low running commentary that I couldn't hear. She finally came over to us and said, "How do you like our star rider?" I realized I'd seen her a couple of times early in the morning driving horses in the road. I answered her, "Wonderful!" and Ginger looked at me coldly.

The woman registered the look and walked away without comment, back out to the middle of the ring. She gave Velvet an instruction I couldn't hear and Velvet began to ride the horse harder; it picked up speed and ran with a loose, elegant gait, throwing its legs around, ambling with speed. Velvet sat up in the saddle and leaned forward; the horse put on more speed. The hair on my neck stood up. Ginger's lips parted and her face glowed; her parted lips stayed quiet, her smile touching her eyes and cheeks only. I realized with a sharp sensation that she looked like she did when she first loved me.

Velvet flew over the first jump and the second, flowing like silk. I made an involuntary noise; Ginger laughed, tiny and delighted.

When she first loved me: her softness emerging as if from hiding, overjoyed to be out in the open, coming to me open-armed. Velvet took the third jump and the horse thundered past us, throwing off heat and breathing with fierce ease. I reached for my wife's hand; she let me. Velvet rode past again, calm and delighted too, her face in an expression I'd never seen on her before, oblivious to everything but the animal beneath her.

Ginger let go of my hand. "She's going to win," she said. "She's going to win."

"You were right to do this," I said. "It's incredible."

"I just want her to win," said Ginger.

And I answered, "So do I."

Velvet

It was not only Spindletop that scared me from competing. Before I even went there I was having bad dreams where I fell in front of people and Fiery Girl fell too, and broke her leg. And there was something else; I don't know what it was, but it made me turn away from competition thoughts fast like a horse turns from a sound or sight. And it was not only Pat's words that changed my mind. When I was riding my horse in the field, there was no nightmare or daymare, nothing but her huge heart with thorns holding me up. Ginger and her strange eyes fell away. Dominic and Brianna's girls were there but floating off the left side of me like a made-up island. When we went for the jump, all of them disappeared.

Then I jumped for Ginger and Paul, and Ginger went back to being her old self, and we went to eat at the pizza place and it was like I was eleven again, and I wished for just a minute that I could stay that way forever before I even knew who Dominic was.

All the way home on the train, I pictured myself at EQUAL on Fiery Girl, running in the practice ring with those beautiful horses. I thought about it so much it was like it already happened. When I got off the train I felt so good I was happy to see my mom, and she saw it because she rubbed my hair and said, "Mi niña" for Ginger to hear. I knew better than to talk about Fiery Girl and the way I rode her. I just leaned against my mom and wrote it on my heart over and over while we went home on the subway.

When we got home I went out because I was in the mood to see people, but I didn't piss my mom off, I just sat on the stoop so as not to miss dinner. I was only there a minute when the Haitian lady passed by with a pink comb in her hair and real shoes, high-tops, on her feet this time. It had been so long, and I didn't know if she'd recognize me, but she right away smiled and said, "Hello, my baby!" I stood up and hugged her and she said how funny to see me because she was thinking about me, she had a dream about me that she didn't remember, but it was something good. She said, "I think something good's coming your way, but don't miss it!"

I was shy to ask her name, but she told me, "I'm Gaby, Gaby Alabre, and I live in the project on the Albany Street side. My name's on the buzzer outside if you want to come see me sometime."

I told her my name too. I wanted to ask her more about why she thought something good was coming, but my mom shouted down and I didn't want her to see me speaking with Gaby so I said I would come sometime and went in.

Ginger

The night she left I went out to the horse barn. It was dark and I could hear the animals react to me when I came in, their silence sudden and massed, like powerful thoughts crowded together, thinking on me. Then I guess one of them grabbed a bucket in its teeth and starting banging it on a wall. Another one snorted and I could feel their thought-shapes part to let me in. Their attention dispersed; they breathed and made quiet noises to each other.

I thought, No wonder Velvet likes it here. It was safe and secret with them, the ground deep under me, under meadows and houses and human things; ant-swarm human thoughts and giant human feelings. Paul, his other woman, Michael, the chopped-up book of my past: wide, clean surges of hope and love forced into weird shapes, breaking free again. Velvet's mother, her crushed little cursing face, her fighter's calm, impassive face; that first time, the way she met my eyes like no one else ever did. *Mi niña;* Velvet; *my* Velvet. The horses.

I went to Fiery Girl. I couldn't see anything but the flash of her eye and the outline of her ears and curious nose. There was a sign on her door; I imagined it still said "Do Not Touch." But Velvet had touched her, rode her, cared for her. I put my hand through the bars and touched her nose. She jerked her head and I pulled my hand back, scared. The horse's teeth flashed and she grunted; I realized she was biting at her door like a cat scratching at wood. I was afraid to touch her again, but I stood there some moments, feeling the animals, calming.

When I finally walked back, Paul was on the porch, waiting. I didn't want to be glad, but I was. For the first time in days, we lay down together—rolled away from each other but together. Michael flitted through me, his artificial kisses I had mistaken for "delicate" stuck together with Velvet trying to call me about her murdered friend, stuck together with the hot-point past where my "self" was crushed into a ball like old aluminum, and I didn't even know what was happening to Michael. My husband lay next to me, blinking loud enough for me to hear.

Velvet

In the school bathroom some girls walked in talking mean shit about somebody's hair, that she bleached it so bad it fell out and she had to wear this crusty ol' wig. I was in a stall. I pulled up my feet and they mobbed up the mirrors goin', "And she like fifty at least and wearin' fake Chanel glasses and that blond wig like she Lil' Kim or somethin'." A girl banged into the stall next to me. "An' I heard she bringin' in retarded AIDS victims to the house?" "Don't be talkin' that way about people with AIDS, and that girl ain't that retarded, either." "And she don't even *got* AIDS, the dude only—" "Yeah, but her own niece pregnant! She should—" "Yeah, but Dominic—" My ears popped open wide; next to me the toilet flushed and the door banged open. "—she say Dominic got somebody else on his mind for real, she can tell." "While she *pregnant*? Word, some bitch gonna die, literally."

That was the last thing they said, but all I heard was *Dominic got somebody else on his mind for real* and *I think something good's coming your way, but don't miss it!*

Except I kept thinking about Brianna pregnant and her crazy aunt and somehow the sick feeling of a retarded girl being raped got mixed in it and why did people think the aunt was bad to help even if she did wear a ugly wig? I didn't want to be the bitch coming in from the side even if I did hate Brianna. So I made myself think about Fiery Girl and how I would see her again soon. But then I just wished I could tell Dominic about the way I jumped her. I wished I could at least text him. But I promised him I wouldn't. So I called Ginger and we read a book called *The Brief Wonderful Life of Somebody* together. Except I couldn't pay attention because of wanting to see him so much it pushed out everything.

Silvia

Dante woke me, but I didn't know it was him at first, just felt something hitting my face—"Mami!" Softly he hit his hands on my face and pulled my cheeks. "Mami, I dreamed Velvet fell off her horse and died!"

"Shh, stop." I pushed away his hands and held his arms at his sides, strong but soft. "Velvet's fine. She's in the next room. Now ssshhh . . ."

"But she said she's going to ride in a contest, and I'm afraid something will happen."

"Don't be stupid. Go back to sleep or I'll hit you!" And I stroked his head and calmed him with my arms. He whimpered to keep me touching him, and I did until he slept.

But of course then I could not. Asleep in the next room, and she deprived me of sleep! He was only dreaming; it couldn't be true. I tried to calm myself and sleep, but anger beat my brain like a drum—that she could do this to me in the middle of the night, get into Dante's dreams and disturb him so he woke me on a work night! I tore off the blanket and went down the hall, threw open her door. I meant to beat her right then, get the truth out of her before she was awake enough to lie, she would stupidly throw it right in my face just to spite me—

But I didn't. My body suddenly felt weak and I just stood and looked at her, her arms and legs wrapped around her pillow, holding it like Dante held me. If I beat her it would take me another hour to get to sleep. I would do it tomorrow. I would find out and then—

"You need to do something different," said Rasheeda. "You beat her ass every which way and she still not doing what you want. You need to get a different idea."

I went out into the living room and sat on the couch, making my body calm. Rasheeda. She said when her daughter was sick she prayed. She believed it was the only reason her grandchild didn't get AIDS. She gave me the prayer she said; it was in my purse, crumpled up. She knew I couldn't read it, but she gave it to me anyway. I got it out of my purse, opened it and held it in my hand. Streetlight flashed on it, and I tried to remember the prayer my mother loved.

Remember, O most gracious Virgin Mary, that never was it known that anyone who fled to your protection, implored your help, or sought your intercession was left unaided. Mary, don't let my daughter die on a horse. Humble her, punish her, but don't let her die. Surely she isn't doing something so stupid. *Inspired with this confidence, I fly unto you, Virgin of virgins, my Mother.* Because she won't listen to me, nothing I do works. *Before you I stand sinful and sorrowful,* punish me, punish her, but don't let her die that way. She is foolish, but not bad except for pride, and it's my fault that she was born wrong, not hers. Forgive, forgive, despise not my petitions, have mercy, hear and answer me.

Velvet

I didn't go find him to take him from Brianna, only to talk to him.
It was my birthday and that made it seem okay. I didn't text or call
because he said not to. I went to the block where we first met and
then met again. When I walked there this time boys looked but
didn't talk to me so much, I guess because it was still cold and my
body was covered and my face was closed to them because I was all
the time calling him, calling him with my mind. I know I was doing
that because he heard me; I know he heard me because he came.

He wasn't alone, he was with another boy—really he was a man,
and he had a hard face. My heart opened too fast, and I said his name
in a voice you shouldn't speak on the street with a hard man there.
And Dominic, he looked at me with his face hard too. His look froze
my heart, but I could not close it. "What you want, girl?" He said it
like he didn't know me.

"Just to say hello. Just to tell you about my horse."

His eyes went soft and then hard again, except not all the way.
The man looked away, bored. "You got business with shawty here?"
he said. "Ima catch you up tha way."

The man left, and we started walking. I hoped he would go to
the restaurant with the lights, but he just said, "So what about your
horse?"

"Ima be in a competition with her."

"Awesome." His voice was sarcastic. I didn't say anything. There
was pounding in my ears and everything seemed like it was moving
very fast. I wanted to say, *Why are you being this way?* I wanted to tell
him about seeing the distance, but I couldn't do that either—his hard
voice made even that stupid. So I just asked, "Who's that man?"

"That ain't your business."

"Why can't I ask that? You said we were friends."

"Not like that we ain't."

"Like what, then? I can't even just ask you who somebody is?"

He stopped on a corner. His eyes went hard/soft/hard/sad.
There were boys like a foot away. "Listen," he said. "I know you

come here and walk around looking for me." His voice was mean, but his eyes looked sad and scared and cut me to the heart so I could not talk. The boys pretended not to see.

"You can't be doin' this," he said. "If I wanna see you, I let you know. You get it?"

"But you told me, you *showed* me—."

"I told you not to bother me!"

Brianna's girls came round the corner. Very quiet, I finished my sentence: "Dominic, you showed me that picture you didn't show nobody else." For about two seconds everything stopped. His eyes said, *I'm sorry, I'm sorry sorry.* But his back was to Brianna's friends, and all they heard was him going, *"Picture?* That wasn't nothin', that wasn't even me, I was just playin' with you! It ain't my fault if you don't know game when you see it!"

One of Brianna's bitches laughed low.

"A'ight? Now you need to go home and not bother people no more."

And he turned his back and talked to Brianna's friends.

Me just standing there. The corner boys watching me. This one bitch grillin' me hatefully. And me ready to fly on her—but like he could feel it, he stuck his arm out between us and pulled the bitch by her shoulders, *pulled* her around, saying to her, *Don't get into that shit, come with us, we gonna*—whatever, I didn't hear. She looked at him sharp, like, *Why do you care,* but still she went. And quick, over his shoulder, he looked back at me.

Me doing nothing. Worse than a beat-down. *You showed me that picture.* Stupid and lame. I hated myself for saying it, more than I hated him for what he said back. If one of them looked at me then and laughed, I coulda run and punched the bitch, but nobody did; they were too busy trying to get attention from him.

The corner boys still stood there. I yelled, "What you lookin' at!" and at least they looked down. But when I walked away I could still feel their eyes on me, like they could see my private body. I felt like I did that time after Manuel, when I wanted to hide in my own house, and now I was on the street and it felt like everybody was looking at my body. All the eyes, and the streets and buildings and cars as far from me as the trees and houses of upstate. But here was no horse to come and touch her face on mine. Fiery Girl, her face on mine—I tried to grab the memory of it. Instead I felt the eyes and remembered the substitute, and Alicia snapping her fingers at his face and Ginger saying, "I'm weak." And my mom saying, "It's not your fault. You have bad blood."

For the first time I understood: She said that to make me feel better. From love.

I went to get Dante from day care. He leaned on me all the way home. I fixed my mind on his forehead and eyelashes until that's all I saw.

Ginger

There is a graveyard in the next town over that I like a lot. It's small and very old, full of thin, crumbling stones so decrepit the names and dates are worn away, slanting sideways or lurching back, some with pieces broken off. There are few big display plots, just these plain, mostly anonymous stones from the 1880s. The living have worn a path through the grass on their way to the drugstore or the parking lot or the diner on the main street—where I'm going to meet Kayla for coffee.

I walk slowly, reading the few legible stones and feeling the gentle humor of the ground beneath me. *As you are now, so once was I / As I am now, so you will be / Prepare for death and follow me*—somebody who died in 1803 wanted his stone to say that. Numbly I smile and wonder how it will be on my deathbed to remember that when I was forty-eight years old I acted in a performance of *A Christmas Carol* with children wearing pajamas and bonnets, and that a Dominican family came from Crown Heights to see it. Where will Velvet be then? What will she remember of our time together? I remember when I talked to her about our periods, and I said, "You're coming up and I'm going down." How she smiled.

Prepare for death and follow me. Church bells ring.

Yes, I am going down. Like every human will, like every woman in particular, as her body splutters and gives out. Nothing wrong with Velvet's satisfaction in the contrast. Maybe my whiteness gives it double meaning, double triumph for her. Whatever. I'm going down anyway, my husband going after somebody younger even as he protests his love. No wonder Becca hates me, Paul left her when she was about my age. He didn't leave her for me, but I am almost ten years younger and must've seemed like a replacement.

A replacement: Michael. The fever-feeling of youth coming up inside me, suddenly animated like a cartoon trying to become human. Sparkling dreams of passion and tenderness unlimited by time and its wounds—stupid for any woman my age to dream of such things. But I did dream, so how can I complain about "cheating"? I didn't get physical with Michael, or at least not genital; we made out like kids. But I tried to start it up again with him; for days, weeks, I e-mailed with him, trying to make it happen again even as he lost interest.

I stop on the edge of the graveyard, paralyzed with sadness and loss. It's dead now, my adolescent longing, and even so I can't help but press it against my cheek one more time, hoping to bring it alive again. Paul is flawed but alive and here I am still rubbing this dead thing on my face—why? How did this dead thing come up out of the past and eat my happiness? Why did I allow it?

I walk out onto the parking lot. People pass me and our eyes do not meet. What will I tell my friend? Nothing. Just that Paul and I are having trouble. It doesn't matter why I allowed it; I did, and so did he, and now nothing will be good again. I am finished. Except for Velvet. Velvet and the horse. Even though she is so aloof now and doesn't tell me anything. Even though Paul is right, everyone is right, the whole coarse world is right: I can't even be her *pretend* mother. I give in. I agree. I'm over. It is what it is. But I can still get her on that fucking horse. I can help her win.

Velvet

For my birthday my mom made asopao with chicken, which she knows I love, and we don't have hardly ever. But that night the delicious taste hurt, like it was love that wanted to protect me but could not and could be torn away like nothing. It doesn't make sense, but that's what it felt like in my mouth and in the way my mom watched me chew.

"What's wrong with you?" she said. "Don't you like it?"

"I like it."

"You're eating it like a robot," she said, and Dante did lame robot arms.

I wanted to be with them, to hide from the world with them. But I couldn't. We were separated even in the same room. Ginger and Pat and Fiery Girl were even further away. The only thing close was Dominic, and he did not want me. He didn't even respect me.

"So," said my mother, "what's this about your riding in a race?"

She looked at me; Dante put his head down. He put his fork down too.

"I'm not riding in a race," I said.

"Dante told me about a race."

"There's a *competition*, but I'm not in it." As soon as I said it, it was true.

"No? The great horsewoman isn't riding in the *competition*?"

Dante's eyes came up to look at me.

"Why not?" asked my mom.

"I don't want to," I said.

They both stared at me. Dante's eyes lost their brightness.

I shrugged. "You don't want me to, Mami."

Dante's eyes said *Liar.* My mom said, "Huh. You finally stopped being stupid."

Dante pushed his food around but did not eat.

"I'm glad," said my mom. "Here." And she dished more asopao onto my plate.

Ginger

Velvet of course needed her mother's permission to enter the competition; there was a form to sign. If I forged the signature and Velvet fell off *or something*, it would be a legal disaster, not just for me but for Paul, and even he didn't deserve that.

"Be openhearted," said Kayla. "Talk to the woman from your heart. She's accepted so much so far—"

"She beats her daughter, Kayla."

"Do it for the girl's sake." She said it like she didn't even hear me. "Give the mom a chance. Let her know you'd love her to come up and watch her daughter shine."

"She doesn't *want* her daughter to shine."

"Give her a chance. Make her feel respected."

But how could I make her feel respected? I'd lied from the beginning—really, why stop now?

I picked up a pen and held it poised over the paper that declared that I, as her parent or legal guardian, understood and accepted that there was a chance of serious bodily injury or even death. Because Velvet was not going to die, she was going to win. Even if *something did* happen, and she broke her arm or her leg or *something*, her mother might not even realize she could sue us.

Judas. I put down the pen, then picked it up. I tried to open my heart. I prayed; I begged the air. I put down the pen. I got on a conference call with the churchy-voiced translator and told her to invite Mrs. Vargas up to see her daughter shine. The ignorant woman sailed forward under the bright banner of her voice, and was cut to pieces before she even got three full sentences out.

"She says no," said the translator. "She says her daughter doesn't want to do it. She's going to put her on so she can tell you herself."

Velvet

She asked why. I said, "I don't want to because my mom doesn't want me to." And I could feel her *trembling,* like, through the *phone,* and I thought how my mother said, "Shut up or I'll give you something to cry about!" Because the trembling was like crying, like how Ginger's face would look when she had *nothing* to cry about, and I was glad to fuck with her like that, to refuse what she gave, my mother beside me with her hand on my shoulder.

But when I hung up I could still hear what Dominic said. I would hear it for the rest of my life. If I went to Williamsburg I would see him and Brianna and their baby and he wouldn't even talk to me. I didn't have him and now maybe I didn't have my horse. Ginger loved me and I disappointed her. Why would she let me keep coming there? I disappointed her all the time. And then I had bad thoughts about her.

I said, "I'm going to sit outside"; my mom said, "Don't go far."

And I didn't mean to go. I only started walking because moving with people, hearing them say shit back and forth, held me down, took the bad thoughts out of my mind. Men's eyes on me made me feel better too, though I don't know why. Because I knew what my mom meant about them now. I knew why she'd been so mean. It was true what my grandfather said when he was still alive, that she said what she did out of love. I felt love for her. I didn't want to make her mad.

But I wanted to see Gaby. That's why I went to find the street she lived on, in case I might find her there. It was where Cookie lived, where my mom told me to stay away from, and I never had a reason to go there anyway. Really, it looked better to me than where we were, with more stores and places to eat and churches, and this store-church had a red electrical sign that said "Mercy Time, 7:00–8:00." I kept going, past the project yard where people were out drinking from bags and little kids were chasing each other, this girl riding on a boy's back.

When I got to Gaby's street I guessed the building and went to find her name on the buzzers. I was just going to find it and go home, but when I did find it, these boys came out the door, almost men, and their eyes were all over me and I went to get in the building past them, mostly just to move, and they blocked me, going, "You coming to see me, beautiful?" "I ain't ever seen you before." "Damn, what I could do with you!" So I pressed the buzzer like I've got business, and one of them said, "Hey, you the little Dominican girl, ain't you? From St. Marks Avenue?" I didn't know him, but I said, "Yea-ah," like, *So what?* And he smiled like I was eleven years old and said, "You and your lil' brother used to know Cookie, right?" I smiled and Gaby's voice came out the intercom; I said who I was but she didn't answer, instead he went, "Cookie said you and him used to talk! He said he gonna wait till you turn sixteen and till then—" Gaby said, "The buzzer doesn't work!" like she was shouting through fuzzballs. "I got it!" said the man, going for the door. "What floor?" I said. I didn't hear what she said. He said, "She on the third floor, number ten" and let me in.

I didn't wait for the elevator because I could hear more people coming from somewhere and I didn't like their voices, so I went for the stairs. I was sorry right away because a light was out and it smelled like a nasty bathroom with disinfectant on top. But it was just the third floor, so I went up anyway.

Ginger

She said it was her mom who said no, but I still thought it had to do with that big fancy barn and big show. Courtesy of Becca's friend Joan who had generously gotten Velvet invited to Spindletop, where her confidence was hurt. Though that was surely *not* the intention; the woman just wanted to be kind, if ostentatiously so.

Which is exactly what Becca was accusing me of when she said I was "playing at being a parent," not to mention exactly why her friend Laura had talked down to me that time outside the drugstore for being—unlike her!—a white person who was "messing with" this non-white woman's child. Judging me like I'm an ignorant racist or just a childless neurotic fool—and now they are proven right, and can smugly nod their heads. The big barn, the big show that a kid from up here would take in stride was too much for Velvet and could only hurt her. Naturally her mother didn't want her to compete because of course it would be threatening to her to see her daughter do something she herself could never do, something only *I* could offer her. And Becca's friends plus Becca herself felt the offense of that right away because after all, they're *moms* like her. I couldn't blame Silvia; she was just protecting her daughter, and even herself, but *them*—how hateful, if I really am so clueless and bereft, to rub it in like that. "Playing at being a parent"—God, I wish I'd said something and not just sat there accepting it like I always do. I wish I'd said, "What are *you* playing at, you mad cow? Being the wounded wife? Is that your reason for acting out the aggression you're so obviously proud of? It's bullshit, you kicked him out before I even met him. You don't care about that except what people think of you, the usual stupid shit: Oh, poor Becca. She's so humiliated."

Of course it did occur to me that Becca was not "playing" any more than I was. That she actually had been humiliated. That she was lonely and sad even now. Even with Edie, even with all those big women around her. Of course I knew it was natural for her to dislike me; it was almost her *job*. But that still didn't stop the cattywampus conversation in my head, back and forth, blaming Becca and then myself, in the house or the gym locker room or driving in the car, sometimes making me smack the steering wheel at the light. I would catch myself doing it and feel crazy and then keep doing it. Until one day I saw her alone in the diner and did it *at* her.

Velvet

I went down halls full of noise and warm food smell to her door. I knocked and when she came she was wearing a bathrobe and these big glasses all crooked on her face, but still she smiled at me and said, "Hello, child. Come in." I did, and a cat ran out of the room; there was another skinny cat with a bad eye on the couch. "Sit down," said Gaby. "I only have ginger ale, you want some?" I said yes, even though I don't like ginger ale. She went out of the room and I heard a old voice asking a question and Gaby saying, "A friend, Mama."

I sat on the edge of the couch. The cat stared the hell out of me with its one eye. It was little like a kitten, but its face was old—its *jaw* was old—and both its eyes cried old greasy tears. There were no lights on and the room was getting dark, but I could see there were pictures of saints on the walls and a picture of Martin Luther King with a white president from a long time ago, their faces pressed together sideways, like they were also saints or old movie stars. Gaby came back in clothes (not her bathrobe), and carrying two big cups of ginger ale. She sat next to me and told me the electric was off, and that she would light the candles soon. I saw the candles, like the ones my mom brought home from work, they were half burned down. My mom would be missing me now.

"You came to see me," she said. "I'm glad. Tell me, how are you?"

I said I was fine. The cat looked at Gaby with love in its one greasy eye.

"I found him on the street," she said. "Both his eyes were shut up so he was going blind, and he was looking up at people and crying on the sidewalk. I don't know why I picked him up, but I did. I cleaned him and fed him and the one eye got better." The old mother's voice talked from the other room; Gaby talked back in Haitian. "My mother didn't even want the one cat. To her animals are just dirty. So I told her I would put him out again when he got better, but I don't have the heart. Look at his little face."

I thought of my mom, looking out the window and seeing I'm not there. It was already darker. I said, "Do you remember the dream you told me you had? That you told me about, where something good happened to me?"

She looked for a minute like she didn't know what I was talking about, but then she smiled and said she did remember. I was hoping she would talk more, but she didn't, she just drank her ginger ale. I asked, "What was going to happen? In your dream?"

"Child," she said, "it was a dream. I told it to you in goodwill so you would know I wish you well from my heart. And because dreams come for a reason, even if we don't know what it is." She got up and began to light the candles. With her back to me she said, "Why do you ask?"

I tried to answer, but the answer felt too big to get out in words.

She sat down again, her eyes soft. "What is it you hope for?"

My heart beat too fast. I said, "There's this boy."

She moved her head; candle flame burned in her glasses. "Yes, a boy?"

"He used to love me." I put my head down to let tears run. But none came. "He used to love me and he don't no more." Her arm went around me. I said, "A long time ago, he stopped this other boy from . . . and now he—" My body went tight like I was crying but still there were no tears, only a numb thing grabbing inside, grabbing and loosing, like I was sick but with no sick coming up. "It's okay," she said. "It's okay. Let it go."

Finally I cried, and I told her. She asked me if I let him have my body and I said no, but I would if he wanted it. She shook her head and said, "It's too soon." She said, "He knew that and he respected your precious body." My tears stopped and I said, "No he didn't. *He didn't respect nothin'.*" She said, "In his actions, he did. Think how much worse you would feel now if it had been the other way."

I didn't answer back to her because I didn't want to tell her what happened. But I didn't think I would feel worse if I'd done more. Because that way I would've been really with him at least.

"He respected you," she said. "Now you have to respect him. What he said today, put it behind you. He needs to care for this pregnant girl as best he can. Leave it be."

She sat back, candlelight shining from her glasses. Her cat stretched its paws to her and she touched its head. "Tell me," she said more softly. "Is there something else that you hope?"

I didn't have time to tell her about the horses, and I didn't feel like it either. So I just said there was a competition I wanted to be in but I couldn't because my mom didn't want me to. She said then I couldn't do it; I couldn't disobey my mother. I said, "I know," and then I remembered my mom and said, "I have to go." She said she would walk me to St. Marks. We were at her door when she asked me, "Is there a man who wants you to enter this contest? An uncle or a teacher, an older brother who might talk to your mother?" I said no, and then her mom yelled at her. She stepped away and yelled back and my phone texted at me, so I looked at it.

It was Dominic.

She came back and said, "What kind of competition you want to be in?" I put my phone away, but I was too messed-up to explain and it came out all wrong—she never heard of the Fresh Air Fund, so she didn't understand about the horses, like where I went to ride them. I could see her thinking, This girl lying or loco, because I didn't make sense, and I was smiling so stupidly even though at the same time I was afraid, because what if he was pranking me or if it wasn't even him but Brianna, or somebody else. What if they were all gonna be pranking me?

Then we stepped out of the building and my heart was wiped clean; my mom was there on the sidewalk. She didn't see me. She was talking to people who obviously could not understand anything she said. She looked small and scared and I was going to call out when Gaby said, "Hola, Mami!" and the people stood back. "Beg pardon, Mami," said Gaby. "I asked your daughter to help me carry some groceries home and she was good enough to take them all the way up the stairs for me."

This lady who cared about right and wrong lied for me and I am pretty sure my mom knew it; she usually does. But because it was in front of people, she had to accept it, and then when we walked away, she couldn't switch out of accepting it. She didn't say anything to me all the way home except "While you were helping the Haitian, our dinner got cold," but not even mad. And I wasn't mad either. She had come to find me, down the street she was scared of.

And also, my phone was texting. I could feel it on my leg.

Ginger

It was rare to see her alone; I don't think it had ever happened before. She was sitting at a table with a cup of coffee and writing in one of those decorative blank books they sell; without her usual prow-like outer focus, she appeared almost gentle. Until I said, "Becca, hello," and she looked up, immediately going haughty and retracted, eyes not quite meeting mine.

"Can I join you?" I asked.

"Actually, I'm waiting for someone."

"Oh. I just wanted to say thanks for the invitation to Spindletop. Very nice place."

"Actually, it was Joan who—"

"Yeah, I know, but I'm just saying it was nice. Although it didn't go all that well for her there."

"Oh, here's Laura!" Her expression went from discomfort to warm and welcoming as she tracked her friend's pleased scarf-flapping, cute-little-bell-on-the-door-ringing entry.

"Oh, hi, Ginger," said Laura. "Do you mind?"

Meaning, *Get out of my way; you're blocking my seat.* And I *did* mind.

"How are you?" gushed Becca as Laura squeezed past me.

"I'm not sure why it didn't go well," I said. "But she seemed pretty upset when she came back."

"What are we talking about?" Laura asked Becca.

"Velvet," I said.

"Who?"

"You know, the girl from the culture I know nothing about, but who I'm messing with anyway."

They stared at me. A middle-aged waitress with stalwart eyes came dragging a bad foot in an Ace bandage. "Are we two or three?" she asked.

They answered together: "Two!"

"Two it is," said the waitress and left with the extra laminated menu she'd brought just in case.

"Ginger—" said Becca.

"I'm going," I said. "And by the way, I wasn't kidding. You did say that, Laura, that I was messing with somebody else's kid."

"I don't remember."

"I'm sure you don't. And I'm sure, Becca, that you don't remember saying to me that I'm playing—"

"This is inappropriate," said Laura.

I flushed. "*Inappropriate*? Well, I don't think it was appropriate to tell me I'm messing with a child I love when you don't know anything about it. Or to tell me I'm 'playing at being a parent.'"

From the look on Becca's face, she *did* remember.

"I understand why you don't like me, and I'm sorry. But you had no right to talk that way to me. You don't know me."

"If you don't like the way we talk, then don't force your company on us and needlessly make a scene," said Laura.

"A scene? This is your idea of a *scene*?" My laugh was empty, and I reddened at the sound of it. "You really are an awful woman—both of you." And I left red-faced and trembling, but also glad, glad that I finally said something, even if it was weak. That at least I didn't just let them treat me like shit again.

But I guess I didn't look glad because when I got home and Paul saw me he said, "Ginger, what's wrong?" and he even sounded like he cared.

"Nothing's wrong," I said. "I just told Becca and Laura they've been total bitches to me and that it's 'inappropriate,' to use their repulsive language."

For a second he looked scared—that was good—but then he put his head in his hand and shook it, like this was just too idiotic to comment on. And I slapped him. I slapped the shit out of him. One, for politely looking the other way while Becca insulted me for years; two, for undermining my relationship with Velvet; three, for being an asshole generally; and four—ooh, let's not forget—for *cheating*. When I stopped, I expected him to start with AA crap, and that made me start looking around for something besides my hand—but he didn't. He stood there holding his face and looking at me like he'd just woken up.

I looked back thinking: Finally the glass is broken. Thank you, Michael. Thank you and fuck you.

Velvet

He texted me that he wanted to see me. He wanted to see me away from Brooklyn so nobody would know. He said just one last time, because it should not end with that disrespect or an apology on text. I said, "How do I even know it's you?" Right away he typed back, "Wherefore art thou?" He said meet him at Riverbank Park up near Washington Heights. He said "plz."

So he picked a time after school, but I didn't go to school. I took the train into Manhattan and went to Penn Station, where I always met Ginger. I bought a Krispy Kreme donut and a soda and stood eating it because to sit you had to show your ticket to a guard who was keeping homeless people out. I looked at the covers of magazines and at the people like me and the people like Ginger walking past each other. I could walk down the stairs and ride through a tunnel to get to my mare and to the house with the blue and white diamond floor.

Instead I paid my last money to see a movie with J. Lo in it, except she got pregnant in like the first five minutes and then died and it was all about white people. I wondered if maybe it was luck to see a movie where a pregnant girl died and then she was just *gone*. I knew that was evil to think, but what a weird thing in a movie. Then I don't remember what else I did until I came off the subway at 145th Street. He said to text him so he could wait there for me and he did. He looked nervous and embarrassed. I was not embarrassed and I was not nervous.

We went to a place by the water. The same water I saw out the train window when I went to see Ginger. He said, "I come here by myself to think."

I said, "It's nice."

We sat on a bench. It was still cold, so not many people were out. The water was blinking and bright in flipped-up pieces. We looked at it and he said, "So you gonna be in a competition on the horse?"

The way he looked at me in front of Brianna's girls. His voice saying *Awesome* sarcastically. "No," I said. "I'm not."

He looked at me quick and then away. "Why not?"

"My mom won't let me," I said.

"Oh."

I said, "So why—" at the same time he said, "You know—" Then he said, "I didn't mean what I said in front a them."

"Then why'd you say it?"

"I told you I couldn't be with you. I know I shouldn't've let nothin' happen, but—" He sat forward with his arms on his legs. The water pushed and pulled, bright and dark like eyes. People went past. A lady smiled.

"But what?" I said finally.

"I had feelings for you."

Had. "Then why you—"

"Because feelings by themself ain't what matters."

"You had feelings for me but it *don't matter*?"

"That ain't what I said!" He got up and I did too. He walked to the water and came back. He came close and I thought he would touch me; I could feel he wanted to. "Just, if you feel one way and what's right is the other way, you gotta do what's right, even if—"

"You made me come all the way out here to say that shit?"

He sat down. "To say I'm sorry. I ain't gonna be able to say it no other time."

I knew what he meant. That he would see me on the street and act like he didn't know me. Even if he had feelings. I said, "You a asshole. You say you love me just so you could get away from the police and—" *Get your dick sucked;* even to think it made me feel like shit. My face flashed hot, and I looked down to hide it.

"You know that ain't true. You know it. I wouldn't be here if that was true. I wouldn't never have come to see you and told you about Brianna. I wouldn't never showed you—"

And he took his Romeo picture out of his pocket. My body shut off; my face went cold. I snatched the picture and tore it in two. His face fell and he stood up. "It don't matter," he said. "I was gonna give it to you anyway."

"I don't want it."

I didn't feel wind, but the torn picture was moving anyway. He said, "A'ight, then." And stood up and walked away. I covered my heart with my hands, like it might cry out. And maybe it did because all of a sudden he stopped. He turned around and came close enough for me to hear him. He said, "You don't have to worry about Brianna's girls. They ain't gonna bother you." He went to go again but then turned back *again* and said, "And also I'm sorry you ain't gonna be in the competition. 'Cause I think you'd win." Then he turned around and left for good. I watched him until he was all the way gone. Then I picked up the pieces of his picture and kissed it and held it to me.

Ginger

"Never again will a disaster of this nature be handled in the terrible and disgraceful way that it was handled."

I sat in the dark watching last years's footage of John McCain talking outside a church in New Orleans. Fast forward to now: there's still crap from broken houses on the sidewalks, and signs for mold removal on telephone poles. What will Obama do?

Paul was cooking in the kitchen, making pasta with the swordfish from last night. I was drinking wine, but he didn't dare say anything. The night I slapped him we did it for the first time in months; he was not going to say anything. Yet.

The phone rang and I got up slowly. *Last year, of course, the house defied the president, preventing the administration from cutting federal spending for the poor.* Halfway up the stairs, I heard Velvet's voice come on the machine; the poor, *my* poor, my poor kid. I thought of her friend, the cruel child in the see-through shirt—Strawberry—stranded on her roof with rising water all around. When I got upstairs, her voice was saying something about her mother changing her mind; I grabbed the phone.

"Changed her mind about what?"

"About the competition. She says I can do it."

"That's so great," I said. "Why did she change her mind?"

"Ah dunno. She's just like that sometimes . . ."

"You don't sound happy."

"I am."

For a strange and active moment I felt my house close around me—water pipes and wires and slow-speaking wood with insects living in it, wallpaper and rugs and furniture, emotions and odors, the air beating with thoughts—and all of it, all of me so far away from the girl on the other end of the phone, even though she had slept and ate and cried here.

Downstairs Paul went, "Ginger?"

"You don't sound happy," she said, and I felt it coming from her

side too: her apartment, her family, her friends, the street outside—the things she never told me but that I could feel in the warm electronic phone dark where the voice is tactile and subtle as an animal.

"I *am* really happy that you're going to do it," I said. "Your mom needs to sign the permission though, like now."

"You can send it, she'll sign."

"That's great. Is she going to come?"

"Ginger, dinner's ready."

She said yes, in the smiling voice she used for lying, and I believed it for the same reason she told it; because believing made the good thing real for a second.

Velvet

On the weekend before the competition, Pat talked to me about what it would be like, the busy parking lot, the horse traffic, the trailers. I didn't tell her I already knew what it would be like, and that I was sending pictures of parking lots and people on carts to my horse every time I put her away for the night.

"You've got an advantage because this mare *does* know how to compete, and she's probably got a taste for it. But you've got a disadvantage too, because her form of competition was racing, not show jumping. You have to keep hold of her, keep her steady and following your instruction so she doesn't just decide to start racing. Use her impulse for speed, but control it. And remember, she's sensitive. Loud noises, unexpected movement, *anything* unexpected could spook her—keep on top of it, keep her steady, take care of her. You're also sensitive, and this will be new to you. *You* can't spook. You've got to be in charge, and give her confidence and comfort, all the way."

Confidence and comfort; she said those words like they were deep, and for me they were. All weekend, when I groomed my mare and tacked her, I would think those words, through my hands to her. And when we were done and I would wash her, I would also think the words that Gaby said to me: *He respected your precious body.* She had said that about Dominic, but I didn't think about him. I thought *your precious body* through my hands to the mare. For confidence and comfort.

I thought those words too when I lay on my couch the night before I went upstate for the competition, but they only helped me fall half asleep; all this other mind-noise kept coming up underneath the words and then real noise from outside. I wanted confidence and comfort and I could not find it. How would I give it to my mare? I tried to talk to my grandfather, but he didn't answer. I listened to the noise from outside: music, cars, and voices—and all of a sudden I remembered something Cookie said forever ago. He said, "I ain't havin' a good time. But I am havin' a time!" That made me smile, and for some reason I finally got calm.

But I only slept two hours, then got up crazy awake, still thinking about Cookie. I went and got my horseshoe from a long time ago; I took it outside and put it under where Cookie's name was written. I put it where nobody would see it and take it, behind the bars of this boarded-up window. I don't know why but it seemed like good luck to do that. When I came back inside my mom looked at me like she knew something was going on, but she didn't know what. I never told her what day the event was and she never saw the paper come because I got it from the box and signed her name and sent it back. But I usually never ask for a doobie wrap to go upstate and I don't usually pack my best silky top with gold rings holding the sides together. She knew *something* and so she picked a fight—like I come out of the bathroom wearing my silky top and she's, "You want to flash your body even up in that sleepy little town? I think those girls there hate you too." All during breakfast and then while I packed my bag she was looking and knowing but not knowing what was up, and going, "How does somebody so scrawny also have a muffin top?" or "You know, I'm going to let you wear that so you'll see for yourself how they laugh at you."

I held back and didn't even look mad at her because she might say I couldn't go, even though she said she was glad I was going because at least I wouldn't be fighting or running down the street to flirt with gangbangers, except why was I wearing that top? Was I looking for boys up there too? And finally it came out of me: "You are crazy, why do you hate me so much? Why did you even birth me? Why don't you call Ginger and ask if I ever even talk to a boy there?" I went into the bathroom with a sweatshirt and came back with it on and threw my good shirt on the couch, which made her yell at me to pick it up.

"Do you even know me?" I said. "I don't care about boys. I go to ride. I'm the best one there, and if I would ride in the competition, I would win!"

My mom's eyes went like prey bird eyes; no feeling, all sight. The TV noise went way up. "Why talk about that, stupid? You told me you didn't want to do that."

"You didn't want me to so I didn't because—" *Because I felt broken.*

"Because I don't want to see you crippled doing something you can't do! Now pick up that—"

"I could do it if you let me. Everybody else says I could win!" *And then I realized I am not.*

She did not go for her belt; she was in too big a hurry. She just took off her shoe and turned her arm into a belt.

Ginger

Right before she came, I saw Becca with Edie at the store. That never happened before, not both of them together. It was pretty awkward; usually when we saw each other, we'd nod only if she couldn't avoid it. If Edie hadn't been there this time I don't even think it would've been that polite. But she *was* there, in the checkout line, meaning Becca was trapped, her body automatically doing its big and important thing while her head looked away, like it was for some reason dawning on her what a gross bitch she'd been all her life. Part of me wanted to make nice; part of me wanted to insult her for real. Since I could do neither, I was prepared to stroll on by, but Edie popped out and said, "Hi! Is Velvet here?"

Was she *furious* at her mom? Or did she just not know what had happened? "Yeah," I said. "She's riding in a competition at Grace Meadow tomorrow." I saw Becca's head come up slightly at the mention of the place.

"Awesome! I was so sorry I missed the other one, this time I'll come; when is it?"

"Tomorrow, starting noon. It would mean so much for her to see you."

"Awww!"

The skinny old cashier (gentle faded eyes, big moles) looked up mid-bag, smiling at the affectionate sound. Becca loaded the belt.

"I even think her mom is coming."

Edie did the *awww* again. Finally her mother turned to look at me, her expression unreadable. Her daughter said, "You should come too, Mom. It'll be fun."

Velvet

She hit me with her shoe, panting so hard spit flew. I hit too, I cried and hit wild, just to keep her off, to keep her words out of me with knife words of my own.

"Why are you so proud? Why do you think you're so special?"

"Because I don't think I'm shit? Because I don't want to think I'm shit? Ginger doesn't think I'm shit, Pat doesn't think it, only you, my own mother!"

"*Ginger?*" She laughed and instead of hitting me, she hit herself, both hands on her face, then me, and then herself again. "Maldita, malcriada! What did I do to make you like this? God help me, what do I need to do to stop you?"

"You've already stopped me, you don't do anything but stop me!"

"Maybe when you're crippled by that horse you'll learn!"

Like a machine that cried tears, I closed my bag up. Crying machine tears, I dragged it down the hall. My mom shouted after me, "At least when you're in a wheelchair, you'll—"

But I was gone.

Ginger

Awww! How do people make this simple noise into such a repulsive mix of real and false, the false mocking the real for the two seconds they rub together, throwing it into high relief that way?

Still, it affected me, the way Becca looked at me; she had never looked at me that way. And then the cashier, smiling to hear that *someone's* mom was coming, that she was "even" coming, meaning that she usually wouldn't, but that now, *now*—

"I don't think she's coming," said Velvet.

"You don't *think?*" I asked.

"She said she might, but I don't think so."

"Why not?" asked Paul, glancing in the rearview.

"She has to work," said Velvet.

I said, "On *Sunday?*"

"That's what she told me to tell you." There was no smile/lie in her voice; she spoke as if a little stunned. "She said she's sorry. She said she'll call me if she can come."

We got home and she went upstairs to settle in.

Paul said, "You know her mother could sue us if we do this without her say-so. Are you sure she gave permission?"

"She signed the form. She knew what it was for."

He didn't say anything.

We had sandwiches for lunch and then Velvet went to practice. I went upstairs and went into her room the way I usually do when she first comes. There was her open bag, her toiletries. There, on the dresser, was a torn, taped-up, wrinkled picture of a beautiful young boy in a costume, holding his arms out and smiling like a lover; there was a real almost completely dried-out sea horse and something I couldn't identify until I picked it up and felt it: a piece of blue seashell. I held it and thought: Her mom has to come. She has to.

I went to call the translator.

Velvet

Pat said we'd walk the course the day of the show, but she wanted me to see it the day before so I'd "have a basic visual." So I was expecting something scary or at least a little big. But it was just a place like Spindletop called Grace Meadow. I wanted to say, *This is it? It's so small!* But I didn't want Pat to know I'd been someplace else. Especially when I saw how she was with the Grace Meadow people. Or even how she was walking from the car to the Grace Meadow office: nervous, in her eyes and hands. I never saw her nervous before. Outside the building, a Mexican guy pushed a wheelbarrow of shavings—he saw Pat and they said hi, they knew each other's names, and I could tell he didn't know what she was even doing there, especially with me. Then she went into the office and introduced me to this lady Grace, who had a face like a muscle and spooky eyes, like if I was a dog and she looked at me, I'd whine or I'd growl. She talked polite to Pat, and to me she said, "What a romantic name"—but she looked like she *did* know what we were doing there and that it was something little and funny.

When we walked out to the main arena, I couldn't help it, I said, "I thought it would be bigger," and Pat said, "Compared to what? This is a schooling show." I didn't say anything. Mexican guys were turning out beautiful horses with thick shiny coats; the horses were moving like they knew they were perfect and the men were their servants. I looked at them and felt like I did at EQUAL, that they were part of some giant *thing* that I didn't know or want to know. I was thinking, It's so small. Why bother?

Until we walked back to Pat's truck and I saw Lexy getting out of her car with I guess her mom. She looked right at me and at Pat too, running her eyes up and down on us. "Hi," she said, meaning, *You're here?*

"Where you know that girl from?" asked Pat.

"Just around," I answered.

Pat didn't say anything. Neither did I. But I was thinking: Yeah. I'm here.

Ginger

It took over an hour for the translator to get back to me and then another hour before she had time to make the call—and then Silvia wasn't home. We tried off and on for almost the whole afternoon; if she really *was* working all weekend, how obnoxious of me to make this call. But still, we made it once more—and she picked up. "Tell her thank you," I said to the translator, "for letting her daughter come." Silvia responded as if she were being nice to an idiot, and then asked, "Is she behaving?" "Yes," I said. "She's sad you can't be here, but I think she's going to make you proud. I am confident she'll win." The translator inflated her voice with "awww" crap; Silvia's silence went dark and hard. I said, "She's practiced so much and gotten so good and it would mean the world to her if you could be here." The translator coughed and tried and—Silvia exploded. She did that thing where she talked so fast it was more sound than words, sound and jagged laughter. "What is she saying?" I asked. "What is she saying?" "I don't know," said the translator. "I can't get her to slow down." And then Silvia was gone. The translator said she couldn't tell if she'd said anything about a contest or permission, all she could really make out was something about "a can of whup-ass."

Velvet

I felt my phone ring in my pocket right before I jumped. I *knew* it was my mom and that snagged my brain and my brain snagged the mare; she started to refuse, but I basically *brained* her forward so she jumped at the last minute, landing too hard in front and throwing me forward then back into the saddle. I didn't care, I had to look, and right after the next jump I did, taking the reins in my one hand and digging for my phone with the other.

Pat went, "You're looking at your phone? *You?* I don't believe it!"

I rode around the next jump, slowing to a trot, then a walk. I said, "It's my mom."

"I don't care if it's President Obama. You don't text while driving or while on horseback, you know that!"

"I wasn't texting, I was just—"

She didn't listen. She came to us and said *Whoa* so strong the mare stopped and let Pat take hold of her. "Give me that phone," she said.

I didn't. I don't know why. I felt mad and Fiery Girl could feel me—she tossed her head and pawed the ground. I don't know if Pat said, Be quiet, *now* or if the words just came off her body. I could feel the mare thinking up at me, *What do I do?*

"Give me that thing or get down and go home."

I thought, I could make Fiery Girl rear up on Pat if I wanted to. I could—

Very low, Pat said, "You need to stop this mess, *now.*"

I sat the mare firm and told her, Whoa. I gave Pat the phone and told her I was sorry.

"You should be. You could've hurt yourself and your horse. Now show me that you're sorry. Do it right. Collect yourself, and by that I mean take whatever crap that's going on in you and get it under you and get it by the reins. And take these jumps without doing anything stupid. Now."

I did what she said. Not just with the horse, but with myself. It took a few trips around the arena, to get it under me. But when I did, it was like I was riding a bullet instead of a horse. Or me and her both were riding it. On the bullet, I counted out the steps like Jeanne told me, rushed seven, slow seven. I released big on the high jumps, small on the lower ones. I stopped her exactly. I did it all in front of Pat, who didn't teach me any of it.

"You ride like a damn dressage queen!" said Pat, and I would've thought she was mad. Except then she said, "You ride like that, you'll take points from those girls like candy."

I said, "Can I have my phone now?"

"Can I please have my phone now?"

I smiled and said, "Please, Miss Pat."

"After you put your horse away."

So I walked Fiery Girl and washed her and dried her and cleaned between her legs with mint. I brushed her and combed out her tail and then took her tail in my hands and leaned back to stretch her spine. These other girls Tracy and Chelsea were getting back from trail-riding and they watched like they couldn't believe she let me do that. She not only let me, she braced her legs so she could get it all the way, and I felt her all the way, to her *eyelashes;* I could feel the soft expression in her eyes and lips without seeing them. Then I wished the day was a normal day. I wished there was no competition tomorrow. I wished my mom wasn't mad at me.

"Good job," said Pat. She gave me my phone.

I said, "Thank you, Miss Pat," and put the phone in my pocket.

"Everything okay at home?" she asked.

"Yeah."

And she kissed me. She kissed me on the forehead and said it again: "Good job."

I walked out and sat on the feedbags on the side of the barn. My mom had called me five times in two hours. The last two times she left messages. My mom did not leave messages. She called and expected you to see it and call back.

I put the phone facedown on the feedbag and watched Chelsea and Tracy get picked up by their moms. They called to each other and waved good-bye as they got in their cars. I called my voice mail.

The first message: *This is what I have to say to you. If you ride in that race, don't bother to come home, because there won't be a home for you anymore.*

The second message: *And don't think your home is there. You are all alone with those people. Trust me.*

I put the phone back facedown. I watched Pat come out of the barn with a wheelbarrow full of dirty bedding, dump it out, go back. I didn't feel anything. I couldn't feel anything. I just thought. I thought about this time when Ginger was driving me back from riding at Pat's: We were talking about tattoos and I said I wanted to tattoo my mom's name on my one hand and Dante's on the other. Ginger pulled over on the side of the road and said, "Don't do that." I asked why. And she said, "Because your mom's name is already written inside you. You don't need to make it literal." "But why?" I said. And she answered, "Because when somebody's name is written on you, that person owns you. Like you're a slave." And I felt sorry for Ginger when she said it, that she would think like that. Now I felt sorry for me.

Pat came out with the wheelbarrow and went back in. The lights went off in the barn. Pat came out, got in her car, and drove away. I got up and went back to the house. And there was Ginger going, "Do you really have permission to compete? Because I talked to your mother and it sure didn't sound like it."

Ginger

"What did my mom say?" she asked.

"I don't know. She was talking so fast, the translator couldn't get it."

"You got the paper, right? You saw she signed it."

"Then why is she sounding so pissed off?"

"Because she's always pissed off, Ginger. After all this time, don't you get what she's like?"

"I think we need to call her again after dinner."

"You call her, I'm not going to. She can't even bother to come see me and all morning she yells and calls me names?"

"Listen," I said. "Do you know what kind of trouble I could get into if I'm acting against her wishes?"

"What kind of trouble?"

"Legal trouble. She could sue me *and* the barn."

For just a split second her eyes changed—*something* changed— then snapped back. She said, "Are you kidding me? She's not going to do that, she doesn't care about me! She told me! She told me this morning she didn't care if I was crippled!"

And she went up the stairs so fast and jerky that she slipped and fell on one knee. "Oh crap!" I said and went to her. She let me hold her. She didn't cry. But I could feel the pain beating against her body like it was too big to get out without breaking her. It made me hold her tighter, and she hardened against my grip.

"Ginger," she said, and her calm was terrible. "I can't talk about my mom no more."

"All right," I said. "All right."

I expected her to keep going upstairs to her room. Instead she said, "Ginger, do you have a Bible?"

"Yes," I said. "Why?"

"Can I just see it?"

We went downstairs and I gave it to her and watched as she flipped through it, clearly looking for something. I asked what it was and she said, "Nothin'." Then she found it and read it intently, moving her lips as she did.

Velvet

Once I heard my mom talk on the phone to this woman Rasheeda, the only black person my mom ever liked. It was when we just moved to Crown Heights, and my mom kicked Manuel out for not paying and maybe for messing with me and he'd come back pounding on the door. I heard my mom say, "It's like there's a hurricane and I'm sitting in my chair holding on with white knuckles."

Now I knew how she felt. I couldn't hear the hurricane and I couldn't see it. But it was there and I didn't even have a chair to hold on to. I had to ride a *horse* through it. I took out my phone and played my mom's message again. *There won't be a home for you anymore.* I knew she didn't mean it, any more than she meant most of what she said. But still, her voice pulled on me and made me want to tell Ginger the truth and not compete, just go back to my mother's hurricane.

That's when I realized: When she said that to Rasheeda, it was only *her* in the hurricane. Like me and Dante were just part of the storm blowing around her with a bunch of other stuff. I turned off my phone and put it in a drawer. I took the piece of blue shell from Providence that I broke off to carry in my shirt pocket while I rode along with the sea horse and with Dominic. I took it all the way out into the field where me and Fiery Girl practiced jumping and I dropped it there. I looked up into the sky; it was cold with purple on the bottom of it. I thought the words I saw on Dominic's chest and then I said them: "You armed me with strength for battle, you humbled my adversaries, you made my enemies run. And I destroyed them."

Ginger

I was 95 percent sure she wasn't telling me the truth—she would've convinced me but for that break in her expression, her *concentration,* then the forceful switch back before she spoke. Still, I didn't make the call. I made dinner with Paul, acted normal, got the chicken in the oven, then went up the stairs to my workroom, address book in hand. I stared at my failed painting of Melinda, the divided face; ugly woman, haunted girl. That break in Velvet's expression, in her concentration, the pain—I had to call, if only to try and make her mother come. Instead I sat and stared at the picture of my dead sister and felt my flesh tingle with the words *no* and *don't.* Over and over: *No. Don't.* The hair on my arm stood up. I heard Velvet come in the door and go into the kitchen. I went back downstairs thinking, I'll do it later.

Silvia

The refrigerator is broken: the seal is worn away and water gathers, I have to clean it constantly to keep black mold from growing, and even so, I can't keep the mold out of the cracks. When I got off the phone I cleaned it again, pulling everything out again, wiping and wiping. I washed the windows, mopped the floor. The whole time I'm thinking, It's no good. We don't belong here. Not in this neighborhood, not in this country, not on this filthy planet where anything good is chopped into little bits trying to join and be whole, but they can't. My prayers are worthless, I have no grace, and my daughter does not respect me because some fool woman has made her into a pet. My son cries, "You think she's going to be crippled but you let her *go?*" I hit him, but I was thinking, Yes, I let her go, like I knew she was sneaking out some nights and didn't stay awake to stop her. A good mother would stop her, a good mother— A good mother wouldn't let her daughter get turned into a pet for a few hundred dollars a month.

"And she's not even *worth* a few hundred dollars a month!"

I said that out loud and shoved the mop so hard I banged a table leg and my only good vase fell and smashed, and I hit myself to not hit Dante again. I felt his fear and then my shame, coming on fast. I shut my teeth against it, pushing it back. Holding it back, I got down on the floor to pick up the pieces of my one beautiful thing, reaching under the couch for it—and saw the blue shell from the beach at Providence. My poor gift for her, the hope of a woman who gets it in the ass with a man who doesn't love her. I would've smashed it, but surprise stopped my hand. What was this thing doing under the couch? I thought she kept it where she keeps her little things, what was it doing here? The beach; the light between water and sky. I sat on the couch and looked at it; it was broken. A big piece was missing, like it had been snapped off. My thoughts sank so deep I no longer knew what they were. The TV was on but Dante was watching me like he could see what was happening, like it was a picture being drawn. And it *was* a picture being drawn. She'd just sent three hundred dollars, and I just cashed it. I had it in my drawer. "Dante," I told him. "Turn that off and get the phone. I need you to make a call for me."

Velvet

I expected dinner to be tense, but it wasn't. Ginger kept drama out of her eyes and Paul seemed happy I was there; he asked me questions about the competition. But when I went back to see my mare again I started to wonder, Why am I doing this? I *am* alone here. I still like Ginger, but I can't talk to her. I love Fiery Girl, but she's not mine. If I win I can't tell my mom, and nobody else where I live cares. I stopped walking and put my face in my hands; I was thinking about my mom hitting herself in the face because of me. She never did that before, never. *Feelings by themself ain't what matters.* Dominic was right and it made me wish I wasn't here on this earth. Not exactly dead, just *not here.*

Still, I went to the barn. And that's when it happened: I heard the horses talking to me like the first time I came. I don't know if I made it up because of being so sad, but it didn't matter—it made me feel better. *Hello, girl! We know you! Come see me! Have you got something for me? What's the matter?* But Fiery Girl didn't say anything. She didn't have to. She just looked at me like she saw me to the bottom, and all her muscles were proud and ready. Like a Jesus heart with *fire* and thorns inside it.

And I knew: I am doing it for *this.* If somebody asked me what *this* was, I wouldn't be able to tell them. But I knew, I knew.

Silvia

With me my son is soft but arrogant too, and I can feel his maleness growing in him; with any other adult or older child, his arrogance hides, and without it his spirit is shy and so soft it has no shape; his words too are so soft they have no shape, and he mumbles like a half-wit. I understand him even in English. But the people he talks to don't and they think he's stupid, then he thinks he's stupid.

So I feel bad to make him talk on the phone with one of these machine people who they get to answer phones—except it turns out, it's not even a machine-person, it's really a machine. Which at least can't think he's stupid as he tries to give machine answers, whispering so the thing can't hear him, finally shouting. "Mami, what do we want, a reservation or a service or something else? Coño, now it's talking about a dining car, it won't let you ask the price—something else, you stupid nonfiction puta, something else! Mami, I can't!" He slammed the phone on the floor so the cap broke off the end of it, and I knocked it on his head, the insane voice talked on and he cried, "Just call the man, Paul. Tell him to call them."

"No," I said. "No."

"Wait," he said and grabbed the phone, listening. "An agent is a person, it says it thinks I want to talk to an agent." He told the phone, "Yes, agent, you puta," and it answered him with music.

Ginger

She was far away when she got ready for bed that night—she didn't even smile when she asked if she could have her favorite towel with the pink flowers on it. Paul said, "She's being amazing. Strong. Considering how disappointed she must be about her mother not coming." "Yeah," I said. *You don't know the half of it,* I didn't say. I called the translator, didn't reach her. I hoped to God I hadn't made a mistake in encouraging this.

The next morning she was still calm, but with something else too, something I could not define. "Velvet," I said. "I know you can win this. I want you to win. But even if you don't? You've still done something incredible to get this far. I'm more proud of you than I've ever been of anyone in my life."

Normally when I would compliment her, she'd smile awkwardly and thank me with a full, tender voice. This time she thanked me with her voice and face so measured she looked like a much older person, almost *middle-aged.* Again I wondered if I had done the right thing. Was any of this right?

But after I walked her to the barn, I didn't doubt. A girl with purple hair greeted Velvet warmly. "Is she competing too?" I asked. "No," said Velvet. "She's just coming to help." I stayed long enough to watch her lead her horse out. The animal seemed to look at me like it knew me and was thinking something very specific. Velvet did not look at me, just at the horse.

It was on the walk home that I finally identified what it was: She looked like her mother. Like her mother the fighter. Except that, unlike her mother, she wasn't in a tank. She was out in the open. I smiled. I knew: I *had* done the right thing.

I knew it even more when Paul greeted me on the porch, phone in his hand. "They're coming," he said. "Dante just called me."

"When?" I asked. "It's starting in like an hour!"

"That's why he called, they wanted to know what time it was. I get the sense it was a last-minute decision. I told them I'm pick them up at Poughkeepsie because it won't cost them as much that way."

Paul

I don't know why I felt glad they were coming. This whole thing—Ginger's "project," as Becca called it—had ruined my marriage, or allowed me to ruin it, and the ruin had just begun. What would happen to Ginger if we divorced? I imagined her in the city, living in a grimy studio in Queens or Brooklyn, maybe *Crown Heights,* trying to find as job (as *what?*) and attempting to maintain a relationship with a family who'd most likely have no use for her—and I sped to Poughkeepsie as if to forestall that future, Polly hurling away from me like a rapidly cooling planet wrenched off its axis.

I got there early but couldn't find a spot in the near lot, had to spiral up the parking structure for a space, thinking weirdly of Ginger's sister, whom I had once compared, after her death, to the Nabokovian character Hazel Shade, an ugly girl who kills herself on being rejected by a cloddish boy. I did not make a direct comparison between live Melinda and the fictional dead girl for Ginger; I just repeated one critic's somewhat quixotically made case that poor scorned Hazel is transformed by death into a Vanessa butterfly, a kind angel who gently guides her father into the spirit world and even comforts the egotistical lunatic (and great rejecter of women) who inadvertently drew her dad to his death.

I heard a train pulling in as I hurried down the concrete steps, feeling that strange gladness in anticipation of the lumpen, frowning woman and her odd boy whom I could deliver to my even more odd wife. Who had liked the connection between her sister and Hazel Shade because she felt that Melinda had guided her to Velvet and Velvet to the horse. And because she believed in transformation, she did not accept that anything just "is what it is"; she always thought it could be something else, something secretly beautiful and glorious.

I made myself visible at the foot of a main stairway, smiling expectantly as the last passengers left the train. My smile stiffened slightly; they did not seem to be there. I went to the other end of the platform, thinking they might be waiting for the elevator. But the conveyance was taking someone up, and I dropped the smile as

I headed back up the stairs. "Pippa Passes"; Nabokov had used that poem wittily in connection with Hazel, Pippa being an insignificant girl who somehow transforms everyone around her into something better than they are. They weren't upstairs either or in the lobby. Exasperated—this was so typical—I reached for my phone, calling as I walked outside, where insignificant people passed and passed.

Dante

He is a funny man, even if he doesn't say anything funny, just the way his hairy uni-blond brows go together when he's trying to think of what to say. Before my mom got her crazy idea of going upstate to open a can of whup-ass, this guy on *South Park* was saying, "Black is beautiful, tan is grand, but the white man is the big boss man!" And I thought of the eyebrows.

But at least when a human came on the phone, she was nice and waited for my mom to find an envelope with the name of their town on it while I told her about going to see my sister race. But I remembered the name of the place anyway—it was like a name in that book about Unfortunate Events. And it was *very* unfortunate, *forty dollars to get there,* not even coming back, and we didn't know where the race was or what time it was or even if it already happened. I expected my mom to say hell no, but she just sat like she was dreaming, and then said, Tell her to make the reservation with the credit card.

But I called Paul before we left and he said to go someplace else, and I didn't tell my mom because there wasn't time to get on the phone again, and then the subway sat in the tunnel and we only had time to get the ticket out of the machine so we wouldn't have saved money, and then my mom didn't understand when we got to Pough-keepsie and I told her, "I think he said to get out here instead." She said, "Why?" and I wasn't going to say "because he wanted us to save money" because then my sister's ass would not be whipped alone. Even if my mom looked like she forgot about that, she just stared out at Poughkeepsie like she was still in that same dream.

So I thought when we get there and he's not there she'll ask me to call him and I will and he will come to where we are. And she won't know I was stupid. Which is what happened. Except the phone was dead.

Velvet

When we got there the parking lot *was* busy, with trailers and cars and horses being groomed and more people coming. When she came out of the trailer, Fiery Girl tossed her head and stepped quick, one foot to the other; her veins were standing out of her silky skin and I was afraid she'd spook. But when I put my hands on her I felt right away that it was something else bubbling up in her, something I didn't know yet.

I wanted to groom her and tack her myself, but Pat said to let Gare do that, we were gonna walk the course. Which was also busy—there were like ten other girls walking it and also their trainers, and I could hear little bits of their talking and it seemed like their thinking too. A couple of them talked loud about somebody's horse being too short-strided or said shit like "Good luck on *that* one," like for me to hear—it was just annoying, and made it hard to count the steps and listen to Pat, even if she was talking like drilling words into my head.

"The first is the simplest, but it's important because it sets the tone," she said. "So you want to giddyup over that, then settle down and whoa a little bit at the second, pick it up again on three—four, look, piece of cake, collect yourself there, check your balance. Five, though—pay attention!" I could see what she meant; the outside fence near five was curved inward to avoid some big trees and there were a lot of trees right up against the fence sideways after the jump, which could make the horse feel like she was jumping into the trees. "Nothing she and you can't do. I'm thinking put your left leg on so you're almost jumping right because she's probably gonna drag you left. And when you land, don't forget the basics: use the corners for balance and take the cleanest lines between the jumps—the ground here is good and solid, so that's a plus."

We walked the course twice and then she made me repeat it all back to her and finally we went back to my horse, and I was glad to kiss her scars and her crumpled ear, and also the beautiful braid Gare did. The show did not seem small anymore, and I realized I was a little bit scared. "Remember," said Pat, "lively on the first jump, a little whoa on the second . . ." Fiery Girl breathed in and out of her open nose and laid back her good ear; she stretched out her lip like she wanted to nibble on me. I thought *confidence and comfort.* ". . . left lead canter to red toward home," said Pat, "hay bales away . . ." Other girls were grooming their horses or leading them to the schooling area—I saw Joanne across the way; I saw Lorrie and Jeanne. I saw Lexy. ". . . outside line away from home, finish with a long ride to white diagonal." Blood filled up my heart and suddenly I knew what my horse felt. I wanted to move, to kick and bite. I wanted to win so much I trembled, and I could not stop. Pat put her hand on my shoulder. "Calm down," she said. "And tell me what you're gonna do."

Ginger

I got to the show at nine o'clock; Velvet wasn't riding until about ten thirty, but she would be there, and anyway, I wanted to see it all. I wanted to see what Mrs. Vargas was going to see when Paul brought her and Velvet's brother. What I saw made me feel satisfaction and vindicated joy: a sunny meadow, horses in spacious pastures, an enormous well-tended barn, tiny girls with bright faces confidently shepherding horses toward two good-sized arenas where families were gathered on a small set of bleachers watching girls warm up. Someone who must've been the judge was sitting in a chair placed on a flatbed truck parked between the two arenas; a middle-aged woman carrying a plastic bucket filled with ribbons walked past me, headed in his direction. Two other women in a dollhouse pavilion talked enthusiastically and half audibly through microphones; I noticed one of them had the discordant profile of a drunk, deranged elf, but never mind—there was a sweet little concession stand selling homemade cookies, and banners with the names of local businesses snapping in the wind. The scene was lovely, proud and modest both.

The stable was open and I walked through it, hoping to find Velvet and tell her that her mother would come after all. But I didn't see her. I asked a couple of girls if they knew her. They said, "Who?" and looked at each other like I must be joking. This bothered me more than it should've. I went to the pavilion and waited to get the attention of the women. The one with the strange face sat back and fixed me with a speculative, quietly malign look that I didn't understand and pretended not to see; did she know me? "Excuse me," I said to the other. "I'm looking for Velveteen Vargas. Do you know who she is?"

"The name certainly stands out," she said. "I don't know her personally, but—" She scanned a list with the help of a swollen finger. "Here she is. She's here with a horse called Fugly Girl."

"Oh," I said, relieved but bothered again. "That's a mistake; that's not the horse's name."

"Well, that's what it says here, that's—"

"Ginger!" I turned and there was Paul saying, "They weren't there. They weren't at Poughkeepsie or Rhinecliff. I checked. I tried to call them several times, but I got no answer."

"There she is!" said the swollen-fingered woman. "There's your girl right there!"

We looked up just in time to see her fighting to stay on her bucking horse, which as I watched, changed tactics, and spun around so hard Velvet lost her seat and fell.

I cried out, and Paul went, "Oh no!"

"Not a big deal," said the pavilion lady mildly. "It's spring, and the animals are—"

I looked at her and saw instead the face of the other, quietly gloating as Velvet got to her feet. That's when I remembered her; the trainer who taught Velvet to ride bareback with a bullwhip.

Silvia

He wasn't there. We walked out of the station with satisfied, idle people who walked well-dressed even if they dressed sloppy. We stood there as they were hugged and kissed by more satisfied, idle people, then driven away in big cars. Or taxis. There were so many people, the taxis took them and came back and took more. Still he didn't come. Soon we were the only ones standing there. Dante was very quiet beside me and I could smell him sweating like he does when he's afraid. Why? And why didn't Paul come? They were always on time. Ginger. Did she tell her husband not to bring me? My face went hot to think she could do that. Dante sweated. One last taxi came slowly back into the station. The driver stared at me through the glass; I saw he was Mexican. Dante said, "I don't think he is coming." The driver rolled down his window and said something to Dante in English; Dante answered him. Then he spoke to me. "You've been here a long time. Do you need a ride?"

I smiled to hear Spanish and said no, we were waiting. Dante said something to him and he asked me what kind of phone I had because maybe he could charge it in his car. When he got out and I could see him fully, I trusted him to let him take the phone. But his charger didn't work on our phone, so he gave it back and asked me where we wanted to go. I told him it was to see my daughter ride in a horse show and, by his face, he didn't believe me. He said, "Where is it?" I took out my envelope with their address on it and showed it to him.

"It's right next to this place," I said, pointing.

"I could take you there," he said. "I could take you for half price."

"Thank you, but our friend said he would take us there. We'll wait."

He shrugged. I expected him to go away, but instead he asked, "Where you come from?" I told him, and he said he was from Bushwick. We talked bullshit about that, and more time went by.

"Look," he said, "why don't you come with me? It's twenty dollars, but for you ten."

"It's still too much."

"Okay, Mami," he said. "Five. For you."

Velvet

When I rode her to the practice arena she moved like on springs, rocking me on her back. It was strange to ride her with her mane braided—her body looked too wide and just not the *same*. We had to stop by the stable to let some other horses pass and Pat saw the Mexican groom from the day before. "Beautiful horse," he said. A girl nearby turned to look and her lips curved sarcastically to see Fiery Girl's scarred face and crumpled ear.

Pat smiled and thanked him. "Put together by committee, this one," she said. "But she's got good heart."

"And good blood," said the groom. "You can see in how she moves."

"Say 'thank you'!" Pat snapped and I did say it. But he already saw the thanks in my smile. Because he said it like it was me who had good blood too, and I wished my mom was there.

But something changed when we walked her past that little house thing where they were going to announce us. I could feel her tense and she kicked up a back leg like to canter. I tightened the reins and she went into a hard trot that bounced me. I felt something behind it, and it bothered me so when I tried to give her confidence she felt bother, and that's when I started to feel the buck coming. I took the reins to the side, pulled her head into my leg. I heard Pat say, "Good, other side!" and I scrunched with the reins to keep her head up. I used my legs, but it didn't work, she half bucked, so I turned her head again and she went into a spin so fast my foot came out of the stirrup. When I grabbed for the mane I couldn't get hold of the flat braid, and then I was on the ground. Pat was right there to take hold of her and she was telling me it was okay, and when I got enough breath back to get up I believed it—until Ginger came running like it was the worst thing ever, which annoyed me and Pat too, and probably the mare.

Ginger

I shouldn't have run up to her like that, but I just wanted to be sure she was safe, to let her know somebody cared about her. But fear was on me, and my feeling was too intense; I just irritated her and the trainer, who looked at me like I was a total fool. But that in a way seemed to strengthen her; I could feel her and the trainer link together against my fluttering presence, and she got up on the horse with a resolve that seemed to calm the animal. Feeling small and worthless, and still afraid because we didn't know what had happened to her mom, I walked back to the bleachers looking for Paul.

But I didn't see Paul. I saw Edie and Kayla with her friend Robin and dour little Jewel. And Becca's friend Joan and—oh my fucking God—Becca. Of course Joan would be there; her daughter rode. But Becca? They were standing there next to the bleachers, talking with casual ease that made me stumble over my feet. They saw me; Edie smiled, Joan said hi, and Kayla hugged me. With an expression I couldn't read, Becca very quietly said, "Hello." I blushed and mumbled. "Where is she?" asked smiling Edie. "Is her mom here?"

"She's practicing," I said, gesturing toward the arena. "Her mom's not here yet."

Joan said something about her daughter hoping to win first place this year. There was nervous quiet.

"Where's Paul?" I said.

"He took a call," said Kayla. "He went over there."

She pointed toward the barn. I said, "Excuse me," and walked off without smiling, almost running into him coming around a corner.

"Ginger," he said. "They're on their way. They took a taxi from Rhinecliff."

Joy spread over my face; Paul mirrored it. "How?" I said. "Why?"

"I don't know, they got off at Rhinecliff for some reason and then their phone went dead. They took a taxi to Pat's barn—"

"Oh!"

"But the driver got our house phone from information and got my cell from that, and I told him how to get here."

He put his hands on my shoulders, and I would've embraced him if I hadn't caught sight of Becca looking at us as she and the others found seats on the bleachers. We joined them right as the woman in the pavilion spoke a daisy-chain of girl-names finishing with "and Velveteen Vargas from Brooklyn, New York, riding Fugly Girl!"

Velvet

Pat said to collect myself and not to worry, this was just the practice time, just sit up straight and aim the mare like a bullet. I tried. I rode into the ring, aiming myself, except I didn't know at what. And I could still feel that something was bothering the horse; her ears were back in that *bother* way. Pat was at the fence, giving me instructions I could only half hear: "Right heel down, eyes up, keep breathing, find your space!" But all of a sudden I didn't care about winning. I rode around the arena while the other girls took the jumps, Lexy and these others I didn't know. I looked at the bleachers, trying to find Ginger or Paul. They weren't there. Only strangers were there. *You are all alone with those people. Trust me.* Fiery Girl bucked up under me so small it was more like bumping, I pulled her head up and scrunched the reins, turning her head good. *If you ride in that race don't bother to come home, because there won't be a home here for you anymore.* "Get her out in front!" yelled Pat. "Don't worry about where her head is!" Fiery Girl went like a question mark under me, and I answered her with my legs. I shut out my mom's voice, put my legs on the mare, and went for the jumps. She hit the first one with her hoof, and she knocked a rail off the second one. That's when I heard them say our names, I heard "Velveteen Vargas and Fugly Girl on deck!" And I knew it was time to go for real.

Paul

I went to meet them in the lot so I could pay the driver; there was something indescribably moving and dignified in the taxi's slow approach up the winding dirt road. "I'm so glad you made it!" I said. "She's just about to do her first event, but she'll go again!"

Dante said hi and looked down. I put out my hand to Mrs. Vargas, but she did not take it. I could not read her face. She was looking off to the side of me with an expression that would've been bewildered except that it was also stiff with purpose, almost robotic. She nodded curtly at me and instead of following me, practically led me back to the bleachers.

But the green meadow, the sky, the small-town banners flying on the wind—even from behind I could feel the softness and novelty of it interrupt her purpose. She looked at some resting horses as we passed the stable, then turned her head to look at the children riding in the arena, parents applauding for them. Dante cried, "There she is!" And Velvet, in the arena, rode right past the bleachers as we approached, her face transformed as it had been on the day I saw her ride. Mrs. Vargas's face lit up in amazement, as before a religious icon come to life. Ginger turned to her and smiled with near-crazy radiance as she made room for us to sit.

"Who *is* that little black girl?" said a woman seated in front of us.

"They said she's from Brooklyn."

"Where'd she learn to ride like that in Brooklyn?"

The horse went into a spirited, near-chaotic trot.

And Silvia's face went dark with anger. It made no sense. She went from joy to rage in seconds. Ginger said to her, "I can't tell what's happening, but I think she just did really well!" Then she registered that Mrs. Vargas looked like she was about to explode. The explosion was diffused, though, when one of the two women in front turned around, beamed, and asked, "Is that your daughter?" She apparently repeated herself in Spanish, because Mrs. Vargas rather sheepishly replied, "Sí." The woman said something else, probably "You must be so proud," then turned around. Whereupon Mrs. Vargas looked

Ginger in the eye and said something that sounded like a curse. Even the women in front of us stiffly cringed; Ginger flinched, then subtly held her ground. It occurred to me that we were looking at a lawsuit.

"Dante," I said, "could you translate what your mother just said?"

He seemed not to hear me.

"Dante," I said, "could you—"

And, with a weirdly *sly* face, he averted his eyes and replied: "She says, 'Black is beautiful, tan is grand, but the white man is the big boss man!'"

A couple of people turned to look at us reprovingly. I felt myself blush.

"Dante," I said, "I don't think your mother said that. It's disgusting."

He said it again, louder.

Velvet

Lexy was in the arena riding and I was last in a line of girls, right after this girl Amber, and my mare was moving her ass around like a volcano was under it, except not like bucking, more like she'd caught some kind of feeling going over those jumps and she wanted to *go*. The girls lined up in front of me were too close for me to turn her; I had to sit her and quiet her. Then that voice called her "fugly" and bad feeling took my heart, like when the branches flew past and I fell off her all alone, up into the sky and then slam on the ground, darkness closing in. Her running away from me. Dominic walking away from me. Everything far away. *You are all alone.*

Silvia

I saw her and I didn't know her. My daughter isn't beautiful. She isn't
strong. Dante said, "There she is!" but instead of my daughter—
who lies and disobeys, who sneaks out to see boys, who gets beat
by girls—I saw a beautiful girl riding like a saint with a sword. Flags
were flying. Strangers told me to be proud. They were coming to sit
with paper plates of food in their hands. I looked again; yes, it was
her, riding like a saint. My face burned; my heart swelled. I turned to
Ginger and said, "If anything happens to her, I am going to kill you."

Velvet

Lexy came riding out of the arena smiling because she knew she was great and people clapped for her. She looked past me like I wasn't there. Amber rode in, people cheering for her. I knew—I *was* alone. I was alone with my horse in a place no one but us could ever be. Like it was when she came back to me and lipped my hair and let me lead her to the fence. When I mounted her bare back and the sky touched me. Yes, I was alone with her in the hurricane, and it was beautiful. It didn't even matter when they called her "fugly" again; Pat said, "Go," and I rode her into the storm.

Paul

Velvet entered the arena at a quick walk that almost immediately turned into a focused, almost delirious trot. Her mother stood and cried out, her voice high and wrenching: "Velvet! Velveteen!" Her voice transfixed us, all of us; as if commanded, Ginger, Dante, and I rose to our feet. "Velvet!" Ginger shouted. "Velvet!" I answered. "Go, Velvet!" As if she could hear us, the girl put on speed, circling the arena with streamlined, almost scary speed. Her mother covered her mouth and grabbed Dante's shoulder. Then the horse went for the jumps like it was on fire, and the bleachers exploded. I heard Edie, then Kayla and Robin and Jewel's squeaky voice and even Becca shouting for her, with Silvia shouting in Spanish, first terrified and supplicating, then in fierce exhortation—Vamos, Velveteen, vamos, tu puedes!—her eyes blazing, moving her knees and fists almost like *she* was running, shouting with growing confidence and finally victory. Because her child was winning; she knew even before they called it from the pavilion: Velvet had won the most points in Jumping. I wanted to hug Silvia, but this small woman suddenly glowed with something you should not touch with familiarity. So I did not, and then she and Dante were up and going toward their child/sister, who had dismounted and was being congratulated by somebody with purple hair. With Ginger of course right behind them.

Ginger

We walked through the milling horses and riders to her, our throats still vibrant with shouting. Horses blocked us from her view, then parted; Velvet stood at the back entrance to the arena with Pat, holding her horse and smiling triumphantly at the girl with purple hair. People blocked us, then parted; she saw Dante, and her smiling lips fell open, then stiffened. She saw her mother and her stiff lips quivered, then her chin. The quivering rose into her eyes, but it did not look weak; her emotion was triumph with its wings open, showing its heart. I felt a second of bitterness that Silvia must be the one to hold this heart, but then—she didn't. She snapped at her daughter, two short lines, fast and cutting. Velvet's soft eyes went shocked and hard; her triumph sank away. I said, "Velvet!" She didn't react. She handed her reins to Pat and, with a stabbing look at her mother, turned and ran down a dirt path that curved behind a broken barn.

"Oh boy," said Pat.

Silvia's shoulders rose and fell with her heavy breath. I came beside her meaning to touch her, but I saw her rigid face and could not.

"Anybody speak Spanish?" said Pat.

"Yes," whispered Dante.

But his mother grabbed his hand and quick-marched him after Velvet. I started to follow, but Pat stopped me. "Let them work it out," she said. She looked down the path at their walking figures, then away. I followed her gaze; a blond girl was stamping her foot and yelling at a dark-haired woman who was trying to calm her.

"Well, at least she won," I said.

"She did. Third place, then first. Blue ribbon."

The blond girl threw her helmet on the ground and walked away. I looked down the path where Velvet had disappeared. I couldn't see Silvia or Dante.

"I just hope it really was her mom that signed that permission form," said Pat. "They'll take away her ribbon if she didn't."

Velvet

"So you won. That's great, Miss Big Shot!"

Those were her words to me. I came off Fiery Girl with my body hammering, Pat and Gare hugging me, my legs trembling and people smiling—except Lexy, who was having a fit, ha-ha—and there was my mother with her face like a wall I could throw myself against forever.

"Miss Big Shot!"

I wanted smart words, *English* words that she wouldn't understand: *Yes, I am a big shot and yes, I won, even with your ugly voice in my head.* Then in Spanish: *Oh, gracias por venir.* But I had no words, and I ran knowing nothing, wanting nothing but air between me and her. I wished I was on Fiery Girl and could ride away like we did that time when everything was terrible and strange and no one was there but my mare. Now no one was there but my mom and she was THERE. I came to thick trees and thorny bushes; I tried to find a way in. I heard them coming, then Dante said, "There she is!"

"Get away from me!" I said, not turning around. "Go away!"

"You lied." Her voice was crooked and breaking, like a witch, like the time she turned into a witch. "You disobeyed me, you—"

"I don't care!" I shouted at the trees and thorns. "I don't want you. I don't want to hear you! I want my horse! I want my ribbon!" I waited for her to curse me, but instead I heard Dante going, "We came all this way for you and you—"

"Came all the way to tell me I'm stupid and ugly in front of people!"

"I came to stop you from being hurt, you stupid girl, I wanted— I came— I came—"

She didn't finish. I heard her hard breath. I wanted to turn around, but I didn't.

"We spent money!" yelled Dante. "We paid for the train!"

"Turn around!" yelled my mom. "Turn around!"

And Dante said in English: "She cheered for you to win."

I turned around. I saw her with her high-heeled sandal to hit me. I saw her face like something crushed but still alive in its eyes. I reached out my hand to her—then she was on me, hitting me wild, shouting, "How dare you treat me this way?" Her blows were so weak, I didn't even lift my arms. She went again, "How dare you?" but crying, not yelling, and the shoe flew from her hand and she raised her fist and I wished she would hit. But she just stood there, fist up, face twisted and crying.

"Mami?" I said. "Mami?" And then her arms were around me and she felt like *her,* strong and angry, and I didn't try to stop my tears. "Little mama," she said. "Sweetheart. You are so stupid and cruel," and she stroked my hair. "You could've died, you can never do this again!"

"Mami, I'm sorry. I wanted you to be proud!"

"Ay, mi niña. Pride is for fools and rich people." She stopped crying when she said that; she wiped her eyes and spoke calmly. "Because of your pride, you will never come here again."

"All right, Mami," I whispered. "Yes."

Then there were no words, just our arms and our chests, beating and breathing into each other. The trees blew in the wind above us. My mami rocked me and said deep and rough: "Your ribbon. Your horse." And I knew: She was proud.

Dante came and wrapped his arms around us.

Ginger

Pat went to walk the horse around. I stood alone as the other riders led their horses—and their parents and trainers—back toward the barn and the parking lot beyond it. I saw Paul coming toward me, and I went to meet him. He said he'd gotten into a conversation with another trainer, that she was going on about how she'd never seen a horse pick up its performance so radically before, that the animal rode like it "was possessed" on that final course. He asked where Velvet and her family were, he said that Becca and Edie wanted to take a picture of us all together, with Velvet and her family too. I felt numb. In the years I had been married, there was no "family photo" with me in it.

"Paul," I said. "I don't think they'll want to."

"Why not?" His face darkened. "She didn't give permission, did she?"

"I honestly don't know."

He didn't say anything; he just put his hand on my shoulder.

And that's when they came back. Mrs. Vargas with her arm around Velvet, and Dante looking quiet and emotional even at a distance. Silvia's eyes fell on me and in them I saw peace with a triumph that sharpened as she came closer. All right, I thought; it's all right. And it was. She embraced me and said something that Velvet did not have to translate: "Gracias."

Then we went to have our picture taken with Becca and Edie—the first time I had ever been in a picture with them. Silvia initially said no, that she was too tired and looked terrible. But she was finally part of it too, and she smiled *big*. It was incredible.

Silvia

She told me that Ginger didn't know and I believed her—I could see it in the way the woman greeted me when she first saw me, happy and ignorant, even when she should've been able to see my face and hear my voice. My daughter was safe and I had her back and they would find out soon enough. My body was tired, but my mind and heart were floating up in the sky. It was fine with me to eat and have my picture taken with Ginger's family. To walk through the barn and see the horses. To have my picture taken with Velvet's horse. It was even a little fun.

Velvet

The pictures they took that day showed a lot. Me and Ginger and Paul and my mom and Dante, then me and Ginger and Edie and Edie's mom, who's got Ginger's head, basically, in a *lock*. Me and Pat and Gare and Fiery Girl. Me and my mom and Fiery Girl. Everybody with my horse, looking at the camera with her head up and sideways, showing her kind but watching eye. Everybody smiling, even Ginger smiling all the way, Dante smiling like Chester Cheetah, and my mom smiling with her eyes closed in like three pictures, the sky very blue behind her, and random people turning to look—even they're smiling, except for the old woman carrying the empty ribbon-bucket someplace out of the picture.

The pictures also *don't* show a lot. They don't show Jeanne from Spindletop telling me I could come train there as a "work-study" and me smiling even though I knew I would never do it. They don't show the sea horse in my shirt pocket, broken into dust except for its nose bone. They don't show Dante looking out the back window laughing at Beverly and Pat in the parking lot, yelling at each other while we drove away . . . or me walking on the block where I met Dominic forever ago, my ribbon with me so if I saw him I could show it to him. How I saw him but he was with Brianna and she was getting a bump. Gaby told me I was young, and I would meet somebody better for me. But my heart hurt, hurt for real, so much it woke me up at night.

When Ginger sent us the competition pictures, my mom framed one and put it on her dresser. The others she gave to me. But after I saw Dominic and Brianna like that, those pictures seemed far away, like something that's only real for kids. Like butterflies bursting out from a shampoo bottle or a cereal box in a commercial. The time I spent with Pat and the things we talked about—it was real. Same with Ginger. Except it can't exist anywhere but, like, in the car when we drove at night, listening to music, Ginger singing in her pinchy voice.

But sometimes when I wake up hurting I think: Fiery Girl. The feel of her body, her neck and the butterfly place between her leg and hoof. That was real. How I took her out at night and she reared up on me and I stayed on her until I *found* her. How she came back to me when I felt worthless and she nosed on my hair. How she wouldn't let me hug her in the field but I loved her anyway. And mostly how I finally had the leg thing with her, in the last part of the competition, *in front of people.* Where my legs touched her sides and it was the best place in the world and we were in it together. Like with Chloe only more strong and deep, too deep to show in pictures or to talk about with Ginger or even Pat. Or anybody except maybe Dominic, and I can't talk to him, maybe ever. Instead I hold on to the leg feeling, and I rub it on my heart like medicine. And it's real then, real in my room, real everywhere. I sit up and look across the street at Cookie's wall with the horseshoe hidden inside it. I don't know when my mom will let me go see Fiery Girl again. But I know I will. Even if I don't, she'll always be with me. But I don't think about that. Because I know I will, even if I have to wait and take the train to see her when I'm eighteen and everything is different. Maybe I'll have my own baby then, or maybe I'll be in college, that would make Ginger glad. But whatever is happening, I know I will see my mare again.

Acknowledgments

I would like to acknowledge and thank the following people and organizations for their moral and practical help in the writing of this book:

Sarah Fink, Celina Martinez, Karen Murphy, Rashena Wilson, Jo Ann Beard, Michael Zilkha, Emma Sweeney, Jean Strouse, Jennifer Sears, T. Kira Madden, Marguerite and Andres San Millan, Peter Trachtenburg, Rima Liscum, Angie Cruz, Ralph Sassone, Peter Franklin, Rene Falcon, Nancy and Catherine Locke of Hyde-Locke Stables, Renee Petruzzelli of Horse Heaven, The Southlands Foundation, The Jentel Foundation, and Ragdale.

Most especially I would like to thank Denisse De La Cruz and equestrienne Sarah Willeman: Your patient, generous help was invaluable.

I would also particularly like to thank David Weiss and Melanie Conroy-Goldman of Hobart and William-Smith Colleges for giving me more time than allotted at the Trias House, essentially providing me with a writing retreat for four months.

Finally, I am grateful to the wonderful children I met through the Fresh Air Fund. This book is not about those children, but it would never have been written if they had not been in my life.

Questions for reading groups

1. "It made you think the beautiful sentiments you pretend to believe in really *might* be true."
   - Here a sentimental song moves Ginger to describe the human need for ideals, whether or not they're realistic. To what extent are escapism and fantasy integral to both Ginger and Velvet's psychological wellbeing?
   - To what degree do you think the novel is about survival?

2. "The dominant mare drives the troublemakers to the outside of the herd. Because that's where the predators are."
   - Velvet draws on her experience with the horses to analyse the behaviour of a clique at school. How is Velvet about to link her experience with the mare, positively and negatively, to her life in the city, with her friends, and at school?

3. Ginger and Silvia offer different experiences of maternal love—what questions does this raise about the nature of motherhood? Is it fair to compare the two?

4. Loyalty to family is arguably the most important factor in Velvet's life; "if I could only get back to her, I would never go to Ginger's again. Even if it meant I would never see my mare."
   - Velvet is securely attached to her mother and consistently loyal. How does the reader feel about their relationship? Is their love for each other mutual? Is it possible for love to co-exist with abuse?

5. "Men are babies screaming for love. They get it, they throw it across the room until it breaks and then start screaming again. And always some dumb woman comes running."
   - The protagonists in this novel are female, but how important is masculinity to the discussion of family and relationships in the novel?
   - How do we see Dante and Paul fulfilling/frustrating gender stereotypes? How do the women react to this?

6. Sexuality is an important theme in the book, and has different connotations for Ginger and Velvet. It can be a source of tenderness, beauty and connection; power and strength; it can also be frightening or shameful.

- How do the characters experience sexuality?
- How is sex part of their coming of age and their understanding of how to negotiate emotion?

7. "Then a man got on ... and I could tell he was Spanish. He was by himself, but he did not look sad or quiet ... He was looking at me like he liked me, like he *knew me*. I looked at him and my sick feeling opened up and became a deep feeling."
   - Identity and community are important themes in the book—to what extent do you think the characters struggle with the labels they are given? Who, in your opinion, appears to struggle most?

8. Paul repeatedly says to Ginger that her relationship with Velvet and her family can't work because she doesn't have anything in common with them. Is this true?

9. "I met my husband, Paul, in AA. I only went for about a year because I couldn't stand the meetings, couldn't stand the language, the dogma."
   - How does the theme of addiction and dependency colour Ginger's interactions with other characters?

10. "It was sentimental and flattering to white vanity and manipulative as hell."
    - How do you think the themes of race and social collision complicate the "normal" trajectory of relationships in the novel?

11. "Mostly she looked immature, more girl than woman—a sad girl trying to be happy."
    - Ginger and Velvet's stories run parallel. To what extent do you believe Ginger is trying to re-imagine her own girlhood, and by extension, her womanhood, through Velvet?

12. Mary Gaitskill often plays with the concept of sentimentality in her work. How do you think sentiment is treated by the characters in *The Mare*?

13. Velvet is a child when she first meets Ginger, and a young teenager by the end of the book. As most teenagers do, she exaggerates and sometimes lies, to protect her own interests, get her own way, or to make herself feel better. Ginger says "If you're going to lie, you should learn to do it better than that ... You keep lying to me, we aren't going to stay close. Lying creates distance between people."
    - Does the way Velvet remakes the stories she tells matter? Does she need to lie to make life feel more acceptable? To give herself hope? Is learning the boundaries of this part of growing up?